W9-BVW-655

PRAISE FOR EARLENE FOWLER'S

Benni Harper Mysteries

Sunshine and Shadow

"A warmhearted spiral that includes the difficulties of marriage, the complexities of a large multiethnic circle of overlapping friends and relations, and old, buried secrets."
—*Booklist*

"Fowler's charm as a storyteller derives from the way she unpredictably sews all these and several other disparate plots together, just like one of those quilts in Benni's museum. Characters' lives crisscross over time, patterns emerge, random actions beget pleasing, as well as ugly, results. And, as *Sunshine and Shadow* suggests, one dropped stitch can ultimately cause the whole crazy-quilt pattern of a family's life to fall apart." —*The Washington Post*

"Each Benni Harper mystery is better than the previous one . . . A five star mystery." —*Midwest Book Review*

continued . . .

Steps to the Altar

"Superior cozy entertainment."
—*Publishers Weekly* (starred review)

"Hoorah! A new Benni Harper mystery!" —*Booknook*

Arkansas Traveler

"A cross between *Steel Magnolias* and *To Kill a Mockingbird* . . . thoughtfully written, laugh-out-loud funny, and powerfully evocative." —*Ventura County Star*

"The sweet sentimentality of this paean to small Southern towns—with shrine-like reverence for Southern cooking, the Waffle House, and the Dairy Queen—is the glaze that holds this story together." —*The Houston Chronicle*

PRAISE FOR THE OTHER
BENNI HARPER MYSTERIES

"Breezy, humorous dialogue of the first order."
—*Chicago Sun-Times*

"Fowler's plots can be as outrageous as Ellery Queen's, her turf is Ross Macdonald's, and her tone is heir to Grafton and Paretsky . . . An up-and-comer worth watching."
—*Nashville Scene*

"Fowler writes beautifully about the picturesque Central Coast, ranching, and local cuisine."   —*Booklist*

"Mayhem, murder, chaos, and romance . . . well-paced mystery . . . fun reading."   —*The Kansas Daily Reporter*

"A lot of fun to read. Fowler has a deft touch."
—*The Wichita Eagle*

"Terrific . . . The dialogue is intelligent and witty, the characters intensely human, and the tantalizing puzzle keeps the pages turning."   —Jean Hager, author of *The Redbird's Cry*

"Characters come to full three-dimensional life, and her plot is satisfyingly complex."
—*The Jackson (MI) Clarion-Ledger*

"Benni is feisty, caring, loving, and one heck of a part-time sleuth."   —*Rendezvous*

"Engrossing . . . a compelling story of families torn apart by divided loyalties."   —*Publishers Weekly*

DON'T MISS THE NEXT
BENNI HARPER MYSTERY

Broken Dishes

SUNSHINE
and SHADOW

Earlene Fowler

MAIN LIBRARY
Champaign Public Library
200 West Green Street
Champaign, Illinois 61820-5193

BERKLEY PRIME CRIME, NEW YORK

If you purchased this book without a cover, you should be aware that this book is stolen property. It was reported as "unsold and destroyed" to the publisher, and neither the author nor the publisher has received any payment for this "stripped book."

This is a work of ct ion. Names, characters, places, and incidents either are the product of the author's imagination or are used fictitiously, and any resemblance to actual persons, living or dead, business establishments, events, or locales is entirely coincidental.

SUNSHINE AND SHADOW

A Berkley Prime Crime Book / published by arrangement with the author

PRINTING HISTORY
Berkley Prime Crime hardcover edition / May 2003
Berkley Prime Crime mass-market edition / April 2004

Copyright © 2003 by Earlene Fowler.
Illustrations by Griesbach and Martucci.
Design by George Long.

All rights reserved. This book, or parts thereof, may not be reproduced in any form without permission. The scanning, uploading, and distribution of this book via the Internet or via any other means without the permission of the publisher is illegal and punishable by law. Please purchase only authorized electronic editions, and do not participate in or encourage electronic piracy of copyrighted materials. Your support of the author's rights is appreciated.
For information address: The Berkley Publishing Group,
a division of Penguin Group (USA) Inc.,
375 Hudson Street, New York, New York 10014.

ISBN: 978-0-425-19528-4

Berkley Prime Crime Books are published by The Berkley Publishing Group, a division of Penguin Group (USA) Inc.,
375 Hudson Street, New York, New York 10014.
The name BERKLEY PRIME CRIME and the BERKLEY PRIME CRIME design are trademarks belonging to Penguin Group (USA) Inc.

PRINTED IN THE UNITED STATES OF AMERICA

10   9   8   7   6

For Gary, Brenda, Heather,
and Erica Fowler
with gratitude for your love
and loyal support

Acknowledgments

During the writing of this book, there were multitudes of people who supported me in both physical and emotional ways. From the heels of my boots to the top of my head, I thank you all.

> *Not to us, O Lord,*
> *not to us but to your name be the glory,*
> *because of your love and faithfulness.*
> PSALM 115:1 HALLELU YAH (PRAISE THE LORD)

Tina and Tom Davis—dearest of friends and dynamite webmasters.

Janice "Beebs" Dischner and Carolyn "Millee" Miller—for your prayers, friendship, and for letting me borrow your names.

Julia Fleischaker—simply the greatest publicist in New York.

Ellen Geiger—the best, most patient agent in the world (thanks for letting me be temperamental once in a while).

Clare Bazley, Karen Grencik, Jo Ellen Heil, AnnE Lorenzen, Jo-Ann Mapson, Helen May, Sue "SueMo" Morrison, and Lela Satterfield—wonderful friends and champion prayer warriors.

Christine "Nini" Hill—who always knows what to say to make me feel whole again.

Debra Jackson—beloved sister and friend.

Dr. John "Mac" McFarland—for theological advice and your always inspiring spirit. I couldn't have invented a better pastor!

Chris and Betty Rodgers—for sharing their personal law enforcement experiences.

Kathy Vieira—dear riding and writing friend and the best darn giant pumpkin grower I know.

Christine Zika—a most wonderful and insightful editor.

To all my fans who pray for me and support my writing not only with their dollars but their encouraging letters and wishes . . . my deepest gratitude.

Always, with love, to my husband, Allen. What a mighty, mighty good man you are.

A Note from the Author

When I started the Benni Harper series in 1992, the first book, *Fool's Puzzle,* was written in "real time." It was 1992 in Benni's life as well as mine. Time in a long-running series is always a tricky thing. Since it often takes a book almost two years from the time the author starts writing it to the point when it is actually in the reader's hands, time sequences can become confusing. Each author deals with this dilemma in a different way. I decided from the beginning that I would age my characters much more slowly than I and my readers were aging. With Dove being seventy-five in the first book, I wanted to keep her active and vital and I also wanted to explore the early stages of Benni and Gabe's relationship. So it has taken me ten years to write a little over two years in their lives. Keep in mind while reading that the books, so far, cover late 1992 to mid-1995. Now, if we could just figure out a way for all of us to age like Benni and Gabe . . .

Sunshine and Shadow is a simple pattern that, nevertheless, has a great deal of visual movement. It is traditionally constructed of small squares of fabric arranged by color and turned on point to form alternating rows of light and dark triangles. Colors expand in a "round" and each round may be a different color or the quilter can repeat favorite colors. Extremely popular with the Mennonites and the Amish, it is often created using brilliant reds, blues, pinks, and aquas as well as darker colors. It has been seen on Lancaster County, Pennsylvania, quilts made as early as 1890. The name and design suggest that human life itself is touched by both sunshine and shadow, the physical and the spiritual, birth and death, and that these elements often intersect. The pattern is also called Trip Around the World, Checkerboard, and Grandma's Dream.

PROLOGUE

March 18, 1995
Saturday
Dove's Wedding Day

"$\mathcal{A}$RE YOU SCARED?" I ASKED MY GRAMMA DOVE AS I
pinned the delicate spray of baby's breath around her
smooth white hair, arranged today in an elaborately
braided bun. She had sent everyone away but me, her
matron of honor and oldest grandchild. Her bright lupine
blue eyes were glassy with excitement.

We stood in the pastor's book-lined office at San Celina First Baptist Church. Muted conversation and laughter
seeped through the thick mahogany door to the sanctuary.
In ten minutes she would walk down the church's center
aisle clutching the solid right arm of her oldest son, my
father, Ben Ramsey. The church, built a hundred years
ago of smooth gray and tan stones dug from the hills of
San Celina County, was filled to almost lawbreaking ca-
pacity with five hundred people, including friends and
neighbors, her children, grandchildren, and great-
grandchildren. They were all excited for this momentous
and unexpected occasion to commence.

"So, are you?" I asked again.

Dove turned away from the round mirror we'd hung

next to the picture of Jesus praying in the Garden of Gethsemane to stare at me with solemn eyes. "Down to my
very toes," she said.

"Isaac loves you," I replied, picking a speck of black
lint off her lacy, sky blue dress. Isaac Lyons, world famous photographer, five-time-married man-of-the-world,
had fallen face-down-in-love with my gramma from the
first moment they met.

"Love isn't always enough," she said flatly, her still
obvious Arkansas accent slightly slurring the words. She
fingered one of her deep blue sapphire earrings, Isaac's
engagement gift.

I pondered her words for a moment, knowing what she
said was true. "But sometimes you have to take that
chance. Sometimes love is all you have."

Her ample chest rose and fell in a sigh. "Maybe so."

"It must be weird, getting married after all these years."

Dove was seventy-seven years old and had been widowed since she was forty-two.

"Thirty-three years I've done as I've pleased." She
turned back to the mirror, critically eyeing her reflection.
With a wetted finger, she smoothed down a stray piece of
hair.

I looked at her reflection in the mirror, rearranged a
small piece of baby's breath. "Isaac won't try to tell you
what to do. He knows better."

She smiled at herself. "Yes, he does." Then her face
turn soft with what seemed like sadness.

"Are you thinking of Grampa?" I asked.

Her eyes dropped, revealing the delicate blue veins on
her eyelids. "How did you know?"

"I thought about Jack when Gabe and I got married."
Jack was my first husband, my high school sweetheart,
who was killed three years ago in an auto accident.

Her eyes came back up and caught mine. "Both
times?"

"Yes." My second husband, Gabe Ortiz, and I had
eloped to Las Vegas, but were married in a second cere-

mony in this very church a little over two years ago. "But especially when I was married here. Jack and I spent so much time here." My own reflection showed a thirty-seven-year-old woman in a round-collared peach dress, reddish-blond hair pulled back in a French braid. I'd worn my hair up when I married Jack, in dancing curls that took a can of hair spray to hold in place.

"I am thinking about your grampa."

"You still miss him."

She ran a finger under one eye, uncomfortable with the mascara she was wearing. "You know how I feel. He was my first love."

I slipped my arm around her shoulder. The stiff lace tickled my palm. "Remember standing in this room with me when I was getting ready to marry Jack? Daddy was so nervous. He still smoked then and I think he had ten cigarettes in ten minutes. He reeked of tobacco when we walked down the aisle." I wrinkled my nose.

We both laughed. I had been nineteen, full of hope and excitement, bubbling over with youthful arrogance. Now I can look back and savor those carefree times, as brief as they seemed now. Perhaps we're given those perfect moments to sustain us through the hard times that inevitably come as we maneuver through this life on earth.

"Your daddy is pacing outside the door right now," she said. "He told me last night that he hopes all the women in his life are settled for a while, that he was tired of all the romantic intrigue."

I grinned at her in the gray-tinted mirror. Part of my smile was hidden by a clover-shaped dark spot in the silver. "He needs some romantic intrigue of his own." It would be hard to imagine my father in love. He'd been widowed himself for over thirty years.

A soft snort came from her pale pink lips. "I'll leave that to you."

From behind the wall we could hear the muffled sound of organ music. The door to the sanctuary opened and MacKenzie "Mac" Reid, our minister, walked in. His six-four, ex-football-player figure seemed to fill the warm room.

"How're we doing, ladies?" he asked, grinning widely from behind his bushy chestnut beard. Forty-three and a widower himself, he was thrilled that Dove had found someone after all these years. "Means there's hope for me," he told us at the rehearsal dinner last night.

"How much time does she have left before walking the plank?" I asked, grinning back.

He glanced at his black sports watch. "Five minutes. Looks like everyone's here." He took both of Dove's hands in his massive ones and gazed down at her with his gentle, pewter gray eyes. "Sister Ramsey, are you ready?"

There was a small moment of hesitation, then a strong, "As ready as I'll ever be, Brother Mac."

"Then I'll see you out there."

After he left, I grabbed her hand. "I'm so happy for you. It's about time you had someone of your own."

Her eyes grew misty. "Maybe this isn't the right thing. Time is so short. One of us will have to survive being widowed again. Isaac has lost three wives to death. I've lost your grampa. I don't know if I want to go through that again." Her normally booming voice was low and afraid. It was a voice that had soothed me and scolded me, threatened me and praised me throughout my life. "I don't know if I can."

I paused a moment before answering, wanting to comfort her, wanting to help her through this dilemma as she had helped me through so many sad and difficult times in my thirty-seven years. She'd essentially been my mother since I was six years old and my own mother died of cancer. Without hesitation or complaint, she'd uprooted her whole life in Arkansas and moved to the Central Coast of California to help Daddy raise me as well as run the Ramsey ranch. She deserved this happiness.

I held her cold hand tightly, trying to transfer my hand's warmth to hers. "Remember when Jack was killed and so many people were telling me that I was young, that I could still find someone, that my life wasn't over, that I shouldn't give up?"

She clucked under her breath. "People never just say they're sorry. Always got to be giving advice."

"Remember when I finally blew up and yelled at you that I was sick of people telling me what I should or shouldn't do, that I never wanted to love anyone again, that I never, ever wanted to suffer the pain of losing someone again? You listened to me rant and rave and then told me that I didn't have to, that I could sit in my room and do nothing for the rest of my life if I wanted and that you'd support me in that decision and would always love me and never nag me to do anything else."

Her pink lips turned up in a smile "I lied. I did eventually nag you to start a new life."

"Yes, but not at first. You let me wallow, you let me *grieve*. You gave me the gift of time. That was what I needed. Time to get used to my new life, a life that didn't include Jack. I had to get used to that life before I could even think about having a life with someone else."

She glanced up at the clock on the wall. Its ticking seemed like a tiny, insistent voice telling us time was running out.

"I know, get to the point. My point is, if you want to ditch this marriage and run back to the ranch, I'll drive you. My truck is right outside. I'll support you in whatever you want to do and I will love you no matter what. Just like you always have me. But first, tell me truly, how do you feel about this man?"

She sighed again. "I've had a long time to get used to a life without your grampa."

"Yes, you have."

"His passing tore my heart to shreds."

"Yes, I know." I continued to hold her hand.

"But I didn't fall apart."

"No, you didn't. Ramsey women don't fall apart. You've told me that more than once."

"We had us some wonderful times, me and your

grampa. Oh, honeybun, I wish you could have known him. He had the most beautiful singing voice. He was always a'singing, when we'd pick cotton and beans, when I was going through labor to have our babies, when they'd get the colic and couldn't sleep. I knew he'd died when he was chopping wood because he quit singing in the middle of a song."

She sang softly, "Blessed assurance, Jesus is mine . . ." She stopped, swallowed hard. "He stopped right there and I knew something was wrong because he never stopped singing in the middle of a song, not in all the years I knew him."

The outside door opened and Daddy stuck his head in. "Dove, we need to get out to the front of the church now. It's time."

The sound of the organ thrummed through the office walls. I could just make out the melody—"We've Only Just Begun." Dove had always loved the Carpenters.

"One last time," I said. "How do you feel about Isaac?"

She looked directly into my eyes. "He pure out gladdens my heart."

I squeezed her hand gently. "Then it's time, Gramma."

For a moment, her pale blue eyes widened and she grasped my hand so tightly I almost winced. "Don't leave me."

"Not a chance," I said, leading her to the door toward my father. "Not until I deliver you safely into the arms of the one who loves you."

"And then?" she asked, her voice reedy with panic.

"Then I'll stick around to make sure he's treating you right. Just like you always have me."

With that, she let go of my hand, straightened her spine, and stepped over the threshold, the old Dove restored. "Then let's get this marriage on the road."

CHAPTER 1

❖

March 31, 1978
Friday

*T*HE SERVICE PORCH SCREEN DOOR OPENED WITH A rusty screech. Heavy boots thumped across the ranch house's creaky linoleum-covered wood floor.

It was a little before 7 A.M. and I didn't have to turn around to see who was behind me.

"Jack Harper," I said over my shoulder, my hands deep in hot soapy dishwater filled with last night's plates and glasses. A sliver of sun was just starting to paint the craggy hills surrounding the Harper ranch with shadows. "Those boots better not have a speck of mud or manure on them. I just mopped this floor." Keeping this seventy-year-old wood frame house clean was a challenge even for the enthusiastic energies of a barely twenty-year-old newlywed wife like me.

A set of muscled arms circled my waist and lifted me up until my feet dangled. He rubbed his scratchy, early-morning stubble across the side of my neck. "Blondie, I flat out love it when you get all housewifey."

"Put me down!" I said, helplessly swinging my legs and giggling. "I swear, Jack, if you don't put me down . . ."

He lowered me slowly, and when my feet touched ground, I swung around to face him. He dropped his hands from my waist to cup my rear end. "Mrs. Harper," he murmured, kissing me. "You have no idea how good you feel to me." He tasted of Clove chewing gum and smelled like worn leather and clean, sweet hay.

"No way!" I said, trying to squirm away. "We have a history class in an hour and a half. We can't—"

He stopped my words with his lips, cool and damp from the brisk April morning air. I rested my wet hands on his darkly tanned forearms, arms made hard and sinewy from years of bucking one-hundred-twenty-five-pound alfalfa bales.

"Jack," I murmured, trying to pull away. But a determined and amorous twenty-year-old male was hard to resist, especially when I'd been married to him for only three months.

"C'mon," he said, pulling me toward the bedroom. "It won't take long."

"What am I going to do with you?" I said, smiling as I let myself be led astray.

He grinned, his warm brown eyes narrowing slightly. "Oh, babe, let me show you."

Twenty minutes later we were in our red Chevy pickup truck with HARPER'S HEREFORDS painted on the doors squealing down the ranch's long gravel driveway toward the highway, a brown dust cloud spiraling behind us.

A quarter mile ahead of us, his older brother, Wade, walked along the driveway toward the new five-bedroom house, a gray-and-white clapboard set a football field's length from our two-bedroom house, the ranch's original homestead. Wade, their mother, Wade's wife, Sandra, and their new baby, Johnny, lived in it now. Six years ago it had been built by their father, John Harper Sr., right before he died of a heart attack, leaving both houses, the thousand-acre ranch, and all their financial problems to his wife and two teenage sons.

Wade was most likely heading toward the huge pancakes, eggs, bacon, and biscuits and gravy breakfast my sister-in-law fixed every morning. My stomach growled, reminding me that because of our early-morning detour back to bed, Jack and I would have to grab breakfast from a vending machine at Cal Poly San Celina, where we were college sophomores. My major was American history with a minor in agricultural management. Jack's was farm management with a minor in animal husbandry.

"Slow down!" Wade yelled as we barreled past him. Though he was only five years older than us, he often acted three times that, having shouldered the responsibility of running the ranch since he was nineteen. The strain showed itself in an anxious expression that never seemed to leave his craggy, strong-jawed face.

Jack slammed on the brakes, threw the truck in reverse, and backed up.

"Where're you two off to in such a hurry?" Wade asked, dipping his head to peer into the truck's cab. Though it was not even 8 A.M., he already looked exhausted. "Did you check on those heifers this morning? I didn't like how that big-eared one looked last night." He tugged at one side of his droopy, blondish-brown mustache.

"Yep, she's fine," Jack said, looking straight ahead out of the windshield. "Gotta go. We're late for history class."

"Again?" Wade said. He turned his head and spit a stream of tobacco juice into a row of white and yellow daisies Sandra planted last week. "Boy, you're gonna get your ass kicked out of that fancy college if you don't start taking things more serious. And that'd be good money being flushed right down the toilet. Money we could've used for a new tractor."

I glanced over at Jack's profile. Minus the mustache, it was almost an exact physical duplicate of his older brother's. His jaw tightened as he continued to stare straight ahead. The conflict between them about Jack attending Cal Poly was a long-running and tumultuous one. Wade believed in learning by doing, that the old ways, the traditions taught to him by their father, a third-generation Texas rancher, was the best way to run the Harper ranch, a cow/calf operation on the Central Coast of California. Jack believed that agriculture's future was in diversification and learning to work the land in a more holistic, land-respecting way.

On the Central Coast, where cattle ranching had been one of the major agricultural strongholds for generations, there were in these last few years of the seventies, rumblings of what was coming, a move away from the family ranch toward corporate ranches that could produce in volume. There was also the new vegetarian craze, fueled by the small, but growing population of ex-hippies and environmentalists, which some ranchers worried might move Central Coast agriculture away from cattle production altogether. The Harper ranch had been losing money since their dad died so Wade had reluctantly given in to the urging of their mother and agreed to let Jack attend Cal Poly to explore new agricultural possibilities.

"All I gotta say is it better not interfere with his chores," Wade had said, his disapproval obvious by the high color in his prominent cheekbones.

Jack relaxed his jaw, then turned to grin at his brother's frowning face. "It's all Benni's fault. She had something extremely urgent she needed me to take care of before we left for school."

I laughed and kicked his Wrangler-clad shin with the side of my brown boot. "You lying hound dog!" I leaned over Jack and said to Wade, "We'll be a little late getting home from our classes today. We're helping to assemble the queen's float for the La Fiesta Parade on Saturday."

La Fiesta de Nuestra Pueblo—The Festival of Our Town—was a week-long celebration of our county's multicultural and agricultural roots. Despite its Hispanic name, it had evolved into a sort of catch-all celebration that involved every segment of San Celina society. It always ended with the Cattleman's Ball on Saturday night after the parade and street festival. This year, my best friend, Elvia Aragon, was voted Fiesta Queen, one of San Celina's highest honors, so I was taking particular interest in the flower-covered float she would be riding.

Still frowning, Wade shook his head and turned away. The social aspects of San Celina County had never interested him. "There's a stretch of fence down over on Miller flats," he called over his shoulder, his rough voice sharp and accusing. "Be nice if you could somehow work that into your social schedule."

"Be nice if you could work that into your social schedule," Jack mimicked as we pulled out onto the highway. "You can kiss my skinny cowboy ass, Wade Harper."

"Jack, don't let him get to you," I said, laying a hand on the back of his warm neck. "That's just Wade."

He slapped the steering wheel with his left hand. "Dang it all, he treats me like I'm five years old. He's nagged me about that stretch of fence ten times in the last two days. I *told* him I would get to it after our classes today."

"So just do what you originally planned and ignore what he says." I reached down and dug through my stained green backpack. "I had a couple of chocolate chip cookies in here yesterday. Did you eat them?"

"Yeah," he said, his face still tense and agitated. "Sorry."

I sighed, resigning myself to the prospect of a stale vending machine sweet roll.

He flipped on the radio and "Stayin' Alive" by the Bee Gees came on. He punched buttons until Merle Haggard's voice sang out of the static-filled speakers. "Disco sucks. Who's been messing with our radio?"

I giggled. "Elvia, who else? You know she refuses to listen to country-western music. She and I went shopping down in Santa Maria yesterday. We finally found the perfect dress for her to wear for the parade Saturday."

He nodded, not answering. The day was cool for early spring, causing me to pull my wool-lined Wrangler jacket closer around me. After a few minutes of tense silence, I leaned over and kissed Jack on the side of his jaw. "Forget Wade. Think about Manifest Destiny and the opening of the American West. We've got a quiz today in history class."

His face lost a little rigidity. "I know. What's after history?"

Even though it was the middle of April and we'd been attending our classes since the semester started in January, I still had to remind Jack of his schedule. I worried that working full time on the ranch and going to school full time was too much for him, but knowing how sensitive the issue was between him and Wade, I didn't dare say so.

"After history," I said, "you have biology and I have sociology. Then we meet at the ag barn to work on the float. It's supposed to resemble the Santa Celine Mission when it was first built in 1775, but it's looking more like a saloon than a mission. To say the least, it needs some work."

"Did you pick up my journal notebook for history?" he asked. "It was the green one on the kitchen table. Professor Hill wants to see proof I'm working on it."

"It's in your backpack. You know, I deserve half the degree you're getting simply because I'm the one who remembers your books and papers." Though Jack always received mostly A's in his classes, he was the most unorganized person I knew. His strength was in relating to people and he knew and used that.

He reached over and squeezed my knee. "Babe, you deserve everything I own and more. I'd be a lost man without you."

I snorted, but was secretly warmed by his praise. Since my own mother had died when I was six and my gramma Dove, who raised me, had been widowed since I was four, I had no idea if I was being a good wife. And being a good wife was really important to me.

"How's your journal going?" I asked. His class project for history, as a substitute for a term paper, was a journal that required him to record for a month his impressions and experiences with people he met, both people he knew and those who were outside his normal circle of family and friends. It was supposed to help improve his observation skills and appreciate the detail of everyday life. Our history teacher, Mr. Hill, was trying to impress on us the importance of recording oral history.

"It's harder than I thought. I'm not that great at putting down my feelings on paper and, I don't know, it kind of embarrasses me to think someone will read it."

"Only Professor Hill," I said. "And he won't laugh. Did I tell you he okayed my term paper?"

"No, you didn't. I forgot, what's it about?"

I dug around in my backpack again and pulled out the small, colorful book I'd stuck in there last night. On the cover a blond girl in blue jeans and a red gingham shirt pulled a colorful crazy quilt from a hole in the wall of a log cabin. A yellow hound dog with a curly tail stood alert at her side. Her rosy-cheeked face looked apprehensive and listening.

He glanced over at it. *"The Secret of the Crazy Quilt,"* he read out loud. "Looks like a kid's book."

"It is. One of Professor Hill's suggestions was for us to pick a person who influenced us as a child and do research on them now. We're supposed to record our memories of what impressed us as a child and compare and contrast that to whatever we can find out about them. It can be someone we knew personally or not."

"Who'd you pick?"

"Emma Baldwin."

"Who?"

I pointed to her name on the cover of the book. "She's a writer. She lives in . . . what are you doing?"

He peered intently in his rearview mirror and started slowing the truck down. "That guy back there needs a ride."

I turned around and watched a sixtyish Mexican man trudge toward our idling truck. "Jack, you know it makes me nervous when you pick up hitchhikers. Not to mention Wade will kill you if he finds out."

"Screw Wade," Jack said and called out the window, "Where're you heading, sir?"

The older man replied with a strong Spanish accent, "Matthews ranch."

"Climb in back," Jack said. "We're going right past there."

"No, we're not," I whispered to Jack. "We're going to be late."

Jack waved my words away with a flip of his hand.

"Muchas gracias, señor," the man said, climbing into the bed of our truck.

"No problem," Jack called out, then winked at me. "Lighten up, Mrs. Harper. You know what Pastor Satterfield said last Sunday about not being afraid to entertain strangers. That old guy back there might be an angel."

I shook my head and didn't answer, silently agreeing with what Wade said, that sometimes Jack was just too trusting with strangers. Wade was always predicting that his habit of picking up hitchhikers was bound to end in trouble. "Jack . . ."

"Ah, babe, he's just a tired old man who needs to get to work. Now what about this lady, Emma whatever?" he asked, trying to divert my attention so I wouldn't lecture him.

I glanced in the side mirror at our passenger. His coppery brown, sun-lined face did indeed look tired, even this early in the morning. He appeared about as dangerous as my best friend, Elvia Aragon's, father. Our eyes met for a moment and we both looked away, embarrassed. I turned to study Jack's profile, the profile I fell in love with the moment he slipped into the desk next to mine five years ago in our high school geometry class. After my initial physical attraction to him, his sense of humor and generous, accepting nature were what truly won my heart.

"Emma?" he repeated.

"Oh, yeah, Emma Baldwin. She wrote a mystery series with a thirteen-year-old ranch girl as the protagonist. They were my and Elvia's favorite books when we were girls. They're set right here in San Celina County and so many things about them were like my real life. Except Molly Connors had two older brothers named Tommy and Andy and both her parents were alive. Her best friend, Lily Waters, was really pretty and lived in town just like Elvia, only Lily's mother was widowed and owned a dress shop. Lily's an only child. Well, that part's not like Elvia though she certainly wished it was. You know how her six brothers have always driven her crazy. Anyway, Molly had a horse named Rooster, a yellow dog named Clementine, and her older brothers teased her all the time just like my uncle Arnie did me."

"Molly? I thought her name was Emma."

"Pay attention. Emma Baldwin is the *author*. Molly Connors is the character she wrote about. Anyway, I found out from Elvia that Emma Baldwin lives here in San Celina County and Elvia's boss, the owner of Blind Harry's Bookstore downtown, knows her personally! He called Mrs. Baldwin to see if she'll talk to me and she agreed to meet with me tomorrow at her ranch up north outside of Paso Robles."

"That's pretty cool," Jack said. "A real author."

A few minutes later we pulled up to the Matthews' silver mailbox. "Here you go," Jack called out.

The man climbed out of the truck's bed and came over to Jack's window.

"Gracias, compadre," the man said, holding out his calloused hand.

"You're welcome, sir," Jack said, shaking the man's hand. "Have a nice day."

We watched the man plod up the long driveway toward the Matthews ranch house. Lloyd Matthews, a friend of Jack's late dad, stepped out on the front porch and saw our truck. He lifted his hand up in greeting. Jack waved in reply.

"We have exactly fifteen minutes to go twenty miles," I said, knowing we were going to receive yet another gentle reprimand and slightly amused look from Professor Hill when we tried to sneak into his class without being noticed. He was my favorite professor and teased me unmercifully about my inability to get to class on time, chalking it up to newlywed distraction.

"We'll make it," Jack said, putting the truck into drive and jamming the accelerator to the floor, tires screeching as we pealed across the highway. "Yeehaw!"

"Jack!" I exclaimed, dropping the book and grabbing the dashboard, laughing in spite of myself. "You're crazy!"

"You bet I am, Blondie," he yelled over the engine's rumble. "Crazy about you!"

CHAPTER 2

❖

April 14, 1995
Friday

"*I*F I'D KNOWN I WAS GOING TO HAVE TO WORK," GABE complained, bringing in another box of books we'd hauled out from the Ramsey ranch, "I would have stayed *at work.*"

It was Good Friday and Gabe had left the police department early to attend noon service. When he'd come home at one o'clock, I seized the rare opportunity of his half day off and sent him out to my dad's ranch for a truckload of boxes.

"Where do you want these?" he asked.

"Just set them down anywhere," I said. We'd had the oak floors refinished two weeks ago so the little bit of organization I'd managed to achieve in our newly purchased fifty-year-old California Craftsman bungalow house had been lost when, as floors were worked on, we were forced to shift furniture from room to room. Though we'd lived in the three-bedroom house for two months already, it still looked as if we had just moved in yesterday.

Gabe placed them next to the dozens of others. Scout,

my chocolate brown Labrador–German shepherd mix, trotted over to the new additions to chaos and started sniffing.

"Scout," I said, "there are no doggie treats in that box. Now get out of there." He wagged his tail and continued inspecting the boxes with the intensity of a drug-search canine.

"No one listens to me in this family," I complained to my laughing husband. Stacked boxes almost completely hid our new cognac-brown leather sofa and loveseat. Sighing, I pushed back a strand of curly, reddish-blond hair that had snuck out of my ponytail. "It's going to take me five years to decide where to put everything."

Since my gramma Dove's wedding to Isaac Lyons a month ago, she'd been on a frenzied cleaning spree out at the ranch. She had informed me a week ago that all the possessions I'd stored in her and Daddy's house and barn for the last three years since my first husband, Jack, died, were my problem now that Gabe and I owned a home roomy enough to store them. Isaac needed the empty space in the barn and any spare closets for all his worldly goods, which included a lifetime of family antiques, photographs, negatives, and developing equipment. Though he'd had at least fifty boxes shipped out already, a moving van with the last of his possessions was leaving his just-sold town house in Chicago today and was due in San Celina in a week.

I'd taken the last two days off from my job as curator for the Josiah Sinclair Folk Art Museum and Artists' Co-op so I could sift through dozens of pasteboard boxes out at the ranch, deciding what to keep and what to donate to the Salvation Army or the Homeless Shelter Thrift Shop. It had turned into a more emotional task than I'd anticipated. Though Jack had been gone for almost three years and I'd been remarried to Gabriel Ortiz, San Celina's police chief, for two of those three years, the moment I opened the box containing Jack's old brown Justin boots and his favorite Western belt with his name carved across the back, my heart lost a little of the joy I'd been taking in my new house.

Gabe pulled a colorful postcard from his back pocket and held it out to me. "Sam is having a ball in Hawaii."

His nineteen-year-old son, who'd been living out at my dad's ranch since last year and attending my old alma mater, Cal Poly San Celina, was on spring break in Hawaii, compliments of Gabe and Sam's mother, Lydia.

"Good for him," I said. "He worked hard this last semester. Daddy says he's the best hand he's hired in years."

"And he still managed to get three B's and an A." Gabe's proud smile was gratifying to see. He and Sam had not had the smoothest relationship in the last few years, but it looked like it was finally on a level plane. For the moment, anyway.

"So," Gabe asked, picking up a book that had fallen out of a box. "Do you really need any help putting any of this away?" The hopeful tone of his voice told me the question was rhetorical.

"Oh, go down to the gym and find someone to play racquetball with," I said, letting him off the hook. Though I could use his help, the truth was, if he actually put anything away, I'd never be able to find it.

He studied the book in his hand. *The Secret of the Crazy Quilt.* This reminds me of my favorite kid's book— *Danny Dunn and the Anti-Gravity Paint.* I loved that book."

"Wow," I said, moving around the boxes to stand next to him. "I haven't seen that book in years. Emma Baldwin, the author, lived here in San Celina a long time ago." I took the small hardback book out of his hand. The once colorful cover was faded with age. "It's a mystery series. They and the Misty books were my favorites when I was a girl."

I opened the front cover and read out loud.

"Oh, Mom," Molly Connors sighed, staring at her long yellow braids in the mirror. Her hair was such a bright shade of gold that her two older brothers, Tommy and Andy, nicknamed her Banana when she was born. "Do I have to put a dress on to go pick up Grandma Connors at the train station?"

Molly had just come in from riding her pinto pony, Rooster. Yesterday was the last day of school and she was looking forward to a long, fun-filled summer at the Triple C Ranch with lots of trips into Santa Regina two miles away to visit her best friend, Lily Waters.

"Now, Molly," her mother said, shaking a playful finger at her green-eyed daughter. "You'll have all summer to traipse around the ranch in your jeans. You are thirteen years old and it won't hurt you to look like a girl for a few hours." She stuck her hands into her red and white gingham apron. "You know, Grandma Connors may not even recognize you now that you are almost a young lady."

"I don't want to be a young lady," Molly moaned dramatically. "I just want to ride Rooster and go swimming in the creek and play fetch with Clementine and have picnics by the lake and spend the night with Lily in town. I don't want to learn how to quilt." Molly hated doing anything indoors, especially during the summer. Her hound dog, Clementine, whined and wagged his tail when he heard his name. His shiny coat was almost the exact shade of Molly's own hair.

Her grandmother, who hadn't seen Molly since she was ten, was coming down from San Francisco to spend the summer at the Connors cattle ranch which was located on the hilly, oak-dotted Central Coast of California. She was bringing the family crazy quilt with the intentions of teaching Molly how to start one of her own.

"You'll have plenty of time to do all of that," her mother assured her, reaching into Molly's closet and pulling out a mint green cotton dress she'd purchased at Lily's mother's dress shop downtown. "And I'm sure you're going to have a grand time showing

Grandma all your favorite places around the ranch. You know, besides loving to quilt, your grandma is still quite a horsewoman. She told me she couldn't wait to go riding with you and she said there might be a chance for you and her to go on an overnight trail ride."

"Really?" Molly said, her green eyes lighting up. She'd been begging to go on an overnight ride, but her mother didn't like camping out and her father, with all of his ranch chores, didn't have time. Maybe this visit from her grandmother wouldn't put too much of a crimp in her summer. "Do Tommy and Andy have to go?" Her fifteen- and sixteen-year-old brothers never let her tag along when they went places. It would be super if, for once, she was the one who was able to go somewhere without them.

"They need to stay and help me with the cattle," her dad said, standing in the bedroom doorway. He removed his white Stetson and ran a hand through hair as blond as Molly's. "Now you'd better get changed, squirt. The train will be here in less than an hour and we don't want to keep your grandma waiting."

"Okay, Dad," Molly said cheerfully. She turned back to the mirror, held the full-skirted cotton dress in front of her and made a silly face. "If Grandma will take me on an overnight camp out, then she deserves to see me in a dress."

"That's my girl," her dad said approvingly.

I looked up when Gabe chuckled.

"I can see why you liked them," he said. "It almost sounds like your life."

"Yeah, I also liked them because she had such a nice mother," I said, looking back down at the book and running my hand over the yellowed pages. My mother died of cancer when I was six years old and I'd always wondered what my life would have been like if she'd lived. "I loved all the popular mystery series—Trixie Belden,

Judy Bolton, Donna Parker, The Timber Trail Riders. But these were my favorites. I even did a term paper on Mrs. Baldwin for my history class when I was a sophomore at Cal Poly. Jack and I had only been married three months." I closed the book, an unexpected tightness narrowing my throat, remembering those days as if they'd happened last week.

Gabe slipped a warm hand under my long hair and gently massaged the nape of my neck. "I know," he said, his voice even and low.

I closed my eyes for a moment, soothed by Gabe's familiar touch, then turned and looked up at him. His blue-gray eyes, eyes that could change in an instant from steel gray to bright blue depending on his mood, glowed against his dark, olive-tinged skin. He was part Hispanic and part Anglo and so handsome that women sometimes turned in the street to stare at him. He possessed the natural social privilege that came in our society to those blessed with physical attractiveness, but it was his inner strength and his honest character that had eventually made me fall in love with him. That and the way he seemed to be able to see inside me in a way no one else ever had.

"The past . . ." His voice trailed away.

I nodded, swallowing hard, appreciative of what he was trying to do, what he was trying to say. In the last two months, we'd gone through a rough time in our still new and fragile marriage. A time when we'd almost broken up because of his own desire to recapture the past, his inability to let history be what it was and not try to relive it. We'd stumbled out of it, both forever branded, but glad we'd somehow not lost each other. Even so, we walked around each other tentatively these days, tiptoeing over eggshell-thin feelings, hypersensitive to the slightest arch of brow or involuntary sigh.

I set the book down and turned around, taking his face in my hands. "Sergeant Friday," I said, using my favorite nickname for him, originally derogatory, now as affectionate as another woman's "darling." "To borrow a phrase from my gramma, you pure out gladden my heart."

He smiled at me and kissed me gently. The feel of his thick, black mustache against my lips awakened in me an undeniable desire, a desire that, even after two years, hadn't seemed to diminish. He kissed me with more passion, finishing by giving my bottom lip a playful nip with his teeth. "You gladden more than my heart, *querida,*" he murmured.

"Hold that thought for later, Chief. Right now, you've got one more trip to the ranch for a load of boxes. Then we can quit for the day." I looked through our living room's large picture window at our deep emerald front lawn. It was a little before five o'clock and long shadows from the hundred-year-old oak tree in our yard were already starting to shade the white camellia bushes lining our deep-set front porch. "Then I promise you a wonderful dinner."

"Great, I'm starved. What are we having?"

"Whatever Liddie's special is tonight."

He gave a little groan. "Again?" He liked Liddie's, San Celina's favorite all-night diner, but this was the fourth time this week we'd eaten out.

"Do I cook after an exhausting day of moving and unpacking boxes?" I took his hand and kissed his palm. "Or do I reserve some strength for later? Your choice."

"Okay, okay," he said. "One more trip then it's dinner and bed. And before you bury your nose in a book or your notes about the museum's exhibits, I need some serious TLC."

I clicked my heels and saluted him. "Yes, sir. Some TLC, sir. Coming right up, sir. Whatever you want, sir."

"Complete and unquestioning obedience," he said, kissing the top of my head. "My absolute favorite personality trait. Especially in my wife."

"Really?" I said, grasping my chest with a spread hand. "I honestly didn't know that about you. I am *so* surprised."

We both laughed, knowing that there was more truth

than fiction in his statement, though he was doing better about changing that particularly stubborn trait. From the moment we met, his difficulty in leaving his police chief persona at work had been more than a slight bone of contention in our relationship.

The doorbell rang and a high-pitched woman's voice called from the front porch. "Hello, hello!"

"Benni, Gabe, are you decent?" another voice called, eerily similar yet just a shade different from the first one.

"Depends on your definition of decent," I called through the open front window.

From the porch came the stereo sound of high-pitched giggles. Scout barked in delight. It had taken him only one time to learn that these visitors were ones who were always good for a treat.

Gabe opened the oak front door. "Come on in, ladies. We're just unpacking boxes."

Our new neighbors across the street, Beatrice and Millicent Crosby (known throughout the county as Beebs and Millee), had known me since I was a baby when my parents moved to San Celina from Arkansas. Their gray-and-lavender three-story Victorian was a San Celina landmark and featured every year in the Christmas home tour.

They owned Crosby's Five and Dime on Lopez Street in downtown San Celina. They had inherited it from their father, Harold Crosby, who'd opened the store in 1928. Long before Wal-Mart came to town, throughout Woolworth's long reign and eventual demise, in spite of all the specialty stores that came and went, Crosby's Five and Dime was the place for locals to buy quilting thread, all sizes of knitting needles, a hundred different kinds of ribbon, birthday cards, children's Halloween costumes, wading pools, handmade Amish brooms, hair nets, and as Millee liked to say, "Every whatchamacallit, widget, doodad, and thingamabob we can find or you can imagine." Its cheery red-and-white exterior was also one of the most popular places for tourists to have their photos taken.

They were identical twins born sometime between the

stock market crash in 1929 and WWII, the exact year being a secret that they claimed even their doctor didn't know. They appeared to be somewhere in their sixties. Both were married and widowed—Beebs three times, Millee four ("either we're awful hard on men," Millee once confided in me, "or God just isn't making them as hearty as He used to"). They'd never had children so had immediately informed Gabe and me that they were adopting us.

"We need *someone* to cook for and worry over," they said the day we moved in. They'd brought an enchilada casserole, a tuna casserole, a macaroni salad, a loaf of zucchini bread, a loaf of banana bread, a dozen homemade rolls, and an angel food cake with orange frosting.

"Just to tide you over for a day or two," Beebs had said.

They always dressed alike and today they were spectacular in bright red satiny athletic suits and purple high-topped basketball shoes. Purple baseball caps decorated with rhinestones topped their heads of frothy white hair. That meant it was Millee's day to pick their outfits. They alternated days, and since they had radically different clothing styles, you could always tell whose day it was. Beebs was more conservative with her choice of outfits, leaning more toward neat pleated skirts and tailored jackets with a sailor or holiday motif lapel pin, where Millee, a frustrated singer and actress, liked bold, bright colors and lots of sparkle.

"We figured you kids might not have thought of dinner, what with all the activity we've been seeing over here today," Beebs said, holding a cobalt blue casserole dish out to Gabe. "It's a baked potato–green chile casserole," she said. "Heat at three hundred and fifty degrees for forty minutes, make yourself a green salad, and you've got supper."

"Thank you and bless you," he said, his eyes lighting up as he took the dish. He gave her his most grateful, devastating smile. She beamed back at him.

Scout whined and pawed at Gabe's leg.

"No way, pal," Gabe said. "I'm not sharing this with anyone."

"Here you go, sweetie," Millee said, pulling a dog treat out of her pocket. "We didn't forget you." She tossed it in the air and Scout caught it with a snap of his strong jaws.

"You two are shamelessly spoiling both of my men," I said, laughing.

"Oh, hush, child," Millee said. "We didn't forget you." She held up a stainless steel cake carrier. "German chocolate. Your favorite. Just like Ed, my second husband." A faraway look came into her gray eyes. "He truly was my favorite. What a dancer. That man could really cut the rug."

"We just got back from visiting the boys," Beebs said. "We're feeling a little nostalgic."

The "boys," as they liked to call their late husbands, were all buried side by side at the San Celina cemetery, where Jack and my mother were also buried. Rain or shine, the twins took flowers to their boys every Friday afternoon.

"Now, don't go eating that cake for breakfast," Beebs said, waggling her finger at me. She knew me almost as well as Dove.

"Oh, little sister, leave her alone," Millee said. She was older than Beebs by two minutes and never let her forget it. "Let the child eat her cake when she pleases."

"I'm just concerned with her health. You know she eats much too much sugar and not enough vegetables. That has always been her problem."

"So make her a carrot cake. A little sugar never killed anybody."

"But she—"

"So, what's new on Canyon Street?" I interrupted. If I didn't, they'd spend the next twenty minutes debating my eating habits. Behind them, Gabe's self-satisfied grin—he wholeheartedly agreed with Beebs—almost split his face in half. I shot at him with a finger pistol.

"Except for the fact that we have a new mailman and he's got great legs, not a darn thing," Millee said. "This place is as dull as yesterday's dishwater. We keep hoping you'll bring some excitement to the neighborhood." Millee had, with great interest, followed my somewhat dubious career of stumbling into crimes. An avid mystery novel reader, she was itching for me to get involved in some kind of intrigue again and include her and Beebs.

"Let's hope she doesn't," Gabe said wryly, handing me the casserole dish. "I'm going out to the ranch for that last load."

"Okay, take Scout with you. He needs the exercise."

After Gabe said his good-byes, I gestured at the ladies to follow me into the kitchen. "So, our mailman's got great legs, huh? I'll have to make sure and check that out." I turned the oven on and slid the casserole in.

"Millee expects life to be like a television show," Beebs said. "Things are going along just fine. We took some chicken gumbo soup over to Velma Richie two houses down because she's down with her gout again and we've been putting the finishing touches on a Road to California quilt that will go to the auction for the Montez adobe renovation. Plus we've finally memorized all the information about the California quilts and the crazy quilts. We're ready for our first tour group."

Beebs and Millee had recently signed up as docents at the folk art museum. In conjunction with the La Fiesta celebration this week, we had acquired a traveling exhibit of California quilts. It was on loan to us for a month from the state historical museum in Sacramento. And in our new upstairs gallery, there was a special exhibit on local crazy quilts that was due to open next weekend. I was just finishing the final draft of the history of crazy quilts to have printed for the exhibit.

"That's great. I'm so glad you two are going to be docents." Because of their vast personal knowledge of local history, they were going to be invaluable additions to the museum staff. "Do you have your costumes for the La Fiesta Parade next Saturday?" The senior citizen center, where they were popular members, was entering their first float, a replica of the Leland/Rodriguez adobe when it was still a working ranchero.

"You bet!" Beebs said. "We're going to be Spanish señoras. I just love my mantilla. Oh, and we bought our tickets to the Cattleman's Ball."

I opened the refrigerator and took out a glass pitcher of lemonade. "Would either of you like something to drink?"

"No time," Millee answered for both of them. "We've got to go peruse our Western wear catalogs again. We're trying to agree on what to wear to the ball. We've waited so long, we're going to have to have it sent FedEx overnight."

The Cattleman's Ball was a long-standing tradition in San Celina started back in the twenties when local ranchers would gather in their finest Western clothes, hire a local cowboy band, and put on a huge Santa Maria–style barbecue. During WWII it turned into a charity event with the money going to war relief and after the war to whatever charity the Cattlewomen of San Celina, who organized and sponsored the event, deemed most fitting. In the last twenty years, La Fiesta Days had culminated with the ball. The Cattleman and Cattlewoman of the Year, a highly prized honor, were always announced at the ball. Dove won Cattlewoman of the Year in 1978, the year Jack and I married. This year she was being given a special Lifetime Achievement Award for her many years of service in the promotion of agriculture and to the citizens of San Celina.

"Millee wants too much Western fringe and spangle," Beebs said.

"Beebs wants too much . . ." Millee thought for a moment, then threw up her hands in frustration. "Whatever the opposite of being spangled is."

"Unspangled?" I said, laughing. "Despangled?

"Spangleless?" Beebs said with a giggle.

"Let's just call it what it is . . . plain as dirt," Millee said, laughing with us. "So, how's Elvia adjusting to married life?" Beebs asked. "Are she and Emory all settled in?"

"I haven't talked to either of them for two days," I said. Not only had my gramma gotten married a couple of months ago, so had my best friend, Elvia Aragon, to my favorite cousin, Emory Littleton. "I was going to walk over to their house after supper and see if they're any further along in getting organized than we are."

They'd just moved two blocks east from us into a beautiful gray and navy blue Victorian house similar to the twins' and had been going through the same possession-weeding process as Gabe and I in the last few weeks. Emory had moved out here from Sugartree, Arkansas, specifically to woo and wed my friend, whom he'd been in love with since he first laid eyes on her when he was eleven years old and spent a summer with me on the Ramsey ranch. Now that his love life was settled, he'd quit his job at the *San Celina Tribune* and was in the process of setting up a West Coast office and a fledgling restaurant for his father's very lucrative smoked chicken business.

"Well," Millee said. "Tell her we're looking forward to Blind Harry's grand opening celebration Saturday. That is tomorrow, isn't it?"

"Yes," Beebs said. "Today is Good Friday, remember? That's why we went to church at noon. Today's Friday so tomorrow's Saturday."

"Thank you, sweetie. I swear, I'm glad one of us is organized. We saw that Elvia's planning a special presentation of local authors downstairs in the coffeehouse. What a wonderful idea!"

Elvia, who had worked at Blind Harry's Bookstore and Coffeehouse since her college years, now completely owned the business thanks to an unexpected wedding gift of the store's deed including its historic brick building from my cousin, who was both extremely wealthy and incredibly thoughtful. She'd decided to host a "Grand Re-opening—Under New Ownership" celebration this Saturday. I agreed with Millee—having local writers talk about or read their work was perfect. I planned on staying for the whole day to listen and help Elvia if she needed it.

"Do you know who's going to be there?" Millee asked.

"She gave me an updated list a few days ago," I said. "But I haven't had a chance to look at it yet."

They followed me into the living room, where I found the list in my purse and handed it to Beebs. "She managed to schedule twelve authors. They're each speaking for a half hour. And there'll be door prizes every hour, refreshments, and continuous activities in the children's department. Elvia's beside herself this week. Frankly, with just getting married and moving into their new house, I don't know why she didn't postpone the grand opening, but she was so excited about owning the store, she couldn't wait."

"Bless her heart," Beebs said. "I don't blame her." She glanced over the flyer with the authors' names listed while Millee peered over her shoulder.

"Would you look at that!" Millee said. "Emma must be back in town. Wonder when that happened?"

"Emma who?" I said.

"Emma's going to be there!" Beebs said. "Oh, my land's, we haven't seen her in years. I wonder how she's doing."

I gazed over Beebs's other shoulder. "Emma Baldwin! That is so weird. Not a half hour ago, I was talking about her books to Gabe. I loved her Molly Connors mystery series. Elvia didn't tell me she managed to get Emma Baldwin to sign at her opening. Didn't she move away back . . . gosh, it had to be when I was in still in college. Not long after I met her."

"It was 1978," Millee said. "Remember, Beebs, how she liked that certain type of notebook we carried at the store?"

"Those black speckled composition books," Beebs said. "We still carry them."

Millee nodded. "Said she wrote her books in them. Hired someone to type them out though. I guess she never learned to type. She came to speak to our Friday morning reading club a couple of times, but never joined herself even though we asked her." Beebs and Millee's reading club was famous in San Celina. It had been going strong for forty-two years.

"Emma always was a bit of a recluse," Beebs said. "I remember her saying at one of her talks that solitude was absolutely necessary for her to be able to write. She moved away in 1978, to the South somewhere, if my memory serves. I don't remember why."

"I do. Her cousin was sick," Millee said. "Emphysema, poor woman, and no one but Emma to take care of her. Wilma, who used to work at Blind Harry's, told us. They apparently corresponded regularly, but when Wilma died in 1984, we never heard what happened to Emma."

"I wonder if she sold her ranch when she went to care for her cousin?" I said. "It was such a cute old farmhouse outside of Paso Robles. The whitest house I ever saw with a shiny bright green roof and matching trim. She described it perfectly in her Molly Connors mysteries down to the gingerbread porch with the lacy lattice work. The first time I saw it, I was thrilled. It was like her books had come to life."

"That house was built in 1885 by her husband's father," Millee said, who had a phenomenal memory of San Celina architecture. "So now she's back. That's odd. I wonder why?"

"It's not odd at all," Beebs said. "San Celina County is a nice place to live. Why wouldn't she want to come back?"

"I interviewed her when I was a sophomore in college," I said. "For my history class. She was really kind to me. I think I totally embarrassed myself by gushing over her books. I just loved them so much. She was very gracious though." I picked up the book Gabe had set down on our coffee table. "Look, she even signed the book I brought with me to the interview." I handed it to Beebs. "I own all ten of her books, but this was my favorite."

Beebs read the inscription out loud. "To Benni, with sincere appreciation with your enthusiasm for my books. Best wishes, Emma Baldwin."

"Perfect and proper. That sure sounds like Emma," Millee said, bending down to retie one of her purple sneakers. "She always was more of a bookworm than a ranch wife."

"The three times I visited her, she served me tea in these incredibly thin china cups with pale orange pumpkins on them," I said. "Earl Grey tea with cream and lemon. I'd never seen anyone put cream in tea before. And she had real crumpets with orange marmalade and tea cakes with pink frosting and scones that tasted like orange and cinnamon. I was so nervous, afraid I would drop my cup and break it. It felt like I was having tea with the Queen of England. The last time I went to see her, I was bringing her a copy of my paper. I wanted her approval, but she wasn't there. I did meet up with her son though. What a creepy guy. Found him skulking about our ranch one time too when Jack and I were out fixing fence. Anyway, I sent her a note after that with a copy of my finished term paper, but I never heard from her again."

"That's odd," Beebs said. "Emma's not a rude person. I can't imagine why she didn't drop you a note or something."

I shrugged. "Who knows? I mean, it's not like we were friends or anything. If she had a family emergency, I would be the last person she'd be thinking about. I could have pursued it further, but I was twenty and just married and didn't much think about it after my class was over. Heaven knows, back then Jack and I flitted around with our heads in the clouds like we were the only ones in the world."

"We remember," the twins said at the same time. We

all laughed. Wasn't almost everyone that self-involved at twenty?

"You certainly have something to look forward to tomorrow," Beebs said. "Renewing an acquaintance with an old friend."

"I doubt that she would consider me a friend," I said. "She probably doesn't even remember me."

"Oh, she'll remember you," Millee said. "And I'm sure she will think of you as a friend. Emma always said that she considered all the young girls who read her books as her secret friends, the daughters she had never had. Why, she told me once when she was at the store that there were times in her life when their lovely fan letters about her books were the only thing that kept her sane."

CHAPTER 3

❖

April 15, 1995
Saturday

$\mathcal{T}$HE NEXT MORNING, HALF DRESSED FOR THE BOOK-
store, I was pouring food into Scout's blue ceramic bowl
when the phone rang. Gabe had already left for his daily
five-mile jog.

"Honeybun, is that you?" Dove asked, her voice sharp
as an ax.

I almost wisecracked and said, "What other woman did
you expect?" but the irritation in her tone told me all was
not well on the Ponderosa and I'd best keep my smart
remarks to myself.

"Yes, ma'am," I answered, hopping on one foot while
trying to pull on a boot and hold the phone at the same
time. Scout raised his head from his dish to watch me
with that questioning, if-you're-in-charge-we're-in-big-
trouble look dogs often give their owners. Rightfully so
sometimes, I must add.

"How hard do you think it would be for the Catholic
Church to annul a marriage?" Her breath sounded slow
and even over the phone.

Her words stunned me silent for a moment.

"I have no idea," I finally said. "Try asking Father Mark." Inhaling deeply, I tentatively asked, "Who wants to know?"

"I want to know."

I sat down hard on one of our pine dining-room chairs. Was she saying what I thought she was saying? "What's wrong?"

"I don't think I want to be married anymore." She paused. "Scratch that. I'm *sure* I don't want to be married anymore."

Thank goodness we didn't have picture phones. My grin right now would have garnered me a swift slap upside the head. "Dove, I am pretty certain you actually have to have been *married* in the Catholic Church before they can annul it." I wasn't even sure what the procedure in the Baptist Church was when it came to annulment.

"Can you still get an annulment if you already consummated the marriage?" she asked.

My face flushed even though there was no one there to see it except Scout. This was getting into territory I really, truly preferred not to imagine. "You know, I think this is something you might need to talk to Mac about."

Poor Mac. This was not the first time she'd challenged our widowed, forty-something minister with a somewhat unconventional request or question. Thank goodness he'd known her since he was in the nursery himself and was used to her wild tangents, as Daddy called them.

"Honeybun, are you still there?" Her voice sounded almost desperate.

I settled back in the kitchen chair and prepared to sympathize with her marriage woes. "Yes, I'm here. What's going on between you and Isaac?"

"Try me and Isaac and Maude and Iris and Louise and Maryjean and Eleanor and Suzanne and Gertie and Lucy and—"

"Whoa, hold on! What are you talking about?"

"My husband's groupies," she snapped. "They call and call and call. Always asking for him, always wanting something. I told him last night I didn't realize I was marrying King Solomon and his thousand concubines."

A giggle tickled the back of my throat and I valiantly stifled it. When she'd married Isaac Lyons, who besides having a public image also had a reputation of being very attractive to ladies of all ages, I'd wondered if she truly realized what a change he would bring to her life.

"Gramma, I hate to point out the obvious, but you've known from the first time you two met that he was a celebrity. I thought you enjoyed his fame."

"That was before it was *my* phone ringing off the hook every blessed minute of the day. I don't know three fourths of the women who call here and the fourth I do know are ladies in this town who never looked twice at me before. Now, all of a sudden, we're the toast of San Celina. We have more invitations to parties and dinners and lunches and brunches than I've had since I moved here in 1964." She took a deep breath and added, "And he *snores*. He sounds like a doggone locomotive engine going up a five-mile grade. I'm here to tell you, honeybun, I haven't had a good night's sleep in a month. And his junk? Heaven's to Betsy, his junk! I'm about ready to light a match . . ."

"I know what you mean about junk. I feel like I'm swimming in it myself." I checked my watch. Without seeming unsympathetic, I needed to find a way to ease myself out of this conversation. There was another frantic woman waiting for me in a bookstore downtown.

"Ha, you're an amateur compared to Isaac. I think we might have to build another barn. And more is coming in a week! Why, I—"

"Dove, I'm sorry, but I have to get down to Blind Harry's. Are you going to Elvia's grand opening?"

"Of course I am," she said. "Isaac's signing his *California Ranch Women* book at three P.M."

"Maybe the three of us can have dinner downtown," I said.

"No chance of *that*," Dove said. "We're booked up for

dinner engagements for the next four months because that man does not know how to say no to anything female. I'll have to pencil you in for mid-August."

"Then how about you and me—"

Her voice went low. "Can't talk anymore. He's back from his walk." She hung up without saying good-bye.

I walked the two blocks to Blind Harry's Bookstore on Lopez Street. One of Elvia's college-age clerks let me in after I tapped on the glass door.

"Where's *La Patrona*?" I asked.

She pointed at the wooden stairs leading to the basement coffeehouse. "Better take your whip and chair," the young girl said, giving me a hesitant smile. She scratched at the green-and-white lily-of-the-valley tattoo on her neck. "She's on a rampage."

"I'll see what I can do," I assured the dark-haired girl, whom I recognized as a new hire. She'd soon learn Elvia's bark was worse than her bite. "Don't worry."

The girl kept scratching, not looking entirely convinced.

Downstairs in the book-lined, nutty-scented coffeehouse, Elvia was, indeed, in fine form. She stood in front of Manuel, her coffeehouse manager and head *barrista*, her five-feet-nothing frame barely reaching up to his broad shoulders. Her arms were moving like little windmills.

"I asked you to double the order for lemon tarts and triple the chocolate croissants, not the other way around!" Her normally elegant, soft-spoken voice had taken on a hysterical edge that told me that lava might be soon erupting from this human volcano. The doors of the bookstore were due to open in less than an hour, but I wasn't sure if Elvia—or anyone else—was going to survive until then.

"Okay, *amiga buena,* let's take a time-out here," I said, gently pulling her around the coffeehouse's blue tile counter. Manuel gave me an amused wink. He'd worked for her for two years and was, thankfully, not intimidated by her sometimes irritable histrionics. He actually seemed to admire them.

"The great ones, they are always like thoroughbreds," he told me once. She was lucky to have an employee who understood her so well.

She didn't protest when I prodded her toward a back table, but her posture was stiff and her smooth brown jaw set in annoyance.

"Manuel," I called over my shoulder. "Could you please bring a couple *decaf* cappuccinos?"

He gave me an understanding nod.

"Elvia," I said, pointing at one of the coffeehouse's library-style ladderback chairs. "Sit down and get a hold of yourself. You know people will eat whatever is here. In terms of tragedy, it's somewhere between the eruption of Mount St. Helens and getting a run in your Anne Klein stockings."

Without a word, she sat down, folded her arms across her chest, and glared at me. Dressed in a Chanel-style burgundy business suit with her glossy black hair up in a French twist, she looked like a finalist for Latina Businesswoman of the Year. Her only jewelry was her new diamond wedding set and a pair of half-carat emerald-cut diamond earrings.

I crossed my eyes and made a goofy face, trying to make her laugh. "I predict, no matter what flavors they are, you won't have two tarts to rub together by the end of the day."

She gave a deep sigh. "You're right. I don't know what's wrong with me."

Manuel walked up with our cappuccinos. "Light foam with a little cinnamon," he said, setting a small white cup in front of Elvia. "Your *favorita*." He placed an identical cup in front of me.

She reached over and grabbed his hand. "Oh, Manuel, *lo siento*."

He patted her delicate French-manicured hand with his own flour-dusted one. "*De nada, patrona.* I know that you are very nervous and excited. We all are excited too. It is finally your own place and you want things right."

In spite of her sometimes military way of running Blind Harry's, Elvia was an unusually thoughtful boss who gave her employees excellent salaries and health care benefits. She also believed in rewarding loyal workers with bonuses and extra vacation time. She'd fought the owner, a wealthy Scottish man in Reno, for those perks when she was manager, justifying it by the store's ever-increasing profits. She was loved by her employees, who tolerated—even sometimes bragged about—their temperamental but hardworking boss.

"*Gracias,* Manuel," she said. "I'll regain my bearings in a moment."

"We're going to be fine," he said confidently, heading back toward the steamy kitchen.

"Oh, Benni," she said, wrapping both her hands around the thick white cup. "I'm so scared about owning this place. What if it starts losing money? What if I can't do this alone?"

I smiled. "You forget, you aren't alone anymore. You've got Emory."

Her face softened, a rare occurrence for my type-A friend. "Sometimes I still have to pinch myself to make sure this is my life. Is it possible for a person to maintain the kind of happiness I feel right now?"

"No," I said cheerfully, knowing better than anyone how tenuous that feeling can be. "But it's replaced by a really nice feeling of peace and, I don't know, a kind of joy. Except, of course, when both of those feelings are replaced by tension, anxiety, irritation, and annoyance."

She laughed. "I guess if anyone knows about the ups and downs of marriage, it's you."

"You're laughing, that's good. Sometimes humor is the only thing that's gotten me through the awful times in my two marriages. That and the occasional mind-boggling quickie."

Her cheeks turned a rosy red.

I grinned. "Caught you! You guys had one this morning, didn't you? You should be more relaxed then."

"Mind your own business," she said primly. "And finish your coffee. I need you to help me set up the book-signing table."

Fifteen minutes later, I was upstairs at the wide oak book-signing desk near the central register attempting to artfully arrange the first author's books, a man who wrote children's books set here on the Central Coast. His protagonist was a mockingbird named Pete who had a cousin named Repete. Pete and his cousin lived in a pepper tree near a fire station.

"Why didn't you tell me Emma Baldwin is speaking today?" I asked, stacking books while Elvia arranged a bunch of pink and white roses in a jade green vase.

"I just received an answer from her on Tuesday. She's only been here a couple of weeks."

"Really? How did you know she was back in town?"

"You know Don Rader, who works the reference desk at the Paso Robles Library?"

"Wasn't he a couple of years behind us in school?"

"Yes, he was sophomore class president when I was senior class president. Anyway, he spotted her last week when she was perusing the new titles and called me. He recognized her because he and his mother, Lucille, are diehard San Celina history buffs. He said he wrote an article about her a few years ago for the Historical Society newsletter. He thought she would be a good addition to my grand opening. She was still there when he called me and he asked her if she would talk to me. I was honestly going to tell you every time we talked this week, but I kept forgetting. I just don't know what's wrong with me these days."

"Newlywed dementia. So, what was she like when you talked to her? Do you remember my interview with her when we were in college?"

"How could I forget? She was all you talked about for weeks. Why didn't you two stay in touch? I thought you hit it off." She pulled out two half-open roses and stuck them in a different place in the vase.

I shrugged and kept arranging the Pete books into what I hoped were attractive piles. "We had those few meetings and then she just disappeared. Don't you remember? I went out to her ranch outside Paso Robles to show her the last draft of my paper and she was gone."

"Vaguely. That seems like a lifetime ago." She pulled some baby's breath from the green florist's paper and started arranging it around the roses.

"It was. Nineteen seventy-eight. Bell-bottoms and puka shell necklaces. Platform shoes! Which you and I loved way too much."

She peered at me over the roses, her full lips turning up at the corners. "You have to admit it was nice being tall for a change. They're back in style, you know."

"Not for this cowgirl. Remember, you *adored* the Bee Gees. You played them all the time in your orange Vega." I sang a few bars of "How Deep Is Your Love."

Elvia put a hand to her temple. Her nails were the same clean white as the flowers. "Please, don't remind me. I can't believe I bought an orange car. Remember how I had such a crush on John Travolta?"

I laughed. "Who didn't? Remember how much Jack hated disco music?"

The worried lines around her deep brown eyes finally relaxed. "I used to reset all the buttons on your truck radio so they'd play it just to annoy him."

"Believe me, I remember. Back to Emma Baldwin. Beebs and Millee said she left San Celina to take care of a sick cousin."

"For seventeen years?"

"That's what they said." I grabbed some baby's breath and started sticking it into the vase. "She must have left in a hurry. I never got a chance to thank her in person for letting me interview her."

"Here's your chance then. I literally begged her to come to the grand opening. I told her she still had lots of fans in San Celina County who'd love to hear from her again. She said she hadn't done any book-signings for years, but . . ."

"But it's hard to say no to someone as persistent as you," I finished.

She tried not to look too smug. "I did bribe her with the fact that you would be here. She said she would be delighted to see you again."

"She remembered me? That's incredible."

"You're not as easy to forget as you think," Elvia said, arching her shapely eyebrows. "And why shouldn't she be delighted, *mi amiga buena?* You're a wonderful person."

"Ah, shucks, I'm just a plain ole country girl," I said, grinning.

She gave me a gentle shove. "Who doesn't know how to gracefully accept a compliment."

I just laughed and shoved her back. We were finishing up the flower arrangement when we heard a sharp tap on the front door.

"We're not open yet," Elvia called out, before she turned around and saw who it was. She walked over to the door and unlocked it.

"Hey, Friday," I said, giving my husband a kiss. He was sweaty and warm from his jog, but the sight of his muscled thighs in his running shorts still had the power to make my pulse skip a beat or two. "How's your town looking?" It was a joke among the downtown San Celina merchants that they knew everything was okay when the chief of police felt secure enough to go for his daily run.

"All is quiet in Dodge City," he said. "I stopped by to see what our plans for dinner are tonight."

"I'll be here until the last author speaks," I said, then turned to Elvia. "When will that be?"

"My last one is scheduled for seven P.M.," she said, wiping the bottom of the wet vase with a paper towel. "But you don't have to stay for all of them. I'll be fine."

"I'm staying until Emory gets here. Where is my flaky cousin, anyway?"

"At his new office. His furniture shipment is coming today," she said with a sigh. "Is that poor timing or what?"

"You know how it is here on the Central Coast," Gabe said. He crossed his arms and leaned against the front counter. "You take things when you can get them."

"I'll go by his office in a little while and see when he can make it," I said. "I'm sure he'll be here by suppertime."

"I don't *need* a baby-sitter," Elvia said, her voice perturbed.

"Yes, *Patrona*," I said, patting her on the shoulder. She swiped at my hand in mock irritation.

"I'll walk you out," I told Gabe.

Outside, he asked, "How's Elvia really doing?"

"She'll be okay, but I just want either me or Emory here to keep her from spinning off into space. She's as nervous as a new heifer. What're you going to do today?"

"I have some paperwork to catch up on at the office and Scout has his rabies vaccination."

"That's right. I'm glad you remembered. So, what do you want to do for dinner?"

"Well, I got a phone call this morning after you left. An old LAPD buddy is in town . . ."

My face froze. This was how our problems started two months ago when an old LAPD friend . . . *female* . . . came into town and disrupted our lives in a huge, almost irreparable way.

". . . and I thought we'd take him out to dinner," Gabe finished. He watched my face intently with a slightly anxious look that reminded me of Scout when I was late giving him dinner.

Him. I let out the breath I didn't realize I'd been holding. Those three little letters made all the difference in the world.

"Okay," I said. "Who is it?"

"Guy named Luke. Luke Webster. He and I worked together in narcotics for a while. You'll like him. He's a transplanted Southerner. Georgia or Alabama . . . one of those states. He's recently retired from the department and started his own investigation firm. Has some kind of case he's working on up here. Why don't we try that new Mexican restaurant, La Casa Buena? I hear they make a great mole."

"Sounds good. Meet me here at four o'clock."

After he left, the time flew by, and before I realized it, it was already one P.M. and the store was packed. I'd spent three hours straight helping at the counter and directing new customers to the author talks downstairs. Even though I hadn't heard one author speak yet, I was glad for Elvia that the grand opening was a success. Every author came upstairs after their talk and had a respectable line of people to buy books so I knew Elvia was relieved. She fretted like a new mother about her authors' feelings.

It was a quarter to two when Emma Baldwin walked through Blind Harry's front door. I knew her right away, and even though I'd been told so by Elvia, I was thrilled and flattered when she did recognize me.

"Benni Harper, is that you?" she said in her distinctive throaty voice. She wore a simple blue denim dress with a silver-and-gold horse lapel pin. Her salt-and-pepper shoulder-length hair was styled in a simple pageboy with bangs. She'd widened a little around the hips and had acquired a few more wrinkles, but her lively blue eyes were as bright as the ones that had greeted me on her shady front porch seventeen years ago. I guessed her age to be early sixties.

"Mrs. Baldwin," I said, coming out from behind the counter. "It's so good to see you again."

She impulsively grasped both of my hands in hers. "Please, call me Emma. Oh, my dear, you haven't changed a bit." Before I could protest, she added, "But, of course, my eyesight is getting a little weak these days." She smiled mischievously and gently squeezed my hands before letting go.

I laughed with her and nervously pulled on my earlobe.

I didn't remember her being this teasing and lighthearted. "Well, my eyesight's fine and you look great. Are you glad to be back in San Celina?"

There seemed to be a momentary hesitation before she answered. "Yes, it is good to be back. A lot has changed, though."

"Yes, it has. And continues to change way too fast for my taste."

Her wide mouth, painted a pale tangerine, moved up slightly in a wry smile. "Much like life. And speaking of life, in the short time I've been back I've read about you in the newspaper. You're quite the society lady these days."

I picked up a red Blind Harry's pencil on the counter and started fiddling with it, uncomfortable, as always, with that aspect of my life. She'd most likely seen last week's photograph of me and Gabe at the March of Dimes Benefit Ball. As was often the case, Gabe had been asked to be the auctioneer for the donated items.

"It's just part of my job of being a police chief's wife as well as curator for our local folk art museum. I'd rather be out vaccinating cattle than wearing cocktail dresses and discussing fund raisers, but I try to do my best at all my jobs."

She gently patted my shoulder. "You are so grown up! And certainly living a different life than when we last met. I was terribly sorry to hear from Elvia about your young husband, Jack. What a tragedy."

"Yes, it was." I gave a little sigh, thinking about those boxes at home containing his possessions. "Believe it or not, I was thinking about you just the other day, before I even realized you were going to be here at the store. My new husband, Gabe, and I bought a house in town and I was unpacking some books. I found my copy of *The Secret of the Crazy Quilt*. The one you signed for me. It was my favorite of all your books."

"Oh, dear," she said, bringing a thin, blue-veined hand

up to her cheek. "That was long ago, wasn't it? I haven't published anything in years."

"I'm sorry," I said, wondering if I'd brought up a sensitive subject. Then again, she *was* here at Blind Harry's to discuss her books and writing. "Will it be hard for you to talk about writing or your books?"

"Not at all," she said. "Talking about Molly and her adventures has always been fun for me. And I've continued to write, though sporadically. My cousin's poor health took up so much of my time."

"How is she?" I asked, then realized the minute I said it that might not be a comfortable subject for her to talk about.

"Adelle died a few months ago," she said softly.

"I'm so sorry," I said.

"I miss her, but am glad she is no longer in pain. She suffered incredibly these last few years. Her emphysema was so advanced she often could hardly take a breath." She looked down at the floor, avoiding my eyes.

There was a moment of awkward silence. "We're having an exhibit of local crazy quilts at the folk art museum," I said, trying to fill in the silence. "It's out at the old Sinclair adobe. Have you seen the museum yet?"

She looked up, her expression overly animated, as obviously happy to change the subject as I was. "No, I haven't and I'd love to. Especially since my crazy quilt is the only quilt I own."

"That's right, your quilt was the model for the one in the book. The clues were in the figures stitched on the quilt." Then an idea came to me. "Emma, would you . . . well, this is sort of last minute . . . but could we use your quilt in our exhibit? I promise we'll take wonderful care of it and the security at the museum is excellent and—"

"I'd love it," she said.

"Great! I'd like to hear some of the history—"

Before I could finish my request, Elvia walked up, her hand held out to greet Emma. "Mrs. Baldwin, thank you so much for coming to our grand opening! I've had so many people asking for you."

"Please, call me Emma," she said, turning to my friend, her cheeks tinged pink. "And I am thrilled to be here though I can't imagine anyone remembering my little books."

"On the contrary," Elvia said. "You have many dedicated fans."

"Elvia and I are your most diehard ones," I added. "We didn't just love your books, we wanted to *be* those characters."

Elvia gave Emma an uncharacteristically shy smile. "She's right. I have my whole collection in my office, which I hope you'll be kind enough to sign for me."

"My dear, it will be my pleasure," Emma said.

Elvia glanced at the large black-and-white schoolhouse clock hanging in the children's department. "There's ten minutes before you're scheduled to speak. Is there anything I can get you, coffee or tea? An Italian soda?"

"Just water, my dear. Perhaps I'll have something else afterward."

"Then we'll just go on downstairs, if you like."

I followed them downstairs and took a chair in back. The room, which could comfortably seat about a hundred people, was over half full. Not a bad showing for someone who'd not published a book in this series for thirty years. Most of the audience were women my age and older with just a sprinkling of young girls probably coerced here by their mothers and grandmothers. When Elvia introduced Emma, the audience grew quiet.

Emma stood up and took her place behind the carved oak podium. Her voice was clear and strong as she began telling us about how she came to San Celina in 1949 when she was eighteen years old from the small Georgia town where she was born. About her adventures waitressing at a diner in Paso Robles when it was a true Western town, how she met her husband, RJ, a local cowboy who fell in love with her on her first day as a waitress and pursued her until she gave in and married him two months later.

She made us laugh with stories about her early days trying to be a good rancher's wife, her first attempts at baking pies, serving a hungry calving crew, and learning to prepare that favorite Western delicacy, breaded, deep-fried prairie oysters. She told us about trying to run the ranch when she was a new mother and RJ was drafted into the Korean War in 1951. She helped the time pass, she said, by writing letters about the ranch to some young neighbor girls she used to baby-sit in Georgia, incorporating some of our county's local legends and history. About eight years later, the girls' uncle, an editor in New York who happened to come for a visit, read some of her letters and contacted her about perhaps turning her stories into a series for young girls, something on the order of Nancy Drew or Trixie Belden.

"I didn't have a clue, no pun intended, on how to go about it," she said, gripping the edges of the podium, "but I went out and read a bunch of Nancy Drew and Judy Bolton mysteries and figured it out. Mr. Vincent liked what I did and so the Molly Connors mysteries were born. The first one came out in 1961."

She had us close to tears with her story of how she was widowed when she was only thirty-four when RJ was killed in a shooting accident while hunting wild pig. She was left with a heavily mortgaged ranch and, with the small advances given by her publisher, not nearly enough money to keep it going. She made a deal with their ranch manager to work for only room and board and went back to waitressing to bring in money.

"Finally," she said, "the ranch started being self-supporting and I quit my waitressing job. It was a hard few years and, unfortunately, my writing is what suffered the most. I wrote a couple of adult books, long out of print now. There just weren't enough hours in the day. That is why there are only ten Molly Connors mysteries."

After her talk, Elvia asked if there were any questions before Mrs. Baldwin signed books. After the usual

"Where do you get your ideas?" and "How long does it take to write a book?" questions, a young preteen girl asked, "Mrs. Baldwin, is your son a rancher?"

For a moment, Emma's face froze. It happened so fast and she recovered so quickly that, afterward, I wondered if I had imagined her reaction.

"No, I'm afraid not," she said.

"Is he a writer like you then?" the young girl persisted.

Emma's face did not reveal one bit of emotion. "No, he passed away a long time ago."

The room went uncomfortably silent. I desperately tried to think of a question that would draw attention away from the awkward moment. I called out, "Would you consider ever writing more Molly Connors books? We all love them so much."

The audience murmured in agreement.

Her grateful eyes found me in the crowd. "I'm not sure about writing about Molly again, but I have been approached to write a memoir of my early years as a ranch wife in San Celina and, perhaps, a book about local history. A young man who owns a lovely local publishing house called Blue Poppy Press has asked me to consider it. I wasn't quite sure anyone would be interested, but after this wonderful day at Blind Harry's, I think I might try."

Her announcement brought a chorus of eager voices encouraging her. Elvia stood up from her seat in the front row and announced, "Mrs. Baldwin will be happy to sign any books you have brought with you and I have managed to locate some used copies of her Molly Connors books, which are for sale upstairs." She turned to Emma. "Thank you so much for taking the time to come help us celebrate Blind Harry's grand reopening." She started clapping her hands and the rest of the audience joined in.

Upstairs, I stood to the side with Elvia and watched the line of forty or so women clutching faded, obviously well-read books inch their way toward a few minutes with Emma.

Elvia bent her head close to mine and whispered, "Thanks for jumping in and saving the day. I didn't realize her son had died."

"Neither did I," I whispered back. "I wonder if it was something violent. He was really creepy, that's all I remember."

"You met him once, didn't you? At her house?"

"Actually, more than once. Three times and every time he was a jerk. It's awful to say, but unless he did a one-hundred-eighty-degree turn around, she's better off with him dead."

Elvia's eyebrows shot up. "Pretty strong words."

"He was trouble, and I don't mean just for her. Remember, I caught him on our property over by Sweetheart Hill that one time. I had the distinct feeling he was casing the section to use it for doing drugs or maybe growing marijuana."

"Hard to imagine someone like Emma having a drug dealer for a son." Elvia looked over at Emma, who was bent forward listening intently to a fan's young daughter. "At least her husband sounded nice. From what she said, he was quite the dashing Western cowboy." She smiled at me. "Just your type."

I laughed. "It was until I was seduced by a handsome, arrogant, Latino police chief."

"Ah, the fickleness of love," Elvia said.

CHAPTER 4

❖

April 1, 1978
Saturday

"THIS WAS NOT FUNNY." I PEERED AT JACK IN OUR brightly lit kitchen through bleary, narrowed eyes. "I'm nervous enough about interviewing Mrs. Baldwin today without your April Fool's Day jokes."

Jack had gotten up early and set out breakfast for me. I thought it was sweet and considerate of him until I tried to pour an empty box of cornflakes, then an empty carton of milk, put a spoonful of salt into a cup that appeared to be coffee, but was actually tea brewed to a muddy, coffee-looking brown. When I spit the salty tea out in the sink and was on my way across the kitchen to strangle the cocky grin right off his face, he pulled out a box of my favorite donuts—maple bars, jelly-filled, and chocolate-iced cake. He'd driven all the way into town to buy them at Leon's Donut-Hole.

"Buddy-boy," I said, dumping the cup of tea into the sink. "Those donuts are the only thing between you and a long, painful death."

"You know you adore me," he said, stopping long enough to kiss the back of my neck on his way out to do his morning chores.

"Right now, that's negotiable," I yelled after him.

At noon, I was driving through Paso Robles on my way to Mrs. Baldwin's house, reviewing my questions over and over in my mind, my nerves as edgy as a new-born colt's.

When I pulled up to her house, about a mile out of town, I sat in my truck for a moment, mesmerized by the sight of the green-and-white farmhouse. It was Molly Connors's house come to life. Every little detail was exactly how she'd described them in her books down to the tire swing on the massive valley oak tree shading her front yard and the Spanish moss hanging from the trees like strands of pale green lace. The early-afternoon air was still and heavy, scented with jasmine and sweet honeysuckle. In the distance a woodpecker's tap-tap-tap punctured the warm silence.

Mrs. Baldwin must have heard my truck's loud engine coming up the drive because by the time I climbed down from the cab, she was coming down the porch steps.

"Welcome, welcome," she said. "You must be Benni Harper."

"Yes, ma'am," I answered. "Thank you so much for letting me interview you."

"It's my pleasure," she said. "Please, come inside where it is cooler."

In minutes, I was inside her living room, filled with simple, Shaker-style furniture, holding a dainty teacup in one hand and a plate of small iced cakes and orange-scented scones in the other. After our first cup of tea, I set down my half-eaten treats and pulled out a notebook. I asked her some basic questions of how she came to San Celina, how she met her husband, what inspired her to write the Molly Connors books. She answered everything with a practiced ease that made me guess she'd been asked these questions many times before. So I branched out into more personal questions, trying to figure out a way to make my term paper more than just a litany of her life and accomplishments.

"Try to find the soul of your subject," Professor Hill always admonished his students. "Don't just record the surface aspects of their lives, but dig deeper and try to discover how they feel about what they've accomplished, the choices they've made. History, when it concerns human beings, is more than just facts, it's also feelings because our feelings about things reflect our times and our experiences in a way that just recording mere facts cannot. And don't forget, sometimes facts lie . . . or rather are not what they first appear to be."

The trouble was, I couldn't figure out a way to do that with Mrs. Baldwin. She was a kind, soft-spoken lady who wrote these books I loved, who lived on a ranch with her husband, RJ, until he was killed. She had a son named Cody. I wondered if he would agree to talk to me.

"Is your son still working the ranch with you?" I asked, desperately trying to think of a way to, as Professor Hill said, dig deeper into my subject. I mentally saw my imagined A dropping down to a C-minus. I stood in front of one of the whitewashed built-in bookcases that flanked the front windows and picked up a fancy silver picture frame. It was obviously a family picture taken before Mrs. Baldwin's husband had died. Her husband was thin and plain-featured and wore a huge white Stetson. He stared, narrow-eyed, at the camera with an intense, though not unpleasant, expression. Her son looked to be in his early teens. Like his father, he squinted at the camera, not exactly smiling or frowning. Only Emma Baldwin's face showed a genuine smile.

"Cody's a grown man now. He left the ranch a long time ago." Her voice was even, noncommittal.

I turned to look at her, holding the photograph in my hand. "What did he think of your books?"

"Did I tell you that I've also written two adult books? One is a novel set in the Gold Rush days up around Grass Valley. Have you ever driven Highway 49 and seen Sutter's Mill? You really must someday. It's quite fascinating. My other book was a novel based on my mother and father. He was a postmaster in a small town called Madison, Georgia, back in the thirties. He met my mother when she tried to talk him into giving back a Dear John letter she'd dropped in the mail slot to an old boyfriend."

For the rest of the interview she steered the conversation toward the Molly books, about what parts of the plots were based on real incidents in San Celina history. Mrs. Baldwin was an avid local history buff and liked using history, as well as local settings, in her plots.

She had to cut our time short because of a prior engagement, but we made a date for me to come by again on Monday.

"I'll show you the quilt then," she said, walking me out to my truck.

I told Jack about my interview that evening at dinner. "It was so weird. She just ignored my question about her son. Wonder why?"

Jack scooped out a second helping of shepherd's pie. "Maybe they don't get along."

"Why didn't she just say so?"

He gave a small chuckle and speared a chunk of gravy-covered beef. "Because people either avoid or lie about their family relationships all the time."

"Why?"

"You know why. No one wants the rest of the world to know how screwed up their own family is. Look at us. All us Harpers go to church every Sunday, all spit-and-polished, nice and shiny. People think we're just as close as can be. But look at what things are like between me and Wade. We barely speak to each other most of the time."

"But that's just squabbles about the ranch. It's not serious. You two really care about each other." I stood up and picked up my empty plate. "Are you finished?"

He scooped up a last bite of gravy and potatoes, then handed me his plate. "Just because people have the same blood doesn't mean they like each other. Frankly, Wade would be the last person I'd ever pick for a friend."

I turned on the water and started rinsing off the plates. "Can you imagine not liking your own child? That would be awful."

Jack carried our glasses over to the sink. "I can if the kid turned out to be like Wade. Any peach pie left?"

"About half. There's ice cream in the freezer unless you finished it for lunch."

"Ate lunch in town. Had to go pick up some feed that Wade was supposed to get because he got waylaid down at Trigger's bar . . . again. Sandra's all riled up about it." He glanced up at the kitchen clock. "It's eight o'clock and he's still not home. He's really going to catch it from Sandra this time. And he talks about *me* being irresponsible."

I started filling the sink with dishwashing soap and water, then turned to Jack. "I'm so glad I picked the good brother."

He reached for the dish towel stuck in the refrigerator handle. "Ha, you didn't think so when I tracked mud in the kitchen the other day. Or when I played my little joke on you this morning."

"You're still a little green-broke, but I'll train you proper yet."

He flicked the towel at my butt. "Don't let Mom hear you say that. She thinks she did a good job."

"Quit that and dry," I said, taking our plates and putting them in the hot water. "Before I'm forced to send you back home and disillusion her."

"Yes, ma'am," he said, laughing.

I stuck my hands in the hot, soapy water. "So, what *do* you think the story is behind Mrs. Baldwin's son? Maybe I should look into that."

He gave me a puzzled look. "Why?"

"I am writing this research paper about her and her books and—"

"What's that got to do with whether she and her son get along?"

I rinsed a plate and handed it to him. "I was just thinking about something Professor Hill said."

"I love his class. I catch up on a lot of sleep there."

I punched his hard biceps with a wet fist. "You should be paying attention. He's says some really interesting things."

"In a voice that sounds like he's set on low idle."

"He's a great teacher!"

"He's a great insomnia cure," Jack said, grinning, happy he'd gotten me riled again. There's nothing he loved better than teasing me.

"Oh, you," I said, punching him again.

He just laughed. "So, what *does* the great Professor Hill have to say that's so dang profound?"

"He says that a person is just as much defined and formed by their conflicts as by their triumphs. That they form the core of a person's character as much, if not more, than the things they profess to love."

"So?"

"So, her conflicted feelings about her son define her and, therefore, her books. If I'm going to write an honest paper about her and how she influenced me, don't you think that how her real life influenced her books, good and bad, should come into it?"

He opened a cupboard and put away the plate in his hands, his tanned face thoughtful. "Actually," he said after a few moments. "No, I don't. What her real life is like has nothing to do with you. Her books are what she wants people to see. Her life is . . . well, *her* life. If she wants it to be private, it should be."

I stopped washing the glass in my hands and turned to stare at my husband's now serious face. As fun-loving and silly as he could often be, sometimes his insight just amazed me. "You are absolutely right. I don't know why I thought I had the right to ask about her private life."

He leaned over and kissed me on the forehead. "Because, as Dove would say, you are as nosy as a chicken."

I made a mock despairing face. "Oh, geeze, I am, aren't I?"

He tossed the dish towel aside and put his arms around me. "Yeah, but not in a bad way. You just like trying to figure people out so you can understand why they do what they do. Maybe you should change your major from history to psychology."

"Maybe I should," I agreed.

CHAPTER 5

❖

April 15, 1995
Saturday

"So, HOW'S MY ADORABLE, YET TEMPERAMENTAL BRIDE holding up?" my cousin, Emory, asked me when he walked through the door of Blind Harry's at three-thirty. "I tried to get here earlier, but the delivery guys were late and I haven't hired anyone yet so there was only me to wait for the furniture." His thick straight blond hair flopped down across his worried forehead in that boyish way that tempted any woman with a shred of maternal instinct to reach up and brush it back.

"She's fine," I said. "Her employees and I have been running interference all day, but she seems pretty calm now. The book talks and signings have gone blessedly smooth and everyone's buying a lot so you know that makes her happy."

"And when *La Patrona*'s happy . . ." he started.

"Everyone's happy," I finished, laughing. "So, when do you start interviewing for a staff?"

"Next week. We want to get a restaurant open as soon as we can. It's a lot easier to convince people to buy your product if they can actually see and taste it."

He and his father, Boone Littleton, owned the biggest wholesale/retail smoked chicken business in Arkansas—Boone's Good Eatin' Chicken—and since Emory had made the decision to move to California when he and Elvia married, he and his father decided to try to market their smoked chicken on the West Coast.

"You know I'll be the first customer," I said, linking my arm in his.

"Yes, sweetcakes, I know. But it's *paying* customers we need."

"Pipe down. You're going to do great in the West. This might be cattle country here on the Central Coast, but there's so many newcomers from the city that I'm sure your chicken will sell like hot . . . chickens." I grinned at him.

"Ha, ha. To spark some interest, I've rented a booth at Farmer's Market Thursday night. I'll be giving out free samples."

"I'll be there with my plate held out."

"I don't doubt that. Did I miss Isaac's talk? He was one person I really wanted to hear."

"It started at three o'clock. I was just going to see if Emma needed anything before I head downstairs to catch the tail end of it."

"Who's Emma?"

I pointed over at the book-signing table, where one last middle-aged woman and her teenage daughter were talking to Emma Baldwin. "She wrote those mystery novels I loved so much as a kid. Remember, the Molly Connors mysteries?"

"Oh, yeah. Arnie used to torture you by stealing them and hiding them in the barn."

I nodded. "Yeah, he was a pill. Daddy sure was glad to see him last month at Dove's wedding, but was just as glad to see him go back home to Wyoming. Looks like Arnie's wife took him back one last time, thank goodness for Daddy's nerves. I think Daddy is about ready to head for the hills if there's one more tumultuous romance in this family."

"Ben's doing okay with Dove's marriage?"

"Actually, Daddy's doing fine. It's *Dove* who's having the problems."

"Already?"

"It's a long story . . . and bound to get longer. I'll come by your office tomorrow with the details. You're in the same building as Amanda, right? Over the Ross Department Store?"

"Temporarily. Hopefully, we'll outgrow them, but there's enough room for ten employees. It's Suite 220."

"Duly noted." I pushed him toward the stairs. "Now, go downstairs and find your sweetie. She'll be ecstatic to see you."

Over at Emma's table, the woman and her daughter had left and Emma was gathering up her purse and jacket.

"You sure had a crowd there for a while," I said. "There's not a book left. Wish we could have found more. Is there anything else I can get you?"

"Not a thing. Everything was perfect. Oh, Benni, I had a marvelous time," she said, her blue eyes bright with energy. "I haven't felt this wanted or inspired in years. Thank you so much. Where is Elvia? I must thank her too."

"She's downstairs. Isaac Lyons is speaking right now."

"I won't disturb her then. This has been a very busy day for her. I'll send a note." She reached out a hand to me. "It was so lovely seeing you again. I hope we can renew our friendship now that we have met again."

I took her hand. "I'd love that, Emma. How about lunch sometime?"

"How about this week? We could meet in Paso Robles and I could bring you the quilt."

Her eagerness to get together so quickly both surprised and excited me. "That would be great! When and where?"

"Are you free on Monday?"

"Yes, the museum's closed on Monday so that's ac-

tually a good day for me. I have a special tour for Constance Sinclair and some friends of hers but that's at nine
A.M. After that, I'm free the rest of the day."

"Let's meet at the Cowgirl Cafe over by the library.
How about noon?"

"I'll be there. I can't wait to look at your crazy quilt
again. I'll make a special display with your book next to
it." Mentally I'd already started composing the story of
Emma and her quilt.

Her cheekbones flushed with pleasure. "That sounds
wonderful."

After she left, as I was arranging Isaac's books for his
signing, Dove sidled up beside me.

"Where have you been?" she asked with a distinctive
hiss in her voice.

I held out my arms. "Right here. At least for the last
five hours."

"You weren't here when Isaac and I came in a half
hour ago."

"Okay, I did go back in the stockroom to fetch more
bags and bookmarks. We must have missed each other.
How's Isaac's talk going? Did you see Emory?"

"It's a madhouse, like always," she said, crossing her
arms over her chest. She was dressed in a pale peach
blouse and new dark blue Wranglers. Her long white braid
was tied with a navy velvet bow.

"You look nice," I said, trying to head off what was
coming. "Is that a new blouse?"

"You know that Ariana Winkle? She's all over Isaac
like white on rice." Dove mimicked Ariana's cultured accent. "Oh, my dee-yah, dee-yah Isaac, the aesthetics of
place and tone of character in your last few photographs
are so illu-mi-nating. Please tell us, does the irony in your
work stem from an organic or conscious source?"

"Say what?"

"My point exactly. They were pictures of cows and
cats, honeybun. Those two speckled-faced heifers and

three calico barn cats. The only organic source in those pictures was the cowpies on the ground."

I couldn't help chuckling. Ariana Winkle was about as opposite to Dove as a person could be. She was the wealthy widow of a San Francisco construction baron and owned spectacular homes in both San Celina County and San Francisco. She had recently won a seat on the city council so would probably be spending much more time here on the Central Coast. Ariana was beautiful, cultured, opinionated, and the new queen of San Celina's small and intensely snobby upper class. And she adored Isaac Lyons. She considered his moving here a real coup for San Celina society and was apparently trying to woo him into her inner circle.

Dove scowled and shook her head at me. Her long white braid flipped back and forth with agitation, reminding me of an irritated mare switching her tail at a pesky horsefly. "I'm glad you find this so funny. I'm about ready to bonk someone on their cultured, organic head."

"Better not." I pointed behind her. "The law is closing in on you fast."

"Abuelita!" Gabe said, putting an arm around her shoulders. "Why the angry face? Is *mi esposa* causing you trouble?" He'd changed from his running clothes into faded Levi's and a gray cotton sweater.

She turned to look up at him. "Well, if you really want to know . . ." she started.

I mouthed at him, *Don't get her started.*

Behind us, the schoolhouse clock chimed. It was four o'clock.

"Quick, help me," I said, grabbing up a bunch of Isaac's books and arranging them on the book-signing table. "Isaac will be coming up here in a minute to sign books."

Between the three of us, we managed to get his stack of books arranged and the author sign switched from Emma Baldwin to Isaac Lyons. I found another chair and placed it right next to Isaac's.

"Here, Dove, sit down next to him. You're in so many of the photographs in his ranch women book, I'm sure some of his fans will want to meet you." I gave her an encouraging smile.

She brushed away my comment with a flip of her hand. "They don't want to see me. They're only here for him."

"Okay," I said. "But if you don't sit next to him, I'm sure Ariana will gladly take your place."

"Over her dead, maggot-ridden body," Dove said, plopping down in the chair and once again crossing her arms over her chest.

"I'll pretend I didn't hear that," Gabe said.

"Dinner still on after church tomorrow?" I asked. Dove had invited us to the ranch for Easter dinner.

"Yes," she said, narrowing her eyes for battle as the sound of chattering women weaved its way up the stairs. "Bring a pie. And some rolls."

"Yes, ma'am," I said.

After we'd escaped outside, Gabe asked, "What was *that* all about?"

On the five-block walk to La Casa Buena, the restaurant where we were meeting his friend, I explained her dilemma.

"How can she be worried he would even look at anyone else?" Gabe said. "He loves her. He married *her*."

I didn't immediately answer because I knew exactly how she felt. "Well," I finally said when we reached the restaurant's bright pink front door. "Sometimes knowing someone loves you isn't enough to make you feel secure."

He stopped in front of the door and looked down at me, his black eyebrows moving together to form a small frown. "Is that how you feel?"

A breeze ruffled our hair and there was a tangy, bitter scent of eucalyptus in the air. I inhaled deeply and could almost taste its mediciney flavor. "Don't we all feel insecure at times about the people who love us?" I stood on tiptoe and placed my lips on his, rubbing them gently against his scratchy mustache before kissing him. "Don't worry about it, Friday. I'm fine. She will be too. Let's go meet your friend."

I turned away from him before he could answer and opened the pink door. Inside the restaurant, it was cool and dimly lit though the decor was cheerful and partylike with vibrant turquoises, pinks, and apple greens. Mexican folk music, heavy on the brass instruments, surrounded us in the small lobby. Gabe slipped his hand underneath my hair and caressed the nape of my neck. Next to my ear, his breath was warm, the feel of it tantalizing on my neck. *"Te amo, mi corazon."*

I turned to look up at him. "I love you too, Chief Oritz."

"Gabe!" A solid-sounding male voice boomed across the noisy restaurant. It came from a medium-built, pleasant-looking man who stood next to one of the colorful booths. Gabe guided me across the crowded restaurant toward him.

"You old son-of-a-gun," the man said when we came within five feet of him. "You look like crap."

"Luke! How are you, man? How's retirement?"

"It's okay. How's being a suit?"

"Pays the bills."

Their handshake moved easily into an embrace, with Gabe and Luke pounding each other on the back in that masculine way that always reminded me of two gorillas who were both greeting each other and marking their territories.

"Hey," Luke said, peering over Gabe's shoulder. "Who's this gorgeous dame? Is she available?" He gave me a long look and a friendly, open smile.

"This ain't no dame, this is my wife," Gabe said, laughing. "And you keep your hands off."

Luke took my outstretched hand in both of his. "The woman who tamed Pancho Villa. I'm impressed." He brought my hand up to his lips and kissed it. "I tip my fedora to you."

"Lips off my wife, *compa,*" Gabe said, still laughing. "Go find your own."

Luke let go of my hand and winked at me. "But it's so much more fun coveting yours."

I laughed hesitantly, not certain how much he was kidding.

"Leave her alone and let's eat," Gabe said, nudging me toward the booth. "I hear the mole is killer here."

Luke slid in across from us and turned his attention to Gabe. While they discussed the menu, old friends, and current jobs, I was able to study him without feeling awkward.

He appeared to be close to Gabe's age, early forties, was about five-six or so with walnut-brown hair, medium-blue eyes, and plain, even features. He was dressed in khaki pants and an off-white polo shirt, and as far as I could see, there was not one unusual or distinguishing feature about him. If he had committed a crime and a group of witnesses were asked to describe him, it would have been virtually impossible, he was that average-looking. He was so average-looking that I felt like I'd met him before, though I knew that was unlikely. Since he'd worked in undercover narcotics with Gabe, I imagined that looking like Joe Everyman would have been an advantage. The perfect undercover officer.

After our food arrived, along with a pitcher of margaritas that Gabe and Luke shared, the conversation moved from a general discussion of their lives to the more specific.

"So, what happened to Lisa?" Gabe asked, taking a bite of his chicken enchilada covered with dark, chocolate-scented mole sauce.

"Shoot, that was two girlfriends back," Luke said, winking at me again. "Try and keep up, old man."

Gabe refilled Luke's margarita glass. "You need to settle down and make yourself a life. You're forty-four, man. You can't live like a twenty-year-old forever."

"Says who?" he replied, draining his glass. His blue eyes laughed at Gabe over the rim.

"Some things never change," Gabe said with a chuckle. "How's the PI biz? What brings you up here?"

"It's boring as a grandma's tea party," Luke said. "I'm beginning to think life is nothing but Workman's Comp scams and infidelity. That's part of the reason why I'm up here. Chasing a middle-aged guy whose rich older wife thinks he has a weekend cutie stashed away in Morro Bay."

"Really?" I said, finally getting interested. "Who?"

He laughed. "Sorry, honey, can't reveal that. Client privilege and all that. You might know her."

"Your experience is wasted doing grunt work like that," Gabe said.

"It pays for the beans and beer, old buddy," he said. "Not everyone's cut out to be a lifetime civil servant. I like being my own boss."

But his face looked thoughtful, maybe even a little sad, when he said it. I glanced over at Gabe to see his reaction. His expression was unrevealing, telling me nothing about whether he pitied Luke or envied him.

"So, you said work was only part of the reason why you're here," I said.

His fork played with the leftover food on his plate. "Got some distant family I'm looking up too. With all the incredible people search software there is out now, I've gotten into geneological stuff."

"I've read about that kind of software," I said. "It's kind of creepy too, when you think about it. If a person has enough money, apparently anyone can be located. And it doesn't take that long to find them."

Luke set down his fork and grinned at me. "That's what I'm counting on."

"Yes, but how do you know if the person seeking another person is doing it for an honorable reason?" I'd read enough articles in magazines to know that many times the people using private investigators were not always seeking people to have loving family reunions.

Luke shrugged and didn't answer, giving me the impression that he was saying that wasn't his problem.

"Benni, I'm sure Luke will be discreet and discerning about who utilizes his services," Gabe said, squeezing my knee under the table.

"Yes, of course," I said, feeling a bit embarrassed. Who was I to question this man's intentions when I barely knew him? "So, what family members are you looking up?"

"Just some distant people from my mother's side."

"Who?" I asked. "I've lived here almost my whole life. I might know them."

He wiped his mouth with his cloth napkin, then looked from side to side. "Oh, I doubt you do."

"I might," I insisted.

Gabe squeezed my knee again, telling me to mind my own business.

I pushed his hand away and changed the subject. "Do you want to come over for some coffee? Our place is still a mess from moving, but the living room does have furniture."

"I'll take a raincheck on that, Benni," Luke said with an easy smile. "I have a lot of things to do the next few days. After that I'll be free to kick back and relax."

So we made plans for him to drop by on Thursday night around six. I promised him I'd make fried chicken, a dish he mentioned he liked.

"My mom's from the South," he said.

"Well, I can't say my fried chicken will be as good as your mama's, but Gabe loves it. And he normally hates fried food."

"*What* is this guy's problem?" Luke said, jerking a thumb at Gabe.

"I have no idea," I said.

"Why do you stay with him anyway?"

"Oh, you know, the usual . . . easy on the eyes, steady

paycheck, good in bed, keeps my windshield washed."
Over the course of our dinner, his easygoing manner had
made me feel comfortable enough to joke with him.

"So, which is more important?"

I didn't even look at Gabe. "I do enjoy the steady paycheck and what woman doesn't appreciate a clean windshield?"

Luke threw back his head and laughed.

"Okay, you two," Gabe said, bumping my shoulder
with his. "I think it's about time to break this ridicule-
Ortiz party up."

Luke held up his margarita glass. "She's a keeper, Pancho. Don't blow this one."

"Up yours," Gabe said, good-naturedly. "Let me hit the
john and then we'll make plans about you coming by the
office next week."

While he was gone, Luke and I talked about retirement,
how he wanted to live near his mother and how expensive
land was getting on the Central Coast.

"It's beautiful up here," he said. "Gabe's a lucky guy."
He grinned at me. "In more ways than one."

I smiled back. "I'm lucky too."

"Well, unless I find someone like you, I'll probably be
retiring near my mother. If she'll have me."

"I'm sure she'll be thrilled," I said. "What mother
wouldn't love having her son close? I think Gabe's mom
has never quite forgiven me for marrying him and sealing
his fate about staying in California. I think after he and
Lydia divorced, she had dreams of him moving back to
Kansas."

Luke ran his finger around the salty rim of his margarita glass, then brought it to his lips. "And we know
how likely *that* was."

"Yeah, but try and tell his mother that. So, I have you
down for fried chicken on Thursday night."

"Absolutely, unless, of course, something comes up
with this job I'm working on."

"Well, if you're in contact with those long-lost family

members by then," I said, "feel free to bring them too. Just let me know how many."

"That's very kind of you, Señora Ortiz," he said.

Gabe walked up and said, "Hate to stop this reunion, *compa,* but I have work to catch up on."

"No problem," Luke said, glancing at his watch.

There was the usual macho squabbling and posturing over who would pay the bill, which I solved by handing my credit card to the cashier.

"She's a real take-charge kinda lady, isn't she?" Luke said as I signed the credit card slip.

"You don't know the half of it," Gabe said, giving a dramatic sigh.

I elbowed him in the ribs. "Look who's talking, General Patton."

"I'll say it again. She's perfect for you, Pancho," Luke said.

Outside on the sidewalk, Gabe handed Luke his business card. "Drop by the station and I'll give you the fifty-cent tour. My office is only about three blocks from here. Where are you staying?"

"Nice little motel in Morro Bay—Morro Rock Inn. Maybe I will drop by if my assignment wraps up early. At any rate, I'll see you Thursday." He leaned close and gave me a kiss on the cheek. "It really was nice meeting you, Benni."

"Hey," Gabe protested good-naturedly.

"Ah, quit being so selfish," Luke said, laughing.

On our walk back, I quizzed Gabe about his friend. There were so many things in Gabe's life that were a mystery to me that whenever someone from his past popped into our lives, I felt as if I was getting one more piece to the puzzle of this man I'd fallen in love with so quickly.

"He sure was evasive about the family he has around here, don't you think?" I said.

Gabe draped an arm around my shoulder and said, "That's Luke."

"Why would he be so secretive?"

"I told you, that's Luke."

"Aren't you even curious?"

He looked down at me and smiled, his white teeth bright against his dark skin. "Not really. I have enough problems with my own family without hearing the sordid details about someone else's."

For not the first time, I marveled at the difference between men and women. The sordid details about our families were a big part of the glue that held many women's friendships together.

"So," I said, going a different route. "Tell me some of the adventures you and Luke had."

"Just the usual. Made drug deals, busted bad guys."

I laughed at his definition of "usual." "Was he good at it?"

"The best."

"He's so average looking that I feel like I've seen him somewhere before. I'm assuming that's a plus in undercover work."

"Yep."

I growled out loud and bumped him with my hip. "Why don't you ever give me more details, Friday?"

He shrugged and stuck his hands in his pockets. "It's cop stuff."

"So I want to hear *cop stuff*."

"Benni, most of it's boring. There's really not all that much glamour to undercover narcotics work. It's a lot of waiting and watching and a few minutes of adrenaline. Most of the people we worked with, you would cross the street to avoid, sweetheart. Trust me on that."

"Okay, then we'll talk about something less boring, like what you're going to wear to the Cattleman's Ball. At Yesterday's Fashions I found this cool Western suit from the fifties with rhinestone horseshoes on the lapels."

He groaned. The Cattleman's Ball was not something he was anticipating with pleasure. "There *was* this one bust involving a heroin dealer where Luke and I had to pretend we were plumbers . . ."

I laughed in triumph and linked my arm through his. "Tell me all about it, Chief."

By the time we got home, he had almost finished the story about his and Luke's not-very-successful charade as plumbers for a Bel Air movie producer who was dealing drugs to subsidize his failing production. In order to get the assignment, Luke had apparently exaggerated to their commanding officer how much he knew about plumbing, and when he was supposedly fixing a toilet in the mansion's basement, he flooded the producer's custom-built movie theater. It took some fast talking on Gabe's part to keep the spitting-mad producer from finding out who they really were.

"We eventually busted the guy," Gabe said while we were getting undressed for bed. "But not before the department had to pay for new carpeting and furniture for his theater. We never let Luke forget it either. He had quite the collection of miniature toilets on his desk by the time he retired."

I settled down next to Gabe in bed. "See, that didn't hurt, did it? I just want to hear things like that. It makes me feel like I know you better. It helps me picture that part of your life."

Gabe pulled me closer to him so my head rested on his chest. "A lot of of my life I don't want you to picture."

I didn't answer because I wasn't certain what to say. Maybe he was right. There were parts of both our lives that were private. Maybe I was pressing too hard. I gave a deep sigh.

"What's that for?" Gabe asked, picking up a file he'd been reading.

"Nothing. I'm just glad you're here with me now."

"Me too, *querida*."

THE NEXT DAY WAS EASTER SUNDAY. I HAD SET THE alarm for five A.M. so I could make a lemon icebox pie and a pumpkin pie. They would be set and ready to eat by the time we were out of church.

"Why didn't you just buy them like you usually do?" Gabe said, coming into the kitchen at seven A.M. dressed for his run. He yawned and opened the refrigerator door. "Are we out of grapefruit juice?"

"There's orange juice. Because Dove will kill me if I *buy* the pies for Easter dinner." The oven timer chimed and I took out my pumpkin pie. "Ah, perfect. I haven't lost my touch."

He came over and kissed me on the top of the head. "I'll see you in an hour or so."

"Okay, I'll make some blueberry muffins. Church is at ten-thirty this morning."

I'd just put the muffins on when the phone rang.

"Hello?"

There was a long silence.

"Hello?" I said again.

Another few seconds of silence, then a soft click.

I shook my head and hung up the phone, annoyed when people just didn't say, sorry, wrong number.

I checked the muffins, saw they still had twenty more minutes. Plenty of time for me to take a shower. I was upstairs taking a shower when I heard Scout barking. That meant someone was at the door. I rinsed off as fast as I could, threw on a terry cloth robe, and ran down the stairs, but by the time I got downstairs, whoever was there had left. On the floor in front of the door was a lumpy envelope that someone had shoved through our mail slot. "Gabe" was written across the front of the envelope with a leaky ballpoint pen. I held it up to the light and could see a folded note inside though the words on the note were unreadable. The envelope felt like it contained a key.

I sighed and set it on the kitchen table, thinking

how different my life with Gabe was compared to the one I'd lived with Jack. If it had been a letter addressed to Jack, I would have opened the envelope without hesitation. There was never anything secret between us. Was it because we'd been together from such a young age or had my relationship with Jack truly been more intimate, more trusting? It had certainly been less complicated.

I went back upstairs to dry my hair and get dressed for church. When Gabe came home from his run, we sat down to eat the blueberry muffins. I handed him the lumpy envelope.

"What's this?" he asked.

"Someone slipped it through the mail slot when I was taking a shower."

He slit it open with his knife and took out a small dark key and a folded note. His face grew puzzled while he read it.

"What is it?" I asked.

"It's from Luke."

"What does it say?"

He handed the note across the table to me.

Gabe, this is to my safety-deposit box. It's in the San Celina Savings across from your office. Thought I'd make it easy for you. You're still my executor. My will and insurance policy is in there. Just in case this one blows up in my face. Thanks, buddy. I've always appreciated your friendship. You've got a real nice wife. I'm happy for you. Luke.

"What's that all about?" I asked.

"I can't believe I'm still his executor," Gabe said, picking up the dark gray key. "After all these years."

"This is kinda spooky," I said, folding up the note and putting it back in the envelope. "I think he sounds a little . . . I don't know . . . scared."

Gabe shook his head and slipped the key back into the envelope. "Don't put too much stock in his dramatics. Luke was always doing things like this when we worked together. He liked the cloak-and-dagger part of undercover work just a little too much, in my opinion. We used to kid him about the things he carried like writing pens that turned into knives and cameras the size of a walnut. His spy gadgets didn't work half the time. We used to call him Maxwell Smart after that character on television." He gave a small laugh. "Luke was also famous for his vivid imagination."

"If you say so. But it still sounds a little odd to me."

"Trust me, it's nothing," he said with a confidence that less than twenty-four hours later he would regret.

CHAPTER 6

❖

April 16–17, 1995
Sunday and Monday

*A*FTER A SEMI-TENSE EASTER SUNDAY DINNER OF Dove's smoked ham and country potato salad, where we were interrupted only twice by phone calls from Isaac's groupies, Gabe and I went home and to bed early. La Fiesta Days officially started Monday morning and we both had a busy week ahead of us. Because of that, the phone ringing long before the sun came up was particularly unwelcome. I rolled over, pulled my pillow over my head, and let him answer it.

"That's it?" I heard Gabe say into the phone. His voice was a muffled grumble through my pillow's feathers. "That's all you found on the body? Give me a description of the victim."

A homicide. I peeked out from under my pillow and glanced at the digital clock on my nightstand: 2:13 A.M. There must have been something special about this one because normally the detectives who caught the case would just leave the report on his desk for him to peruse first thing in the morning.

"I'll be right there," he said, hanging up the phone. He

flipped on the bedside lamp and pulled himself into a sitting position, his back against the oak headboard. A tiny muscle in the side of his cheek throbbed as he stared across the room at our tan bedroom wall.

I sat up, suddenly alarmed. "Who was killed?"

His lips tightened for a moment. "Sounds like Luke."

"Oh, Gabe, that's awful. What happened? How did—?"

He interrupted me, his voice curt, businesslike. "They found a John Doe lying in the creek over by the Mission, under the footbridge. He'd been stabbed. Only thing in his pockets was a matchbook from La Casa Buena and my card. Looks like a robbery."

I stroked his cold forearm. "I'm so sorry."

His face softened and he covered my hand with his. "I need to get down to the scene."

"Of course." I threw back our comforter and reached for a pair of sweatpants and a sweatshirt. "You'll need some coffee."

The coffee was on and I'd mixed some orange juice by the time Gabe came into the kitchen. He wore a dark green flannel shirt, Levi's, and hiking boots. I sat at the kitchen table, my hands wrapped around a warm mug, trying not to shiver.

"Coffee's done." I stood up and reached into the cupboard for his travel mug. "Drink some juice before you go."

He poured coffee into the mug. The refrigerator cycled and turned itself off, leaving the kitchen in silence. Outside, the sad cooing of a mourning dove seemed eerily appropriate.

He cleared his throat and took a sip of coffee before snapping the lid on. "I have to find out what he was working on, check his safety-deposit box, talk to his mother . . ."

"His mother," I said, closing my eyes for a second, concentrating on the dove's persistent cry. A phone call like that had to be the worst thing for any mother to experience. Like an electric current, a sharp memory flashed through my mind—Wade's stuttering words telling me Jack's Jeep had crashed, the throbbing sound of the refrigerator, Dove's voice, full of tears, saying my name over and over. I remembered how cold my bare feet had been, the floor like a sheet of ice. Why is it that bad news learned early in the morning always seems so much worse? Maybe because the dawning of the day should be a hopeful time and when, for some reason, despair hits, the wrongness of it all seems that much more shocking.

I poured myself another cup of coffee, knowing I wouldn't be able to go back to sleep. "He never mentioned whether he had any children."

Gabe shook his head no. "He was married twice, but never had kids. His older brother died in Vietnam. His dad died a couple of years ago. As far as I know, there was just him and his mom."

"Will you have to tell her?"

"Once I find out where she lives, I'll probably call the local police chief. News like this is better coming in person."

"You know, he never said where she lived in the South."

"I'll have to make a call to LA and see if anyone there knows." He swallowed a large gulp of coffee.

I grabbed his free hand. "Is there anything I can do for you, Friday?"

He brought my hand up and ran his lips over it, back and forth. "I'm fine, *querida.* I just want to find who did it. He was my friend and this is my home. He was killed on my watch."

"It's not your fault."

"Every crime that happens in this town I take personally."

I sighed, knowing I'd not be able to talk him out of feeling responsible. "Do you think that his murder might have something to do with his undercover days?"

He looked at me for a long moment, his deep-set eyes

glazed with some kind of emotion I couldn't fathom. "What do you mean?"

I felt foolish, but said anyway, "Like someone who wants revenge."

"You've been watching too much television. Most bad guys are too busy trying to pull another scam to worry about getting back at the cops who helped put them away." He opened the lid on his travel mug and topped it off with more coffee. "I'd better get over there. I'll be back home when they're through with the scene to change for work. Will you iron a shirt for me?"

"Sure. If I'm gone when you get back, I'll call you later."

After he left, I went upstairs and ironed a white shirt for him. Then, too agitated to settle down, I puttered around downstairs, arranging my favorite books in the built-in bookshelves next to the fireplace and moving some of the lighter boxes of books to one of the upstairs bedrooms, which would serve as our library/office. At six-thirty, when the blue morning haze started turning a delicate peach, I took a shower and changed into black Wranglers and a tan cotton sweater. My first stop would be Liddie's Cafe. A good hot breakfast was what I needed before going to the folk art museum and facing our illustrious patron, Constance Sinclair, and whichever of her cronies she had invited to a preview of our new exhibit.

Liddie's Cafe (Open 25 hours!) had been a beloved San Celina landmark for so long, it was almost impossible to find someone who was around when it wasn't. The coffeeshop was originally owned by a Portuguese immigrant named Buck Vieira. Liddie was his first wife, who died giving birth to his son, Buck Junior, whom everyone still called Junior even though he was going on sixty years old. Junior was a watercolor artist who lived in Cayucos, a small coastal town north of Morro Bay, and made an appearance at Liddie's only once a year when they served their famous free Thanksgiving dinner to the homeless. In its eighty-two years of operation, its bright red, six-person booths had comfortably and equitably seated ranchers and politicians, students and secretaries, lawyers, cops, firemen, and even the occasional visiting dignitary. It was rumored that William Randolph Hearst used to eat over-easy eggs and crispy hash browns here with his architect, Julia Morgan, while they were planning Hearst Castle and that Jimmy Carter, while stumping for the presidency back in the seventies, told Junior Vieira that their fluffy baking powder biscuits and bacon gravy were as Southern as his own Georgia gramma's.

Like most residents of San Celina, I had a special place in my heart for Liddie's—early-morning breakfasts with Daddy when I was a little girl and he met with other ranchers, lunches with Dove and her historical society friends after a meeting, late-night study sessions with Jack and Elvia during college. Liddie's half-pound hamburgers, skin-on French fries, and straw-collapsing strawberry malts were as comforting and well known to me as Dove's chicken and dumplings. Even my relationship with Gabe began here in one of the familiar back booths. Our first kiss, as confusing and tumultuous as our relationship was destined to be, had been in Liddie's shadowy parking lot on a chilly, white-breath of a winter night.

I stood for a moment in the small foyer, inhaling Liddie's comforting, beefy, deep-fried aromas.

A loud cackle from Nadine greeted me. "Lord help us, the world is coming to an end," she said, pulling a bright yellow pencil from behind her ear. "Benni Harper is out and about before the chickens are scratching." She picked up a pot of coffee and followed me as I slid into my favorite window booth.

Nadine Brooks Johnson had been head waitress at Liddie's since before I could saddle my own pony. She was dressed in her customary pink waitress uniform with a white apron and a plastic name tag pinned to the lacy handkerchief on her lapel. Her style hadn't changed in all the years I'd been coming here even though all the other waitresses through the years had worn a variety of clothing styles.

"You don't know Dove's chickens," I said, smiling. "Gabe and I were woken up around two this morning. But then, you already know that, right?"

Not much happened in this town that Nadine wasn't privy to. Her sources of information were rivaled only by those of Beebs and Millee Crosby. Nadine's white eyebrows arched above her pale blue cat's-eye glasses. "Sorry piece of business, that man getting killed. Only two blocks from here too." She shook her head disapprovingly. "Took everything in his pockets, I heard. Dopehead looking for money, most likely. We never had these kind of problems until the locusts moved in."

The locusts were what she called all the people moving in from the cities. In the last few years, San Celina County had been discovered by retirees from Southern California and the San Francisco Bay Area. The sudden influx of new citizens had taxed the county's public services to their limits and driven housing prices so high that many local people couldn't afford to buy here now. And the new citizens brought a big-city attitude that didn't always set well with the natives.

"They don't really know what the story is yet," I said amicably, uncomfortable about taking sides since I was married to someone who hadn't lived that long in the county. "He was an old cop friend of Gabe's."

"So I heard," Nadine said, flipping over my cup and pouring me some coffee. "Drink this. The bags under your eyes are over the highway weight limit."

"Thanks, Nadine. You're always so good for my ego."

She pulled a new order pad from the pocket of her white apron. "Is my boy okay?" Like many women in San Celina, she adored Gabe and made no bones about showing it.

"He's fine. I'll have a short stack and a side of chicken fried steak."

"So who was this fella who got killed?" she asked, writing down my order.

"His name was Luke Webster. We had dinner with him Saturday night."

"Wife and kids?" Her wrinkled face was sympathetic.

"He was divorced with no children. He just had his mother. She lives somewhere in the South."

"What a cryin' shame." She leaned closer, her slightly bulging, tobacco-brown eyes eager for some tidbit to entertain her customers with today. "What else do you know about him?"

I realized then that it probably would be better if I didn't reveal too much information about him, at least until I could ask Gabe what was okay to say. "That's about it. He and Gabe just rambled on about old times. You know, cop stuff. He seemed like a nice man."

She nodded, pushing her glasses up her bony nose. "You tell my boy that I'll set aside a nice piece of rhubarb pie for him. Cook fresh-baked it this morning."

"I will if I see him. We might not cross paths until this evening. I'm giving a museum tour to Constance and her gang this morning then I have a lunch date with Emma Baldwin in Paso Robles."

"I heard Emma came back to town. Hasn't been in here once." Nadine's face looked a little grumpy. She took it personally if any locals, even ones that had been gone a long time, didn't drop by Liddie's to have a bite and say howdy.

"Give her some time," I said in Emma's defense. "She's only been in town a few weeks."

"Wonder why she's back," Nadine said, adjusting her crooked eyeglasses.

"She didn't say in her talk at Blind Harry's yesterday. Just that she was glad to be back. Remember when I did that term paper on her back in college?"

She pointed her yellow pencil at me. "What I remember, missy, is you and Jack practically living in this very booth and not buying much.

"You know Jack and I never had any money. We *always* left you big tips when we had it. And don't I get credit for making up for it since?" I always left Nadine generous tips even though she teased me all the time about stiffing her. It was a running joke between us.

"What a sweet boy, that Jack," she said, not about to admit that I wasn't as cheap as she liked to make out. "Seems like a hundred years ago since he passed on." Nadine's thin, lined face softened in memory.

I propped my chin up with my palm. "Yes, it does." Then I said, "Did you know that Emma's son was dead? She mentioned it yesterday during her talk."

Nadine shifted from one bony hip to the other. "No, I didn't. He was a strange one, that Cody."

"No kidding. I had a few choice encounters with him myself."

"Never had a smile on his face. Cheap tipper too." She narrowed one eye at me. "That tells a lot about a person's character."

"I am not a cheap tipper!" I protested.

She cackled and bopped me over the head with her order pad. "My auntie's quilt look okay?" Nadine had loaned the museum her great-aunt Melba's crazy quilt for the display in the upstairs gallery.

"It looks great. Come out and I'll give you a personal tour."

She rolled her eyes skyward and stuck her pencil behind her ear. "I'll try, but Junior never lets me have any time off."

I smiled, knowing, as everyone else in this town did, that Nadine was like his own mother and he would steal the moon and stars out of the sky for her. She was the one who couldn't tear herself away from the cafe.

After she left, I pulled my notes for the tour out of my purse and reread them. We had twenty-five quilts in the California Quilts exhibit, fifteen of them from a collection owned by a state-sponsored folk art museum in Sacramento. It had taken quite a bit of wrangling and political clout for our little county museum to borrow this collection. We'd been required to have an alarm system installed which, thanks to Constance's personal favors list, was donated by a local alarm company.

Constance and I had agreed on a name for the exhibit: "With a Banjo on Her Knee—A Retrospective of Early California Quilts." I had intermingled some of San Celina County's own historical quilts. One had actually traveled with a woman from Alabama to California in 1888, just like the banjo in the song, "Oh, Susannah!"

I was on my second cup of Liddie's mud-thick coffee when I heard a familiar male voice over the soft buzz of early-morning conversation.

"Hey, Miguel," I called to one of Elvia's younger brothers and a San Celina police officer. He was standing at the counter waiting for a carryout order. He raised his hand in acknowledgment and, when he'd finished paying, headed back to my booth.

"Hi, Benni," he said. In his dark blue police uniform, his chest looked as broad and solid as a bass fiddle. Now in his mid-twenties, he'd been an officer long enough to have lost the adolescent excitement of a new rookie. His face had acquired a hardened expression that came from observing too many drunks, crazies, and domestic disputes. Had I really once given apple juice in a dribble cup to this sober-faced cop? "You're out early."

"Got woke up early, as you know," I said. "What's going on at the crime scene?" Even though he wasn't directly involved, a homicide was an odd enough occurrence in our town I knew that he, as well as all the other street cops on duty, would find some reason to drop by and take a look.

"Not much. Chief's really gotten involved with this one."

"Luke was an old friend of his," I said, sipping my coffee.

His equipment belt squeaked as he shifted from one foot to the other. "Whoever did this was royally pissed."

"Why do you say that?"

"Heard one of the detectives talking. Guy was stabbed more than they thought at first. Fifteen, sixteen times, I heard."

"That seems rather excessive," I said. "Not your average robbery."

He nodded again. "One of the detectives, Stan Westmont, said it looked personal. He majored in psychology so he's always looking for things like that."

My thoughts jumped back to my statement to Gabe. Could it be a revenge killing? Maybe my theory wasn't as ridiculous as he said it was. My heart fluttered in my chest for a moment, worrying about Gabe. Was it someone he and Luke were both involved with?

"They'll find out who did it," I said confidently. "You know *mi esposo,* he won't rest until it's solved." I sighed inwardly, knowing from experience now what was ahead of me—the late nights, the obsessive attention to this and nothing else.

After he left, Nadine came back with my pancakes and chicken fried steak. As the dollop of pale butter slowly melted on my pancakes, I fought my feelings of guilt. Though I was proud of what Gabe did for a living and how seriously he took every crime that happened in our town, it still sometimes troubled me that our life often took second place.

I was halfway finished with my breakfast when my new stepgrandpa, Isaac, walked into Liddie's. When he saw my raised hand, he headed toward me, calling out to Nadine, "Western omelette with extra cheese, wheat toast with real butter, and a soup tureen of coffee."

"You got it, honey," she called back.

He slid into the booth across from me, his blunt-featured face troubled. Deep, defined wrinkles, as if drawn by a child, radiated from his small, raisin-colored eyes. His long gray braid was a bit crooked and he was dressed in a pair of wrinkled blue jeans and an extra-large seafoam green fisherman's knit sweater. For the first time since I'd met him, he was without an earring, which led me to believe he had rushed out of the house in a hurry.

"Help me," he said, pulling at the fleshy earlobe that usually held his earring.

I gave a nervous laugh. "Do what?"

"Understand your gramma. She's the most difficult, frustrating, crazy-making woman I've ever been married to." His dark eyes glowed with misery. "She's about ready to toss me out on my ear and I don't know what to do."

"Well," I said carefully, wanting to choose my words right. "Maybe I'm not the best person to ask advice about relationships." My own marriage had been pretty rocky these last few months and the only thing I could safely recommend was to take each day as it came with as much grace as you could muster. That didn't seem like what Isaac wanted to hear.

"You know her better than anyone else. Why can't I make her happy?" Before I could answer, Nadine walked up to our table with a full coffeepot. She flipped his white mug over and poured it to the brim.

"Bless you, Nadine," he said, wrapping both of his ham-sized hands around the mug.

"Your omelette's on its way," she said. "What's wrong with your bride that she's sending you out this early without a decent meal? I'm just going to have to nag at her about that."

Isaac's face blanched with panic. Being a native of Chicago and a professional photographer living all his life on the road or in one big city or another, he was still adjusting to the invasive lack of privacy in small towns. Especially when you were married to a well-known and much-loved citizen like my gramma Dove.

"No . . . I . . . uh . . . She . . ." He struggled to find an answer that would both satisfy Nadine and hide what was going on between him and Dove.

Pure empathy caused me to jump in with a small white lie. "Because she's been hogging him all to herself and I figured it was about time he had breakfast with his new granddaughter. Besides, Dove's all wrapped up in getting the historical society float done for the La Fiesta Parade this Saturday. I heard that they're making a model of the old Montez adobe . . . or what it will look like when it's done. Are you going to the work day at the adobe on Friday?" I'd learned from experience that the best defense to nosiness was distracting the inquirer with lots of questions, information, or if you were lucky enough to have it, a juicier piece of gossip.

Nadine filled my coffee cup back up to the rim. "Wallowing around in mud is not my idea of a fun day off. Got enough weeding to do in my own little patch of wilderness, thank you very much." She patted Isaac on the back with her free hand. "You tell that new bride of yours to give me a call. We haven't had a good hen session in a monkey's year."

"You bet." When she was out of earshot, he whispered to me, "Thank you. Tell me, will my life always be this much on display?" He leaned over his cup and let the hot coffee warm his face.

I shrugged and speared my last piece of chicken fried steak. "Only as long as you're married to Dove."

"Benni, *what* am I going to do?" He took a long drink of coffee. "Nothing I say or do makes her happy. I'm seventy-six years old. I'm an old man. Old men snore. And I have a lot of stuff. Who doesn't at my age? What does she want from me?"

I pushed my plate aside. "You've been married before—wasn't it like this with the others?"

He shook his head no. "I was always traveling. And my other wives were more . . . I don't know . . . easy to please."

I raised my eyebrows. "In other words, they molded their lives around yours."

He nodded, his face flushing slightly.

I wiped my mouth with my napkin, trying not to smile. "I know you and Dove didn't date long, but did you honestly expect her to be like your other wives? Wait on you hand and foot? Change her life to suit yours?"

His face grew stubborn. "No, but I do expect some compromise. After all, I'm the one who up and moved his whole life. *She* hasn't had to change a thing."

I didn't answer, not entirely agreeing with him, but not about to debate that statement. I reached across the table and took his hand. "Pops, I know it's rough, but all I can say is give it time. This'll all work out."

"I suppose. But you know, we don't have as much time as you and Gabe. I hope she realizes that."

Remembering what she said to me on their wedding day, I said, "I'm sure she does."

After breakfast, I went by Stern's Bakery and bought some plain and lemon-filled croissants and chocolate chip scones in case any of Constance's friends wanted something to nibble on after the tour. Then I headed for the museum. When I passed the Farm Supply, one of the museum's neighbors on what had once been a lonely highway out of town and was now slowly growing into a semi-industrial area, I spotted Daddy's white Ramsey ranch truck. I couldn't help wondering how Dove and Isaac's marriage tensions were affecting him. That went on my ever-growing list of things to do—talk to Daddy about Dove. It was seven-thirty when I pulled into the empty parking lot of the folk art museum. I parked in the back, next to the carved-up old oak tree, so the closer spots would be free for Constance and her friends.

The old Sinclair hacienda, which had been in Constance Sinclair's family since the Spanish land grant days, was looking spectacular due to the excellent care it was receiving from my assistant, D-Daddy Boudreaux. He kept the adobe walls patched and painted, the red clay tile roof repaired, and the old wine barrel planters filled with native wildflowers like wild sweet peas, pink prickly-phlox, and two-toned Chinese Houses. Before he'd retired to the Central Coast, he was a shrimp boat captain in Louisiana and there was no doubt he'd run the most ship-shape boat on the Gulf of Mexico.

Inside the museum, the air was cool and quiet. The silence in the main exhibit room surrounded by all the old quilts and soft grayish-white adobe walls, soothed my soul. Usually my day started around nine o'clock when the museum was already open by our head docent and the artists' co-op located in the old stables behind the hacienda bustled with people. This rare solitude inside the museum gave me the opportunity to take one last look at both quilt exhibits to see if they needed any final adjustments. I was looking forward to acquiring Emma's crazy quilt for our new upstairs gallery. It would enhance the exhibit with a needed focal point and add a touch of local celebrity that always intrigued people. I just wish we'd had it earlier so we could have advertised it in the publicity flyers.

The California quilt exhibit needed only a few little repairs. One of the quilts was sagging so I found a ladder in the artists' studios to fix it. It was an 1849 Shoo-fly pattern signature quilt made by the young ladies' Bible study class of the First Methodist Church of Stevens Point, Wisconsin. The quilt was made for one of their classmates, Madeline O'Brien, who was traveling to California to marry her fiancé, Jonathan Marker, a young attorney who worked for a shipping company in San Francisco. After readjusting the padded wooden clamps D-Daddy had made to hang the quilts on the museum's adobe walls, I stood back and gazed at the primarily red-and-white quilt, reading again some of the sweet and innocent endearments embroidered in the center of each square.

Along the trail West, don't forget who loves you best.
                                        —Laura Wingfield, 1849

On the darkest day of December, send me some sunshine if you can remember.
                        —Jean Stein, Steven's Point, Wisconsin

On May the First, I did begin, To make this Square,
For Madeline.

　　　　　　　　　　　　　　　—Loretta Foreman

Good luck and God Watch Over You.
　　　　　　　　　　—Susan McCoubrie—July 1849

Back then, when someone moved out West, there was
a good chance they would not see their family and friends
for many years, if ever. How different our lives were now
with jets and telephones to keep us connected with distant
family and friends. How brave those women were to take
that adventurous plunge into marriage and a new life so
far from that which they'd grown up knowing. Would I
have had that sort of courage?

I breezed through the exhibit and checked the other
quilts. Everything looked in order. In the place of honor,
because of her generosity toward the folk art museum, the
first quilt to be viewed on the tour was made by Constance
Sinclair's great-aunt Marylee from Virginia. It had been
sent West by train and stagecoach to Constance's great-
grandmother, the original Constance Sinclair. A traditional red, green, and white Baltimore medallion quilt, it
reminded me of Constance herself—perfection bred from
time and money.

Though as a curator I appreciated the almost flawless
preserved quilts in this collection made in the East by
talented, affluent women and sent West to family and
friends, it was the quilts actually made here in the West
or along the trail to a hopeful new life that touched my
heart. For a rich woman to make a quilt in her many hours
of idle time and using the best fabrics money could buy
was impressive, as many in this collection showed, but
what really moved me was the brilliantly executed, but
obviously used quilts made by everyday women. Women
who traded fabrics, waited for that right piece of calico
red or indigo blue, and worked on their quilts in the eve-

nings after all the real labor of building a life in the new land was finished.

Part of my talk included pointing out the caste system in quilting back then. Much of what is preserved, so therefore what we see as historical record, are the unused quilts made by a certain upper class of women because many of the quilts made by women in the lower classes were used until they wore out. That was the reason, some quilt historians speculate, that so few slave quilts survived, that is, quilts made by slaves for their own use. It made me think of the old folk saying from the thirties, one that Dove had raised me on: *Use it up, wear it out, make it do, or do without.*

Upstairs in the crazy quilt exhibit, the docent talk that I'd written would take on a lighter tone. I didn't want to upset the affluent women of our county *too* much. They were, after all, a good part of the financial and emotional support of this museum and artists' co-op. I'd come to understand and reluctantly appreciate the mutual reliance that affluent patrons and struggling artists have for each other and that part of my job was to facilitate those relationships. Sometimes my own working-class sensibilities interfered with that task, especially since Constance did have her patrician nose so far up in the air sometimes that I was sure if it rained hard enough she'd drown.

The crazy quilts showed everything that was wild, creative, and rebellious in the quilting world. I had to admit, though I loved the neat and eye-pleasing old-fashioned patterns in the California quilts exhibit, the Victorian crazy quilts just delighted me. Their pure love of color, sensual use of velvets and silks, wools and cottons; their erratic and joyful placement of embroidered birds, animals, names, dates, flowers; the maker's spontaneous addition of buttons and ribbons and gewgaws always left me with a smile. My hope was that would be how the exhibit would affect our visitors and patrons. Though often not accepted in the quilt world as "real" quilts since technically they were tied, not quilted, they represented a freedom of expression not often seen in earlier quilts.

From a historian's point of view, they were both intriguing and frustrating since they represented an actual change in women's lifestyle coming along when early mass-marketed products gave women in the middle and lower classes the luxury of leisure time once reserved for the upper classes. To prove that their "leisure" time was well spent, women did many hours of needlework to produce these quilts for their parlors.

The frustrating part for historians was dating them. It was almost impossible to exactly pinpoint a crazy quilt's "finished" date since the fabrics used often spanned a hundred years in age. To make it even harder, dates and events were often embroidered on quilts years after the actual events took place in the quilter's life and the fabric they were embroidered on could be decades older than the inscriptions themselves.

Still, they gave us a peek into the daily lives of women from the late 1800s to the early 1930s. They'd recently come back into vogue and there was actually a crazy quilt guild here in San Celina called the Victorian Krazee Ladies, who had contributed some modern crazy quilts and crazy quilt clothing to this exhibit. They would be thrilled when they learned that Emma would be showing the quilt that was featured in her first Molly Connors mystery.

I was back in my office, going over my notes one last time, when my phone rang. It was Emma Baldwin.

"Benni, it looks like we're going to have to postpone our lunch date," she said.

"Oh, that's too bad. Is everything okay?"

"I'm fine, it's my car that's sick. It won't start and I've called the Automobile Club. They'll have to tow it into town to the garage. It shouldn't take too long. I'm afraid since I've been gone, the town has moved a little closer to the ranch."

"You still own your ranch?" I asked, surprised, but glad.

"Yes, but it's much smaller than when you last saw it.

I've been selling the land off little by little to help support me and Adelle. My old friend and ranch manager, Lou, has lived here for years. I only have the house and three acres left. I'm surrounded by neighbors now."

"I'm glad they didn't get Molly's . . . I mean, your house," I said.

She was quiet for a moment. "Well, I've been approached by developers again and I may have to sell."

"Oh," I said. That seemed to be the way everything was going in San Celina County these days. I thought for a moment, then said, "I have an idea. How about I come by and pick you up? We'll go to lunch in Paso Robles and maybe, by the time we're through, they'll have your car fixed. If not, I'll take you home."

"Benni, that is so sweet of you, but it's so much trouble."

"No, not at all. It's actually doing me a favor. I've already made a space for your quilt in the exhibit and this way I can pick it up. And besides, I was really looking forward to having lunch with you."

"If you're sure it's not too much trouble . . ." Her voice was hesitant.

"I swear it's not. Is noon still okay?"

"Wonderful. Do you remember how to get here?"

"I think so. Go up Highway 46 out of Paso Robles, turn right on Bantam Road, left on San Bruno Road. Your house was emerald green and white with gingerbread lattice work on the front porch. Is it still green and white?"

"You have a wonderful memory. Yes, it is. A little faded, like myself, but still the same." Her throaty laugh echoed through the phone line, then it abruptly stopped. "I'm afraid you might be disappointed if you haven't been here for a while. I'm not exactly in the country anymore."

"I might be disappointed, but not surprised."

"No, I suppose you wouldn't be. You've been watching this happen for years."

I had to admit I was actually glad for the change of events, even though I felt bad about her car troubles. I wanted to see her house—Molly's house—again, to see where she'd written the books I'd loved so much as a girl. I wanted to see it before it was possibly bulldozed to make room for a million-dollar tract home.

After arranging the baked goods, napkins, cream, and sugar on the table in the co-op's small kitchen, I started the coffee. I was wiping up some spilled coffee grounds when Constance's shrill voice rang across the main room.

"Benni Harper, are you here?"

"Yes, ma'am." I walked out into the spacious main room where our quilting bees took place. "I was making coffee. Maybe you and the ladies would like some coffee and pastries after the tour."

"Oh, I don't think so." She sniffed the air as if she smelled something bad. "We have reservations for brunch at the country club."

I sighed inwardly, wishing I'd not jumped the gun and bought two-dozen pastries. Oh well, D-Daddy and who-ever showed up to work in the studios this morning would appreciate them. He certainly deserved them. D-Daddy worked harder than any twenty-one-year-old I'd ever met.

Behind Constance, the object of my thoughts appeared.

"Miz Sinclair," D-Daddy said in his sexy, Cajun-tinged drawl. "*Bon jour.* It's so fine to see you. How's my favorite *belle?*" He took her hand, bent deeply at the waist, and kissed it.

Constance's greyhound-thin, porcelain face lit up at his flirting. "Oh, you old fool," she said, unable to keep from smiling. Though in San Celina's social class system, they were about as far apart as her namesake Lady Chatterly and her randy gamekeeper, D-Daddy's thick white hair and old-fashioned manners charmed Constance as they did every woman he encountered.

He winked at me over Constance's champagne-blond bouffant hair. "I come to tell you, *chère,* your ladies are arriving," he said.

"I'd better get out there," Constance said. On her way

out, she called over her shoulder, "Are you ready to conduct our tour, Benni?"

"Yes, ma'am," I said, feeling for my notes in the back pocket of my Wranglers. I hoped I wouldn't have to use them, but just having them there made me feel more secure. "I'll meet you out front."

"Ah, coffee," D-Daddy said, gazing past me to the kitchen.

"Pastries too," Constance called from across the room. "We'll be coming here after Benni's tour. Will you join us?"

"But, of course," D-Daddy said.

After she left, I complained to him. "She wouldn't come within ten feet of the pastries when I offered them!"

He just grinned, well aware and quite proud of his charms.

"You'll have to entertain them if they stay too long," I said, wagging my finger at him. "I have a lunch date in Paso Robles at noon."

"Who's in Paso Robles?" he asked, pouring himself a cup of coffee.

After explaining about Emma, he said, "Then, *ma chère 'tite fille,* I'd best be getting out there and fixing your truck or you won't be going nowhere fast, you."

"What's wrong with my truck?"

"Flat tire."

"What? Those tires are brand new!"

He held his coffee up to his face, inhaling its scent before sipping. "Probably picked up a nail. Don't worry, by the time the ladies be in here drinking coffee, it'll be done."

I gave him a hug. "D-Daddy, what would I do without you?"

After the tour, I left Constance and her ladies in D-Daddy's capable and entertaining hands and headed out to my truck.

"I changed your tire," D-Daddy called to me. "Don't forget to get the other one fixed."

"I won't." Another item to add to my mental list of things to do.

He hesitated, a troubled look on his craggy face.

"Really, D-Daddy, I promise to get it fixed right away."

"It's not that, *ange*. I'm worried, me. That tire, it was slashed."

My mouth opened in surprise. "It was?"

"You be involved in any shenanigans?" That's what he called my occasional forays into crime.

I held up my hands in innocence. "No, I swear, I'm clean."

He shook his head. "You best tell the chief. Maybe some ornery kids."

"I will," I said, patting his upper arm.

The drive to Paso Robles took almost twice as long the usual forty-five minutes because of the traffic that was getting heavier and heavier every year. They'd started work on widening the two lanes of Interstate 101 over Rosita Pass that connected north and south San Celina County, but I'd heard it was going to take at least three years to complete. I inched my way up the hill thinking about all I had to do this week.

Tonight was the Zozobra bonfire and barbecue at the Elks Club. It was a tradition that had been a part of La Fiesta Days for as long as the event had been celebrated. The bonfire was built for "The Burning of Old Man Gloom." Those who wanted to participate wrote their fears on a small piece of wood and tossed it into the raging fire. Tradition stated that this helped everyone get rid of unhappy thoughts and feelings, making them free to enjoy La Fiesta's week-long activities.

I had agreed to help Elvia, who as a former La Fiesta Queen, was one of the people handing out the flat scraps of wood. We were supposed to meet there at six o'clock. That gave me plenty of time to see Emma, drive back to the museum, type up her biographical display card, and hang her quilt in the museum. Opening day for the exhibit was tomorrow and we had three senior citizen groups scheduled for tours.

After breathing the toxic fumes of a truck loaded with tomatoes for twenty minutes, the traffic jam finally broke at the top of the pass and I drove at just over the speed limit to Paso Robles. The way to Emma's house came back to me as easily as if I'd driven it two days ago instead of almost seventeen years. After the citylike traffic on Rosita Pass, the drive along the widened highway going out of Paso Robles didn't do much to soothe my fears that San Celina County was turning into a suburb of San Francisco or Los Angeles. I hadn't been this way outside of Paso Robles for a couple of years. What had once been miles of almond and walnut orchards, old barns with still-working wooden calf chutes, and the occasional sweet-smelling grape field were now one-acre ranchettes with fancy, million-dollar pseudo-Spanish-style homes with perfect lawns and elaborate sprinkler systems.

I turned left on San Bruno Road and my heart jumped with gladness when I spotted Emma's house. It hadn't changed as much as I'd imagined. Though, as she had said, the paint was a bit faded and it was surrounded by fancy homes rather than the oak trees and almond orchards of my memories, it was exactly like the house she described so well in her Molly Connors books. Maybe that was why when I first saw it when I was twenty, I felt such a shock of recognition. I dug through my backpack, found my copy of her first book and read the first page.

The Rolling C's ranch house was at the end of a wide, gravel driveway. It was a two-story white clapboard with a slanting emerald green roof and two red brick chimneys. The front windows were long rectangles framed by green and white gingham curtains. A long front porch ran the length of the house. Wooden railing cut like fancy lace corralled the white wicker chairs on the porch. The front door was a bright mint green with a brass horse head door knocker. Next to the house, a

huge sycamore tree with a black scar from a lightning
strike the year Molly Connors was born shaded the
front yard.

THE SECRET IN THE CRAZY QUILT—
A MOLLY CONNORS MYSTERY.

I sat for a moment staring at the house. Though it happened less and less as time went on, occasionally there
was a shock of memory that brought my life with Jack
back into sharp focus. The last time I'd seen this house
I'd been an optimistic, twenty-year-old newlywed. What
had I truly expected life to hold? I honestly didn't remember thinking about it much. I only remember worrying
about getting my term paper done and working on the
ranch with Jack and occasionally contemplating us as
older people. I remember thinking the first time I met her
how Emma Baldwin was so much older than me, though
she was only in her late forties. At the time, I couldn't
even imagine being that ancient age. Resting my arms on
my steering wheel, I smiled to myself. Gabe turned forty-
five this year. Mid-forties definitely seemed less ancient
than when I was twenty.

By the time I stepped out of the truck, my arrival had
been announced by the sound of determined, high-pitched
barking. The wooden screen door opened and Emma
stepped out on the porch. A chubby wiener dog dashed
out ahead of her and barreled toward me, its ears stream-
ing behind giving a comical illusion of speed. He stopped
two feet from me and continued to bark a shrill warning.
I laughed at his sincerity, always impressed by the bravado of dachshunds.

"Hello, Benni," Emma called from the porch. "Don't
mind my little protector. He's definitely more bark than
bite. Now, you hush. Benni's a friend."

The dog gave one more suspicious bark. I bent down
and stuck out my hand. He moved tentatively toward me,
gave it a disdainful sniff, then turned back and trotted over
to stand next to Emma.

She beckoned me up to the porch. "That was about as friendly a greeting as I've ever seen Plug give. He must like you."

"Plug?" I replied, laughing. The name fit him perfectly.

"His actual name is about two feet long. Believe it or not, both his parents were champions. But poor Plug was too ornery and too chubby to be a show dog." She gestured at me to follow her. "Let's go inside and get the quilt. Then we can be on our way. The Automobile Club arrived thirty minutes ago and took my car to the repair shop. I do appreciate you rescuing me."

The house inside was decorated as I remembered, neat and simple with Shaker-style furniture. In the living room, the quilt lay across the back of a new-looking navy blue sofa. In a flash of memory, I was twenty again, sitting on a sofa very much like this one, studying the quilt's intricate embroidered squares.

CHAPTER 7

❖

April 3, 1978
Monday

"*I*T'S BEAUTIFUL," I SAID TO MRS. BALDWIN TWO DAYS later during our second interview. I ran my fingers over a red velvet triangle. She'd brought out the quilt that had inspired her first Molly Connors mystery. Near the center, in the middle of one red velvet triangle, she had embroidered a spider. Its body was a shiny silver bead, its legs stitched with gold thread. It crawled toward an iridescent spider web stitched with both silver and gold thread.

"Spiders are very traditional in a crazy quilt," she said.

"Wait, let me take notes." I pulled a spiraled notebook out of my green backpack and started writing.

"In Europe," she continued, "they are considered to be good luck when used in needlework."

"Is Europe where crazy quilts came from?" I asked.

"Historians are not quite sure where crazy quilts originated," she said, running a hand over the quilt, caressing it as if it were a beloved child's head. "They think the crazy quilt fad may have started during Queen Victoria's rule in the early nineteenth century. She collected so many mementos and memorabilia of her late husband that she eventually ended up having to hold court in the corridors of Windsor Castle because her rooms were too crowded."

I shifted the quilt so I could study another section of it. "She was a pack rat. Just like my husband, Jack. He drives me nuts because he saves everything."

She laughed and ran her fingers over an embroidered fan. "Ranchers and Queen Victoria. Who would have ever thought there was a common denominator? My husband, RJ, was the same way." She made her voice deep and gruff. " 'Emma, don't you dare throw out that three feet of rusty barbed wire. I might need it someday.' "

"That sounds just like Jack!"

She leaned closer to me, as if to tell me a secret. "And what's most irritating is they are so often right."

"Yeah, but we don't want *them* to know that." My eyes skipped from one intricate, colorful square to the next. "This is so interesting. I want to use this somehow in my term paper, but I'm not sure how." I thought for a moment, then asked, "How exactly did this quilt influence your writing?"

"As you can tell by the title of the book, it was the object that inspired my first Molly Connors mystery. When the editor asked me to turn my ranch stories into a mystery series for young women, I was in a quandry. I was sitting in the living room here adding something to one of the squares on the quilt when it came to me that it might make an interesting story, using a quilt to hide messages for Molly and her chums to solve. I couldn't have any sort of violent plot. My editor made it clear that she didn't actually want a murder, but a mystery that would keep young readers interested, but not scare them or offend their parents. I'm sure you remember, children were much more innocent back in the fifties and sixties than they are now. A clue in a quilt about the stolen diamond necklace seemed just the key."

"I've read all your books more than once and loved them all," I said while writing down her comments. "But *The Secret of the Crazy Quilt* is still my all-time favorite.

I never guessed that her friend's uncle was an undercover G-man. I thought he was one of the jewel thieves."

"Thank you, my dear. It is special to me, of course, not only because it was the first, but because it was such a thrill to see my quilt on the cover. You know, this quilt is actually the only scrapbook I have of my life. Every date or incident that is of importance to me is represented somewhere on this quilt. It is my most precious possession."

"May I take a picture of it?" I asked, putting down my notebook.

"Certainly."

We spread it across the dark blue sofa so I could take a good photograph of the whole quilt. "Now," I said, "one with you holding it."

After the pictures, I asked her a few more questions about what writing a book was like, how much of Molly was her, how her fans influenced her, and whether she would ever write again.

"Perhaps," she said, her eyes growing vague. "There's so much to do running this ranch. We put in walnuts a few years back and they take quite a bit of work. I still run some cattle and I don't have to tell you how much time that takes. Right now, it is all Lou and I can do to keep this place going."

"Lou is . . . ?" I flipped back through my notes.

"My ranch manager. He's helped with the ranch for a long time. If it hadn't been for Lou . . ." She paused for a moment, overcome, it seemed, by emotion. She inhaled deeply. "If not for Lou, I might have lost this place when RJ was in Korea and then again after he died."

I glanced over at a black-and-white picture of her on a side table. It showed Emma, her husband, and a scowling boy about twelve years old.

"Is that your son?" I asked.

She nodded, her face expressionless. "That was taken a long time ago. He's a grown man now."

"Does he help you with the ranch?"

Her face stayed bland and she stood up. "He has occasionally worked on the ranch. Let me make us some tea. Then I'll show you the original manuscripts of my books. I wrote them in these little speckled composition books that Crosby's Five and Dime stocks for me."

"That would be great," I said with exaggerated enthusiasm, feeling slightly ashamed for asking about her son. There was obviously some difficulty between them. Remembering Jack's admonitions about delving too much into her private life, I tried to push my curiosity aside.

Just as she was standing up, the front screen door slammed opened. Both startled, we turned to stare for a moment at the scowling man standing just inside the farmhouse's small entryway. He looked to be in his twenties, had long, stringy hair, and was gaunt as a scarecrow.

She jumped up. "What do you want?" Her even voice became high and nervous.

"Who's that?" He flicked his bright blue eyes over at me. They held a distinct challenge though I had no idea why.

"Cody, honey, let's go outside," she said, not looking back at me.

So this was the son. He sure looked like a jerk. She'd obviously not used him as a model for Molly's two mischievous, but caring brothers.

He gave me one more unfriendly stare. I frowned back at him, not about to be intimidated by some long-haired hippie freak. There was a long moment of silence. The Shaker-style grandfather clock struck three o'clock, its chimes echoing in the quiet house.

Finally I snapped, "What are you looking at?"

"Apparently one of my mother's pathetic little groupies," he said in a nasty tone.

Before I could answer, Emma grabbed her son's arm and pulled him out on the porch. "I'll be back in a moment, Benni," she called.

"Okay," I called back, suddenly ashamed of how I'd reacted to her son's unfriendliness. If Dove had been here, she'd be telling me to show some compassion for Emma and turn the other cheek.

I could hear his harsh voice yelling at her on the front porch, and a part of me wanted to rush out and defend her. But what went on between her and her son wasn't any of my business.

Trying to tune out their fight, I turned my attention to the crazy quilt. Though it was pictured along with the cover artist's interpretation of blond-haired Molly Connors on the front of her book, the cover didn't do justice to the quilt's multidimensional beauty. The actual quilt was slightly larger than double bed size and was almost overwhelming in its complexity. I took out my notebook and started listing the embroidered objects. Even though I'd taken photographs, for me, putting things down in words seared them more into my memory.

Things on quilt: two fans—small and large, spider and web, embroidered pine tree, satin stitched lily, handkerchief with peacock printed on it, lace, ribbon, ivory button that looks like a turtle, real 1888 gold coin with hole drilled on top, printed picture of cowboy (looks like flannel), red and white flower made with small, Indian-type beads, the silk lining of a man's hatband, a ribbon embroidered with lilies of the valley, embroidered teapot and cup, small four-string guitar with a date embroidered on it, porcelain horse button, embroidered Monarch butterfly, a political ribbon supporting Eisenhower, a Paso Robles football ribbon, an embroidered sea gull . . .

My hand started cramping and I realized that there was no way I'd be able to write down everything that was stitched on this quilt. I'd just have to enlarge the photos I'd taken and hope that they came out clear. Just in case, though, I quickly listed all the dates she had embroidered so far.

July 1, 1931; June 22, 1949; August 17, 1949; May 1, 1950; March 23, 1951; December 28, 1951; October 25, 1952; August 1, 1953; September 12, 1961; March 24, 1965; June 14, 1968.

I put down my notebook. It had grown too quiet out on the porch and I wondered if I should go out and check on Emma. A minute or so later, the front screen opened and she stood in the molded entry of the living room. Her face was a shade paler than before, but otherwise, she appeared composed.

"Would you like some tea, Benni?" she asked, not saying a thing about her son.

"Yes, thank you," I replied, taking my cue from her that we weren't going to talk about what had just happened.

"I'll be just a minute."

When Emma came back with the silver tea tray, I concentrated on trying not to drop my teacup or make a mess eating the tiny lemon and ginger cookies she served. "I wrote down all the dates on the quilt," I said, figuring the kindest thing would be to get back on the topic of my term paper. "What do they commemorate?"

"Different highlights of my life," she said. "They start with my birthday, July first, and the rest are things like my son's birthday, my wedding day—RJ and I were married in the summer, two months after we met, right out in front of this house. One is the day RJ left for Korea and when he came home, another the day my first book was published, the dates of RJ's and my mother's death. Things like that." She sipped her tea. "Those dates are really only important to me. That's the whole point of a crazy quilt. It is your personal history, your life lovingly stitched."

"Your life lovingly stitched. I like that. Can I quote you?"

"Absolutely."

After our tea, I thanked her profusely for taking so much time to talk to me, then made another date for next Friday to show her a rough draft and make sure I had quoted her correctly.

"That would be lovely," she said. "It has been such a pleasure talking to you, Benni. I hope we can continue our friendship."

"Me too," I said.

On the way out, we were met on the porch by a rugged-looking, middle-aged man wearing a stained and battered straw Stetson. When he saw us, his sun-browned face drew up in a striking white smile.

"This the girl you was telling me about, Emma?" he asked, giving me a friendly nod. He looked somewhat familiar.

"Yes, it is," Mrs. Baldwin said, beaming back at him. "Benni Harper, this is my ranch manager, Lou Chesterton."

"Pleased to meet you, young lady," he said, touching his hat with two dirt-stained fingers. His honey-brown eyes were friendly. "You any relation to John Harper?"

"He was my father-in-law," I said. "I'm married to his youngest son, Jack."

He gave a curt nod. "Know the boy. We've talked a time or two at the Templeton stock auction. Knows his cattle real good."

"My dad's Ben Ramsey."

His grin widened. "You're Ben's little girl? Why, he's just proud as punch of you. Talks about you all the time at the feed store in Paso."

I smiled back at him. That was probably where I'd seen him, the few times I'd had to go to the Paso Robles feed store because ours was out of something. Like our feed store in south county, there was always a bunch of grinning, chewing old guys there shooting the breeze, catching up on the local ag community gossip. I thanked Mrs. Baldwin again and promised her I'd come by to show her my term paper once it was finished.

As I backed out of the gravel driveway, I watched her say something to Lou, then her hand come up to her face in a familiar gesture of despair.

That night at dinner, I told Jack about the uncomfortable incident with Emma's son. "He is the biggest creep you can imagine. And there's something fishy going on with him. What do you think they were arguing about out on the porch?"

Jack cut a piece of steak and stuck it in his mouth. "Blondie, who cares if she is having problems with her son? I'll say it again, what does that have to do with your term paper?"

"Nothing, I guess." I sat for a moment with my chin in my hand watching him eat. "But I still think there's more there than meets the eye."

He pushed his empty plate aside. I stood up and started to pick it up, but he pulled me down onto his lap. "And I think you've been reading too many of her mystery novels," he said, kissing the base of my throat.

"It honestly might be something more . . . I don't know what . . ."

"Sinister?" He threw back his head and gave a big laugh.

I laughed with him. "A fancy word for such a good-looking, yet simple-minded guy."

"Hey, I *is* getting college educated."

"Really, I do think there's more there than it seems."

"And I still think it's none of your business. Now, let's talk about what's for dessert." He opened the top snap of my shirt and nibbled on my collarbone.

I swung my left leg around and straddled him. "Jack Harper, I swear you are worse than one of your bulls. Is this *all* you ever think about?"

He grinned and, using both hands, unsnapped the front of my Western shirt with one pull. "Yeah, pretty much."

CHAPTER 8

❖

April 17, 1995
Monday

"*E*XCUSE ME FOR A MOMENT," EMMA SAID. "I NEED TO finish getting ready. Perhaps I should bring a sweater and a book. Who knows how long I'll be waiting for my car."

"That's a good idea," I said.

While she was gone, I wandered around the room, looking at the titles of books in her bookcases and glancing at the dozen or so silver-framed family photographs. On the end table next to the sofa was a leather notebook with several sheets of paper sticking haphazardly out of it. Was she writing again? Maybe the authors' day at Blind Harry's had inspired her. I certainly hoped so.

Temptation almost overcame me. I wanted so badly to open the notebook and read what she was working on. "Oh, have some class, Harper," I muttered, trying to content myself with imagining what new stories she might be concocting.

When Emma came back carrying a large canvas tote bag, she scooped up the notebook and its contents. As she did, a flurry of papers fell to the oak floor.

"Oh, dear!" She stooped down and started frantically

gathering them up, her panic an overreaction to the accident.

"Let me help," I said, bending over to pick up an envelope. I glanced at the return address. LAPD? Why would Emma have a letter from them?

"Thank you, but I've got it," she said, snatching the letter from my hand and stuffing it into her tote bag.

At the Cowgirl Cafe, a new diner in Paso Robles, she and I settled down in a brown vinyl booth and caught up on everything that had happened in our lives since we'd last seen each other seventeen years ago. The urge to ask her about her son's death was almost overwhelming, but since she didn't bring it up, I didn't either. She did ask me about Jack and I had no reason not to tell her the whole story.

"After their father died, when Jack was sixteen, he and his brother Wade never agreed on how the ranch should be run," I said, sipping my Coke. "When I first met you, I was twenty. Their dad had only been dead for four years, but the ranch was already failing. It took fifteen years for it to actually give up the ghost, and by that time Jack and Wade were barely speaking. They had a fight one night in Trigger's, a bar by the Interstate that's closed now. Jack didn't usually drink much, but that night he was drinking with a friend of ours. He and Wade argued, then Jack and his friend left and they flipped Jack's Jeep out on old Highway One."

I stopped for a moment and swallowed. Though it had been almost three years, it was still hard to just come out and say. "Jack was killed. It's still unclear which of them was driving." I stared down at my hands and realized I'd unconsciously shredded my paper napkin. Thinking about that night still caused my insides to turn cold and hard. "I left the Harper ranch shortly after that and moved to town. That's when I started as curator of the folk art museum. A little less than a year later, I met Gabe." I squeezed my napkin shreds into a neat ball and pushed it aside before looking up at Emma. "I love Gabe very much. He's a wonderful man."

"I am so sorry about Jack," she said, her eyes liquid with sympathy. "You two were so much in love."

"Yes, we were." I picked up my tuna sandwich. Talking about him was still difficult so I understood why, during her speech at Blind Harry's, Emma hadn't wanted to talk about her son. "What have you been doing for seventeen years? Beebs and Millee said you had a cousin who was sick?"

"Yes, I spent a good deal of these last years taking care of Adelle. Emphysema and then cancer. She had her share of troubles and no real family but me." Behind us, someone put money in the jukebox and Patsy Cline's mournful "Sweet Memories" started playing.

"Listen," I said to Emma. "That's certainly appropriate."

Tears softened her eyes. "It certainly is."

"Where did Adelle live?"

"A small town in Georgia. Dawson."

I smiled and bit into my sandwich. "You know, I thought I detected a slight Southern accent in you, but I wasn't sure."

She picked up a salt shaker and lightly sprinkled her chef salad. "I guess I never lost all of it, and being back there, it snuck up on me."

"Are you glad to be back?"

She contemplated the sliced eggs and ham in her chef salad, then looked over at me, her eyes still glassy from unshed tears. "Yes, I am, though I miss Adelle terribly. She was like a sister to me. She was there for me at a time in my life when I really needed someone. But it is good to be living at the old place again. Lou worked the land the years I was away and did a fine job keeping it up. I hate the thought of having to sell."

I didn't answer, unable to even imagine what it would be like to sell the Ramsey ranch house, much less with the thought that our house would be demolished.

"Lunch is on me," I said, picking up the bill as we stood up to leave.

"No," she started to protest.

"I insist. I hope I'm not being presumptuous, but you can get it next time."

She smiled. "I'd love for there to be a next time, Benni. I've enjoyed our talk immensely."

As I was paying the bill, she said, "I need to run across the street to the pharmacy."

"Okay, I'll wait for you in the truck."

I was leaning next to the truck, talking and petting Scout in the bed, when she came out of the small pharmacy. She waved and was halfway across the street, when, it seemed, out of nowhere a small white car darted in front her, missing her by only inches. It was gone as quickly as it appeared.

"Emma!" I ran across the street where she stood frozen, her face in shock. "Are you okay? I swear, it looked like that car was aiming for you!"

She allowed me to lead her to the sidewalk. "There's a lot more traffic than there used to be here in Paso Robles. I guess I should have been paying more attention."

"Nonsense," I said. "That car was definitely in the wrong. Are you sure you're okay?"

She brought her hand up and nervously patted her hair. "Yes, yes, I'm fine. Just a little shaken up."

"I'll drive you to the repair shop," I said, glancing up the street where the car had disappeared around a corner.

At the shop we found out that the car's problem was the alternator and they would have it fixed in a couple of hours.

"I'll wait," she said, sitting down on the lobby's nubby sofa. "I did bring a book." She held up her tote bag. I noticed that her hand still shook a little.

"Are you sure you're all right to drive home?" I asked.

"Absolutely."

"Please come by and see the quilt exhibit when you

have time. I'll treat you to the two-buck VIP tour of the museum."

"That would be wonderful. I'll give you a call."

Thankfully, the drive back over the pass to the museum was much quicker. I spent the rest of the afternoon typing up Emma's biography sheet to hang next to her quilt and hanging the quilt itself. About four o'clock I called Gabe at his office.

"Want to meet at the Elks Club?" I asked. "I'm helping Elvia hand out pieces of wood for the Zozobra fire so I'll be there early. I'll save you a piece of wood."

"You'd better save me a two-by-four," he said, the weariness in his voice obvious.

"How's it going on the investigation?" I switched the phone to my right ear and leaned back in my chair. "I saw Miguel and he said that it might have been someone Luke knew rather than a plain old robbery."

"The multiple stab wounds do indicate a suspect who is emotionally involved with the victim, but it could also just as likely be some idiot high on PCP."

"Are you okay?" I asked, knowing it was a futile question, but I'd felt compelled to ask it anyway. Gabe's feelings about his friend being murdered would take weeks or even months to surface and not always in a predictable fashion. I was slowly learning to accept that fact about my emotionally complex husband.

"I'm fine," he said, just as I thought he would.

"Did you get in touch with his mother?"

"You know, that's a really weird thing. She's from Alabama, by the way. A little town called Eufaula. And she's dead."

"What? Are you sure? At dinner he talked about her as if she were still living. No, wait, he distinctly said to me that he was going to retire near her. It was when you were in the bathroom."

"She died of a heart attack six months ago," Gabe said bluntly.

"Why would he tell me she was still living?"

"I don't know, but if he doesn't have any other family, that leaves me to deal with his effects."

"What are you going to do?"

"My investigators are searching for other family members though they've come up empty so far. I've also sent an investigator down to his office in Santa Monica to haul back all his files. Maybe there's something in them that will give us a clue about who killed him."

"Don't you think it more than likely had to do with whatever case he was working on up here?"

"There's no telling. We've brought in everything that was in his motel room in Morro Bay and we're going through it."

"Well, good luck," I said, not knowing what else to say. I wanted to comfort Gabe, but I also knew that when he became like this, all business with his emotions packed down tight, the best thing to do was wait him out and just be a sounding board.

"If I don't make it to the bonfire, I'll see you at home," he said. "I'll call if I'm going to be past ten o'clock."

After we hung up, I realized I hadn't told him about my slashed tire. Oh well, I thought, it's not all that important considering what he was dealing with right now. I'd tell him tonight and ask him if they could have a patrol car drive by the museum a little more frequently. My purple truck sitting out there by itself was probably just a tempting target for a bunch of bored teenage kids.

I arrived at the Elks Club before Elvia. The club sat across the street from the San Celina Cemetery and was already crowded with hundreds of people, forcing me to park three blocks away. Before Elvia arrived and put me to work, I headed over to the row of steel barrel barbecues to buy a tri-tip steak sandwich from one of the Elks members who were cooking the hunks of top block beef and thick ribs over the blazing red oak fire. The juicy, meaty scent immediately started my tastebuds watering.

"Billy Johnson, this is my lucky day," I said to a square-shaped, gray-haired man with black-rimmed

glasses. Billy had attended high school with Jack and me.
He and Jack had team-roped at local high school rodeos
for a few years. "I want . . . no, make that *need,* a tri-tip
sandwich."

He gave me a wide, gap-toothed grin and wiped one
hand on his stained apron, which showed a giant pink pig
in a chef's hat proclaiming EAT BEEF! "Benni Harper, you
sweet young thing, you not only can have a steak sandwich, you can have my heart."

"No, thanks," I said, pulling a ten-dollar bill out of my
pocket. "Never have liked organ meats."

He laughed, waved away my money, and handed me
a foil-wrapped sandwich. "It's on the house. Heard you're
working the wood table tonight."

"Yeah, I'm slaving alongside our most famous former
Fiesta Queen."

"Shoot, that's right, Elvia was Queen. When was that,
1977?"

"Nineteen seventy-eight. Hard to believe so much time
has passed. Why, I remember you when you had brown
hair."

He ran a rough hand through his thick gray hair. "That
was before seventeen years of marriage and four kids. I've
earned every last one of these gray hairs."

"Seventeen years? Wow, I didn't realize it had been
that long for you and Susie."

"Got married the same year you and Jack did. Two
months before. Remember?"

"What I mostly remember is Jack getting pie-eyed at
your bachelor party when he was way under the legal age
to drink."

Billy waved his tongs at me. "Not my fault. Blame my
older brother."

"Always trying to pass the buck," I said, shaking my
head. "Thanks for the sandwich."

He bowed, showing me the top of his gray head. "My
pleasure."

At the wood table, Elvia was already arranging the thin

pieces of pine and black felt pens for people to write their fears with.

"I should have realized where you'd be," she said, glancing down at the steak sandwich and can of orange soda in my hand.

"Hey, you know what the lines will be like if I waited. I wanted to get a sandwich before the crowds descend upon us." I held the foil wrapped sandwich out and wiggled it at her. "Do you want half?"

"Actually, I do," she said. "I'm starving. But let's get everything set up first and then we can sit back and relax."

Once all the flat pieces of wood were set out for people, we sat back and shared my steak sandwich and drink, occasionally having to explain to first-timers the purpose of the wood pieces. Across the parking lot, in the middle of a grassy area, we could see the Elks members setting up the bonfire. Out on the street, as a precaution, sat a shiny red San Celina fire truck.

"What are you going to write on your wood?" I asked, taking a bite of my sandwich.

"I can't tell you," Elvia said. "That would make it invalid."

"Says who? This isn't like wishing on a star or blowing out birthday candles. What's your biggest fear?"

"You first," she said.

I picked up a flat piece of wood and a felt marker. "Shoot, this sliver isn't big enough for all my fears."

She smiled and smoothed back a strand of black hair blowing across her face. The sharp, cool breeze reminded us that it was still early spring. Over by the fire, just now starting to dance and glow yellow and orange, a few of the firetenders were harmonizing a Spanish song with a melody that was as familiar to me as one of Dove's country lullabies. It spoke of God's protection, the power of St. Michael, the archangel, and the love of mothers for their children.

Elvia tilted her head to listen. "Remember Mama singing that to us when we were girls and wouldn't settle down and go to sleep?"

I nodded. Many nights of my childhood had been spent at her patchwork house in town, eating cinnamon toast and fresh tortillas for breakfast, sleeping in her pink canopy bed, sharing her hairbrush, my blond hairs intermingling with her black ones. "When you hear that song, it's hard to be afraid of anything."

She leaned her head back and sighed. "I guess my biggest fear is that Emory and I won't stay as happy as we are right now. Something this good just can't last."

I raised my eyebrows and didn't answer. She was right—it wouldn't last in the exact same way she was experiencing it now. But from my own life, I know one thing: Even if it changed, it could still be good, maybe even better. I reached over and patted my friend's cold hand. "I think my biggest fear is that things will stay the same, that Gabe and I won't grow and change. Even if things seem good, being static isn't. So, let's ditch both those fears and wish that both happiness and change will come into our lives."

"That's a deal," she said, grabbing my hand and holding it for a moment.

When the fire had reached its zenith, we all took our pieces of wood, and after a lengthy speech by El Presidente, the head of the La Fiesta de Las Pueblos celebration, the current Fiesta Queen threw in the first piece of wood. In an orderly fashion, watched over by the San Celina Fire Department, we all took our turns throwing away our fears. When the last piece of wood had been thrown in the fire, a mariachi band struck up a cheerful song and El Presidente and his executive committee burned an effigy of Old Man Gloom, who bore a striking resemblance to the scarecrow in *The Wizard of Oz*. Soon a few of the older couples started dancing to the band's mariachi music.

Elvia and I were sitting on a brick fence watching the dancers when my cousin, Emory, showed up.

"Ladies, how was the fire dance?" he asked, coming over and giving his new bride a long and enthusiastic kiss. He looked every inch the successful businessman in a custom-tailored gray suit and pale green shirt, except for his gray-and-green, modern-art-inspired, Jerry Garcia tie.

"It's not a fire dance," she said, pushing at his chest. "How did the meeting go?"

"Great, the store down in Santa Barbara looks like it'll open about a month after the one here in San Celina. Which is two weeks from Saturday, by the way, ladies."

"I'll be the first one in line," I said.

"No doubt, sweetcakes," he said to me, loosening his tie before leaning over to kiss me on the cheek. "Where's the chief?"

"He couldn't make it. He's working on a murder investigation."

"I read in the paper that some guy was killed down by the creek, but I thought he hired people to do the grunt work."

"This one's personal. I'm sure the paper hasn't found that out yet." I quickly explained about Luke and Gabe's past relationship.

"That must be hard for Gabe," Elvia said. "Do you think his murder had to do with what he was investigating here?"

I shrugged. "Luke was very close-mouthed about who he was following. He said it was a job concerning a cheating husband, but who knows? He worked undercover narcotics with Gabe so I have no idea how much of what he says is real or part of that whole secretive, cop thing."

"The undercover guys can be as tight-lipped as nineteenth-century schoolmarms," Emory agreed. "I found that out real quick when I worked at the *Tribune*. So, what have you dug up?"

I wrinkled my nose at him. "Not a thing because I'm not involved with this. I'm just being a caring, supportive wife who listens to her overworked husband when he trudges home from the salt mines."

Emory and Elvia shot each other an amused glance.

"You two stop that. I'm not involved nor even want to be. Even though I met Luke, it's none of my business. Actually, I'm not that interested."

They glanced at each other again and laughed out loud this time.

"You know," I said, "I'm almost regretting bringing you two together. Being ridiculed in stereo is annoying. Especially when I'm being absolutely sincere."

Emory came over to me, pulling me up by my hands. He kissed one cheek, then the other. "My deepest apologies, dear cousin-o'-mine. We don't mean to ridicule you, I promise."

"We just know you," Elvia said, still smiling.

"This time you two are just wrong, wrong, wrong," I said with exaggerated haughtiness. "I'm too busy with my own stuff this week to be a part-time PI."

"And I'm sure the chief is mighty relieved," Emory said.

"Suck eggs, Emory Delano Littleton," I said. "You now owe me five free chicken dinners for your poor treatment of your favorite cousin."

He squeezed my hands. "You've always known that my chickens are your chickens."

"You fool," I said, rolling my eyes. I turned back to Elvia. "Will you be at the children's costume parade and piñata-decorating contest tomorrow evening? The historical society talked me into taking pictures of it for them."

One of the La Fiesta events was a parade down by the Mission, in which children were encouraged to dress in the costumes of their heritage and show off the huge piñatas that different groups of children—Girl Scout troops, Boy Scout troops, public and private school classes, and 4-H groups—had decorated. The piñatas would be featured on a float in the parade and then were for sale at the historical society's booth at La Fiesta Mercado on Saturday. The money earned went toward summer arts and crafts programs.

"Yes, three other former queens and I are judging both contests," she said.

"I love being able to say I'm married to a queen," Emory said, teasing.

"Have you seen the pictures of her as the 1978 Fiesta Queen?" I asked.

"No, she won't let me."

"Come by the house, I have copies. She was one hot *mamacita* in her Chantilly lace empire dress and three-inch platform shoes. The gargantuan can of Final Net hairspray it took to keep her dancing curls up would be against almost all of our current air quality protection laws."

"Big-haired women have always revved my engines," Emory said, winking at me.

Elvia stood up, giving us both a withering look. "If you two are going to make fun of me, I'm leaving."

"Ha," I said, "You can dish it out, *mi hermana,* but you can't take it."

She just murmured something in Spanish and bumped my hip with hers. "If we're going to start showing ugly pictures, don't forget I have your fifth-grade masterpiece. I could have it framed for Gabe's office."

"I remember that one," Emory said, groaning. "Orange freckles and Little Orphan Annie hair. You'd've scared the crows out of the cornfield."

"Okay, okay," I said. "Picture truce."

At Elvia's little green 1959 Austin Healy, we parted ways. After kissing her good-bye and telling her he'd meet her back home, Emory turned to me. "I'll walk you to your truck."

"That's okay, I'll be fine. It's not too far." I pointed across the street to the cemetery. "It's down past those pepper trees."

"It's dark. I'll walk you." His voice gave no compromise.

"Geeze Louise, being a married man has made you as protective as Gabe."

"You say that as if it's a bad thing."

I linked my arm through his. "I guess it isn't. Let's go."

On the walk down the street we talked about the opening of the chicken store and cafe. He was worried that bringing the business west would take up more of his time than he wanted. "Elvia and I hardly ever get to see each other," he complained. "Much less do anything fun."

"Welcome to adulthood, my late-blooming cousin," I said. "Wait'll you have kids."

His face turned thoughtful. "Kids. That's hard to imagine, me somebody's daddy."

"Not so hard," I said, looking into his green eyes. "You'll be a wonderful daddy."

"You think so?" His voice sounded wistful.

I turned to answer him, but before I could, he took his arm out of mine and slipped it around my shoulder, pulling me close to him.

"Oh, Lord," he said under his breath, more a prayer than an oath.

"What is it?" I asked, turning my head to look.

My purple truck sat comically low, its four tires completely flat. But worse than that, spray-painted in bright red paint across the side, were words describing me that were so vile and filthy my head buzzed with fear.

CHAPTER 9

❖

April 17, 1995
Monday

"*M*Y TRUCK!" I WAILED AND STARTED TO DASH TO-
ward it.

"No," Emory said, grabbing my shoulders and stopping
me. "We need to call Gabe."

Before I could wail a second time, he had me turned
around and walking back toward the thinning crowd of
people at the barbecue a couple of blocks away. I kept
turning my head back to look, propelled by a morbid com-
pulsion to read and reread the repulsive words and threats
painted all over my truck.

When we got back to the still glowing fire, he sat me
down on a wooden bench, found me a Coke, and was
calling Gabe on his cell phone. By that time, though my
anger was still there, a sliver of fear was starting to wind
its way through my veins. This was much worse than
someone slashing one of my tires, much more than just a
teenage prank. Because I knew it was the first thing Gabe
would ask, I racked my brain trying to think of who might
hold a grudge against me. I honestly couldn't imagine. In
an unbelievable ten minutes, Gabe was there and holding
me against his chest.

"Are you okay?" he asked, rubbing his lips across the top of my head.

"Yes," I said, my face muffled against his cold denim shirt. I pulled back and looked up at his set jaw. "But someone ruined my truck!"

"The truck can be fixed," he said, his lips a grim, straight line.

Then it occurred to me. What if I'd walked up while they were vandalizing my truck? I gave a violent shudder. Gabe's arms tightened around me.

"I'm going on home," Emory said behind me, his hand touching my back. "Call me tomorrow."

I turned and gave him a hug. "I will. Don't worry, Gabe'll find out who did this."

He gave Gabe a worried glance. "I know."

By this time the incident had spread around to the remaining Elks and firefighters. From across the street, I could see my truck was being inspected by dozens of people, and the back of my neck started to warm with embarrassment. My reputation for stumbling into crimes, which the local newspaper loved to exaggerate, was definitely being discussed when Gabe and I started toward the truck. When we walked up, the half-dozen or so men studying it suddenly shifted their eyes away from us and fell silent. Gabe tightened his arm around my shoulders.

One of the two patrol officers who'd pulled this shift strode over to Gabe, his nightstick bouncing against his leg. He was very tall, thin as a new sapling, and wore a blond crewcut and black-rimmed glasses. He stuttered slightly when he said Gabe's name.

"C-Chief Ortiz, sir. What would you like us to do?"

"Just take your usual report," Gabe replied. "Then have the vehicle taken to the police yard. Make sure and take enough photographs."

While I answered the questions for the report, Gabe walked around my truck, inspecting each painted comment closely. He was followed by a couple of firemen he knew from the gym. He kept glancing over at me, a troubled expression on his face. Cold strings of fear shot through me every time he scowled at one of the comments.

A half hour later the city's flatbed tow truck arrived. I'd already cleaned most of my belongings out of the cab and shoved them into every nook and cranny of Gabe's 1968 Corvette, then slipped into the passenger seat. After a final discussion with the tow truck driver, Gabe climbed behind the wheel.

"I need to get another car," he said for the hundredth time in the last two months. He'd told me that he wanted to buy a new car and store his old Corvette to eventually give to his son, Sam. He just hadn't decided on what kind of car he wanted yet.

"What about my truck?" I asked, not wanting to hear at this moment his never-ending litany of the pros and cons of various makes and models of cars. "Can someone get those words off? Can they paint over them? Is my truck ruined? What are we going to do? What am I going to drive?"

"After they check it completely out at the yard, I'll call the dealer and see if they can recommend a place to have it repainted," he said, shifting the car into first gear. "You can drive either the Corvette or my dad's truck until then."

"You know I hate driving the Corvette. It shifts funny and I stall out at every light. I'll drive your dad's truck until mine is fixed." His dad's old 1950 Chevy pickup had been lovingly restored by an old friend of his father's back in Kansas, but its heater didn't work that well and it didn't have a radio.

"Okay." His eyes stared straight ahead at the dark road.

I turned to him and touched his warm forearm, rubbing my hand across his coarse black arm hair. "I don't know who could have done this, Friday. Honestly, I'm not involved in anything remotely criminal."

"I know." His bottom lip disappeared under his thick black mustache, a sure sign he was agitated.

"Really," I said, still feeling as if I needed to defend myself.

"I *know*," he repeated, his voice slightly sharp.

We were both quiet for a moment. I studied the palms of my hands, damp and white in the darkness. Finally, I couldn't stand it. "Then why are you mad at me?"

His head turned to look at me, his expression inexplicably sad. In an instant, he pulled the car over to the curb and stopped even though we were only a few blocks from home. He unbuckled his seat belt, turned to me, and took my face in his warm hands. His deep, long kiss left me breathless.

"Sweetheart," he said, still holding my face in his hands. "I'm not mad at you. I'm mad at myself."

It took me a moment to realize what he was saying. "You think someone is trying to get back at *you?*"

He nodded, kissed me again gently before rebuckling his seat belt. "When you mentioned it the other day, I didn't want to scare you, but it has always been something that has worried me. Luke coming through here reminded me of the possibility that there are a lot of people who hold a grudge against me."

"Do you think this might have anything to do with his murder?"

The shadows from the streetlight made his face appear as finely etched as a marble statue. "Maybe. Or it could just be some punk here in San Celina who wants to get back at the police. I and, therefore, you are very public figures. What better way to give society the finger?" He turned on the ignition. The Corvette's heavy rumble vibrated through my already jittery stomach.

He didn't look at me, but pulled slowly into the empty street, looking intently into his rearview mirror. "I have to figure out a way to keep you safe until I can find out who is doing these things."

When we got home, he took Scout for a quick walk. Though I hated admitting it even to myself, the short ten minutes he was gone I sat in the living room with all the lights on, too nervous to start my shower until he returned.

"Come here," he said to me in a husky voice the min-ute we crawled into bed. We made love slowly, deliber-ately, without many words. We both seemed to need the physical closeness, the reassurance that only another hu-man being's touch could provide.

Afterward, while he lay on his stomach, drifting toward sleep, I traced the greenish-gray tattoo on his solid back, the only physical souvenir he had brought home from Vietnam. I ran my fingertip over the snarling bulldog's face, around his oversized helmet, tracked the words USMC—FIRST IN, LAST OUT. As hard as it might be for some people to believe, this tattoo was a surprise to me on our wedding night. We'd met in November, married the next February, and I'd never seen him without his shirt. To this day, it both facinated me and broke my heart. It symbolized all the things about this man I might not ever know.

He was almost asleep when I remembered the slashed tire. Though I hated telling him about it right then, I also knew he'd want to know.

"Why didn't you tell me this before?" He turned over on his side and scrutinized me in the dark.

"With all that was going on with Luke's homicide, I just forgot. To be honest, I thought it was kids fooling around."

He didn't answer, but I could sense his tension. It seemed to fill up our new bedroom, sucking the room of oxygen, making me feel as if I should take only short, shallow breaths. He turned over and lay on his back, star-ing up at the dark ceiling.

"Friday," I said, nuzzling his arm until he lifted it and I crawled under, laying my head in the crook of his shoul-der, one leg intertwined with his. The lengths of our bod-ies fit comfortably together now like two age-softened puzzle pieces. "This isn't your fault."

He still didn't answer.

I kissed his neck, then gave it a small lick. He tasted,

as always, like a gingery spice, his late-night stubble rough on my tongue.

His voice was flat, emotionless when he finally spoke. *"Querida?"*

"Yes?"

I closed my eyes and remembered the first time he'd called me by the Spanish endearment. I was sitting on the fence at my dad's ranch. I didn't know then what it meant—its literal translation is "dear," but when said in a certain way, by a man to a woman, it means "lover." We had not been lovers the first time he called me *querida;* but the minute the word fell from his lips, I knew we would be.

"Do you ever regret marrying me?" His voice was soft, but tinged with a rough agony.

I waited a moment, then said, "Sometimes. But I've never regretted loving you."

"Gracias," he whispered.

I hugged him and didn't answer, not quite certain if he was talking to me.

CHAPTER 10

❖

April 18, 1995
Tuesday

"DOES YOUR DAD'S TRUCK HAVE GAS IN IT?" I ASKED the next morning at six A.M. while pouring myself a cup of coffee. I'd gotten up earlier than usual because of my overloaded schedule.

"Full tank," Gabe said. He sat hunched over the kitchen table, reading the paper and eating a bowl of oatmeal.

"Good, I've got a lot of places to go today."

His spoon stopped halfway to his mouth and he slowly lowered it back down into his cereal. "What are your plans?"

We had been up a half hour and had studiously avoided talking about what happened last night. Now that I was actually going to be out of his sight, anxiety darkened his eyes.

"Here it is in a nutshell. From seven to nine, I'll be working on the Montez adobe. Then I have one quick tour at the folk art museum at ten-thirty. At eleven-thirty I'm supposed to meet Elvia at Cal Poly to help work on the queen's float. Three o'clock I have to go to the Mission

Plaza and help with the children's costume parade and contest. We're serving refreshments and it looks like there will be about two hundred kids. That should be over at five-thirty. How about chili for dinner? I can put it in the crockpot before I leave."

He stared down into his hardening cereal. "I suppose asking you to stay home today would be—"

"Out of the question," I finished for him. "Gabe, I know that thing with my truck last night scared you. It scared me too, but I'm not any safer staying home alone than I am going about my regular business. I have a cell phone. I'll take Scout with me everywhere. And I'll keep my pepper spray ready."

His voice was stiff and stubborn. "I'm just worried."

I reached across the table and took his hand. "I'll be very vigilant about watching my back."

"Don't be alone. Not anywhere, not at any time. Carry your cell phone *turned on*. Keep it where you can get to it. Don't forget your pepper spray. You have my cell number on automatic dial, right?"

"Yes, I do. And if at all possible, I won't be alone."

"Not at all." His voice held no compromise.

I inhaled deeply, glad he was concerned, but slightly annoyed that he felt I was incapable of being cautious. "*Sí, sí, Papacito.* Not at all."

After he'd dressed, he came back into the kitchen to kiss me good-bye.

"What will you be doing with Luke's case today?" I asked him while wiping off the counter top.

"Like I said last night, we sent a man down to Santa Monica yesterday to collect all of Luke's office files. Detectives will be going through them and so will I, even though I have three meetings and a quarterly budget proposal due to the city manager in two days. I probably have a better chance at spotting a connection than anyone."

"Do you actually have some names that are possibilities? I mean, do you remember the guys you helped put in jail?"

"Some of them," he said.

"Their actual faces?"

He lifted his eyebrows slightly. "Maybe. People change, get older."

I felt a pang of anxiety, more for him than me. "But you were in disguise when you worked undercover, right? Would they recognize you?" Though I knew being a cop was dangerous, I'd only known him as a chief, a relatively safe position. The thought of someone from his past hurting Gabe was something I didn't like to even consider.

"Maybe, maybe not. They could find out my name and whereabouts easy enough, if they wanted to, especially these days with the Internet."

The fearful expression on my face caused his eyebrows to move together in concern. "Benni, trust me, most of the dirtbags I busted just aren't that smart. The smartest ones are the ones who didn't get caught."

I frowned and pulled a paper towel off the roller to dry the counter. "That makes me feel *so* much better. Then they're out there walking around in society."

"But with no grudge against me," he pointed out.

"What about Luke's funeral?"

"I'll be taking care of it, but not until the autopsy is done."

"I forgot to ask last night, did you ever find any other family members?" The thought of having a funeral service for Luke with no family to mourn him was one of the saddest things I could imagine.

"No, only his mother. There's his ex-wife, but she remarried and I have no idea what her new name is. There might be some record of it in his personal effects though he didn't mention her in his will. I'm not sure she'd want to come anyway. It wasn't an amicable divorce." He leaned back against the refrigerator door. "As a matter of fact, I went and opened his safety-deposit box yesterday. He had a ten-thousand-dollar insurance policy and his will in it. I'm his only heir."

My eyes widened slightly. "You? Were you two *that* close?"

He folded his arms across his chest. "Not really, but I suppose I was as close to him as anyone. We talked about four, five times a year. We met for lunch in Santa Barbara a couple of times in the last year."

After he'd left, I fried ground sirloin, chopped onions, and gathered all the ingredients for my ten-alarm chili. After putting them in the crockpot, I went upstairs, pulled on a pair of beat-up Wranglers, a faded blue sweatshirt, and my oldest boots. I stuck a newer pair of jeans, a turquoise sweater, and my good black boots in a duffel bag to change into at the museum. Before I forgot, I dug through my purse and found the pepper spray attached to my key ring. I stuck it in my back pocket. Not a .357 magnum, but it was certainly better than nothing.

It was almost seven o'clock, and as I was just opening the front door, the phone rang. Even though we had an answering machine, without thinking, I dashed across the oak floor, slipping and sliding across its highly polished finish, Scout bounding and barking next to me, excited by the game.

"Hello?" I gasped, trying to grab Scout's snout and stop his enthusiastic barking. He kept darting out of my reach.

"Is Benni there?" a male voice asked. It had a peculiar, throaty timbre, as if he was just getting over a cold.

Because of what had happened last night, I hedged my answer and said, "Who's calling?"

He gave a low laugh and hung up.

I held the phone a moment, my heart beating fast. When Scout's nose bumped my leg, I jumped and let out a small yelp. Scout moved back, whined in his throat, and wagged his tail in apology.

I slammed the phone down, bent over, and called Scout to me. "Sorry, Scooby-Doo," I said, scrubbing the silky hair under his chin. "You just startled me." He licked my hand in understanding. Only then did it occur to me that these days, what with cell phones and all, the caller might be parked right outside my house.

I rushed to the front door and locked it. Then I peeked through the lacy living room curtains. Three cars were parked within two blocks of my house, all ones I recognized. Could the guy be parked farther down the street out of my eyesight, but where he could observe Gabe driving away?

"I'm going to have to tell Gabe about this, you know," I said to Scout. He leaned against my right leg, his strong tail thumping on the wooden floor.

"But not right now. He'll just get all agitated and overreact and leave work. I'll go to the Montez adobe. There'll be lots of people there and I'll drop by the station after my shift and tell him then. How does that sound?"

Scout rumbled deep in his throat.

"Okay, you're right. I'd better call him now."

I picked up the phone and dialed his direct line. Maggie, his assistant, answered.

"Chief Ortiz's office," Maggie answered in a clipped, professional voice. She was a no-nonsense, black woman who often seemed able to keep my husband in line better than I could. I teased her by saying that was because finding a good assistant was much harder than finding a good wife.

"Honey," she'd say to me, "you just aren't firm enough with him. All he needs is a good smack with a rolled-up newspaper every once in a while."

We'd laughed at her humorous remark. The truth was she had a great deal of respect for Gabe and took pride in making sure everything ran smoothly with his schedule.

"Hi, Maggie. Sorry to bug you so early but has *El Jefe* arrived yet?"

"No problem, Mrs. Chief. He's been here and gone. He's over at city hall in a meeting with the district attorney. Want me to page him?"

I hesitated, then said, "No, it's not a dire emergency,

but would you please tell him to call me as soon as he can?"

"Sure will. How's that new bull doing?"

Maggie had grown up outside of Reno, Nevada, and was a ranch-raised girl like me. She and her sister owned a few head of cattle on a small ranch outside Santa Flora in north county. We spent a few minutes catching each other up on our respective bull's breeding foibles and then said good-bye.

After making sure every door and window in the house was locked behind me, I headed out for the Montez adobe. Every minute or so I glanced in my rearview mirror, scrutinizing every vehicle that pulled up behind me.

At the adobe, which was located about three blocks from the Mission, next to San Celina Creek and only one block from where Luke's body had been found, a group of twenty or so volunteer workers were already assembled. I left Scout in the back of the truck, clipped my cell phone to my belt, touched the pepper spray in my pocket for assurance, and joined the group.

The leader of the work crew, Stan, a local contractor who was also a history buff, was already handing out assignments. I was given a rake and the job of clearing brush on the north side of the half-acre property. The vine-covered Montez adobe, built in 1858, was in severe need of restoration, which was why I volunteered a couple of hours every month. There were only a few original adobes left in San Celina County and they were such a vital link to our Spanish ranchero past that I wanted to do my part to preserve them for future generations.

The Montez adobe was originally used as a kind of lookout for the Mission. Much of the white plaster, vital to the protection of the clay bricks, had melted away and there were large holes chipped by vandals into the two-feet-thick adobe walls. Adobe was very soft and pliable, swelled up when it got wet, and shrank when it dried so it needed constant work to keep from deteriorating, something I had learned when I became curator of the folk art museum. Keeping the Sinclair Hacienda's walls repaired was something that, thankfully, D-Daddy Boudreaux took great pride in doing.

"We'll be making adobe bricks as soon as my guy gets here with the cement mixer, sand, and straw," Stan said. "Our goal today is to make enough bricks to shore up the north wall. Until then we can work on getting the branches and roots cut away from the adobe itself so they don't do any more damage. Anyone need gloves?"

I pulled my stained chamois leather gloves out of my back pocket, took my rake and shovel, and found the section assigned me. Though I knew a few of the other volunteers enough to say good morning, nobody was a close enough acquaintance for me to feel obligated to strike up a conversation. I was thankful for that because I had a lot on my mind with that troubling phone call. If Gabe didn't call before long, I would try and reach him again once my two-hour volunteer stint was up.

I was struggling with pulling out a thick clump of rootbound weeds when a leather-gloved hand reached from behind me, grabbed the clump, and yanked it straight out with one mighty pull. Caught off balance, I stumbled back slightly against the person, who steadied me by placing the palm of their hand between my now-damp shoulder blades.

"Thanks," I said, giving a small laugh and turning around to see who helped.

"You're welcome, sweetcakes," my cousin Emory said.

"Hey, what are you doing here?"

"Just doing my bit to help save the adobes," he said, leaning against his shovel. "I'm a part of this community now and I want to be a good citizen." He smiled. "Besides, my wife has a special feeling for this adobe. Apparently her mama and papa lived here when they first moved to San Celina after the war. It is rumored that a certain beautiful young lady whom I happen to be in love with might have been conceived inside these very adobe walls."

"Really? I didn't know that. They've lived in their yellow-and-white house for as long as I can remember." I pulled at another stubborn clump of weeds. An explosion of pollen caused me to sneeze twice.

"Bless you. They moved into the yellow house right before Elvia was born. Señora Aragon said that this adobe once had a beautiful garden that she did her best to keep up. See that trellis by the front porch?" He pointed over at the rotting wooden trellis. "It was all covered with wisteria. Did you know that this is the first building in the county to have a Monterey-style veranda? That's a staircase that leads up to an outside balcony."

I laughed at my cousin's enthusiasm for early California architecture. "Yes, I know. I'm a history major, remember? Plus we learned all about adobes and mission-style architecture in fourth grade."

"Well, don't forget I grew up in Arkansas. We learned about the Civil War and the battle at Pea Ridge in the fourth grade."

"So you'll have to make sure your kids learn about both California and Arkansas state histories," I said.

A huge grin spread across his face. "Guess I will."

We worked together for a few minutes in silence. Then he asked, "What's going on with the investigation into the vandalism of your truck?"

"I have no idea. I've got a call in to Gabe so I'll ask him when he returns it." I inhaled deeply, hesitating for a moment, not certain if I should alarm Emory by telling him about the threatening phone call I'd just received.

He stopped digging and came over to me. "Okay, spill it. What's wrong?"

I gave a half smile. "Can't hide anything from you."

He threw his arm around my shoulder. "Or anyone else, Miss Not-So-Poker-Face. Why the worried look?"

His smooth cheeks narrowed slightly when I told him about the phone call. The lines around his thick-lashed eyes deepened. "I don't like the sound of that."

"Neither will Gabe. He's worried it's someone from

his past out to get back at him by harassing me. This phone call certainly supports his theory. He's going to feel horribly guilty."

"I can understand why. No man wants to think someone he loves will be hurt because of something from his past. You need to go right from here to the police department."

"I know."

We finished the rest of our section in silence. I was glad that my cousin was there with me even though there were plenty of people working at the adobe this morning.

He walked me back to the old truck, reminding me that I was supposed to work on the float at eleven-thirty.

"I know, I'll be there. The big Cal Poly ag Building, right?"

"Glad I brought it up. It's not at the college anymore. We moved it to an empty warehouse down by the bus station. The one with the blue stripes on the side next to the self-serve car wash."

"The old Butterfield Bread Building. Why'd you have to move?"

"Another float claimed our space inside the ag buildings. The Butterfield property's being sold, no one's using it right now, and the owner is a big La Fiesta booster. It's big enough for the float to be inside, which, I don't have to tell you, is important in April."

Both of us grimaced at the idea of soggy tissue paper flowers. "I sure hope it doesn't rain this Saturday. Did you get in touch with everyone?"

"Everyone I could. I left a note on the ag building and told the people working on the other float to send our people over to the Butterfield building."

"Gosh, it's been a long time since I worked on a float. I love the idea that they're having the former queens in this parade."

"You and me both. I'm looking forward to seeing my bride in her queenly dress and crown."

I laughed. "She really hates that dress, but I'm impressed that it still fits."

"It wouldn't dare not fit our queen," he said with a laugh. "See you later. *Be careful.*"

On the way to the folk art museum, I drove to the plain brick police station, one of the few county buildings that didn't adhere to San Celina's mission-style theme, to see if Gabe's Corvette was parked in his space. It was, so I found a spot under a tree about a block away, rolled down both windows, and left Scout in the front seat to stand guard. Inside the lobby, the clerk behind the glass immediately recognized me and buzzed me in. Gabe's office door was closed and Maggie's desk empty, so I wandered down to the break room to get a Coke. Maggie stood in front of the snack machine perusing its salty, sugary selections.

"His meeting should be over in about five minutes," she said when she saw me, then continued studying her choices with the intensity of someone on a diet. She was tall and broad-shouldered, physical assets I would have loved to possess, and looked perfectly proportioned to me. But like all of us, she struggled with what society deemed the right weight and shape. "What has more calories, a Hershey bar or a bag of Doritos?"

"I have no idea," I said. "Are you craving salt or sugar?"

She sighed. "Both. Maybe I should just get the chocolate-covered pretzels."

"Sounds like a good compromise," I said, laughing. "Does Gabe have a few minutes free? I need to talk to him."

"For you, honey, I'll call the mayor and tell him to wait a half hour." She put three quarters in the machine and pressed two buttons.

"No, that's okay. I can—"

"No problem at all. I think it'll do the chief some good to talk to you. He's been a little agitated all morning."

"What I have to tell him might not help."

She turned to look at me, her coffee-colored face interested. "Anything you care to share with sister Maggie?"

"Sure, it's not a secret." I told her about the weird phone calls I'd received—the silent one the morning after they'd found Luke's body that I realized now might have been this person and this morning when the caller had grown bolder and asked for me by name.

"That's downright creepy. Especially after what happened to your truck. You'd better get in there right now and tell him. He'll want to know." She tore open the bag of chocolate-covered pretzels and held it out to me. "Want one?"

"No, thanks," I said, my stomach suddenly feeling queasy.

Gabe was predictably upset when I told him about the phone calls.

"Why didn't you tell me about the first one?" he demanded, leaning forward in his black high-backed leather chair.

"I didn't realize then it was anything to worry about. I just thought it was a wrong number or something."

"I'm going to step up patrols around our neighborhood and dig deeper into what Luke was working on. It can't be a coincidence that this happened just when he came to town."

"Do you think it has to do with some old case you two worked on?"

He stood up and walked over to the window that looked over the police yard, his hands deep in his pockets. "Luke and I worked together on lots of busts. We were in undercover for three years. It could be any one of a number of people."

I went over and stood next to him. "Do you think he followed Luke up here? Or do you think that Luke was working on something that involved this person?"

"I just don't know, Benni. I don't even know if the case he said he was working on up here was bogus or not. There wasn't any record of this man supposedly cheating on his wife in Morro Bay, no contract with the wife, no notes, nothing."

"So whatever he was working on was all kept inside him."

"Apparently. Which wouldn't be unusual for Luke."

Or you, I wanted to add. I felt like there was something more Gabe wasn't telling me, but I also knew if I accused him of that, he'd get irritated and deny it. I'd grown to know one thing for sure about my husband: He was as stubborn as the sun was hot and nothing would make him do something he didn't want to do.

"How can I help you?" I asked, laying my hand on his forearm.

He leaned over and kissed the top of my head. "Just stay around people. Watch your back. Keep telling me everything."

"Okay," I said, leaning my head against his shoulder. "Now, I have to make tracks or I'll be late for my tour."

Outside, the sun was shining bright and warm. By the time I got to the folk art museum at ten-thirty, I was glowing with perspiration. I quickly changed clothes in my office, just pulling on my sweater as someone knocked on my door.

"Benni, your tour group is here," the voice called.

The group consisted of a quilt guild from Salinas who'd chartered a bus for the day. They were mostly senior citizens, a lively bunch, full of opinions and comments on California history. Two of them were docents at the John Steinbeck House, where Gabe and I had once eaten lunch after touring the Steinbeck Museum. Most of them remembered Emma Baldwin and her books though what they remembered was buying them for their daughters, so they were particularly interested in her crazy quilt.

"Has someone recorded what all the dates on her quilt are for?" asked one lady in a long white blouse with a red hibiscus lapel pin. "It's so important to get that information written down somewhere."

"Leonora is our guild historian," another lady with pale

pink hair explained to me. "She's been making us write oral histories for all our quilts."

"Or trying to anyway," another woman said with a laugh. The others joined in the laughter.

"This bunch," Leonora said, her voice as loud and insistent as a goose's honk. "They're worse than a gaggle of schoolgirls trying to avoid memorizing their times tables. It's important we get these histories down before people start keeling over with heart attacks. Think about all the quilt histories lost from our mothers and grandmothers simply because someone didn't take the time to ask them about the details and write them down."

One of of the ladies reached over and patted Leonora's back. "We know you're right, sweetie," she said. "We're just procrastinators, you know that. We're lucky we have you to keep us in line."

Another woman said to me in a low voice, "Leonora was a third-grade teacher. She likes things in their proper order."

"She's right," I said, turning to look at Emma's quilt. "Being a history major myself, I know how important it is to get oral histories written down. I'm not sure if Emma has the corresponding events to these dates recorded somewhere, but I'll certainly ask her the next time I see her."

By the time the ladies left, I was already ten minutes late to meet Elvia. On the drive there, I dialed her cell phone. "Hey, girl. Have you had lunch yet? I could pick up something for both of us to eat while we're working on the float."

"That would be perfect," she said. "I've been seeing book reps all morning and have only had three cups of coffee."

"Are you at the float yet?"

"No, I'm still at the bookstore. Are you?"

I sighed. "I'm on my way. It's been one of those mornings."

"Tell me about it."

"I'll buy some food at Taco Town and meet you at the warehouse."

"Get me a *horchata* drink. No more caffeine for me today."

I beat Elvia to the old Butterfield Bread warehouse down by the bus station. There were already six other people working on the float, making tissue paper flowers and tying them to the chicken-wire frame that was only half filled. It would fit on a flatbed trailer, which would be pulled by a one-ton pickup loaned to us by the local Chevy dealer.

"Hey, Benni," one of the other ex–La Fiesta Queens said. Her name was Josie and she'd been the 1942 Queen. She now volunteered at the Chamber of Commerce and worked part time at a local travel agency. I dealt with her frequently, arranging tours like the one from Salinas today. "Is Elvia coming?"

I nodded, looking for a free table to set down my Taco Town bags. "She'll be here soon. I held up the white-and-orange bags of food. "I bought extra tacos and chips at Taco Town. Anyone hungry?"

A couple of people took me up on my offer. While Josie munched on chips and salsa, she said, "Oh, someone left this for you." She reached into the pocket of her loose denim jacket and handed me a white envelope.

"Who?" I asked, taking the envelope marked with my first name.

She lifted one shoulder. "It was taped to the door when I got here."

I held it up to the bright warehouse overhead light, trying to make out what was inside. Paranoid, maybe, but after the incident of my truck and this morning's threatening phone call, I was suspicious of everything. It looked and felt like a photograph. I took a pair of scissors, cut one end of the envelope, and gingerly dropped the photograph on the ground. I bent over and picked it up. It was a cheap Polaroid, the colors blue-tinged and the photograph itself blurry.

"What is it?" Josie asked.

I shoved it back into the envelope. "Just a picture my cousin took of me and . . . Gabe," I lied.

"Oh," Josie said, turning back to the chips and salsa.

I stuck the envelope in the back pocket of my jeans, trying to maintain an attitude of nonchalance. "I'll be back. I need to make a phone call."

Out next to the old truck, I called Gabe's office. His voice mail answered. Apparently both he and Maggie were out of the office. I hit the button to speed-dial his cell phone. Another voice mail. Dang, I thought, annoyed and just a little fearful. What good are cell phones if no one was where they were supposed to be? What if there was an emergency?

I pulled out the photograph and stared at its blurry image. The sour, salty taste of tortilla chips and salsa hovered at the back of my throat as it constricted in anxiety. It was a picture of me and Emma hugging outside the Cowgirl Cafe. Across the entire photograph, with a black felt pen, someone had drawn a circle dissected by a slash.

CHAPTER 11

❖

April 3, 1978
Monday

*A*FTER MY INTERVIEW WITH MRS. BALDWIN, I headed for Cal Poly Agriculture Department's biggest barn to meet Elvia, Jack, and a bunch of other students to work on the queen's float. Elvia and Jack beat me there.

"You know, we could use some masculine brawn over here," she was nagging at him when I walked into the large, airy building. Jack sat with his back against the wall, writing in his journal and pretending he hadn't heard her. "There's a reason it's called *homework,* Mr. Harper," I said, reaching down and flipping off his bright green John Deere cap.

"Yeah," Elvia echoed. She, along with three other girls, were attempting to lift the tissue-paper-flower-covered chicken-wire frame of the queen's float onto the back of the flatbed trailer loaned to us by Rob's U-Haul-Urself truck rental yard. "Get up off your worthless butt, Harper, and help us out here."

"Listen to her," he said, tossing the notebook aside and standing up. "Already acting like she's Queen Elizabeth or something." His grin softened his words. He loved teasing Elvia about her prim and proper ways. "I was up hours earlier than the rest of you fixing fence. That's why I'm trying to catch up on my homework. Professor Hill wants to see our journals tomorrow."

"Get a clue, plowboy," Elvia said. "No one cares. We are only interested in your brawn, not your brains."

He gave an exaggerated bow and clicked the heels of his manure-caked boots. "I serve at the pleasure of my queen."

"Refresh my memory," Elvia said to me, her long dark hair styled in a perfect Farrah Fawcett winged haircut. "What is it you see in this guy?"

"Nice pecs," I said, laughing. "And he can rebuild a carburetor with a bobby pin and a screwdriver."

"Always a plus for a ranch woman, I suppose," she said.

"You two are so funny I forgot to laugh," Jack said, coming up behind us. Without a bit of effort he lifted the heavy back section of the almost finished float out of our hands and shoved it into place on the flatbed trailer.

"And that's a cliché," Elvia said, rolling her black-rimmed eyes at me.

"Excuse the heck out of me, Miss Literature Expert," he said. "From now on, I'll just keep my big dumb country-boy mouth shut and only lift heavy objects."

Elvia giggled. "Oh, Jack, you know we all love you for your good looks *and* big muscles." She could tease him like that only because he carried a grade point average almost equal to her straight A's. He and Elvia both liked to spar about his "good ole boy" image.

"You know," I said, "you should read some of the entries he has in this journal he's keeping for his psychology class. Jack could be a writer."

His face turned a dull red. "Ah, Benni, don't be reading my journal. It's embarrassing."

I waved away his comment. "C'mon, Jack, you should get used to it. Professor Hill's going to read it. Let me read some of the sections to Elvia."

"That's his job, and no, I don't want anyone else reading them." He gave a small irritated grunt and walked away, shaking his head.

Elvia raised her dark eyebrows in question.

"They really are good," I said. "He seems to get right to the heart of people. I never realized how much attention he paid to little things."

She flipped her head, the perfect wings of her hair not moving one inch. "Jack fools a lot of people. He's deeper than most people realize. But don't tell him I said that."

"Speaking of fools, my cousin Emory called me last night. He said to tell you hi."

She wrinkled her nose as if she'd smelled something bad. "That four-eyed nerd."

"Hey, watch it. Emory's my favorite cousin. And he just got contacts, I'll have you know. He's actually kinda cute now."

"Yeah, right. What did he want?"

"Just wanted to say hi and tell me about his fraternity doings at the University of Arkansas. He's on the debate team."

"Well, goody for him." Though Emory had carried a crush the size of Alaska for her ever since they first met when he was eleven years old and spent the summer with me at the Ramsey Ranch, she would have nothing to do with him.

"He's thinking about majoring in law," I said.

"Emory a lawyer?" she said in a scathing tone. "Maybe contract or real estate law. Some place far away from the courthouse. I know you love him, Benni, but honestly, he scores a zero on the charisma scale. Atticus Finch he isn't."

I laughed and threw a stray tissue paper rose at her. "Someday you're going to change your tune about him, Queen Elvia."

"Not in this or any other lifetime, *gringa loca*," she said smugly.

CHAPTER 12

❖

"So, WHERE SHOULD I PUT THE RED FLOWERS?" ONE of the float workers asked me. For some reason, the group of volunteers inside the old Butterfield Bread warehouse had started asking me questions about what went where on the float.

"Sasha's in charge," I said. "She should be here any minute." At least I hoped so. "I guess we could always make more flowers."

While they wandered over to one of the long, foldout tables covered with pliers, thin wire, and stacks of rainbow-colored tissue paper, I pulled the photograph from my pocket and studied it again. Whoever was stalking me was getting bolder. Scout lay over in the corner, his head on his paws, watching my every move, making me feel a little more secure. He was good protection from almost everything except a bullet.

"I found a computer picture," one of the volunteers called. "The red flowers are for the bougainvillea on the Mission walls and the dark green and plum are—"

"For the olive trees," Elvia said, coming through the

warehouse's double doors. "It's an exact copy of the float I rode on when I was queen. The olive tree goes to the left, the bougainvillea across the right hand side on back."

I stuck the Polaroid picture of me in my back pocket. "You actually remember what the 1978 float looked like?"

"My *quinceñera* and being elected La Fiesta Queen were the highlights of my mother's life until my wedding. She has satin-covered albums of each event that she brings out every time her *tres hermanas* come up from Mexico. Frankly, I think I would have married Emory just so Mama would have new pictures to show Tía Maria, Tía Ofelia, and Tía Lupe."

"I'm sure the wedding pictures will satisfy her for a while. Until she starts nagging you about not having baby pictures to show your aunts."

"Until?" Elvia said, rolling her eyes. "She started on that exactly two minutes after Emory and I exchanged vows."

A few minutes later, Sasha arrived. She was a twenty-two-year-old graphic arts major who promptly organized us into teams of two and situated us at different points of the sparsely decorated float. Elvia and I were assigned the west wall of the Mission. My best friend, not one who works well with others unless she is in charge, grumbled slightly under her breath as we started attaching green, white, and red tissue paper flowers, representing the bougainvillea bushes surrounding the mission gardens.

"She's certainly bossy," Elvia whispered to me.

"Hmmm," I answered noncommittedly. She reminded me a lot of Elvia.

"What's going on with Gabe's friend's murder?" she asked.

"Not much yet." I hesitated, then decided to show her the picture found on the door of the warehouse.

She stared at it, her dark eyes widening. "How did he know you were going to be working here?"

"He's obviously following me and somehow knew about me working on the float." The hair on the back of my neck prickled, as if someone had shot me through with an electric current.

"But we changed where we were meeting."

"Emory said he put a note on the ag building at Cal Poly telling everyone who is working on the queen's float to come here."

She stared at me, then crossed herself quickly, saying a quick prayer to Saint Michael for my safety. "It seems like he is two steps behind you."

"Or rather two steps ahead," I said.

"You need to show this to Gabe right away."

"Just as soon as we're finished here."

"You're sure no one saw anybody?"

"Josie said it was taped to the door of the warehouse when she arrived."

Elvia bit the inside of her cheek. "This really scares me. That man's murder, your truck, the phone calls, this picture."

I twist-tied another flower to the Mission's chicken-wire wall and tried to calm my racing heart. "We don't know yet if they are actually related."

Her red lips straightened. "Of course they're related."

I didn't look at her. I didn't even want to think the word I'd been studiously avoiding the last twenty-four hours—stalker. I've never been the kind of person who liked movies where people, usually women, were being stalked, even when the stalker inevitably got captured.

There was something so primitive, so insidious about the crime of stalking. I'd experienced it once before in a slightly less scary way when I'd inherited a house in Morro Bay, though by the time I found out about it, the man stalking me was already dead. The thought of some-one watching my every movement made me want to run home, lock the doors, and take the phone off the hook. I glanced over at Scout for reassurance. His head was still resting on his big paws, his eyes closed. If there was any danger, he wouldn't be so relaxed. I was beginning to understand, in a miniscule way, how dependent physically challenged people were on their helper or seeing-eye dogs.

Yes, I was nervous, bordering on flat-out afraid, but a part of me was pissed too. Not living your life as usual gave people like that exactly the power they wanted and something contrary in me rebelled against that. After I worked on the float, I would go back over to the police station, dutifully give Gabe the photo, and then get on with my normal business.

In between bites of tacos, Elvia and I finished our section of the float. At one-thirty we parted ways, agreeing to meet at the Mission at three o'clock for the judging of the children's costume parade and piñata-decorating contest.

"Be careful," she said, hugging me tightly in a unusual display of affection. "I love you, *hermana*." Being married had really loosened up my emotionally private friend.

I hugged her back. "I love you too."

The public parking lot and the street in front of the police station were packed, so I parked two blocks away, rolled down both windows halfway, and again told Scout to guard the car. I would be safe inside the police station and I didn't want anything happening to Gabe's truck. Scout laid down on the seat, his tongue hanging out the side of his mouth. His gleaming white canines were big enough, I hoped, to scare any potential car vandal.

"I'll only be a minute, buddy-boy," I told him, scratching his favorite spot on his broad, brown chest. Just as I started walking down the sidewalk toward the station, my cell phone rang. Though "Happy Trails" sang out on my phone, the person on the other end was definitely not singing that tune.

"That's it, I've had it," Dove said. "I'm down to my very last nerve."

I leaned against the truck's fender. This would probably take a while.

Dove took a deep breath. "I cannot take one more society dinner, one more night of snoring, one more load of his junk! I missed the Zozobra bonfire for the longest, dullest, most tiresome evening I've had in the whole of my life at Ariana Winkle's house in Cambria. And I needed that fire this year with the load of troubles I'm toting. I'd liked to died of boredom listening to her whiny voice. And you know what Isaac said when I told him what I felt? That this was a part of his life and I'd just have to accept it. We'll see about that! I'll be over tonight to stay with you and Gabriel until Mr. Big-Man-on-Campus can figure out how to fix this groupie addiction he has."

"Let's think about this first," I said slowly, trying to decide which problem to tackle first. This had definitely gotten to the point where I'd have to call Daddy and see what we could do.

"Nothin' to think about. I'm so sick of his social following I haven't answered the phone all day. There's fifteen messages a'blinkin' away on the phone and I don't care to hear what any of 'em has to say."

"But why should *you* leave? It's *your* house," I said, not following her logic.

"Yes, honeybun, but he has no place else to go now. I can't very well kick him out in the streets. And people will talk if he goes to a hotel. You *know* how the flapper-mouths in this town like to rattle away."

So, she still cared enough to protect his reputation. That was a good sign. "I won't be home until about six o'clock. You have a key . . ." Then I remembered the stalker. I didn't want Dove in any danger and I also didn't want her worrying about me. "You know, I have a better idea. My guest room is still in shambles. That work we had done on the floor really threw our house into a mess. Why don't you stay with Emory and Elvia? Their place is in much better shape for visitors. And they have four guest rooms for you to choose from. I think you'll rest much better there and it sounds like you could use a good night's sleep."

"I can help you get organized," she said.

"Maybe after this week. You and I both have a ton of things to do for La Fiesta." I held my breath, hoping she'd buy the excuse.

"You're right," she said, a slight tone of suspicion in her voice.

"I'm making chili for dinner," I said. "I'll call Elvia and tell her you'll be coming over and invite them to dinner too. And I'll call Beebs and Millee. It'll be fun." I tried to make my voice light.

"I'll whip up some cornbread," she said, warming to the idea of a party. "There's a blackberry cobbler in my freezer that'll be perfect. I'll buy some of that vanilla bean ice cream Gabe likes so much."

"Great," I said, glad she was distracted from her marriage problems for a moment. "See you at six-thirty."

After she hung up, I called Elvia at the store and explained the situation. "She doesn't know a thing about Luke's murder or about this person who's been harassing me and I don't want her to know."

"We'll be glad to help," Elvia said. "I'll just keep her talking about her problems with Isaac's girlfriends. That'll keep her occupied."

"Call them his girlfriends and I guarantee you'll be up until one A.M. listening to her rant and rave."

Her laugh was a tinny sound in my cell phone. "Who would have ever thought we'd be helping Dove hide from her husband?"

"I doubt that where she's going is a secret from Isaac. They might have a lot of problems in their relationship, but communication is definitely not one of them. She will probably tell him exactly where she'll be and what he'll have to do to get her back. Don't be surprised if there is a *Streetcar Named Desire* scene happening in your front yard."

"Can you picture that? Isaac acting like Marlon Brando and standing in my front yard yelling—Dove! Dove!"

"That would give the town gossips fodder for a year, though it might be a few days before we experience that little scenario. From what Dove said, Isaac's own dander is ruffled. It sounds like it's a standoff."

"Poor man. He doesn't realize who he's up against."

"No, and I'm not going to be the fool who breaks it to him."

I stuck my cell phone into my purse and started up the street toward the police station, glancing around me, trying to appear aware, but not paranoid. Was this person watching me right now? I passed by six cars before reaching the front steps of the police station, all of them empty.

"Go right in, Benni," the front desk clerk said, buzzing me in. When I came to Gabe's office, again the door was closed and Maggie's chair was empty. I grabbed a piece of paper from her message pad and was writing a note when Gabe's door opened. Captain Jim Cleary noticed me before Gabe did.

"Benni," he said in a full, rich voice that was the pride of St. Stephen's Baptist Church, where he was head deacon and a baritone in the choir. "Haven't seen you in a month of Sundays. How are you?"

"Just fine, Jim," I said, giving him a hug. He'd been a good friend to both Gabe and me many times in the last two years. He was second in command at the station and there was no doubt in my mind that Gabe's job would be a hundred times harder without Jim's easygoing personality and practical wisdom. Jim's wife of thirty years, Oneeta, had also been a good friend to me. Without her patient and good-humored advice about what loving a police officer entailed, I'm not sure Gabe and I would have made it through our courtship, much less the first six months of marriage. "I just talked to Oneeta last week and she told me you are expecting another grandbaby. Congratulations!"

"Thank you. That will be number four for my oldest son and his wife. We're tickled to death about it though I may just have to have a little talk with the boy and tell him exactly what causes this to happen."

"I'm seeing Dove tonight so we'll have to start planning a baby quilt."

After he left, I threw away my half-written note and followed Gabe into his office.

"You told Jim we're seeing Dove. Is there some reason we're going out to the ranch tonight?" Gabe asked, settling down in his leather chair.

"No, she's coming to us. Or rather to Elvia and Emory." I explained the whole situation. "I haven't told her about your connection to Luke's murder or about this person who's been harassing me. I don't want her to worry." The small Polaroid in my jean's back pocket felt as big as an eight-by-ten. Gabe was going to hit the roof.

"She'll know by tonight then," he said.

"Not if we don't tell her."

"Too late." He handed me today's edition of the *San Celina Tribune*. On the front page was a color photograph of my purple truck being towed. It was taken at an angle so that the vilest language couldn't actually be read. I scanned the story which, not surprisingly, had sketchy details since I knew Gabe was attempting to keep this as quiet as possible. Pretty hard to do considering his position and the public place where the vandalism happened.

"Not one person mentioned this to me today," I said. "I guess Dove hasn't had time to look at the paper and Daddy very rarely reads it anymore. He mentioned last week that a good half mile of fence needed fixing up on Condor Hill. I wouldn't be surprised if, cold as it is, he went up there and camped out in the old miner's shack just to get away from Dove and Isaac. I've been meaning to call him and see what he thinks about their problems."

"I'm surprised one of her friends hasn't told her," Gabe said, leaning back in his chair.

"She hasn't answered the phone all morning," I said.

He pulled at the end of his mustache and gave a small chuckle. "Then she must be *really* upset."

I inhaled deeply. "Speaking of upset . . ."

His smile faded and he sat forward. "What's happened?"

I pulled the photograph of me and Emma out of my pocket and handed it across the wide expanse of his desk. "This was taped to the door of the warehouse where I worked on the float this afternoon. One of the workers found it when they arrived."

He stared at the picture for a long moment before speaking. "You need to leave town," he finally said.

"No way," I said.

"Yes."

"No."

We held a staring contest. His eyes, dark gray now with apprehension and anger, broke eye contact first to look out his office window. A muscle twitched in the side of his locked jaw. I followed his gaze. A lone sycamore tree at the edge of the enclosed city yard rustled in the slight afternoon breeze, showing the yellowish backs of its leaves. I could see the tail of my truck sticking out from a garage port. Next to it, two city mechanics stood over the open hood of a patrol car discussing some mechanical problem. Gabe stood up and came around his wide desk, taking the other visitor chair, turning it so we faced each other, knees touching.

He leaned close and took both my hands in his. "I want you to be safe. I don't have any idea who this might be and . . ." His voice grew harsh and he choked slightly on his words. "I'm afraid for you."

I brought his hands to my lips, kissing their roughness. "And I'm afraid for *you.* Not to mention for the rest of my family and friends. If this guy really is someone from your past, then my leaving would either, one, make him follow me and I'd be that much more vulnerable away from you and your protection or, two, he'll transfer the harassment to you or Dove or Daddy or Elvia or Emory or who knows who. Gabe, I couldn't bear it if something happened to any of you because I took a powder. Please, don't send me away."

He gave a half smile. "Took a powder?"

I smiled back. "Okay, bad television dialogue, but you know what I'm saying."

He mulled over my words, his eyes studying each part of my face. "You probably will be safer here."

"Just tell me what I can do to help find this guy so our lives can get back to normal."

He shook his head. "There's not much you can do. An ex-undercover buddy of mine in LA is searching old records of our biggest busts trying to figure out if anyone's been released from prison and, if so, where they are now. Just keep your eyes open and tell me if you see anyone who appears suspicious. I might have some mug shots to show you soon. Maybe you've seen this guy and not realized it."

"Too bad they don't have people's voices on file. I'm pretty sure I'd recognize his voice again if I ever heard it, not to mention his laugh." That sound was one I hoped I never heard again.

"Screen every call. I mean *every* one. Maybe we can get his voice on tape. That would help."

"I can't believe he'd be that stupid to leave a message."

"Often it's one stupid thing that trips a criminal up," he said in a grim voice. "To be honest, sometimes that's the only way we managed to bust a lot of them."

"Anything more on Luke's homicide?" I asked, wanting to change the subject, though that wasn't much of an improvement.

"Not really. I'm still leaning toward it being either something he was working on now or one of our old busts."

"Even though he was stabbed so many times? What about what that detective said about it being personal?"

Gabe lifted his eyebrows. "To a lot of these scumbags, getting busted and being sent to prison for years is personal."

His intercom buzzed. Maggie's rich alto voice said, "Sorry to interrupt, Gabe, but you have a meeting in five minutes down in the conference room with the mayor and the Neighborhood Watch team leaders. Then you have a meeting with the city manager about the street officers' dental coverage."

Gabe leaned over and pushed the answer button. "Thanks, Maggie."

We both stood up and he pulled me into a tight hug, burying his face in my hair. His breath was warm on the top of my head. "Be extra careful, sweetheart. Don't hesitate to call me if something . . . *anything* . . . looks strange or you feel threatened."

"I won't." I tilted my head and kissed the bottom of his chin. "Don't worry. I'll have Scout with me every minute." I patted my back pocket. "And my trusty pepper spray. But you know, you could get me a permit to carry a gun."

"I could, but I won't. I can protect you."

"Despot."

"Vigilante."

"Love you, Friday."

"Te amo más, niña bonita,"

A few minutes later, I was opening the truck's door, talking silly talk to an abnormally excited Scout, when an elderly man across the street called out to me.

"Miss, can I talk to you a minute?" His voice was raspy with the broken resonance of a longtime smoker.

He stood in front of a small wooden bungalow with a porch that stretched the length of the house. An ancient Basset hound stood next to the man, his tail wagging slowly. Behind him, the porch was almost swallowed up by morning glory vines as deep green as fish tank algae.

Keeping my distance, I inspected the man for a moment. He was dressed in starched slate gray Dickie work pants and shirt, clothing that his generation used for its intended purpose and Generation X used as casual wear. He looked to be at least eighty years old and his slack-jawed dog looked to be the equivalent in dog years. He appeared to be harmless, and besides, it was broad day-

light with my own dog sitting in the front seat of my truck
and the police station two blocks away.

I walked across the street and stood at the edge of his
square patch of mottled St. Augustine grass. "Good afternoon. Is everything okay?"

"Just thought you'd like to know that some fella tried
to break into your truck, but that ole hound of yours got
a chunk of him before he could."

My heart started beating faster. "Did you get a good
look at the man?"

The man's eyes bugged at me from behind one-inch
thick glasses. From across the street, he most likely hadn't
gotten a great view. "Sure did, but my eyes ain't as good
as they used to be."

"What did you see?"

"I was sitting here on the porch with Rebel." He
pointed up to a porch lacy with overgrown ivy. "I heard
your pup down there commence to barking. Even got old
Rebel worked up and that's hard to do these days." Rebel
wagged his tail once as if to agree with the old man.
"Anyways, I came out to the porch to see what was happening and I saw this young fella reaching inside your
truck. Guess your hound must've been lying down on the
seat and the fella didn't see him because the fella yelped
a good one when your hound grabbed his arm."

"Did you see what the guy looked like?"

He scratched behind one of his oversized ears. "Mostly
saw the back of him. Maybe a little of the side of his face.
Was too busy watching him dance like a puppet trying to
get his arm out of your pup's mouth." The man gave a
huge, yellow-toothed smile. "That'll teach that boy to
reach inside someone else's truck. It's a fine one you got
there. What is it, a 1950?"

"A 1950 Chevy. It was my husband's father's first new
truck. A friend of his father's restored it for my husband.
Oh, I'm Benni Harper."

"Will Rogers."

I laughed. "Really?"

"Yes, ma'am. Though no relation, sorry to say."

I walked over to him and reached out my hand. "Nice to meet you, Mr. Rogers." I laughed again.

"Yeah, I get that too," he said, laughing with me. "Worked awhile with the Welcome Wagon crew, and people always got a big kick out of my name."

"Would you be willing to talk to a detective about what you saw? My husband is Gabe Ortiz."

"The chief of police?"

"That's him."

"Why, I saw in the newspaper what someone did to your little purple truck." He shook his head, his hand scratching behind the other hairy ear. "What is wrong with our town when our police chief's wife's truck is vandalized like that? What's this world coming to?"

"Can you give me an idea about age, hair color, whatever you remember about this guy? It might be the same person who spray-painted my truck."

"Well," he said, bringing his sharp-nailed old hand to a whiskery chin. "I'd say he looked about your age. Had brownish hair. Jeans. Some kind of sweatshirt with writing on the back. Couldn't make out what it said."

"What color of sweatshirt?" I asked.

He shrugged. "Dark. Blue, black, green, maybe."

That wasn't much help.

"You said you got a glimpse of his face."

He lifted his shoulders again, gave a wet cough. "Kinda average looking, what little bit I saw. He was on the passenger side and I was at the back of my porch so's he couldn't spot me."

"After Scout bit him, what did the man do?"

"Once he got his arm back, which took a little bit, mind you, he took off like a bat out of Hades up the street there." He pointed in the direction away from the police department.

"Would you be willing to talk to a detective about this?" I asked again.

"Sure, though I couldn't tell them any more than I just told you."

"Let me go check on Scout and I'll call the station. I'll let you know when someone will be coming by."

Back at my truck, Scout didn't appear any worse for the wear from his encounter with my stalker . . . at least that's who I assumed it was. This man was starting to grow bolder and that was a frightening thought.

After checking Scout all over to make sure he was not hurt, I glanced around the seat and floor to see if the stalker had left anything behind. Down on the floorboard lay a small piece of cloth. I picked it up and scrutinized it. It was appeared to be something Scout had ripped off the guy. A piece of a sweatshirt fabric. Dark green. The same dark green that was one of Cal Poly's school colors.

"Good boy," I said, rubbing his chest and chin briskly. "You got the bad guy. Extra treat for you tonight."

At the scent of the cloth, Scout started barking and whining.

"I know, I know," I said, rubbing his chest to calm him down. "You want to get him. So do I. But we gotta let Gabe know about this."

I glanced at my watch. It had been almost an hour—was he still in the Neighborhood Watch meeting or now with the city manager? I contemplated calling with this new informaton, but I was sensitive to the fact that the city manager, who was technically the person who could fire him, was not happy with the publicity I'd garnered on some of my other escapades into crime solving. He was an uptight, traditional kind of man who believed that wives and children should be seen and not heard. I'd met his wife at a few of the city functions and she was a thin, pinch-faced woman who always looked as if she were going to stab someone any minute.

"There's a woman plotting an escape," Maggie had whispered to me at last year's Christmas party. "Ten dollars says she divorces him before their twenty-fifth wedding anniversary and joins the circus."

No, I didn't want to give this man more fodder than today's front page newspaper article to make my husband feel like he couldn't control his wife, much less a city. I wasn't in any immediate danger so I decided to go back inside the police department and report the incident in person to Jim Cleary.

"I don't want to interrupt Gabe," I explained. "I'm okay."

"Good idea," Jim agreed. "Leonard Neely is not someone Gabe needs snapping at his heels right now. Especially since Gabe's trying to get across-the-board raises and dental coverage for all the patrol officers and Leonard's fighting him on it."

"So, could you send someone over to talk to Mr. Rogers? And tell Gabe when you see him that I'm fine. Scout has obviously proved himself to be a capable protector."

"I sure will. Now, you be real careful, Benni."

"I won't be alone for a moment, I promise," I said. "Now I'm off to photograph some piñatas."

CHAPTER 13

❖

April 5, 1978
Wednesday

"*W*ANT TO COME FIX SOME FENCE WITH ME TODAY?"
Jack asked the next morning.

"I thought you did that fencing yesterday," I said,
cracking four eggs into a bowl. I added a little milk, salt,
and pepper and started beating the mixture with a fork.

"I did, but Steve Malcom told me yesterday there's
another stretch of fence down over near Sweetheart Hill.
Steve saw it last weekend when he was searching for a
couple of his steers. I thought I'd fix it as a favor to your
dad."

Sweetheart Hill was on my father's property. It was
called that because of an ancient blue oak tree at the top
of the two-hundred-acre parcel that had a heart-shaped
knothole in its wide gray trunk. It was not land that was
easily reached, most of it accessible only by foot or
horseback.

Jack flipped one of our high-backed pine kitchen chairs
around and straddled it. On the back of his head, a clump
of his walnut-brown hair stood up in a cheery cowlick.
"We can trailer the horses out to that turnout on Highway

One and Lowell Road and ride in from there."

"That's nice of you to do that for Daddy," I said, looking out the frosty window. "He'll appreciate it. Sure, I can help. I don't have any classes today. Guess we better bring jackets. Looks kinda cold."

"Great, I'll saddle up Buck and Sheba after we eat breakfast. Buck's been cooped up too long and he's getting kinda goosey. He needs a good hard ride."

"I'll make us a lunch." It had been weeks since I'd worked outside on the ranch, and besides, any time I managed to spend with Jack was always fine with me. I smiled across the table at my husband.

After breakfast I gave the dirty dishes a solemn promise to meet with them tonight and fixed ham and swiss cheese sandwiches, cut up apples, put trail mix in baggies, and filled our large Coleman thermos with hot coffee. I added a couple of Hershey bars and a package of graham crackers and started across the yard. Wade and I almost ran into each other as he barreled out of the barn.

"Hey, brother-in-law," I said cheerfully, jumping out of his way. "How are you?"

"Fine," he grunted and didn't slow down his determined stride.

Jack had Sheba tacked up and was haltering Buck when I walked into the barn. His face, genial only moments ago in our warm kitchen, was rigid with anger.

"What's up?" I said lightly though I had no doubt by Wade's grumpy answer to my greeting that they'd argued again.

"Wade's just being an asshole, as usual," he said, attempting to slip the bit into Buck's mouth. Buck gave him a little hassle, then took the bit, grumbling cranky little horse grunts. "Quit it," Jack snapped at the horse. "You're beginning to sound like Wade."

"Hey, Sheba, girl," I crooned, walking over to my easygoing five-year-old buckskin mare. "You ready to ride today? You're a sweet little lady, you are." I stroked her chest and scratched a favorite spot on her withers. "What happened?"

"He wanted me to work on the tractor's engine today. It's eating too much oil again. I told him that this fence was down and I wanted to help Ben. He told me that Ben has hired help and that Ben doesn't pay my college tuition." He lifted the stirrups and checked the saddle cinch, loosening it slightly for the half-hour ride to the section of land we were working. Buck blew his lips and grumbled.

"Wade's a jerk," I said, though I knew encouraging Jack's anger would only make it worse.

"He's an ass."

I started packing our lunch into my saddle bags. "You could work on the tractor at night."

"*That's* what I told him. Or I could do it this weekend. But he just likes being Mr. Bossman. I also told him I am part owner of this ranch, that I'm of legal age now and he couldn't tell me what to do."

So that was why Wade was grumpy. Jack had never, until this moment, challenged Wade with the fact that, now that Jack was over eighteen, he did legally have as much right to make decisions about the ranch as Wade or their mother. I held back any more comments, not wanting to agitate Jack further. This day had always lurked just around the corner. Jack was a high school boy when his father died so his part had been under his mother's trusteeship, but now he was legally one-third owner of the Harper ranch. There was no doubt this power struggle was just beginning.

I finished packing our lunch into my saddle bags, then checked Sheba's cinch, making sure it was comfortable for the drive. Sheba gave a little whinney and blew a quick puff of cold white air from her nose.

"That's my girl," I crooned to Sheba, then turned to Jack. "You know this'll blow over just like it always does. You guys love each other." I'd never had siblings and it pained me to see the two brothers at odds.

Jack frowned at me. "Yes, but it will happen again over some other stupid-ass thing. And again and again." He started putting fencing tools into his saddlebags. "I swear, Benni, if it wasn't for Mom . . ."

"I know." If it wasn't for his mom, we would have left the ranch a long time ago. This was something he'd said many times in the last year though deep down I didn't think he meant it. He loved this ranch, this land, maybe more than his brother did. Jack had been only fourteen when their father, John Harper, had fought with his own brother back in Texas, sold off his half of their family ranch to his brother's biggest rival, and bought this ranch on the Central Coast. Wade had been nineteen and hadn't wanted to leave Texas. He'd never bonded with the land or the community here in California the way Jack had.

After we had coaxed the horses into the trailer, we pulled slowly out on the highway. Once on our way, I tried to stay off the subject of Wade by encouraging Jack to talk about his journal. I'd kept my promise not to read it, but I loved hearing him talk about what aspects of his life he wrote about. Of course, the biggest reason I wanted to read it was obvious.

"What have you written about me?" I tried to pry out of him.

"Not telling, but I promise, it's X-rated."

"Jack!" I poked him in the side.

He grinned and jerked away, trying to avoid my finger. "Don't you want me to get an A? I'm sure Professor Hill would love to read about what we did last night."

I felt my face grow warm. "You'd better not have."

He laughed and winked at me, before pulling slowly onto the highway, checking his rearview mirrors to make sure the horse trailer was turning smoothly.

"Seriously," I said, after we'd been on the road for a few minutes. "Tell me what you wrote about last." The day was cloudy and cool, but the newscaster on the radio had promised the sun would break through by mid-afternoon.

"Dove," he said.

"What did you say about her?"

"I ran into her at the Farm Supply yesterday and listened to her give Bill grief about the last bunch of chickens he sold her. Apparently they aren't laying very well and she claimed he knew that before he sold them to her. I wish I could have captured how she kept accusing him of pushing inferior fowl. It was pretty funny how she said it. You had to be there."

"Are you going to let her read it?"

He turned his head and grinned at me. "No way, José."

"I want to read it."

His face colored slightly. "Nah, it's kinda dumb. I just couldn't get how funny it was on paper." We came to the turnout for Sweetheart Hill so he slowed down, turning onto the gravel road with careful ease.

"C'mon, it's me, the woman who's seen you naked. Why can't I read them?"

"Someday, if you're good."

"How good do I have to be?" I asked, teasing, knowing I was setting myself up.

He raised his eyebrows.

"Ha!" I said, sitting back in my seat. "You'll get that only *after* you let me read your precious journal. And the parts about your beautiful, smart, sweet-natured, and long-suffering wife better be accurate."

His laugh echoed through the small cab. I was glad he was back in a good mood. One of the things I loved most about Jack was his easygoing, positive nature. Nothing kept him down for long.

He stopped the truck in front of the entrance to this section of my dad's ranch. The PRIVATE PROPERTY—NO TRESPASSING sign seemed to have a few more bullet holes in it, but the metal gate was unharmed.

I jumped out and unlocked the gate, opening it all the way so Jack could pull the truck and trailer through. It was then I noticed the cut fence. I walked behind the truck, waited until he stopped, and went over to the driver's door. "Hey, come look at this."

"What's wrong?" He turned off the truck and climbed out.

"Someone's cut through the fence here." I pointed to the barbed wire fence attached to the gate. About a foot of the wire was cut and the green weeds and brush around it flattened, as if someone had dragged something over it. It stopped at the gravel road. A piece of cloth was stuck to the barbed wire. I reached down and pulled it from the twisted wire. It was a piece of worn denim. I held it out to Jack.

He inspected it a moment, then turned to look up the gravel road to Sweetheart Hill. "Hope the trespassing son-of-a-gun lost some skin too."

"Think he's still there?" I asked, looking nervously up the road.

Trespassers were usually just stupid tourists who didn't understand the meaning of the words "private property." We'd come upon them dozens of times over the years, both on the Harper ranch and the Ramsey ranch and politely asked them to take their picnic lunches and lovers' trysts off our land. Twice in my life I'd had to spend long scary nights fighting potentially devastating grass fires that had been caused by ignorant campers. And it never occurred to them that if they were hurt on our land, we were financially liable. Whenever they hassled us about leaving, I would ask if any of them owned a house or a condo. If they said yes, I'd politely ask them how would they like it if someone broke into their backyard and set up camp. That usually shut them up. The principal was the same—the only difference was the amount of property in question.

The last few years, with the crazy sixties not that long behind us, we'd had to worry about marijuana growers who tried to hide their illegal patches on desolate pieces of ranch property. Things happened on our land after dark these days that twenty years ago would have never occurred. Scary, terrible things from the stories many of the local ranchers loved to talk about at brandings and barbecues.

"Nah," Jack said, pocketing the piece of fabric. "I'd be willing to bet it was just a bunch of hippies looking for a place to smoke dope. But if there is anyone there, they'll have to deal with my buddy here." He reached inside the cab for the carved leather holster that held his Colt .45 pistol. He wore it whenever he rode out and didn't expect to be back until after dark. Though some ranchers thought him paranoid, Jack felt these days a rancher didn't dare ride alone in the more desolate parts of the county without protection of some kind.

We climbed back into the truck and drove another half mile to the old miner's shack where he and I had spent many hours making out when we were dating. The advantage ranch kids had over town kids was we had dozens of private places like this at our disposal, much to the dismay of our parents.

We unloaded the horses, tightened their cinches, then started up the steep trail to Sweetheart Hill. In twenty minutes we were there and we spent the good part of the next four hours following the fence line and fixing the places torn down by cattle, humans, or weather. By two o'clock the cool morning haze had turned to warm sunshine. We finished mending our last stretch of barbed wire and were riding back to the truck when about a hundred yards beyond the miner's shack, in a thick clump of brush, I saw something shiny flash in the now bright sun.

"Jack, wait," I called, pulling the reins for Sheba to stop and swinging off to inspect the shiny object. It lay next to a sturdy old sycamore tree which was surrounded by flowering sage and small clumps of purple nightshade.

"What is it?" Jack called.

He came up behind me and swung off Buck. We both stared at the crude circle of blackened stones that held the remnants of a campfire, the empty cans of stew and baked beans, a crumbled blue-and-yellow potato chip bag. Jack went around me and hunkered down to take a closer look. With a long stick, he dug around, then leaned closer and picked up a small object.

"What is it?" I said, stooping down beside him.

"Roach clip," he said, holding up a small, dirty metal clip. "Hope they were only passing through." He stood up, stuck the clip in the pocket of his dusty Wranglers, and stared off toward the dense, rugged hills. "If someone's growing marijuana on our land, I swear, some ass is gonna get kicked."

"Look," I said, pointing toward a clump of silver lupine flowers. "There's something else."

We walked a few feet over and Jack kicked at the paraphernalia with the toe of his boot. There were some shoe strings, a couple of bottle caps, some cotton balls stained an ugly brown, and a fire-blackened spoon bent at an odd angle.

"Crap," Jack said, swearing softly under his breath. "That's heroin stuff." He glanced around, his hand instinctively touching the gun strapped to his muscular thigh.

"We'd better tell the sheriff," I said.

"We'll see what your dad says," Jack answered. "You know what a hassle it is when the law starts trampling around on your land. You get marked and they always look at you a little funny. Remember the Jordans."

Langley Jordan was a longtime rancher up in Monterey County who, in an effort to pay the overdue taxes on the land he'd inherited from his father, had attempted to make a quick buck by growing marijuana. He'd ended up in jail and lost his land anyway. This had happened only a few months ago, so all the ranchers on the Central Coast were sensitive about any hint of impropriety concerning their land.

We mounted our horses and rode silently back to the truck. After we'd watered and fed the horses, we settled down on an old army blanket under the cool, dark shade of an oak tree that had probably been an adolescent when California became a state in 1850. The day had grown warmer than we had anticipated and we'd both peeled down to our jeans and off-white thermal underwear shirts.

"We need to fix that fence by the gate before we go," Jack said in a drowsy voice after we'd eaten our lunch. He leaned up against the scratchy trunk of the oak. I rested my head in his lap, staring up into the leafy tree top. Slices of white-blue sky, so bright it pained my eyes, filtered through the greenness.

"I hate it that someone is using our land for smoking dope," I said. "What do you think Daddy will want to do?"

Jack stared out toward where we'd discovered the drug stuff. "Most likely just keep watching this place. Wade will hassle me about taking the time to help your dad, but that's tough." Jack's voice wasn't bitter this time, just resigned and, a little tired.

"If you come out here alone, bring one of the dogs with you. And your pistol. And be careful. Those dope-heads are crazy."

"I will."

"I hate how everything is changing so fast. I wish things never, ever had to change."

"Me too, babe," he said, smoothing away some stray strands of hair the wind had blown across my face. His rough fingertips gently scratched my cheeks, tickling it in a not unpleasant sensation. His tender brown eyes looked down into mine.

After a bit of napping, Jack said, "I want to check that section of fence near the north meadow. It'll only take a half hour or so."

"I think I'll stay here," I said, standing up. "I'll get Sheba loaded up."

After he left, I realized that we'd forgotten to repair the small section of fence down by the gate. I mounted Sheba and trotted the half mile to the entrance. I'd almost finished the repairs when the car drove up.

I turned to face it, squinting in the bright, early-afternoon sun, wishing I hadn't left my sunglasses back in the truck. There were three figures in the beat-up car, whose tinted windows made it difficult to see their features. My stomach lurched in anxiety, but like I'd been taught, I straightened my spine and stepped forward to confront them.

"What do you want?" I said in my most assertive voice, wishing I had Jack's pistol strapped to my leg to give it more authority.

No one in the car answered. They didn't even roll down a window.

I stepped closer and saw it was three men.

"This is private property," I said louder, more aggressively. "You need to leave."

The driver, a Hispanic man, turned and said something to the person in the back seat of the car. There was a muffled burst of laughter. I felt my stomach tighten.

Clutching the fence-mending pliers in my hand, I turned and walked back to Sheba, tied a few feet away. I mounted her and turned to face the car.

"I'm fetching my husband and his friends," I yelled at them. "We have guns. We'll call the police on our CB radio."

At that, the car slowly backed up, made an awkward turn, and started driving away. As it did, a face appeared in the back window. A hand came up and gave me the finger. When the hand lowered, I caught a glimpse of his face and gasped out loud.

It was Emma Baldwin's son.

CHAPTER 14

❖

April 18, 1995
Tuesday

I PARKED THE TRUCK INSIDE THE MISSION PARKING lot, normally reserved for church workers. Father Mark would understand my current need for caution. I used my cell phone to dial the twins at Crosby's Five and Dime Store to invite them to dinner tonight.

"Oh, that sounds delightful," Beebs said. "What would you like us to bring?"

"Just your lovely selves," I answered. They would ignore my answer, of course. Even if their lives depended on it, Beebs and Millee couldn't visit anyone's house without bearing a gift of food.

"We'll bring a pie," said Millee, who'd picked up the other line.

"And a fruit salad," Beebs said. "Gabe loves ambrosia. I make it with pecans instead of walnuts."

"That's fine," I said, laughing at my ability to predict them.

"What's going on with our case?" Millee asked eagerly.

I hesitated a moment, not certain if I should tell them

about the man who'd tried to break into my truck or the photograph.

"Dear heart, we won't tell your gramma," Beebs said, reading my mind. "We know you don't want to worry her. We saw today's paper. We left the Zozobra fire early so we missed the hullabaloo. That's terrible what happened to your little truck. My heavens, a person just isn't safe walking across the street these days."

"Yes, just tell us all the details so we can pray accurately about it," Millee said.

I laughed again, knowing her motivation was twofold. Though I knew she and Beebs would, indeed, pray for my safety, I also knew they were as nosy as new kittens. I filled them in on the whole story of my stalker, Scout's possible encounter with him, Mr. Rogers's witnessing of the incident, and the piece of evidence I had in my possession.

"Hurrah for Scout," Millee said. "Extra biscuits for him tonight."

"That's what I told him."

"What's next?" Millee asked eagerly. "Is the chief rousting out known criminals, trying to get them to confess? Has he got the bloodhounds out searching for clues? Has he called the FBI? Does he need help canvassing the neighborhoods to question possible suspects or witnesses? I could take a day off work and help."

I laughed and said, "Millee, you watch too much television. Actually, he's in a meeting with the local neighborhood watch groups and he's working on the department's budget."

"It's not just television," Beebs said. "She's been like this ever since she subscribed to the Mystery Guild Book Club. If she doesn't get a mystery to solve before long, I do believe she's going to pitch a fit of Alaskan proportions."

"Hush, sister," Millee said. "You devour those books just like I do."

Beebs gave a small hmph over the phone. "Yes, but I

don't actually believe they bear any resemblance to the
way real life works. That piece of cloth Scout tore off of
your stalker. Shouldn't you give that to a policeman?
That's what the detectives would do in one of Millee's
books."

My stalker. I sure didn't like the way that sounded.

Millee chimed in. "They would not! They would have
kept it for themselves and developed other clues."

"I'm giving it to Gabe tonight," I said. "Not that it'll
be much help. It's green. Like the Cal Poly sweatshirts
they sell everywhere." Cal Poly's school colors were dark
green and gold.

"Which will make him impossible to pick out around
here," Millee said, her voice disappointed. Then her voice
brightened. "There's always DNA . . ."

I checked my watch. "Whoops, I'm late, girls. We'll
have to continue this conversation later. But not tonight.
Like I said, I'm trying to keep all of this from Dove."

"Talk about impossible," Beebs said.

"I know," I said. "But I'm going to try."

❖

"You're late," Elvia said when I walked into the
small office behind the Mission gift shop.

"Only five minutes," I said. "And I have a good reason
that I'll tell you when we can catch a breath. Now is there
anything you want me to do before I start taking pictures?"

She handed me a stack of paper. "Make sure all the
piñatas have an entry form filled out. It's going to be hard
to pick a winner. All of them are pretty cute. Could you
count them? We can run off more if we need to."

I had just finished counting the stack when my cell
phone rang.

"What's going on?" Gabe's voice barked. "My cell

phone's been acting up. Lousy piece of junk. I just got your message from Maggie."

"Nothing that I can't handle," I said and quickly told him what happened with Scout and the man in the green sweatshirt. "Right now I'm surrounded by people at the Mission, so don't worry."

There was a long silence.

"Gabe, I'm fine. Really."

"Okay," he said, his voice subdued. "Just . . . be careful."

"I am, Friday. I promise, I am."

"I'll go talk to Jim and see what they found out from the old man."

"Good idea. Be home by six. We're having guests."

Inside the Mission office, Elvia and the three former La Fiesta Queens were perusing their rating sheets. There was Elaine Gardiner, now an interior decorator; Maria Padilla, a famous local sculptor; and Rosalee Jaramillo, who owned a vintage clothing store downtown.

"Everyone set?" Elvia asked. "Any questions?"

All of us murmured no.

"Then let's go judge the costumes and piñatas."

Elvia was right about it being a difficult task. The kids who'd entered the piñata-decorating contest had really outdone themselves. We had thirty entries, most of them from Boy Scout and Girl Scout troops, 4-H clubs, public school classes, and even one from the Headstart day care center down by the homeless shelter. The papier-mâché creations depicted everything from purple cows to jukeboxes to fire trucks to palm trees. I was especially impressed with the detailed piñata of the Santa Celine Mission complete with a tiny Father Serra in the entry to the church. A bright pink-and-orange alligator had a mouth that would open and shut every time the piñata moved, revealing all the goodies in his stomach through a clear plastic wrap barrier.

"I love the alligator," I whispered to Elvia.

"It is adorable," she said. "But make sure and give

every piñata a good look. Some of them are very clever, but you have to look closely."

After I'd taken photographs of all of them, while Elvia tabulated the votes, I helped the other volunteers oversee a coloring contest, helped kids pose for free photographs with Father Serra (a grinning Father Mark in sandals and a scratchy-looking brown robe tied with a thick, wheat-colored rope), and gave out iced, bell-shaped butter cookies and Hawaiian Punch. Scout, my constant shadow, was in seventh heaven from all the hugs and head-patting, not to mention the occasional dropped cookie.

Though it was hard, we finally picked a first, second, and third place and gave pink YOU'RE SPECIAL ribbons to all the rest. The prizes, donated by one of our local businesses, San Celina Homestyle Ice Cream, were coupons for three free ice cream sundaes to each of the winners and a free single scoop cone to every child who participated. Plus all the piñatas would be part of the parade on the ice cream store's float and would be sold at La Fiesta Mercado on Saturday with the money going toward a summer arts and crafts program for low-income children.

"Guess I'd better get a move-on," I said at five o'clock as I helped Elvia clean up the last of the punch and cookies and store the piñatas in the back office of the Mission gift shop. After she had locked up, we started walking through the cool and shady Mission Plaza. The thick bed of dry eucalyptus leaves crunched underneath our feet. "I have a busload of people for dinner."

"Should I bring anything?" she asked.

"No, ma'am," I said. "It's enough you're taking Dove into your home. I'll owe you a month of dinners for that."

"It's no problem at all," Elvia said. "You know I love your gramma. We haven't really visited since we've both gotten married."

"You can exchange honeymoon stories," I said, laughing. "I've heard all her Hawaii stories a hundred times now."

We parted ways at her little green Austin Healy.

Long shadows from the buildings shaded her troubled face. She gazed up and down the still busy street in apprehension, "Are you going to be okay? Where are you parked?"

"In the lot around the corner. There's tons of people around and I have protection." I held up Scout's leash. His heavy tail banged against my leg.

"Just be careful," she said, her face still not convinced.

"For the hundredth time, I will." I gave her a quick hug.

I glanced behind me twice while walking the long block to my car, though I knew if the man stalking me was anywhere close, Scout would scent him. I didn't want to admit it to anyone, but this person had changed my perception about my hometown, about the safety and security I'd always taken for granted. It made me scared, it made me sad, and most of all, it made me angry. And for right now, I decided anger might best serve to keep me sane so I concentrated on that feeling and tried to push the others away.

I was almost at my car when simultaneously my cell phone rang and a woman called my name. While fumbling for my phone, I turned around to see who was yelling for me.

"Benni Harper, I need to talk to you," said Sissy Brownmiller. She strode toward me, her long beige cloth coat flapping like a superhero's cape behind her flamingo legs. Not that Sissy would ever be mistaken for Wonder Woman or Supergirl.

I finally found my phone, punched it on, and held up one finger to her. "Hello? Oh, hi, Gabe."

"Are you okay?" Gabe asked.

"I'm as fine as I was an hour ago when you called. I'm going to see you in a few minutes." Before he could launch into another lecture on me being careful, which I didn't think I could take right now without screaming, I asked, "How did the meeting with . . ." I remembered that Sissy was standing only a foot away. "How did it go?"

That diverted his attention from my safety for a few minutes. "You'd think I was asking him to pay for my patrol officers' raises right out of his personal checking account. Sometimes I hate this job. Give me a good, straightforward bank robbery/hostage situation any day."

"I'm sorry," I said, smiling and nodding at Sissy while she looked impatiently at her watch. "One minute," I mouthed to her.

"I just read the interview sheets of the old guy who saw Scout bite our suspect. Anything you want to add to it?"

There was no way I was going to talk to him about my suspected stalker in front of Sissy Brownmiller, the empress of San Celina gossip. "I'll be home in ten minutes and we can talk about it then."

"Tell me now. I'll talk you home."

"It's dangerous to talk on a cell phone and drive, sweetheart," I said in a syrupy tone.

"Sweetheart? You never call me that. Is someone with you? Are you okay?"

"I've got Scout with me and I'm fine," I said, thinking if I had to say that one more time I would start stomping my feet and screaming like a two-year-old. "I have to go now, Sissy Brownmiller is waiting."

He chuckled. "That's why you sound so funny. Okay, I'll see you in a few minutes. Good luck."

I stuck the phone back into my purse and smiled at Sissy. "What can I do for you?" I instantly regretted my poor choice of words since Sissy usually did have some tedious task she wanted me to perform.

A cool breeze rushed through the half-empty parking lot and she pulled her cloth coat closer around her gaunt frame. "I've just gone to see the new exhibit at the folk art museum," she said.

I steeled myself for her criticism. Sissy Brownmiller, though a hard worker and an ardent supporter of local history and the historical society, was one of the most negative people I'd ever met. She never had anything good to say about anything or anyone, which is probably why after running for historical club president four times she'd never won.

"It looks wonderful," she said.

I almost fell over in shock. "Uh, thank you," I stammered.

"But there's one thing I'd like to ask you to do."

I knew it was too good to be true. "And what might that be?" I struggled to keep my words from sounding sarcastic.

She glanced at me sharply, her round, walnut-brown eyes narrowing while she tried to discern if my tone was being disrespectful, a particular complaint of hers about "young people these days."

I gave a wide, phony smile in an attempt to soften my snippy words. Sissy Brownmiller did do a lot of volunteer work at the museum and was a regular financial contributor. Though she drove me nuts, like Constance Sinclair, our most generous patron, the museum needed her and part of my job was to appease people like her.

She gave a quick nod, apparently satisfied I wasn't being impertinent. "Well, I do love the crazy quilt exhibit and am photographing all of them for the historical society's archives, but I find the written history of some of them to be quite skimpy."

"The information there is all that the quilters gave me." I lifted up my shoulders and gave a palms-up, what's-a-person-to-do gesture.

"For the historical society's purposes, I'd really appreciate you calling the women back and finding out a little more information. You know, so many of the quilts of old have had their histories lost simply because someone was too lazy to press for a little more information."

I bit my tongue to keep from snapping at her. Who was she calling lazy? Silently, I counted to ten, then said, "Which quilts exactly were you speaking about?"

"The one from Eleanor Rolly up in San Miguel and the baby quilt made by Loversa Levy's grandmother, Jolene Espinoza's quilt, that sort of odd-looking one from Charlene Michaelson, I don't know what she was thinking putting all those coffins and skeletons on her crazy quilt."

"It's a commemorative quilt of all the people who've passed away in her family," I said patiently. I'd actually thought it was interesting, reminding me of the Day of the Dead celebration that was so popular among San Celina's Hispanic citizens.

She gave a small shudder. "I find it morbid. And, of course, Emma Baldwin's lovely quilt."

"What about Emma's quilt?" I asked. I understood about the others—the women had given pretty skimpy details and maybe I'd not pushed as hard as I might have to find out the full story behind the quilts, but Emma's quilt history was one I'd worked on for a long time and it seemed very complete to me.

"I think it would be nice for the patrons and for the historical society's records if there was some indication of what those dates on her quilt are for."

"She told me they were personal milestones in her life. I listed a few of them."

"Exactly," Mrs. Brownmiller said. "Which, because she was such a historical figure in our county, don't you think *all* of them should be listed?"

"I suppose."

"So you'll rewrite her display and put what the dates represent?"

"I'll call Emma Baldwin and ask her," I said firmly. "Don't forget, Sissy, those are personal to her. Maybe she doesn't want them listed."

"Why ever not?" Sissy said, bringing a thin, large-knuckled hand to her chest.

I looked at her through narrowed eyes. It was becoming clear to me now. Sissy was just nosy about Emma's life. "I don't know how she feels about listing what the dates represent. I'm just saying that's a possibility."

"I can't imagine why she wouldn't."

"I'll let you know," I said, inching my way backward.

"I'll call you tomorrow afternoon," she persisted.

"Okay," I said, still inching away. "I'm sorry, but I really have to go. I have company coming for dinner."

"Who?" she called after me, ever curious.

"Family," I called back and hurried toward my truck.

I unlocked the truck's passenger door and was in the process of unhooking Scout's leash when a deep rumble sounded in his throat and he jerked his blue nylon leash out of my hand and took off, the leash dragging after him.

"Scout, come!" I screamed, shocked at his unexpected behavior. "Come back here! Scout, stop!"

I ran after him as he dashed into the middle of the street and chased a white car as it turned the corner. Scout rounded the corner after the vehicle. When I made it to the corner, I stopped, my heart beating wildly, and watched the car and my dog turn right at the next corner and disappear from sight.

"Dang," I said, stomping my foot in frustration. "Dang, dang, dang." I still couldn't believe it. Since I'd first owned him, Scout, who had been obviously very well trained by the man who left him to me, had never disobeyed one of my commands. What had gotten into my dog?

Then it occurred to me. Only one thing might cause him to react like that. He'd obviously smelled or spotted the man he'd bitten earlier today.

Breathing heavily, I walked back to my truck and pulled out onto the street where Scout had started chasing the car. Though I knew Scout would eventually come home or be brought home by one of the many people who knew him in town, I decided to at least drive around the general area and see if I could find him. If this guy stopped, which was unlikely, I hoped, there was no telling what he might do to Scout.

I drove slowly, scanning the bushy and shadowed front yards. When I turned down a street three blocks from where I originally parked, Scout was trotting on the opposite sidewalk, his tongue dangling. I pulled over, stopped the pickup, and opened the passenger door.

"Scout Harper Ortiz, get your butt in this truck right now," I yelled at him.

He dashed across the street and jumped up into the passenger seat, a panting, satisfied doggy-smile on his furry face.

"You are a bad dog," I said, unhooking his now-muddy leash and throwing it on the floor. "A bad, bad dog. What was that all about?"

He whined and lay down on the seat, placing his head on his paws, looking up at me with pleading eyes that said—I just couldn't help myself.

I looked down the street and saw that it was one that ended at a dangerously short entrance to the 101 Freeway as many of our streets do here in San Celina, where the freeway had been built long after the town existed.

"At least you were smart enough not to follow him onto the freeway, you dumb mutt." Unable to be angry at him for long, I reached over and scratched behind his ear. "If you were Lassie, you'd be able to bark out the numbers of his license plate." His tail thumped in either appreciation or apology.

My cell phone rang just as I was pulling up to our house.

"I'm in the driveway, Friday," I said, knowing who it was.

He walked out on the porch holding his cell phone, still dressed in gray suit slacks and one of his white cotton dress shirts. He closed the phone and stuck it in his pocket. "Where have you been?" he called to me before I was completely out of the truck.

"Gabe, it's only been twenty minutes since we talked."

He frowned. "And it should have taken you ten minutes to get home."

"I had a small incident . . ."

Before I could say more, he was down the steps and next to me. "What happened?"

"Inside, you mangy mutt," I told Scout. He bounded

up the porch steps and scratched at the door. Dove opened it, waved to me, and let him in.

"We'll be in to dinner in a minute," I called to her.

"No hurry, honeybun," she called back. "The cornbread's got fifteen more minutes."

"What happened?" Gabe repeated, placing a large hand on my shoulder and squeezing it.

I told him about Scout's unsuccessful pursuit of the white car. "It had to be my stalker. Oh, and I don't know if it's a help or not, but here's some cloth I think Scout took from the arm of the guy's sweatshirt."

He took the piece of cloth and swore softly in Spanish.

"What is it, Friday?" I asked, placing a hand on his forearm. Even after working all day, his shirt felt crisp and clean. I could feel his sinewy muscles through the thin cotton.

He looked down at me, his eyes now a murky gray. "I feel helpless." It was an intimate and difficult thing for him to admit to me. "I want to protect you, but I can't figure out how."

Though his statement chilled me, I didn't want to add to his fear by panicking myself. "You're doing all you can. Short of hiring a bodyguard to be with me at all times—which I won't allow—you are doing all that is humanly possible. I'm being careful and I have Scout and my pepper spray and my cell phone with me all the time. What else can we do?"

"I still think it might be good for you to go away."

"That is impractical and you know it. First, for how long? We don't know how long it'll take you to find this person. And second, I'll say it again, if he's watching me that closely, then he'll see where I'm going and that could put me at worse risk. Third, I'd be tons more scared away from my home turf. Here I feel like there are dozens of places, hundreds of people I could run to for help. If I was in some strange place . . ."

He held up his hand for me to stop. "*Querida,* I know

you're right and I agree with you. I was just reaching for straws."

I slipped my arms around his waist and lay my head on his chest. His heartbeat was slow and steady, but his breathing came in quick, shallow spurts. His arms encircled me and I could feel his breathing start to slow down and his body relax. He started rubbing his lips across the top of my head, a gesture I'd come to realize he did when he needed comfort.

"I'll be fine," I said. "Don't worry. Really, at this point all we can do is just trust God to handle it."

"Let's go inside," he said. "When everyone leaves tonight, I have something I need to tell you."

"About what?"

"Later."

I pulled out of his arms and looked up at his face, having every intention of haranguing him about setting me up with a remark like that and then making me wait. The serious look on his face stopped me.

"Okay," I just said, suddenly feeling more fearful than I had all day.

Once everyone had arrived, the evening turned out to be a light, relaxing one, though, like a tumultuous rain cloud, Gabe's mysterious comment hovered over me. After dinner, Emory, the perennial camp counselor, had us all playing Pictionary and charades, even managing to get a nervous and cranky Gabe involved and laughing.

When Dove and I begged off one last game, we took everyone's empty dessert bowls into the kitchen to rinse off and put in the dishwasher.

"Where's Isaac tonight?" I asked, my back to her while I rearranged dishes in the dishwasher.

"I don't know and I don't care." She stretched plastic wrap over the remainder of the blackberry cobbler. "Where's your dish soap?"

I gestured to the cupboard under the sink. "You do too. Care, I mean."

She lifted the ceramic liner of my crockpot out,

squirted dish soap in it, and took it to the sink, filling it
with hot water. "That's all you know. I really don't care
where he is tonight or any night, for that matter."

"But you care about *him*."

"Hmph," she just said, turned off the water, and started
scrubbing the liner.

"I had breakfast with him yesterday morning."

"Goody for you."

"Nadine was fishing around trying to figure out why
he was out so early and why you hadn't fixed him breakfast."

"Nadine Brooks Johnson is an undegenerated gossip."

I gave a half smile and leaned against the kitchen table.
"I think you mean unregenerated."

"Don't correct your elders," she snapped. "I raised you
better than that."

"Yes, ma'am."

I turned back to the dishwasher and started loading
glasses into the top rack. "All I have to say is he loves
you and that he's miserable and I think you're miserable
too. Maybe you should to talk to Mac about this."

"Mac doesn't know squat. He's been widowed for six
years, has a secretary to take his phone calls, and *he* gets
a good night's sleep."

I took a deep breath. "Sorry, just trying to help."

"Speaking of that, you need any help down at the museum?"

I didn't answer. Oh, Lord, please get them back together, I prayed.

Without her own house to run and staying as a guest
at Emory and Elvia's, where there was nothing to do because of their excellent housekeeper, Dove was going to
be bored silly. And a bored Dove was a problem I didn't
have time for this week.

"Actually, I'm pretty caught up. Except for doing a
little more work on the crazy quilt histories—Sissy
Brownmiller thinks I didn't get as much historical information about them as I could have—I'll probably be

hanging around the house here, trying to get organized."

"I could help with that," she said, her voice brightening. "I could get you organized in no time flat."

"Oh, well . . ." I stammered, trying to figure out a way for her *not* to help me. Dove and I worked well together in some areas, but how we organized a house, that was where we parted ways. Besides, I didn't want her staying in this house alone with that stalker hanging around. That would defeat the whole reason she was staying at Emory and Elvia's.

"I think Emory could use some help at his office," I blurted out. Emory was going to kill me, but it was all I could think of to appease her. "The restaurant is opening in a few weeks and he can use all the help he can get."

"I'm not surprised," Dove said. "I can't believe how much he and Elvia have taken on, being newlyweds like they are. They need to spend more time with each other and not so much time working."

"Hmmm," I said, trying to avoid getting back on the subject of newlyweds.

After Dove and I had finished kitchen detail, we went back into the living room for one last game of charades. I begged off however, and grabbed my cousin's arm. "You can sit this one out too, Emory. I have a book upstairs I've been meaning to show you."

Out of Dove's earshot, I explained what had happened today and why I wanted Dove as far away from my house as possible. "I'm sorry I said you needed help, but it was pawning her off on you or Elvia and I'm more scared of Elvia."

He laughed and hugged me. "You and me both, sweetcakes. That's okay. I do have a lot that needs to be done. I'll get her busy organizing the kitchen at the restaurant. I'll tell the manager he can change it all back once she's gone, but it'll keep her busy for a day or two."

"Thank you, thank you. I'm hoping Isaac comes up with some solution soon to lure her back home. He's miserable and I suspect she is too."

"Though she'd never admit it."

"Amen to that. She's nothing if not stubborn."

"Unlike you or I," he said, grinning.

I punched his arm. "Let's not discuss disagreeable family traits right now."

"Speaking of stubborn, I'm not sure this time if Gabe's not right," he said, in that typically convoluted, double-negative Southern way that I totally understood. "Maybe you should leave town for a little while."

I leaned against the book shelf and crossed my arms. "Let me ask you something, cousin dear. Would you leave town, leave Elvia all alone, leave your family and friends alone, if you were being stalked knowing that the stalker might follow you or, even worse, he might turn his harassment to those you love?"

He shoved his hands deep into his dark brown corduroy pants. "Okay, I get your point. But what can I do to help you be safe? I'm worried sick about this."

"There's nothing anyone can do that isn't already being done. We just have to wait and see if Gabe or his detectives can find out anything."

His eyebrows came together in a troubled scowl. "Or he strikes again."

"Or that," I said, wrapping my arms around myself and meeting my cousin's worried green eyes.

CHAPTER 15

❖

April 18–19, 1995
Tuesday and Wednesday

$\mathcal{T}$HOUGH I WAS TEMPTED TO GRAB GABE THE MINUTE everyone left and demand he tell me what he meant earlier in the front yard, I waited until he took Scout on one last walk and we were settled down in bed. He switched off the light, bathing the room in a pale, milky moonlight. It divided the room into light and dark spots, like the markings on a wild animal's back.

"You've had me on pins and needles all night," I said, turning to him and propping myself up on one elbow. "What do you need to tell me?"

He turned on his side and looked at me. His thick, black hair was disheveled, sticking up in places like a boy's. I reached over and brushed the cowlicks down. He grabbed my hand and kissed my palm gently. I scooted closer, attempting see his face better in the semidarkness.

"When I came up here to take over Aaron's job . . ." he started. For a moment, he was struck silent, his eyes blinking quickly.

Gabe still had trouble talking about his best friend. Aaron Davidson had been Gabe's first partner when he joined the LAPD. Gabe was twenty-one years old and Aaron thirty-eight. Aaron left Los Angeles a few years later and began working for the San Celina Police Department. He was at San Celina PD for fourteen years, seven of them as chief, when Gabe first came to San Celina almost three years ago. Not long after Gabe and I had married, Aaron died of liver cancer.

"Yes," I said, stroking his cheek with my fingertips.

"When I came up here that November it . . . it wasn't the first time I'd lived in San Celina."

I pulled my hand back from his face and sat up, crossing my legs. For a moment, I didn't know what to say. It was a long running and touchy issue between us, his difficulty in revealing himself to me, his reluctance for emotional intimacy. His argument was always the same.

"There are too many things I've seen . . . I've *done* . . . that I don't want you to know about," he'd say.

My argument that I would love him no matter what he'd done in his past didn't faze him. He determinedly kept whole parts of his former life, his life before he moved to San Celina, in a secret place inside him, the door closed tight with a steel lock to which only he knew the combination.

"When?" I finally asked, trying not to let the anger that was starting to simmer inside me come to a rolling boil. With what was going on in our life right now with this stalker, we didn't need to be at odds with each other. We needed to work as a team.

"In 1978. Aaron was a captain here. He'd left LA about two years before and moved up here. He wanted to raise Esther in a safer environment. And Rachel liked it up here."

"I was twenty years old." A sudden flash of memory crackled across my brain. Jack and I lying in bed discussing our plans to buy new porch furniture. Green wicker that I'd seen in a garden shop in town.

Gabe's voice brought me back a split second later. "I'd just started work in undercover narcotics. I was twenty-eight and had been in the squad for about six months when Aaron called my commander. They were old buddies from before I was on the force." He sat up and leaned back against the headboard. "They were starting to have problems with drugs up here. Heroin mostly, but lots of marijuana too."

A shiver darted up my spine, stopping at the base of my skull in a hard, cold knot. I pulled the comforter over my shoulders. "Jack and I used to find places on our ranch where people did drugs, but we could never catch them. It drove us nuts."

He ran his fingers through his hair and stared down at a spot on the bed. "They wanted to arrest the dealers. Especially the top guy. But the San Celina Police Department was much smaller then. Anyone they could use in undercover would probably be recognized. That's why Aaron borrowed me from LA."

"How long did you live here?"

"A little less than three months."

"Where?"

"You know that trailer court over by the bus station?"

I nodded. It was a rougher side of town then and still that way now. I was silent for a moment, thinking about how strange and unnerving it was that he and I had possibly passed by each other on the streets of San Celina never guessing that someday we would be married.

"So, what happened?" I asked in a slow, careful voice.

His arms came up and wrapped around himself as if he were cold, a vulnerable gesture I'd never seen him do. "I screwed up, blew the sting, and was almost killed. My memories of San Celina are not proud ones, *querida*."

I wanted details, but knew he wouldn't reveal them. At least not tonight. I wanted to be angry, but seeing him hug himself like that, a young boy's comforting gesture, softened my heart and my anger at feeling, again, so much on the perimeter of his life. I slid across the bed and put my arms around him, touching my forehead to his.

"You were young," I said.

"I had a wife and a son. When I think now about the chances I took . . ." His voice cracked.

"Gabe, they're okay. You're okay. *Everyone's* okay. We've talked about this before. You have to let the past go." I inhaled deeply, thinking, knowing, that unless he talked about it, he probably never would. "If you can't talk about these things to me, then go to Father Mark . . . or Mac . . . or some counselor. *Somebody.* I think it would help you."

"This situation now," he said, ignoring my plea. "It might involve that assignment."

I rubbed my hands over his forearms, trying to massage some warmth into his cold skin. "Can you get the old records for it? Find out if any of the people who were involved are back in this area?"

"We're doing that. Back in '78, after what happened, I left in the middle of the assignment. But there were dozens of people involved, close to fifty, maybe."

"But there are written records, right?"

"Yes, and I have a guy down in LA checking out where all these people are. But it was seventeen years ago. It's a long shot."

"Do you really think that this guy might be one of those people who was busted?"

"There's a good chance. But it could also be hundreds of others. I was undercover for eight years. Right now, I'm just grasping at whatever seems the most logical."

"But why would they target you? I mean, if you blew it . . . ?" The instant I said the words, I wanted to snatch them back.

Gabe's face grew stiff and hard. "I blew the assignment, but not before I was able to tell Aaron who the major players were. They weren't caught that time, but because they'd been identified, it eventually caught up with most of them."

"I'm sorry," I said, taking his hand and touching the top of it with my lips. "I didn't mean that the way it came out."

He squeezed my hand in reply. "I can't talk about this anymore."

"Okay." But I couldn't resist asking one more thing. "Do you think that this might have something to do with Luke's death? I mean, it is sort of weird, Luke worked with you undercover, he comes to visit you, is murdered, and now I'm being stalked."

"There's no reason to believe that his death and this stalker are connected," Gabe said, sliding down under the covers. "Luke didn't work that assignment with me, and as far as the LAPD's records show, he was never involved with anything on the Central Coast. I think the timing of Luke's homicide and your stalker is pure coincidence."

"So what are you going to do?" I asked, snuggling up next to his warm body.

"What we always do. Keep digging."

The next morning I made Gabe's favorite banana pancakes and held back the urge to revisit the subject of his past.

"What are you going to do today?" he asked, looking up from the newspaper. Luke's murder had already been replaced on the front page by the latest budget crisis in Washington.

"I'll probably spend most of the day at the museum," I said, buttering my pancakes. "Sissy Brownmiller is insisting that some of my quilt histories aren't thorough enough for the historical archives of San Celina so I'll be on the phone trying to pry more information out of the quilt owners in question."

"Are things pretty busy down at the museum?" He studied me over his gold wire-rimmed eyeglasses, the shadows under his eyes causing them to appear deeper set.

I poured maple syrup over my pancakes. "Don't worry, there will be plenty of people around. I repeat, I have my cell phone, my pepper spray, and my personal bodyguard, Scout Harper Ortiz."

From under the table, Scout's tail thumped the kitchen

floor. I ran my bare foot over his silky back.

"Of course I'll worry," he said, taking his glasses off and massaging the bridge of his nose. "I'll send a patrol car around a couple of times today to check on you."

"If it makes you feel better." I certainly wasn't going to argue with that. Frankly, right then I wouldn't have minded it if one parked right in front of the museum all day.

"It will. And it will show this guy that I'm keeping close tabs on you. He might think twice before trying something again."

He left for work a half hour later, but I puttered around, taking my time since I didn't have any pressing business at the museum and, frankly, was not looking forward to calling those quilters and trying to coerce more information out of them. I unpacked a few more boxes, avoiding the three boxes that contained Jack's things. Just going through one of them a few days ago out at the ranch was too emotional for me. With my nerves walking on a thin wire like they were, I couldn't deal with the emotions that seeing his possessions would surely cause to surface. So I shoved those boxes aside and started sifting through my old high school and college papers, deciding what to keep and what to throw away.

At the bottom of the first box I came across an envelope labeled EMMA BALDWIN. I undid the clasp and pulled out my old term paper and the photos I'd taken of her quilt. The date on the essay was April 17, 1978. A lifetime ago.

I set the essay aside and looked at the photographs. A friend in the photography department had enlarged them to eight-by-tens for me. I stuck them in my leather backpack to take with me to the museum. It would be interesting to compare them to the actual quilt. I picked up the essay and started reading.

The first time I saw Emma Baldwin's house it felt as if I'd been there many times before. And when I met Emma Baldwin, it seemed as if I were talking with an old friend. Such is the power of fiction that touches our souls.

I smiled at my innocent, slightly pretentious prose, though I understood and still mostly agreed with my youthful self. Certain fiction does touch us in a special place, though the sentence I wrote about her feeling like an old friend was a bit fictional itself. In reality, I remembered being in awe of the person who'd written the books I loved and scared to death she'd think I was a total goofball.

I was skimming over the essay, thinking the B-plus it received was certainly generous on my professor's part, when the doorbell rang. Scout, who'd been dozing in a spot of sunlight next to me, jumped up and ran over to the door barking. My heart started pounding. Did Gabe lock the door after him?

My heart settled down as soon as Scout's tail started swinging back and forth, his bark friendly rather than threatening. I shoved the essay into my backpack along with the photographs. Even though it was obvious Scout knew whoever was outside, I looked out of the peephole.

"Daddy!" I unlocked the door and swung it open. Scout darted out and nosed my father's leg.

"Howdy-do, you old hound," he said, scrubbing the top of Scout's head. He stepped over the threshold and gave me a big hug. "How're you doing, pumpkin? What's this I hear about some hooligans messing with your truck?"

"Come in and I'll tell you all about it. Do you want some coffee? Are you hungry?" I glanced over at the mantle clock. Ten o'clock. He'd most likely eaten breakfast at five A.M., his normal rising time, so ten o'clock was practically lunchtime.

"I could eat," he said.

"Bacon, scrambled eggs, and toast?"

"Sounds good." He took off his straw Stetson, stuck it on the oak hall tree, and followed me into the kitchen.

"So, what's the story on your truck?" he asked. He sat at the kitchen table with a cup of coffee in front of him. "I just got back from the hills last night and didn't read the paper until this morning. Does your gramma know about this? And where is she anyway?"

"She didn't leave you a note?" I cracked three eggs into a blue ceramic bowl.

"No, ma'am. Their bedroom door was shut last night when I moseyed in about nine so I assumed they were both in there. When I got up this morning, Isaac was fixing the coffee, and when I asked after Dove, he just grunted and said she was gone. That's all he'd say. I went out and fed the horses and checked on those two orphan calves, then came back to the house. Figured he'd be a little more awake by then and tell me what's what, but he was gone. I figured you'd know what was going on."

He sipped his coffee, his weathered face grumpy and annoyed. Daddy hated breaks in his or the ranch's routine, and the last few years, thanks to me and Dove, there'd been far too many of them.

I peeled off four strips of bacon and set them to frying while I whipped the eggs with milk, salt, and pepper. Without asking, I refilled his cup of coffee. Then I decided to just spit it out.

"Well, Daddy, besides everything I need to do for La Fiesta Week, it seems that I'm possibly being stalked by some drug dealer Gabe helped convict seventeen years ago, a friend of Gabe's was murdered right after we had dinner with him the other night, and this friend may or may not be involved with the reason the stalker is stalking me, and Dove has decided she wants her marriage annulled because Isaac snores, owns too much junk, and has too many groupies."

He shook his head and gave a big sigh. "I wish y'all would get your ducks in a row and settle down. I don't know if my nerves can take any more hullabaloo. I swear, I am as confused as a termite in a yo-yo. This is one of them times when I purely wished I still smoked."

I stuck two slices of wheat bread in the toaster and didn't answer.

"What're you going to do about your gramma?" he asked.

I melted a pat of butter in the frying pan, then dumped in the egg mixture. "What in the heck do you expect me to do?"

"I don't know. Talk to her. Talk to Isaac. And you'd best be carrying Jack's pistol with you."

I stirred the eggs and flipped the bacon. "You know I can't do that now that I'm married to Gabe."

He slapped his hand down on the table. "That just don't hardly make any sense to me. Now that you're married to a cop, you can't protect yourself from some yahoo who wouldn't be after you if you wasn't married to a cop. Tell me how that makes any sense at all."

I inhaled deeply, wishing I'd not been so lazy and gone ahead to the museum at my normal time. Maybe I could have avoided this conversation.

"Daddy," I said patiently, not turning around. "When I carried Jack's pistol before, it was against the law because I didn't have a permit to carry. If I'd been caught, I could have gotten into big trouble. It is still against the law, and if I was caught carrying it now, I would still be in big trouble, and worse, it would reflect badly on Gabe."

"But you'd be alive."

It was hard to argue with that logic, skewed as it was.

"Please, just let me and Gabe handle this. Trust me, no one wants me safe more than he does."

"Why don't you come out to the ranch for a while, at least until this blows over?"

I turned to look at him. "Because I wouldn't be any safer there than here."

"Yes, you would because I'd put a load of buckshot into any jackass who was harassing my girl." His tanned face grew stubborn.

I went over and kissed his cheek. "I know you would, Daddy. But I have to stay here. Really, you have to trust me and Gabe on this." I turned back to the stove, filled his plate, and set it front of him. "Boysenberry or strawberry jam?"

"Strawberry."

I set the jam jar and butter dish on the table, poured myself a cup of coffee, and joined him. "Now that we have me settled, we have to figure out what to do about Dove and Isaac."

"Far as I'm concerned, they can both move out," he said, sprinkling Tabasco sauce over his eggs.

"You know you don't mean that. There must be a way to help them work this out."

"You figure one out, you let me know," he said, chewing a piece of bacon. "I've given up trying to make sense of your gramma and the bugs she gets in her craw years ago."

He'd finished breakfast and we were both walking out the front door when we saw Dove coming up the street from Elvia and Emory's house. The determined expression on her face, not to mention the newspaper in her hand, instantly made me feel like a teenager caught sneaking into the house after curfew.

"She kinda looks ready to chomp down on someone," he said, settling his Stetson firmly on his head.

"And I'll bet that someone is me," I said. "She probably just now saw yesterday's newspaper."

He turned, gave me a kiss on the forehead, and said, "Good luck, pumpkin. I think I'll head on back to the ranch. You be careful now, hear?"

"Yes, sir, I will."

"Mornin', Dove," he said, going down the steps, touching a finger to his hat brim.

"Mornin', son," she said. "I'll be staying with Emory and Elvia for a few days."

"So I heard."

"Water my kitchen plants. And don't forget to feed the chickens."

"Yes, ma'am."

I watched him walk toward his dusty white Ramsey ranch pickup, wishing I was going with him.

"I was just leaving for the museum," I said to Dove.

"We have to talk, young lady. They'll just have to wait for you."

"Yes, ma'am," I said meekly, sitting down on the porch swing and waiting for the coming lecture. She tossed the newspaper in my lap.

"Why didn't you tell me about this and why are you trying to hide it from me? If I hadn't taken out the trash this morning, I'd've never seen this."

"Gabe and I are taking care of it . . ." I started.

"What is going on and did you really think I wouldn't find out?" She flopped down next to me on the swing.

I sat back and started rocking, hoping it would soothe her ruffled feathers. "We knew you would. We just wanted to keep you from worrying as long as possible." Trying to keep the details as spare as I could, I explained about Gabe's confession about living here in 1978, the drug bust he was involved with, the possibility that someone was getting back at Gabe through harassing me.

"I'm coming to stay with you," she said.

"No, you're not. Anyone who is around me might be in danger."

"I can take care of myself. And you too, for that matter."

I took my gramma's hand. Its soft, thin skin made my heart ache. The thought of something happening to her frightened me more than anything that could happen to me. "Dove, I'm not going to argue with you. I arranged for you to stay with Emory and Elvia and that's where you're going to stay. You're close, but not in danger. Please don't fight me on this. I'm upset and worried enough."

She covered my hand with her other one and studied my face gravely. Only someone who knew me as well as she did could see how close I was to breaking down, in spite of my assurances to everyone that I was fine. "Okay, honeybun. I don't want to make things harder for you. I'll trust God and Gabe to take care of you for me."

"Thank you," I said.

"But I'll be keeping my eyes open," she said. "The guest room I'm in on the second floor has a direct shot to your house. I'll be over here in two seconds if I see something going down."

"Something going down?" I said, smiling. "I think you've been watching too much *NYPD Blue*."

"Never you mind, young lady. I know what's what and I can make those two blocks pretty darn fast with my shotgun if I had to."

"You have your shotgun with you?" I asked, wondering if Emory and Elvia knew about that.

"No, but I'm going out to the ranch to get it now that I know you need protecting."

I didn't try to talk her out of it, knowing that would be fruitless, but I was also not going to tell Gabe about it. "Now that we have *my* life and safety discussed, let's talk about your life. What are you going to do about Isaac?"

She stood up, patted me on the shoulder, and started down the porch steps. "That's none of your business. You be careful now, hear?"

"Hey," I called after her. "No fair. We dissect my life and you avoid yours?"

"Like I always say, 'fare' is something you pay to ride the bus," she called back to me, wiggling her fingers in good-bye. "See you later."

"She's going to drive me all the way to crazy town someday," I told Scout after I had closed and locked the front door and opened the truck door for him to jump in. He grumbled deep in his throat in reply.

At the folk art museum, there was no doubt that I'd be safe at least for a few hours. The place was a madhouse. I had to wedge Gabe's truck into a space between a red Honda and a tree stump at the very back of the lot, then weave my way through the cars and three small buses that filled the lot.

"What's going on?" I said to the silver-haired woman behind the gift shop counter, a new docent I only vaguely recognized. "I practically had to park in the Farm Supply's hay barn next door."

"A couple of impromptu tours," she said. "They were here from Bakersfield on a wine-tasting tour and one of the wineries suggested they come by and see the crazy quilt show." She smoothed down the side of her black San Celina Folk Art Museum T-shirt. "And two quilt guilds are using the big room to try and finish quilts to raffle off at the La Fiesta Mercado at Farmer's Market tomorrow night."

"I'll be in my office if anyone has any problems."

"Will do," she said cheerfully, turning to a customer, who asked to see one of the handmade patchwork dolls in the glass case behind her.

It took me fifteen minutes to finally reach my office since I had to greet and talk to both quilt guilds and admire the quilts they were stitching. One was a replica of the Frida Kahlo painting called "Fruits of the Soil" that was breathtaking in its attention to detail; the other was a Mexican Star quilt in red, green, and white, the colors of the Mexican flag. Both guilds were donating the profits from the raffled quilts to Los Niños Health Cooperative, which provided basic health care and medicine for migrant workers' families.

In my office, I first called Mrs. Rolly in San Miguel, who told me that, as I suspected, the information she'd given me was all she had on her mother's crazy quilt.

"I'm so sorry," she said. "We just never thought to ask any questions about quilts back then."

"It's okay, Mrs. Rolly. I was just double checking because some, uh, interested member of the historical society thought maybe I hadn't dug deep enough." I fiddled with the pencils in my pencil cup, irritated that I was having to waste Mrs. Rolly's time as well as my own.

"That Sissy Brownmiller," Mrs. Rolly said, laughing. "You just can't satisfy her. I swear, if she gets to heaven, she'll ask to see the upstairs."

I laughed along with her, but didn't verify that Sissy was the actual culprit. "The crazy quilt exhibit looks like it might be our most popular one yet. You should see how crowded the museum is today."

"I'll drop by next week when I come south. I have some quilted potholders and tea cozies to drop off at the gift shop."

"That's great. If business stays as bustling as it is now, the gift shop will need restocking soon."

My next phone calls to Mrs. Levy, Mrs. Espinoza, and Mrs. Michaelson were almost identical to Mrs. Rolly's. Except for a nice little anecdote by Mrs. Espinoza about her quilt being lost to the family for twenty years, only to be found again when one of her daughters spotted it wrapped around a refrigerator on the back of a pickup truck driving up Interstate 5 outside of Fresno, there was nothing else to report on the quilts.

My final phone call was supposed to be to Emma Baldwin. I had purposely saved it for last, because I was reluctant to take up her time. I remembered what she had said about it being hard to write when life interceded. I wasn't quite sure what she meant by that. Maybe people calling her disturbed her train of thought and she couldn't write. I had no idea what was involved with writing a novel, and even though we'd had lunch and she was so easy to talk to, I was still a little in awe of her and her profession. Like a lot of people, I was curious as to how a person took a blank sheet of paper and put letters and sentences together to create something that put images in my own mind. It seemed so miraculous and impossible to me—though I imagined it was something like making a quilt, which I had done many times, taking a pile of fabrics and cutting and rearranging the pieces into another form altogether. The truth was, with quilts you started

with something physical. With stories, you started with
nothing except a blank sheet of paper.

Remembering how I had struggled with my term papers in college, not to mention grant proposals now, I was
reluctant to disturb Emma unnecessarily. So I decided to
try and figure out as many of the dates as I could on my
own, then verify them with her and not take up as much
of her time. One way I could accomplish that was to compare the old photographs that I'd taken seventeen years
ago with the actual quilt.

It was a little after noon when I walked across the vine-
covered path connecting the artist studios to the museum.
A little jasmine had intermingled with the honeysuckle
and the air's sweet, flowery scent reminded me of my
ladies at Oakview Retirement Home, where I oversaw a
quilt guild meeting once a month. Since it was lunchtime,
the crowds had thinned, with only a few people wandering
through the exhibits and gift shop.

Emma's quilt was displayed in the center of the upstairs gallery along with her history and a copy of the
book cover the quilt had inspired. I held my old college
photograph of the quilt next to the original. I compared
the photograph to the quilt in sections, trying to spot any
additions. As far as I could see, there was only one—July
15, 1978.

I went back to my office, took out a lined legal pad,
and listed the dates, trying to discern what was what from
the conversations I had had with her and my old essay.

July 1, 1931. That was an easy one—her birthday. June
22, 1949. I chewed on the end of my pencil. That would
have made her eighteen years old. I remember her saying
she was eighteen when she met her husband, RJ. I wrote
down: *First came to San Celina or first met RJ or first
date?* I'd have to verify that one.

I settled back in my office chair. This was kind of fun.
Like piecing a puzzle together or cracking a code. August
17, 1949. I knew that one—her wedding day—because
she'd said she'd married in the summer right after she

met RJ. May 1, 1950. That had to be when her son, Cody, was born. A May Day baby. March 23, 1951. That sounded familiar. I checked my old essay. Her mother died back in Georgia. December 28, 1951. That was when RJ went to Korea. What did that feel like, watching your husband leave for a war halfway around the world knowing that you might not ever see him again? I couldn't even imagine.

August 1, 1953. That had to be when RJ came home from Korea. Then she must have been too busy with her life to work on the quilt because the next date was September 12, 1961. That one was in my essay. It was the day her first Molly Connors book was published. March 24, 1965. That one I knew—RJ's death. There weren't any dates again until June 14, 1968. That had to be her son's high school graduation.

The last date was July 15, 1978. The only date she'd added since I first saw the quilt when I was twenty. It was over three months after I'd interviewed her in April. Could that be the day that her son died? That would be a hard one to ask her and I dreaded doing it, not even certain if I should press for the date's meanings no matter what Sissy Brownmiller wanted for the historical society. There were no more dates embroidered into the quilt after July 15. Was it because she felt as if, when her son died, her family's life had essentially ended, that her family history was complete? I was certain she'd eventually add her cousin's death. Had nothing significant happened to her in the seventeen years between her son's and her cousin's deaths?

I chewed on my pencil for a good half hour trying to decide whether I should call Emma and ask her about the dates in question. To some degree, I understood what Sissy Brownmiller asserted, that if we don't find out all the historical details about quilts when the people who made them are alive, then the stories will be lost forever. These stories would be very important to a future historian. Too many women's histories had been lost simply because those in charge and often the women themselves did not consider the milestones of their lives worth recording.

I decided to call our hall of records here in San Celina. A friend of mine from school, Denise, worked as a supervisor. If Cody had died here in San Celina, it would be recorded.

It took me only fifteen minutes to find out that Cody's death was not recorded in this county. Wherever he died, it wasn't here in San Celina. I glanced over at my computer. If I had the time, I could get on the Internet and start researching. But I didn't. It really would be easier just to ask Emma . . . or better yet, tell Sissy to mind her own dang business. I knew, though, if I didn't somehow find out about this date, Sissy wouldn't hesitate confronting Emma, most likely in front of people. I wanted to save Emma any more embarrassment or heartache.

My stomach rumbled and I glanced over at the clock on my wall. It was almost two-thirty P.M. I could either make the phone call to Emma before I went to lunch or have it hang over my head all through my meal. The phone rang just as I was reaching for it.

"Benni?" Emma Baldwin said.

"Oh," I said, shocked at the coincidence. "I was just going to . . . Oh, hi. I mean, yes, this is me."

"I'm sorry, did I catch you at a busy time?"

"No, no, not at all," I stuttered. Hearing her voice definitely threw me for a loop. "What's up?"

"I have a dentist appointment today in San Celina and I thought since I was in town we could possibly get together for coffee and maybe you could give me that tour of the folk art museum."

This was too good to be true. Actually standing in front of the quilt would give me just the opening I needed to broach the question of the quilt's embroidered dates.

"Absolutely. I was just getting ready to go into town myself for a late lunch. Have you eaten yet? Would you like to join me?"

"Thank you, no. I've eaten already. My appointment is at three o'clock. What do you say I meet you at the museum between four and four-thirty? I'm just having my teeth cleaned so it shouldn't take longer than an hour."

"Sounds perfect. I'll see you there."

I sat back in my chair, relieved at my unexpected good fortune. I wouldn't have to worry about interrupting her writing now, and there certainly was some tactful way to find out about that last date. After informing D-Daddy, who'd be there working all day on the temperamental plumbing in the co-op's kitchen, that I'd be back about four o'clock, I headed to Liddie's. My favorite booth was free and my clam chowder and sourdough roll had just arrived when a familiar, but unwelcome voice called my name.

"Benni Harper," Sissy Brownmiller yelled from two booths over. "Did you call those quilters?"

I contemplated ignoring her, but half the customers in the restaurant turned their heads to hear my answer. If I didn't, she'd keep screeching like a owl going after a three-legged field mouse. Feeling as helpless as that struggling mouse, I took a quick bite of my buttered roll and slid out of the booth.

"Yes, I called the quilters," I said, standing in front of her table. She sat with two women I recognized by sight from historical society meetings. "I filled in the histories as much as they knew."

"What about Emma Baldwin's?" she said eagerly.

Engaging my tongue before my brain, something I'd yet to conquer, I said, "Don't worry about that. I'm meeting her at the museum . . ."

Dang, what made me say that?

"When?" she asked. Her round, sparsely lashed eyes glittered with anticipation.

Would it be okay to tell a small lie if I was protecting Emma from Sissy's predatory clutches?

"Four, uh . . . thirty," I said weakly, my lie just the palest of eggshell white. "But she and I—"

"I'll just drop by and say hello then," she said, dabbing at her pursed mouth with her napkin.

"She's only going to be there a little while," I said curtly, trying to grab back some kind of control. "She's a very busy woman."

"I *just* want to say hello," Sissy said, frowning at me. "You know, we met at her signing and I invited her to a historical society meeting. She and I had quite the connection, I think."

"I'm sure you did," I said, thinking the current only flowed one way on those wires, honey.

"You know, I did quite a bit of personal fund raising to get the money for that exhibit." Her pinkish, rabbity nose twitched in irritation.

"Yes, Sissy, I know," I said, wishing I could just go back to my table and jump into my bowl of clam chowder. Or better yet, throw Sissy Brownmiller into it. I painted a crazy, but enjoyable picture in my mind of her floating in a white ocean of chowder, clinging to a bobbing oyster cracker.

"I'll just drop by around four-thirty then," she said, picking up her tuna melt. "I'm sure Emma will be glad to see me."

I murmured a noncommittal sound. Back at my cooling soup, I fumed at myself for allowing her to manipulate the situation like she did. More and more often these days I wished I'd never accepted the job at the folk art museum. If I went back to work for Daddy, I'd have only him and a couple hundred cattle to worry about pleasing.

I tore another piece of my roll off and chewed it. Then again, did I really want to be out at the ranch dealing with Daddy, Dove, and Isaac? Not that living in town had made it impossible to draw me into their dramas, but at least I had a good distance between us.

I was halfway through my chowder when Isaac walked by the window carrying a small aqua shopping bag. He saw me, held up his hand, and mouthed: *Don't leave.* He hurried around the corner and came through Liddie's empty lobby, only briefly acknowledging Nadine as he propelled himself toward me like a pelican diving for mackerel.

"Just the woman I've been looking for," he said, sliding into the bench seat across from me. "I need your advice."

"I have no opinion about anything," I said, pushing my soup aside even though I was still hungry. It didn't look like my peaceful lunch was going to happen today.

"Look at these and tell me which one Dove would like better." He pulled two jewelry boxes out of the aqua Tiffany's bag.

"How'd you get something at Tiffany's?" I said. I didn't even know where the nearest one was . . . Los Angeles, San Francisco?

"I have an account with them. Had them sent FedEx from the New York store." He pushed the two dark blue velvet boxes toward me. "Which one will lure her back home?"

I opened one—it was a heart of diamonds dangling from a delicate platinum chain. The second box held a platinum dinner ring—a deep ocean blue sapphire surrounded by blue-tinged diamonds.

"Oh," I said, a bit overwhelmed.

"The necklace?" he said, his voice desperate. "The ring? Both? I can give her both. What do you think? Both? Should I give her both?" His dark raisin eyes pleaded with me.

Taking one last look, I closed both boxes and pushed them back across the table.

"Well?" he said.

I hesitated, then gave him the bad news. "Neither."

The weathered creases on his face seemed to deepen. "Neither?" he said in a low, agonized voice.

I reached over and took his huge, wide-fingered hand in both of mine. Feeling his large, slightly arthritic knuckles, I realized in that moment how much he'd come to mean to me, how much I'd taken this big, white-haired, earring-wearing, ponytailed man into my heart.

"Isaac, you know jewelry isn't the way back into Dove's heart. You *know* that."

"It's always worked before."

I smiled. "There just ain't no before when it comes to my gramma. Let me ask you something. Were your other wives married before they married you?"

He nodded. "Except for my first wife, Lilith. We were only twenty when we married."

"Were any of them widows?"

He shook his head no. "No, they were all divorced, like me."

"Okay, here's the deal. Dove's not like your other wives. She was widowed in 1962. As far as I know, she didn't even look twice at another man until you came into her life thirty-three years later. Think about that. Maybe this relationship is just a little bit more of an emotional risk for her than you."

His face grew stubborn and I held up my hand before he could argue. "I'm not saying she loves you more than you love her. I'm just asking you to consider what a change this is for her. All her dreams, expectations, pent-up emotions are centered around you. You've been married five times. No offense, Pops, but this isn't all that different for you. It's a whole new world for her." I rubbed his hand, feeling the rough hair against my palm. "Give her some time and space. She's going to come back, I promise. She's just feeling a little . . . unsafe at the moment."

He inhaled deeply, then smiled at me, his old face relaxing a little. "Okay, kiddo, you're right and I should have known all that. So what exactly do I need to do to make her feel safe?"

I let go of his hand and pointed at the velvet boxes. "Don't treat her like any of the others. Remember, she waited for you for thirty-three years. That makes her pretty special, if you want my opinion."

"You are a living doll. I'll do it."

I laughed. "Do what?"

He beamed at me. "I have no idea yet, but it's going to be spectacular."

After we parted ways in the parking lot, I started back toward the museum discussing the whole problem of Sissy Brownmiller with Scout, who, like all good dogs, agreed with everything I said.

"You know, I shouldn't let her push me around like that. When am I going to learn? Why do I lot people like her get away with the things like that? Where is my backbone? You want to find it for me? Somebody obviously buried it. Go find me my backbone, Scout. Right now."

Scout grumbled in the back of his throat, then barked once when I let my voice go high and silly at the end of my sentence.

"Scooby-Doo, I really think you should bite her the next time you see her. Just bite her in her skinny leg and send her packing. You want to do that for me, boy?"

He whined in reply.

"Good dog," I said, pulling into the museum's parking lot at about five after four. "You're the best." Emma's car was already parked in the middle of the parking lot, almost empty now with only two remaining cars, probably artists working in the back. Emma had obviously arrived when the parking lot was more crowded. The museum's off-season hours were nine A.M. to four P.M. Tuesdays through Fridays so, by now, the docents had already left. Even D-Daddy's gray pickup truck was gone. Until Sissy arrived at four-thirty, and I was praying for a huge traffic jam to delay her, I would have time alone with Emma.

Emma sat in the small lobby on one of the two bent-willow chairs next to the double doors. She stood up when I walked in. She was dressed in a loose black dress and red canvas espadrilles. Her silvery hair glinted in the lobby's fluorescent light.

"I'm so sorry I'm late," I said. "I hope you weren't waiting long." "Scooby-Doo, go lie down." He trotted over and flopped down on the red tiles.

"No worry, I've had a fine time seeing the exhibit at my leisure, though I'm anxious to hear more about each quilt. Your nice handyman, the French gentleman, told me I could wait here when I was through."

"That's D-Daddy Boudreaux. He keeps this place from falling around our ears."

"He was very accommodating and personable."

"Not to mention quite the looker," I said, grinning. "I've not had a bit of trouble recruiting docents from the senior center since he started working here."

She gave a cheery laugh. "I don't imagine you have."

I turned to lock the museum's double doors behind me and said, "We can safely put our purses right here behind the counter."

"Wonderful," she said, setting her black leather hand-bag on the credenza behind the counter.

I started the tour with the California quilts from our sister museum in Sacramento. Though I could tell she appreciated the work that went into the quilts, she was much more interested in the stories behind them. Considering her literary background, that wasn't surprising.

"Such a shame that some of the histories are lost," she said as we contemplated a Star of Bethlehem quilt dated between 1830 to 1850. The radiating diamonds were made of brown, yellow, pink, and blue tiny print calico fabric with appliqued pomegranates in all four corners and a finely sewn sawtooth border. The artistic skill and talent of the quilter was obvious throughout the square quilt. "Look at this. All we know is the name of the quilt owner's grandfather and that the quilt was made by some-one in the family. What a shame that this woman will never get the credit for something that has endured so long."

I almost couldn't contain myself. "Emma, I'm so glad you brought that subject up. I couldn't agree with you more. So I was wondering . . ." But before I could finish, a pounding at the door interrupted me. Scout jumped up and started barking. His tail was standing straight out and not wagging.

"Stay here," I told Emma, walking across the museum toward the door. I felt in my pocket for my pepper spray. "Who's there?" I called through the door.

"Benni Harper! Why is this door locked? Benni Harper? Are you in there?" Sissy Brownmiller's reedy voice pierced the hacienda's thick wood doors like a flaming arrow.

"It's okay, Scout," I said, unlocking and swinging the door open to reveal a red-faced Sissy in a loose navy dress, her gray, shoulder-length hair a bit messy. "Friend," I reluctantly added only so he would stop barking.

"Will that beast bite?" she asked, looking down at Scout, whose tail was now waving back and forth in a friendly manner. Her strong flowery scent seemed to burn the back of my throat.

"Not unless I tell him to," I said in a tone as sweet as her perfume.

"Don't we have rules about allowing animals in the museum?" she said in a nasty tone, her sloped, pump-handle nose quivering in distaste. Obviously not a dog person.

"He's my helper dog," I said through clenched back teeth. That wasn't an actual lie. Scout was extremely well trained and he helped me a lot.

She gave him a suspicious look, but didn't press it. "Is Emma here yet?" she asked, stepping over the threshold. She looked over my shoulder and her face lit up.

I turned and watched Emma walk in from the main exhibit room.

"Well, hello . . ." she said to Sissy, then paused for a moment, her eyes narrowing slightly as if she were trying to remember something. "Didn't we meet . . . ?"

"At Blind Harry's," Sissy said, pushing me aside and moving toward Emma. "I'm Sissy Brownmiller. We talked about the historical society."

Emma's face relaxed. "Oh, yes, I remember." Then she

looked confused again. "Why are you here?"

"Benni invited me," Sissy said, not even looking at me.

My hands tightened into fists at the blatant lie. "Actually, I—"

Sissy spoke over me as if I wasn't there. "I haven't seen the exhibit myself and I'm dying to see your quilt. Tell me, have you thought about my idea about incorporating that story about my father into your new book? I distinctly remember him being there when your poor husband was killed. He told me and Mother all about the tragedy. She and I didn't care much for rodeos. I still don't. So smelly and dusty. Not to mention the beer drinkers. And what about the year I was Strawberry Queen?" She gave a huge sigh. "Nineteen forty-one. Now that was a year to remember. Our country ruled the world back then."

So that was her intention. Sissy was trying to wrangle her way into Emma's memoir. Sissy's father, Dr. Brownmiller, had been one of San Celina's most revered citizens until he died twelve years ago at the age of ninety-six. When he retired at seventy-nine, it was on record that he'd delivered a good quarter of the citizens "of a certain age" walking the streets of San Celina. He'd been loved by at least as many people as tried to avoid his only daughter.

"Well, I . . ." Emma said, looking at me in desperation. "I haven't really decided what to include . . ."

"Let's continue the tour," I said, rescuing her. "Unfortunately, I only have about an hour because I have a dinner date."

"Oh, certainly, we mustn't take up too much of your time," Emma said, standing aside so Sissy could walk ahead of her. "After you, Sissy." When Sissy's back was to us, she mouthed *Thank you* to me.

I gave her a palms-up apology, hoping she understood that Sissy had invited herself.

As I tried to make it through the rest of my rehearsed tour of the California quilts as well as the crazy quilts, Sissy kept up a constant monologue about her own quilting experiences and family history. With each crazy quilt, Sissy had some remark or piece of gossip about the local quilter and her family. By the time we had reached Emma's quilt, which I'd purposely saved for last hoping that somehow Sissy, like Zechariah in the Bible, would be struck completely dumb, she was in supersonic mode.

"Emma," she said. "I cannot tell you how much I dearly love this quilt. It is just exquisite and what an addition to the annals of San Celina history! As a matter of fact, though it took some doing on my part, if you don't mind me tooting my own horn, I managed to convince the advertising committee to consider your quilt as the cover photo for our next historical society book—*A Century of San Celina Arts.* That's not the final title, of course. We're trying to come up with something more catchy, but your quilt on the cover would just be so appropriate, what with you being one of our most famous citizens. And of course, we're so excited at the historical museum for the chance to write about it. We'll devote a whole article to the wonderful story of the quilt and your wonderful life and wonderful accomplishments. Why, it will just be—"

"Wonderful?" I supplied.

Emma's eyes twinkled in amusement, a smile tugging at her lips.

Sissy turned to look down at me. "Well, Benni, yes, it would. You young people and all your nasty rapping music and comic books and MTV don't understand that there has been and is a real art world here in San Celina. Not that crazy stuff you call art."

I stared at her for a moment, tempted to burst out laughing. No doubt there was nothing I could do to convince Sissy Brownmiller that, at thirty-seven, I was definitely not in the rap music, comic book, MTV crowd. I imagined she lumped everyone under the age of sixty-five into the category of "young people." I couldn't hold back a small chuckle.

"What's so funny?" she snapped.

"I'm sorry," I said, holding up my hand in apology and trying to cover my indiscretion. "What was it you were saying about rap music? I was thinking of something Gabe said to me this morning."

She gave me another suspicious look. Fortunately for me, Sissy didn't like to stay off her favorite subject—herself—for very long. She turned back to Emma. "Of course, we'll need much more information about your life than what Benni has so skimpily provided."

Emma's obviously distressed expression was the only thing that kept me from snapping at Sissy.

"What do you mean?" Emma asked. Her voice seemed to flutter.

"We need much more than is here if we're going to feature it in our book and, did I forget to mention, our new brochure? For example, we absolutely need an explanation for every date embroidered on the quilt, which Benni was supposed to ask you about but apparently hasn't."

"For cryin' out loud, Sissy," I said. "You just asked me last night! I was going to call Emma and then she decided to come by the museum . . ."

"Whatever," Sissy said, brushing my explanation away with a flip of her spindly hand. "So, Emma, what do all the dates correspond to? Benni, do you have some paper? Write these down."

Emma's face blanched and her eyes blinked rapidly at Sissy's aggressive assault. "Well, I . . . they are personal dates that mean . . . I . . ."

That did it. I grabbed Sissy's upper arm firmly and said, "Sissy, I'm afraid that this tour is over. Emma and I will get back to you with the information you need but right now I must insist on closing the museum. Gabe is waiting for me."

Sissy stared at me as shocked as if I'd spit in her face. "It will only take a few minutes . . ."

"We don't have the time," I said, pulling her toward the door. Emma stood there watching us, her face frozen

with some emotion—shock, fear? Whatever it was, Sissy
had brought it on and I wasn't going to let her bully
Emma or me any longer.

Though her sputtered protests were almost taking
chinks out of the adobe, I pulled Sissy to the door and
out on the front porch. Dark clouds had moved in during
the time we were inside. The craggy hills surrounding San
Celina were slashed with shadows and the air was cold
as well water. The sky had turned a deep plum color, and
in the eucalyptus trees that lined the parking lot, birds
chirped and chattered the way they do right before it rains.
They reminded me of Sissy's voice.

"Let—go—of—my—arm," she said, jerking it out of
my grasp. "What is wrong with you, Benni Harper? I
swear, Dove never did discipline you properly. You do
not treat your elders with one ounce of respect."

"Sissy, I treat *everyone* with the respect they earn. I'll
get you the information you're asking for if and when
Emma decides to give it. Until then, I must ask you to,
please, leave her alone."

Her nose went up and red roses bloomed on her deeply
lined cheekbones. "And who appointed you her personal
guardian? You know, Constance will be hearing about
your insolence, young lady. I think you've let your position go to your head." She started walking toward her
car, which was parked next to Emma's. "You young people today . . ."

Before she started another rant about the foibles of today's youth, I heard a sharp *crack*. In a split second I
knew what it was. Without thinking, I made a flying leap
and tackled Sissy.

A surprised quack came from her throat. We hit the
gravel with a hard thump. My heart pounded like a kettle
drum.

Another *crack*. The sound of a car engine. I lifted my
head in time to see the taillights of a white car.

In the next second, Emma came running out of the
museum. "I heard a noise! Are you both all right?"

"Get back inside," I yelled. "Call 911. Tell them there's a shooter at the museum."

By the time I helped a trembling Sissy up and into the museum, a couple of artists had run in from the studios in back.

"What happened?" asked Will, a duck decoy carver. "I heard gunshots." He'd been a deputy sheriff near Bakersfield in Kern County for twenty years before retiring to the Central Coast. He'd know the sound of gunshots. Behind him was two other carvers, both retired men in their early sixties.

"Someone tried to shoot me!" Sissy said. "I swear, ever since those city people started moving into San Celina County, it has turned into a ghetto."

"Oh, my dear, let me help you," Emma said, brushing the gravel off the front of Sissy's navy blue dress. "Are you hurt?"

"Except for the fact that Benni probably broke a dozen bones in my body, I don't think so," Sissy said, putting a shaky hand up to her mouth.

Before I could point out that there was a good possibility I had saved her life, two San Celina police officers called out, "Police!"

"Come on in," I called back. "It's Benni Harper. The shooter's gone."

"Hey, Benni," said the willowy, dark-haired woman who entered the lobby first, reholstering her pistol when she stepped over the threshold.

I nodded at her. "Hi, Pam. Glad you're here."

Pam Munns, one of Gabe's most experienced street cops, had moved to San Celina from Fresno, where she'd worked the street gang detail for ten years. Her partner today was about ten years younger than her thirty-six years. He was a handsome Hispanic man with hands the size of Frisbees and a skull-baring Marine haircut. "Everyone okay? Dispatcher called and said there were shots fired."

We all murmured that we were fine.

"Good. This is my partner, Juan Rodriguez. Juan, this is Benni, the chief's wife."

I nodded at his unsmiling face. "Hey, Juan."

"What happened?" Pam asked me. Her even, All-American-girl features were neutral.

"Everything okay?" a deep male voice called from the door. Another two San Celina officers walked in.

"Yes," Pam told them. "Shooter's gone. I was just getting a statement from Ms. Harper here. Maybe you can check up and down the street and see if any of the other businesses saw or heard anything. Call dispatch and tell them no more officers need to respond."

The two officers nodded and walked back out.

She turned back to me and raised her neat eyebrows. "Sorry."

"No problem. I was walking Mrs. Brownmiller out to her car and—"

"And I was almost killed by a drive-by assassin," Sissy interrupted. "And just exactly what are you going to do about it? I am a tax-paying citizen of this county and I am outraged . . ."

Pam, the calmest, most easygoing cop I'd ever met, held up her hand for Sissy to stop talking, but softened the firm gesture with a wide, attractive smile. "Ma'am, I'm going to let you tell me your story in just a minute. But I need to hear from Ms. Harper first." She turned back to me, winked, and told me to continue.

I tried not to grin at her. "Like I was saying, I was walking Mrs. Brownmiller out to her car and I heard a pop. I pushed her to the ground—"

"And ruined my hose," Sissy interrupted. "And they were a pair of my good support hose too. They're not cheap, you know."

"And," I continued, trying not to turn and glare at her, "when we hit the ground, there was a second shot. I glanced up in time see the taillights of a car."

"Definitely a car?" Pam asked.

"Yes and it was white. That's all I could see from the

distance we were from it. It never pulled into the parking lot. It was out on the street."

Pam's mouth straightened out and she shook her head, gripping the nightstick at her side. "Too bad you didn't at least get a partial plate."

"Sorry, that would have taken the eyes of an eagle."

"No matter. Just glad you're okay. Any ideas who it might be?"

"Crazy city people," Sissy muttered.

"Well," I said, glancing over at Emma, Sissy, and the three woodcarvers. "You know, I think you'd better talk to Gabe about this."

Pam's eyebrows went up slightly, picking up on my cue that there was more to this than I wanted to talk about in front of everyone.

"Juan," she said. "Take statements from Mrs. Brown-miller and the rest of the folks here while Benni shows me outside exactly what happened."

"Sure," he said and pulled out a notebook.

Pam closed the museum doors behind us and gestured at me to follow her out to where their patrol car sat behind Sissy's sky-blue Ford Taurus. She leaned up against the patrol car and I joined her. The storm clouds had blocked the setting sun, causing an early dusk and the museum's automatic security light to come on, illuminating us like targets. I glanced out at the road, where an occasional car drove by. Surely this person wouldn't try anything with a cop car out here? Probably not, but I still felt rather like a sitting duck. The flashing of her patrol car's red and blue lights soothed me somewhat.

Pam glanced up at the clouds. "Looks like we're in for some rain."

"Yep," I said, suddenly feeling so shaky I almost couldn't stand. The adrenaline that had powered me minutes before was starting to dissipate. I leaned against the side of her blue-and-white cop car.

She folded her arms across her chest and lifted one

shapely eyebrow. "Okay, Benni, what's really going down here?"

I explained to her about my stalker and the possibility that this might be him.

She jerked her head over at the museum. "No chance that it might be someone who just wants to silence Mrs. Motormouth in there?"

I gave a small smile. "It's possible, I suppose. But as irritating as Sissy Brownmiller can be, I doubt that someone would take out a hit on her." Above us, a flock of birds burst out of the eucalyptus trees, taking flight over the museum's tile roof. I gave a quick startled laugh, then glanced at the highway again.

"Don't worry," Pam said. "He probably won't be back to bother you tonight."

"Not here anyway," I said.

She lifted one eyebrow. "You really think it was your stalker?"

I stared down at the toes of my good black boots. The left toe had been scuffed when I tackled Sissy. No amount of polish would repair the torn leather. I looked back up into Pam's concerned face. "I can't imagine why else someone would be taking potshots at the museum. And it was pretty obvious that the person was waiting for someone to come out before firing."

At that moment, Gabe's Corvette screeched into the parking lot, the portable flashing light attached to the roof of the car. He jumped out and ran over to me.

"What happened?" he asked, his hands gripping my shoulders.

"Someone took a potshot at me and Sissy Brownmiller," I said.

He stared down at my face a moment, his eyes narrowing in anger. "Tell me exactly what happened."

I told my story again.

"Where were you standing?" he asked.

I showed him where on the porch I was when the first shot happened.

"Where was the car?"

I pointed to the spot on the highway, right in front of the museum's driveway. He walked out there, looked back at Pam and me next to her police car, then came back.

"What?" I asked.

His hand rested protectively on the small of my back. "Let's go back inside," he said, nodding at the museum's front door. "I want to talk to everyone involved."

Once inside, I introduced him to Emma Baldwin and stepped aside while he questioned both her and Sissy Brownmiller. Sissy followed his every movement and utterance with the intensity of a cobra. She'd had a crush on Gabe from the moment she first met him at a historical museum fund-raiser.

"What are you going to do about this, Chief Ortiz?" she said in a voice that managed to be both flirtatious and demanding.

"I'll make sure my officers follow you home, Mrs. Brownmiller," he said in his most soothing, politician's voice. He turned to Emma. "And you too, Mrs. Baldwin."

"Thank you," she said, her voice subdued. "But I live all the way in Paso Robles."

"No problem," he said. "Let me just make a phone call." He pulled out his cell phone and called dispatch asking for another patrol car. "Ladies, we'll look into this, but I believe this was just a random act that most likely won't be repeated."

"I would hope not," Sissy said. "Why, we are taxpaying citizens who have lived here for years and we expect—"

Before she could start on another rampage, Gabe placed a gentle hand on her shoulder and said, "Mrs. Brownmiller, you are absolutely right and I'll personally get on this right away."

Her finely etched face softened in satisfaction, like a dog who'd buried a particularly special bone, and she allowed Pam and her partner to escort her out to her car. In a few minutes, another patrol car arrived and Gabe instructed them to follow Emma Baldwin home and make sure she arrived safely. This, I knew, was way beyond the call of duty and that Gabe was doing it to make me and the ladies feel better.

"Will you be okay out there alone?" I asked Emma as I walked her out to her car. Her face was still pale and her hands shaky when I helped her into her small white car.

"Yes, I'll be fine. I'm not completely alone. Lou lives in the bunkhouse and we keep a loaded shotgun handy."

"Good," I said. "And of course, there's Master Plug the bad guys would have to get past."

That made her smile. "Dear, sweet Plug. The heart of a lion . . ."

"The body of a frankfurter," I finished.

After Emma and Sissy had left, I locked up, then turned to Gabe and said in a light voice, trying to keep the tremble out of it, "So, Chief Ortiz, do I get an official police escort home too?"

He pulled me into his arms and laid his cheek on the top of my head. "*Querida,* you get a police escort all the way to your bed."

CHAPTER 16

❖

April 6, 1978
Thursday

$\mathcal{T}$HURSDAY MORNING WHILE EATING HIS CORNFLAKES, Jack said, "You won't believe what Wade told me about the Malcom ranch while were were doing chores."

"What?" I said while packing a grocery bag full of the extra bags of sugar, flour, and spices that I'd bought yesterday. Today Elvia and I were helping her mother make *pan dulce* to sell at the Mission Ladies Altar Society booth at Farmer's Market tonight. Señora Aragon was in charge of sweet breads and had finagled me and Elvia into helping her.

"John Simpson called Wade this morning. Last night the sheriff found almost an acre of marijuana plants out over by Lion Flats. That's only a little ways from Sweetheart Hill. Wonder what your dad's thinking."

"I wonder if he knows."

"You can bet he does thanks to the good old ranchers' grapevine." He took another spoonful of cereal and chewed it, a thoughtful expression on his face. "Kind of makes you wonder about who's growing it, doesn't it? That was obviously their stuff we found the other day.

You know, that land's pretty hard to get to."

I shrugged, contemplated what I'd packed into the gro-
cery sack, then added another five-pound bag of sugar.
Better too much than not enough. "I bet those three guys
I told to get lost at Sweetheart Hill yesterday are con-
nected with it. I can't believe one of them was Emma
Baldwin's son. I wonder if she knows."

"If he was one of the guys caught, she sure does by
now. I'll also bet my last dollar that other locals are involved too. Probably ranchers."

I looked up from my bag of groceries. "No way."

Jack lifted his eyebrows. "I can think of a few ranchers
I'd suspect. People are getting pretty desperate, would do
about anything to save their land."

I folded the top of the paper sack over. "That's terrible.
I'd rather lose our ranch than sell drugs to keep it going."

"I agree, babe, but I'm saying that there's others who
would do anything to keep theirs. I think we'd better
spend some time riding around on both ranches and making sure it's not happening on our property." His mouth
straightened out into a grim line. "And just hope my own
brother isn't involved."

"Jack!" I said, shocked. "How could you say that about
Wade?"

His bottom lip grew stubborn. "Because it's true. He'd
do anything to make this ranch succeed."

I shook my head. "I don't believe that."

He stood up and came over to me, kissing me on the
forehead. "That's because, Blondie, you're too trusting
and innocent."

"I am not!"

He hugged me, chuckling under his breath. His denim
workshirt smelled of clean detergent and warm sunshine.
Underneath was the faint scent of Old Spice and sharp
clove. "Yeah, you are, but that's okay, you just stay that
way. I'll be the cynical one in the family. Will you still
let this old cynic crawl into bed with you tonight?"

"Yes," I said, burrowing my face into his hard chest.

"But you're wrong. I don't want to believe that anyone we know would willingly sell drugs, not even to save their land." But deep inside, I knew what he said was probably true.

"I sure hope I am wrong."

"You know," I said, listening to the strong beat of his young heart. "The one thing I've always felt on our land is safe. I hate it that something like this can affect how I feel. Things are changing too fast. Why can't things just stay the same?"

"Because life just doesn't, babe."

"Well, I don't like it."

He hugged me hard. "Neither do I, but the truth is, we don't have much choice in the matter."

CHAPTER 17

❖

April 20, 1995
Thursday

*A*FTER HIS INITIAL QUESTIONING OF ME, GABE deliberately refused to talk about what happened at the museum or about the stalker for the rest of the night.

"You're safe right now," he said. "And there's nothing we can do at this moment, so psychologically, I think it's best if we act like this is a normal evening."

"Okay," I said, knowing he was right, that if I kept talking about it and speculating on possible scenarios, it would make both of us only more agitated and jumpy. Though I was tempted to ask about the investigation of Luke's homicide, I held back. We'd discussed enough stressful subjects for one night. If he'd found out anything big, I was sure Gabe would tell me. At least, I hoped he would.

We ate dinner, watched some television, and went to bed about ten P.M. I had a big day tomorrow because I was getting up at six A.M. to go with Elvia to her mother's house to bake *pan dulce* for the Mission Ladies Altar Society booth at Farmer's Market that night. It was something that we did every year and I looked forward to the day spent in Señora Aragon's red-and-gray chile-scented kitchen.

The constant activity in the Aragon household hadn't changed much since I was a girl despite the fact that of their seven children, only their youngest, Ramon, still lived at home. Elvia often told me that I wouldn't have found the abundance of human beings so charming if I'd grown up fighting for my fair share of hot water for a shower or the last burrito in the refrigerator.

But at four-thirty, long before the alarm went off, something woke me. A sound, a fragment of a dream, the wind rattling our bedroom windows. My eyes flew open and I lay there, Gabe's arm thrown protectively over my chest, trying to stop myself from trembling. Holding my breath and listening, all I heard was the pepper tree branch scratch against the window, Gabe's even breathing next to me, and Scout's soft, doggy snuffling in his cedar bed. Whatever disturbed my sleep was obviously internal or Scout and Gabe, both light sleepers, would have awakened.

I lay underneath the warm down comforter and tried to retrieve whatever vestige of thought or dream had startled me awake. I replayed the shooting in my mind, pictured myself going outside, hearing the first crack, tackling Sissy, the sound of her squawk, the tangling of her thin bones and my more solid frame. Something bothered me about the situation, but I couldn't put my finger on it.

The car had been so far away, the museum parking lot lit only by one security light. Had it even come on yet? I couldn't remember. It was dusk, the sun down behind the hills surrounding San Celina, but the sky not quite black, more a hazy purple-blue. How well could the shooter have seen me and Sissy? And the nagging thought that the first shot was at her. Granted, I was on the porch, but partially obscured, I was certain, by one of the hacienda's heavy posts.

I sat up, too awake now by my troubling thoughts to fall back to sleep.

"*Querida,* what is it?" Gabe said in a groggy voice, reaching his hand under the covers to touch my bare thigh, assuring himself I was still there.

"Nothing," I whispered. "Go back to sleep. I'm going downstairs to get a glass of water."

Satisfied I was okay, he murmured some incomprehensible reply and burrowed back under the comforter. I crawled out from the warm covers, quickly pulled on thick sweatpants and a sweatshirt, and went downstairs. Scout, ever vigilant, woke up when I climbed out of bed and followed me downstairs.

While he munched on a dog cookie, I watched coffee drip into the pot, trying to wrap my sluggish brain around the thought that hovered at the edges of my consciousness. Something, something . . .

Then it occurred to me. Their dresses.

If someone had been watching, they would have seen Emma and me both enter the museum. Emma and Sissy were almost the same height, had similar color and style of hair. Although ten years apart in age, that wasn't something obvious from the street. And yesterday they wore similar plain, sacklike dresses though one was black, the other navy blue. Something that could easily be mistaken from a distance.

Then I remembered Emma's close call in Paso Robles the other day. A white car almost missed her. Was it the same car? Could it have been on purpose?

Maybe I wasn't the target.

Emma's pale, frightened face came back to me. Could the shooter have thought Sissy was Emma? And an even bigger question, why would this person want to shoot Emma? Her panicked look when Sissy was insisting they needed to know what every date stood for on her quilt. Were there dates on there that corresponded to things that weren't necessarily happy events? Things in her life that might come back to haunt her? I wondered about her son's and her husband's deaths. Was there anything suspicious about either?

I poured myself a cup of coffee, not even taking the time to put in milk and sugar. After one cup of straight caffeine, my mind really started moving. What did I really know about Emma Baldwin? I knew I had loved her books as a child, that she owned a ranch in Paso Robles, and that she had a few mysterious holes in her background.

I poured myself a second cup, shaking my head at my vivid imagination. Still, it was something I should tell Gabe, wasn't it? After a few minutes, when I decided to present my cock-eyed theory to Gabe, I formulated a plan. Baking powder biscuits and bacon gravy were one of Gabe's guilty pleasures, and if I was going to lay my wild early-morning thoughts on him, it might go down better with a hot, flaky biscuit smothered in peppery homemade gravy.

Hearing a car drive by on the street, I cautiously peeked through the blinds covering my kitchen window, half expecting to see a face staring back at me. Whoever this stalker was, he was making me angry that in such a short time he could rob me of even the small freedom of pulling up my kitchen blinds without a thought.

Across the street at the twins' house I could see Beebs in a pale blue quilted housecoat moving around in their brightly lit kitchen. Either they were very early risers or I was obviously not the only one with insomnia. She was talking at the floor, to one of their three cats, I guessed. Millee came into the room wearing a red-and-gold housecoat. She held up some clothing, something that appeared to have fringe. I narrowed my eyes, trying to see it better. They must have decided on their costumes for the Cattleman's Ball. Only two more days until the ball and Gabe and I still didn't have appropriately dressy Western wear. I'd better start working on that today.

At five-thirty, just as the oven timer went off and I'd finished frying the bacon to add to the gravy, Gabe am-bled into the kitchen. Without speaking, he poured himself a cup of coffee and sat down at the pine kitchen table. His sleep-grumpy face brightened when he saw me take out the pan of biscuits.

"Why did you get up so early?" he asked.

I shrugged and turned back to the frying pan where I was making bacon gravy to pour over the biscuits. "Bad dreams, I guess."

I could sense his eyes scrutinizing my back.

"What do you have cooking, Benni?" he said, his voice suspicious.

I didn't turn around. "Biscuits and gravy."

His chair scraped against the tile floor and I felt him come up behind me. He slipped his hands under my sweatshirt and pulled me up against him. His large hands felt comforting against my bare skin, his solid chest even more so against my cold back. "Very funny," he said.

"You're darn lucky your hands are warm, Friday," I said, laughing softly as he caressed my midsection. "Or there'd be gravy all over this kitchen."

"Let's hear the truth now," he said, nuzzling my neck. "What's got you all agitated?"

I gave the gravy one last stir, then took it off the burner. Then I turned and kissed his scratchy chin. "Go sit down. Breakfast is ready."

Once he'd eaten a good part of his breakfast and finished the sports section of the newspaper, I said, "I was thinking this morning and have come up with an idea about last night's shooting."

He peered at me over the tops of his wire-rimmed glasses. He didn't have to say a word; his dubious expression said it all.

I gave him a hard look. "Quit being so condescending. I have a very credible theory."

"I didn't say a thing," he protested.

"Not in words, you didn't. Just hear me out, okay?" I quickly told him my idea about the shooter mistaking Sissy for Emma and about how a white car almost missed

Emma the other day in Paso Robles. To his credit, he
didn't interrupt me once during my speech though he listened to me with that blank expression that always made
me want to shake him.

When I finished, I waited for him to tell me I was
crazy.

He took another bite of biscuits and gravy, took a sip
of his coffee, and said predictably, "I think you're crazy."

"Aren't you even going to consider it?"

He rubbed his stubbled chin with one hand. "Sweetheart, it's just that it's far-fetched. I think you're grasping
for reasons why this person isn't after you. Not that I
blame you, but I'd be irresponsible if I let you think that
you weren't still in danger. You might relax your guard
and that's too risky right now."

"But—"

He held up his hand. "I don't want to argue about this.
We'll proceed as we have been, assuming this is someone
from my past and that you are the target. I love you and
I won't let you pretend this is less serious than what it
is."

We finished the rest of our breakfast in silence.

I stacked our empty plates and took them to the sink.
"For all we know, there could be something in Emma's
background that would cause someone to shoot at her."
He picked up our coffee mugs and brought them over.

"I'll do the dishes," he said.

I stepped aside so he could rinse them off. "You're not
even going to consider it?"

He turned on the hot water and waited for it to warm
up. "Okay, I'll consider it. How's that?"

"Will you question her?"

He started rinsing the plates and loading the dishwasher, his face irritated. "It's a little premature for that."

"But you said you'd—"

He turned and pointed a greasy butter knife at me. "I
said I'd *consider* your theory. Just be careful today and

we'll talk about it again tonight after I've thought about it."

I swiped at the knife with my hand. "What if I want to question her?"

He shrugged and turned back to the dishwasher, saying over his shoulder, "She's your friend. But I'd tread carefully, if I were you. People are very touchy when it comes to their past. We all have things we don't want others to know about. It could end your friendship."

I stared at his back, knowing he was right, but still not certain she wasn't somehow involved. Maybe I could question her so subtly she wouldn't realize what I was doing.

Right, I thought. With my proven inability to hide my feelings on my face, that was probably impossible. But still, it was worth a try. Anything was better than doing nothing.

My mind darted a million miles a minute as I showered and dressed. How would I approach Emma? What should I ask her? Timing was everything in a situation like this.

I was blow-drying my hair, trying to figure out a way to see her again that didn't look suspicious when it occurred to me I was becoming way too excited about this. Why was I so thrilled about her possible connection in this? Why was I treating this as a lark? Sometimes my own self-centeredness and one-track mind just floored me.

"What is your problem?" I asked myself in the steamy mirror.

I wiped a clear place in the condensation with my palm. Hazel eyes, glossy and wide with fear, stared back at me, the truth visibly apparent. As much as I liked Emma and as much as I never wished this upon anyone, Gabe was right. I wanted the stalker to be after someone else rather than me . . . or Gabe. I wanted this to be something from her past, not his.

I sank down on the bathroom floor, finally giving in to the emotions that had hovered over me ever since my truck was vandalized. My head fuzzy with fear, I brought my knees to my chest and hugged them. The truth of the matter was, right at this moment I was terrified to walk out my front door.

"Querida!" Gabe said when he came in a few minutes later and saw me sitting on the floor. He dropped down beside me and circled me with his arms. "Don't be afraid, *mi amor. Que te apoyas en mi.* I'll make sure you are safe. I won't let anyone hurt you. I'm sorry, *lo siento, lo siento, querida,* I'm so very sorry. How I wish me and my problems had never come into your life."

The sadness and regret in his voice broke something inside me, and in that moment, fear was mixed with another emotion . . . anger. How dare this stalker think that he could enter our life and tear it apart with his cowardly acts of harassment. I would not let him do this to us, not now when Gabe and I were just becoming secure with each other again. If I had to question Emma and make her hate me, so be it. If me being out in public drew this guy out so Gabe could find him, so be it. I made the decision right then to go about my life as normally as possible and not give this unknown stalker the power he thought he had.

"I'll be okay," I said, pulling out of his embrace and putting my arms around him. "It's not your fault and I do not regret for one moment that you walked in my life, Friday. I'd never wish that away." I rubbed my lips across his muscled forearm.

"Keep your cell phone on," he said. He stood up and held out his hands to me, pulling me up. "I'm going to call you every hour to make sure you're okay."

"I will," I said, not arguing with his overprotectiveness this time. We went into the bedroom and started getting dressed. "But you don't have to call me every hour. I'll call you whenever I move from one place to the next, okay?"

He thought for a moment, then nodded.

"Okay, here's a rundown of my day. First, I'm walking down to Elvia's and we're driving over to her mother's

to make *pan dulce* for the Mission Ladies booth tonight.
Then I'm going to try and talk Elvia into taking a few
hours off and go shopping. I have some things I could
possibly wear to the Cattleman's Ball this Saturday, but
you don't. Then I'm going to help Señora Aragon and her
ladies set up her booth and also help my artists set up
theirs. I'll be working the folk art museum booth tonight
at Farmer's Market."

He pulled a white shirt out of the closet. "Want to have
lunch together? I'll be leaving for Santa Barbara at one
and won't be back until seven o'clock." His face grew
troubled. "It's our monthly California Police Chiefs'
meeting. Maybe I should just reschedule it."

"Don't be silly. It's only two hours away and I'll be
with people that whole time. Not to mention you have all
your officers on alert. I'll be fine. How about I bring lunch
to the office?"

He nodded gratefully. "I have a ton of work. When I
come back from Santa Barbara, I'll look for you at Farmer's Market. Is Señora Aragon making *chamucos?* She
makes them just like my *abuelita Juana* did. As for the
Cattleman's Ball, I have that cowboy hat and boots I
bought in Kansas. Isn't that enough?" He considered his
light gray Brooks Brothers suit, then decided on the dark
gray.

"A Western-style jacket might be nice."

In front of our long mirror, he pulled on his slacks and
tucked his white shirt inside the waistband, shaking his
head at my reflection behind him as I put on Wranglers
and a white T-shirt. *Waste of good money,* his eyes were
saying as he smugly tied his conservative blue-and-gray
diamond-patterned tie.

"I saw that," I said, smacking his shoulder with the
back of my hand. "A nice, conservative Western-style
jacket would look wonderful on you and should be a part
of your wardrobe if you're going to stay married to me,
buster. Maybe a grayish tweed? Or black? Maybe a classy
Western shirt."

"I have that blue shirt I bought at Shepler's in Kansas."

"That's not dressy enough."

He inhaled deeply. "Sweetheart, I'll wear whatever you buy me and talk steer prices and heifer weights with whoever wants to discuss them. I'm only going to see Dove given her Lifetime Achievement Award and to protect my most precious possession."

"I promise I'll find something you'll feel semicomfortable in." I smiled up at him, then thinking about Dove, I made a face.

"What's wrong?" he asked, picking up his leather briefcase.

"I just hope Dove and Isaac have made up by Saturday night. This is such a big night for her, I'd hate for it to be marred by Isaac's absence."

Gabe kissed my temple, then my lips. "They'll be fine and probably dancing the tango by Saturday night."

"It's two-step, you goofball," I said, smiling. "Or the Cowboy Cha-Cha. No self-respecting cowboy or cowgirl would dance the tango at a Cattleman's Ball."

He smiled. "There's no Cowboy Tango?"

"Not that I've ever heard of, but now that you mention it, it might not be a bad idea."

"Well, you know me, I'll be at the punch bowl watching the rest of you scratch up a perfectly good wood floor, as my grandpa Smith would say."

"For someone with the wonderful natural rhythm you have in other *physical things,* I just don't understand why you can't dance."

"That's an old wives' tale." He wiggled his eyebrows like Groucho Marx. "Just because a man doesn't dance a good cha-cha doesn't mean he can't perform an excellent horizontal mambo."

I stood on tiptoe and kissed him. "Your arrogance is in fine form today, Friday."

His face changed quickly from amusement to indecision and worry. "Maybe I should drive you to Elvia's."

"It's two blocks away. I refuse to let this yahoo make

me afraid to walk two lousy blocks to my best friend's house."

I locked the door after him and through the front window watched him walk down the steps toward the Corvette. I said a quick prayer for his safety as I did every morning. He was so worried about this person hurting me when, the truth was, he might be in as much danger as I was.

I sat down and had another cup of coffee. Though I fought it, the minute I was alone, all the bravado I felt only a half hour ago melted away. Every unfamiliar sound startled me, and frightening scenarios started painting themselves in my mind. And though I had no trouble praying for Gabe and the rest of my family, I had a hard time asking for help for myself. So unable to talk to God about my fear, I chose the next best thing.

"Hey, Brother Mac," I said minutes later, glad that my pastor was an early riser and was in his office. "What's new?"

"Hi, Benni, great to hear from you. Not much. Grandma Oralee's supposed to ride in the parade this Saturday on the old timers' float, but she's refusing to until they change the name. Says she's not a bottle of whiskey."

We both laughed and compared notes about our respective grandmother's latest shenanigans. Though Oralee was almost ten years older than Dove, they were good friends and very similar in their outlook on the world. Many times when Mac told me about Oralee's dilemmas, it felt like a peek into my own future.

"Did Dove contact you about—"

"Her annulment?" he finished, giving a hearty laugh. "Yes, I told her I'd check into Baptist doctrine, that I'll call some of my former professors at Baylor."

"And is she buying that crock of cowpies?"

"Oh, I think she's just biding time. You know she and Isaac will work this out. She just needed someplace to let off steam. A lot of people do that with me."

"I bet they do," I said, glancing down at my hands.

He was silent for a moment, then said, "Benni?"

"Yes?"

"Is there something you need? Are you okay? Dove called me this morning and told me about this person who was stalking you. Is there anything I can do?"

"Yeah, if you see him, tackle him and knock him silly. Or better yet, load your sawed-off shotgun and . . ." I didn't finish. What was wrong with me? I was asking my minister to blow someone away?

"It's okay to be afraid," Mac said softly. "It's a debatable point, but there are some Bible scholars who believe that Jesus was actually physically afraid himself in the Garden of Gethsemane. At any rate, he certainly understands your fear."

"That's what I don't get," I burst out. "If God does understand our fear, then why doesn't He do something about it? The Bible says 'Fear not' and to trust God, but in real life, down here on earth, God doesn't always protect us. Why do we pray for protection and then deep in our hearts wonder if, when the rubber meets the road, God will really be there? The truth is people cry out to God all the time and still get raped and killed and hurt and die and . . ."

I choked on the salty lump at the back of my throat. Hot tears ran down my face, tears I could shed only because Mac couldn't see them. "I'm sorry, but I don't believe God always . . ." I stopped, unable to actually say it, especially to Mac.

"Those are very legitimate questions, Benni," he said, his voice unruffled and kind. "And to be honest, smarter and wiser people than me have never been able to answer them adequately. You know, faith is something like a football."

In spite of my tears, I couldn't help giving a small laugh. Mac loved sports analogies and used them often in his sermons.

He chuckled at himself. "Now, hear me out. This is a good one. It's like this really high-quality pigskin football that has sprung a slow leak. It doesn't mean the football is no good, it just means that before it can be put back in play, the leak has to be fixed and air pumped back into the ball."

"So you're saying I'm a flat football." I was trying not to be annoyed, but this wasn't doing much to make me feel safer.

"Not a flat one. Just a little soft. This person who has invaded your life has punctured a hole in your football, your faith. You're feeling vulnerable, a little flat, but those are the times when our faith is tested. How does faith grow except through adversity? If everything went smooth in our lives, we'd stay like little children, never knowing if we could rise to the test or not. Faith is taking that step out into the unknown, like Peter walking on the water. If all we ever walked on was solid ground, we'd never know what we are truly capable of doing or feeling or being." He paused for a moment. "Okay, let me bring this closer to home. If you hadn't taken a step of faith in marrying Gabe, think of all the joy you would have missed."

"And the pain," I pointed out.

"Yes, but you know that you can't have one without the other."

I thought for a moment about what he'd said. "But I'm still afraid, Mac. And I can't . . . God is . . ." I'd never articulated this before to anyone, but deep inside I was thinking, God was the one who let my mother be taken when I was so young. How can a God like that protect me?

For not the first time, Mac seemed to know exactly what I was thinking and feeling. "Benni, I can't tell you God's thoughts. No one can. I only know deep in my own heart that there is a reason for everything, even this insidious thing that has disrupted your life. He does protect us . . . just not always in the way we think we need protecting. And I promise you that He's in control. You know, a pretty smart guy named Einstein once said this about God, 'I am convinced that He doesn't play dice.'

Think about what he's saying. God doesn't gamble with the universe or with our lives. I agree with Einstein. God knows how this will end and He'll be right there beside you the whole way."

I sighed and didn't answer.

"I'm sorry if what I said doesn't help," Mac said, sounding sad.

"I know you're right, but I was just hoping for . . ." I let my voice trail off. Actually, I wasn't quite sure what I was hoping for.

"A force field that protects us when we're in danger?" Mac said.

"That *does* sound pretty good right now."

"Yes, it does, but then you wouldn't need faith, would you?"

"I guess not. Thanks, Mac." The lump in my throat did seem a little smaller. "Let me know what happens with Dove and Isaac."

His laugh this time was gentle, reassuring. "Oh, I imagine you'll find out before I will and I have a feeling it won't be long. I'll be praying for you. Sometimes, when we're afraid, we can't pray for ourselves. That's when you need someone else pumping air into your football."

"Thanks, Mac. Really, thanks."

"Thank you for trusting me with your fears," he answered.

"C'mon, Scout," I said, after hanging up. I was still afraid, but somehow, Mac's words had helped a little. "We're going to one of your favorite places. You love Señora Aragon. She's the one who always gives you those wonderful meat scraps."

At Elvia and Emory's house, I had another cup of coffee with my cousin while Elvia finished getting ready.

"I hate you," I said to my cousin, sitting across from him in their green-and-white sunroom. Scout sprawled out in front of us on the dark green tiles, enjoying a patch of sunlight. "Everything in your house is always so perfect."

He rocked slowly in the hickory Appalachian rocking

chair that had been his mother's. "I think our housekeeper has a day free in her schedule."

I shook my head and laughed. "That would just cause me more work because I'd have to clean every week before she came."

"So," he said, stopping his chair mid-rock. "What's happening with this stalker business?" His sandy brows plowed a worried furrow between his eyes.

I shrugged and picked at a stray thread on the green-and-white-flowered chintz loveseat. "Not much. Gabe has some ideas about who it might be. It could be someone he helped bust when he was in undercover, but there were so many it's like finding a needle in the proverbial haystack." I told him about the man reaching into the truck and Scout's encounter with him. When his name was mentioned, Scout lifted his head and thumped his tail.

"Yes, you're a good, brave boy," I said, reaching down to stroke his silky head.

"I sure don't like the sound of that," Emory said, leaning forward and resting his elbows on his knees. "The guy's getting bolder."

"He might think twice now after Scout snagged a piece of him."

"Or he might try something worse, like a mail bomb or taking a potshot at you."

Though I tried to look neutral, the expression on my face obviously gave me away.

"Dang it! He already has?"

I told him what happened yesterday at the folk art museum.

Emory's scowl deepened. "What's Gabe doing about this? I think I should hire a bodyguard for you."

"You are *not* hiring a bodyguard. My gosh, you are worse than Gabe. He's doing everything humanly possible. Having a bodyguard will not make a bit of difference. How would a bodyguard have helped last night when he was shooting at me? I'm being very careful and—"

"And nothing," my cousin said, jumping up. He started

pacing back and forth on the sun porch, his hands shoved
deep into the pockets of his dark wool slacks. "I will not
stand by and watch you get hurt just because of your
stupid independence."

I stood up and went over to him, touching him on the
shoulder. Even though I was scared too, I couldn't bear
to see Emory so upset. "It's not stupid, it's practical.
Think about it, if he wanted to hurt me, he could have by
now. He could have the first time he tried something. Who
knows how long he's been watching me and Gabe. I think
this is just some cruel game he's playing to torture Gabe,
to make him nervous."

"It's working . . . on all of us," Emory said, turning to
me and putting his hands on my shoulders. "But, sweetcakes, if anything happened to you, if he hurts you . . ."
His green eyes grew flinty as cut emeralds.

"Emory, I'll be fine."

And, I thought to myself, if I said it enough, maybe
I'd even start believing it. I contemplated for a moment
telling him my theory that I might not have been the target
last night, but at that moment, I was just tired of thinking
about it. I needed to concentrate on something totally shallow and unimportant.

"Enough about me," I said, giving him a quick hug.
"Scratch that, I do need to talk about me again, but it's
actually about me and Gabe. I need some fashion advice,
cousin. What are you wearing to the Cattleman's Ball this
Saturday? I'm in a quandry about what to do about me
and, especially, about Gabe."

His face relaxed and he gave me a huge alligator grin.
"Glad you brought that up. This is something I *can* control. Last week when I was back in Little Rock, I made
a short detour to Nashville . . ."

"Emory, what did you do?"

He held up one finger and said, "Sit tight and I'll show
you."

He left the room and came back a few minutes later

with two maroon garment bags. The gold lettering outside of the bags stated simply MANUEL.

I squealed, jumped up, and grabbed the smaller one. "You didn't? You did! You went to Manuel's. You shouldn't have." I hugged him, crushing the bag between us. "But I'm so glad you did." Manuel was *the* tailor of custom Western clothing. His shirts, dresses, jackets, and suits were worn by almost every famous Western star alive today.

My garment bag revealed a midcalf, pearl-button, plum-colored dress with navy blue piping. The cowboy yokes were embroidered with pink and navy blue flowers and moss green leafy vines. Gabe's bag contained a plain black Western cut wool suit that was cowboy enough to pass muster Saturday night, but would not upset his conservative Brooks Brothers persona and a crisp, white, pearl-button cowboy shirt. I hugged my cousin again and kissed him on the cheek.

"You are the prince of the world. Thank you. They are too expensive and I know I shouldn't accept them, but I'm so grateful to have this taken care of, I won't protest one bit. How did you know Gabe's size?"

"You're not the only detective in the family." He grinned again. "I borrowed one of his suits when I was helping y'all move and had my tailor measure it."

I zipped the garment bags closed and laid them across one of the dark green wicker chairs. "Now that our clothing problems are solved, maybe you can solve an even bigger one. *What* are we going to do about Dove? And where is she, by the way?"

He sat down and crossed his legs. "She left early this morning for some Cattlewomen's meeting. As for what to do with her, I haven't a clue. She's welcome to stay here as long as she wants, but—"

"She needs to be back with Isaac at the ranch," I finished, sitting down across from him. "Yes, I know. It's just making that happen is the hard part."

"Have you talked to Isaac?"

"Yesterday. He was going to try and bribe her with jewelry from Tiffany's."

Emory whistled low. "Bad idea. Too much like what he'd do for his other wives."

"That's what I told him. He says he has something else up his sleeve."

"What?"

"I have no idea."

We looked at each other and burst into laughter.

"How much do you want to bet he reveals it Saturday night at the Cattleman's Ball?" Emory said, kicking the bottom of my foot with the toe of his leather loafer.

"I'm not taking that bet, cousin, 'cause you'll get all my money."

"Why is he getting your money?" Elvia asked, coming into the room at the tail end of my statement. She was dressed casually in dark brown jeans and a camel-colored cashmere sweater. Her black hair was pulled up into a high ponytail, psychologically subtracting ten years from her age. Her Chanel No. 5 perfume mixed not unpleasantly with the fragrance of the sun porch's flowery scent.

"Isn't my wife just the cutest thing walking?" Emory said, jumping up and moving swiftly across the room to pull her into an enthusiastic hug. He lifted her up until her feet dangled over the floor.

"Put me down, you *tonto*," she said, pounding him gently on the back, softening her words with a smile.

He planted a noisy kiss on her neck, then did as she said. "I love it when you talk Spanish to me."

"He's *loco*," she said to me. "I can't believe I've married a crazy man."

"You're telling me something I don't already know?" I said. "I was just hoping you wouldn't notice how crazy he was until you married him. We've been trying to pawn him off on any woman who'd take him for years. If you didn't marry him, our next step was locking him in the attic like all good Southern families do with their nutty relatives."

"You two are just a riot," Emory said. "I think I can even arrange an audition for *Saturday Night Live*. Now, run along, little ladies, and bake us hardworking men some sweet breads for our supper."

"Come over here, my sexist cousin," I said. "And stoop down so it's easier for me to slap you upside the head."

Elvia just laughed and patted Emory on the cheek.

"Are you ready to go?" I asked.

"Yes," she said. "Mama's already called twice. She's already made the *campechanas* and the *negritos*. She says she's waiting to make the *monos* and *cuernos* until we get there. And she has ten special orders for *libros*." Señora Aragon loved baking all the different varieties of *pan dulce*.

"*Libros* are my favorite," Emory said. "Bring me home a dozen."

Libros, glazed rectangles of pastry with many "pages" or layers of dough, were one of my favorites too. Señora Aragon made them once in a while for Blind Harry's events, usually for a new author who might not draw a big audience. They were always certain to get a good crowd when Elvia advertised that Señora Aragon's *libros* were being served. And once the customers were there, they were too intimidated by Elvia not to buy the new author's book. Señora Aragon's *libros* had helped along more than one author's budding career.

"We'll bring home a little of everything, *mi esposo loco*," Elvia said. "Now get to work."

On the drive to her mother's house, I filled her in on everything that had happened since we last talked.

"*Chica,*" she said. "How do you manage to get embroiled in such things?"

"Not entirely my fault this time, my friend," I said, deliberately making my tone light and flippant. "Then again, I did choose to marry a man with a past so I guess it's time to pay the piper."

She glanced over at me, her eyes bright and shiny with worry. "Life certainly turned out more complicated for both of us than we ever expected, didn't it?"

"You can say that again, Sister Elvia."

Ten minutes later we walked into her mother's warm, steamy kitchen and the familiar scents of cinnamon, cooking beans, and sugary caramel greeted us. A wonderful feeling of calm washed over me. Next to Dove's kitchen, there was no place on earth I felt more comfortable or safe than in Señora Aragon's red-and-gray dominion. Though her husband, six sons, and numerous grandsons and sons-in-law with their loud masculine voices, macho posturing, and testosterone-ladened bodies were allowed access to her kitchen for a bite to eat or a short visit, it was definitely her domain in their rambling, five-bedroom, patchwork house and she ruled it with a crushed-velvet fist.

More than one crying woman, including me, had been soothed and strengthened by Señora Aragon's sweet, spicy Mexican hot chocolate and tender "*Mija, mija,* do not be so sad. He cannot help himself, he is just a man. They do not have the same hearts as we women. We must forgive him and pray to the Virgin to change his heart."

Her words and a bowl of *atole,* a thin vanilla pudding made with pineapple chunks, had helped mend more than one shaky relationship. To Señora Aragon the old Mexican folk saying—*La conversacion es el pasto del alma*—Conversation is food for the soul—was more than just a homily; it was how she lived her life.

"*Mijas!*" she said when she turned from the open oven door and saw it was us. "You are just in time. The *rosas* are ready to be made and I have no more space to put things." She held a pan of the swirly-shaped rolls in her hand. They were always my favorite as a child because of their sugary pink icing. Every counter top and the whole gray Formica-topped kitchen table was covered with pans of Mexican sweet breads.

"Okay, Mama," Elvia said, hanging her jacket on one of the brass hooks next to the kitchen door. "Benni and I will start putting them into boxes."

For the next hour, Elvia and I packed the pastries into white bakery boxes and listened to her mother tell us the latest news about the Mission's parishioners.

"Señora Jimenez." Elvia's mother lowered her voice even though we were the only ones in the kitchen. "She is having the operation." She pointed at the area below her stomach.

"A hysterectomy?" Elvia said. "That's too bad. But maybe she'll feel better after she does. You said she's been in a lot of pain since her last baby was born."

Her mother nodded. "Yes, it will be a blessing to her. And Señora Carrillo has been blessed with twin grandsons!" She crossed herself and gave Elvia a penetrating look. "Her *hija* is thirty-five and had given up hope. It is a miracle. The doctors, they say it is harder the longer you wait."

"*Sí,* Mama," Elvia said, concentrating on packing another box of sweet breads and not meeting her mother's eye.

"Benni?" Señora Aragon said, hoping to gain my support in her quest for a grandchild from her only daughter.

"I have to go to the bathroom," I said, jumping up. There was no way I was getting into the whole having babies conversation right now. "Excuse me."

Elvia shot me an evil look as I backed out of the kitchen. "Traitor," she mouthed behind her mother's back.

On the way to the bathroom, located off their huge family room, I came upon Miguel in a pair of sweatpants and a navy blue San Celina Police Department T-shirt sitting in a recliner watching a movie that was low on conversation and heavy on crashing cars and gunfire.

"Hey, Miguel, what're you doing here?" I asked.

"I'm on nights this month. And my VCR broke last night. I wanted to watch this movie before I had to return it today."

"Not to mention that your mama is baking *pan dulce* and you wanted to get your fair share."

He grinned and pulled the recliner to an upright position. "You know how fast they sell at Farmer's Market. If I don't get some before they leave her kitchen, I don't get some."

"Are you working tonight?"

He nodded yes. "I've been off three days so I'm pulling a double shift. Chief's putting twice the number of officers downtown tonight. It's spring break so the kids who didn't find someplace else to go to get drunk and wreck things will be puking their guts out on our city streets. And we've heard some rumblings that one of the north county gangs is out to get down with one of the south county gangs."

"He never mentioned that to me," I said, then sighed. "But that's nothing new."

He shifted the remote control from one hand to the other, his young face uncertain about what he should comment to a childhood friend about her husband who was now his boss. "Maybe he didn't want to worry you, what with that guy stalking you and everything."

I smiled at him, letting him off the hook. "You're probably right. Well, I'm sure all you fine men and women in blue will keep us safe tonight."

"Just remember to hit the ground if you hear gunshots," he said.

"Count on it." I gave a small chuckle even though my heart was beating like a trapped rabbit's. He obviously hadn't heard through the police department grapevine about what happened to me last night.

When I returned to the kitchen, the baby conversation had either run its course or been nipped in the bud by Elvia. Señora Aragon was now talking about one of her friends in the Altar Society.

"Señora Gonzalez, she has the troubles," she said, her thick, black eyebrows pulled close together in a sympathetic frown. "She's the one with the *cicatriz*." She gestured at her cheek.

I looked at Elvia in question.

"Scar," Elvia said, closing the lid of a box packed with

a dozen assorted Mexican pastries. She marked $5.00 on top of the box. "What about Mrs. Gonzalez?" She handed it to me and I stacked it on top of the other boxes.

Señora Aragon shook her head, her unpainted lips making soft tsking sounds. "Her son, Luis, he goes to prison again. He sells dope and then is caught by the *policia.* He will be in the prison for many years. She has much *tristeza* in her heart."

"She should be mad, not sad," Elvia said. "That Luis has been a pain in her side since the day he dropped from her womb. She should have kicked his butt out years ago and not looked back."

Señora Aragon clucked under her breath and touched the top of the *rosas* to see if they'd cooled enough to spread the bright pink icing. "*Mija,* you'll find out when you have *bebés* that it is hard to be so harsh when they are your own. You learn about *la gracia de Dios* when you have *bebés.*"

"*Sí,* Mama," Elvia said, rolling her eyes at me.

"Don't with the eyes," Señora Aragon said, picking up a clear glass bowl. She started whipping the pink frosting with a whisk. "You will see."

After we had finished frosting all the *rosas* and packed them in bakery boxes, Señora Aragon insisted on fixing us lunch.

"I'm supposed to have lunch with Gabe at noon," I said, sitting down at the kitchen table. "But I suppose I could eat a little something."

Elvia laughed, knowing as well as I did that her mother wouldn't let either of us out of her kitchen until we were groaning from stuffed stomachs.

"I will send lunch to Gabriel," Señora Aragon said. "Now sit down, *mijas,* and rest."

While Elvia and I discussed the opening of Emory's new chicken restaurant and the latest computer program she had installed at the bookstore, her mother made *pollo verde,* refried beans, spicy Spanish rice, and handmade tortillas fresh from the frying pan.

I left with plastic containers of everything we'd had, including a dozen still-warm tortillas wrapped in aluminum foil. I gave Señora Aragon five dollars for one of the boxes of Mexican sweet breads. She put two extra *chumucos* in a white bag. The rich cinnamon smell of them immediately tempted me to eat one on the way to Gabe's office. He would never know.

"You leave the *chumucos* for Gabriel," Señora Aragon scolded me. She handed me one wrapped in a white paper napkin. "Here's one for you to eat."

"Gracias, Mamá Aragon," I said, laughing. She knew me too well.

Elvia dropped me and Scout off at my house, where I picked up the truck and drove to the police station. The heavenly scent of Señora Aragon's still-hot food almost got me mugged by the office staff as I walked through the labyrinth of hallways to Gabe's office. Maggie was obviously at lunch, but Gabe's door was open so I walked in. It was empty too.

Figuring he'd be back shortly, I set the bag of food on the oak credenza behind his desk and wandered about the room. After inspecting photographs I'd seen a million times before, I stood for a moment in front of his new framed Albert Einstein poster—"I want to know God's thoughts. The rest are details." It reminded me of my talk with Mac.

I glanced over the paperwork on his desk. A plain manila file with Luke's name on it immediately caught my eye. I was staring at it, fighting the temptation to pick it up, when Gabe walked in.

"Something smells delicious," he said. "And you can look at Luke's file if you want."

"I didn't touch it, I swear," I said, coming around the desk to hug him.

"But you were struggling with the desire," he said.

"But I *didn't* give in to it. At least up until the point you walked in."

"Just in time to save you from yourself." He laughed

softly, then turned to inspect the grocery bag on his credenza. "Don't tell me Señora Aragon . . ."

"Yes, she made you lunch and sent sweet breads too. You are one spoiled *hombre.*"

He looked up at the white tile ceiling. *"Gracias, El Señor."*

As he unpacked the bag, I went to the break room and bought us two Cokes. Since I'd just eaten, I read through Luke's file while Gabe had his lunch.

"Not much here," I said, glancing over the details of his case and noting his vital statistics—born December 21, 1952, married March 10, 1973, divorced in May 1982, retired October 30, 1994, died April 17, 1995. His whole life reduced to five significant dates. I quickly read over the report written by the officers first on the scene and then the updates by the detectives. Then I noticed his name. "Hey, there's a typo here."

Gabe took a bite of rice. "So what else is new? Sometimes if the clerks are too busy, my detectives have to type out their own reports. I'm sure they aren't the best typists in the world."

"They could at least get his name right." I turned the file around and pointed at the top of the report.

He glanced at it and then smiled. "Oh, that. No, that's right. That's Luke's given name."

"Lute?"

"Yeah, he really hated it too. Said it was a little too William Faulkner for his tastes. He always introduced himself as Luke."

I'd never known anyone named Lute, but it was true that Southerners did dream up some odd names. Albenia, for example. There was something about his name though, something that seemed, familiar. "Was it a family name?"

"I have no idea."

"Not much here," I said again, closing the file and laying it on the desk.

"Tell me about it," he said, taking another big bite of Señora Aragon's pollo verde. "Thank goodness you came by with this food. Otherwise lunch would have been a protein bar. I'm still not certain I should go to Santa Barbara."

"Look, I'm with people every minute this afternoon. Go to your meeting. We'll be in touch by cell phone and you have your whole department on alert. They could get to me faster than you could anyway."

He looked at me across the wide expanse of his desk with unblinking eyes. "I don't have to remind you to stay around large groups of people at all times, right?"

I picked up a rubber band sitting on his desk and shot it at him. "I think you just did."

"I mean it, *niña*,"

"Yes, *papacito*," I said and made a silly face. I was determined not to let him see how nervous I was.

After lunch, he walked me and Scout back out to the truck and we kissed good-bye.

"I mean it," he said. "Be careful."

"Yes, yes, yes, yes, *yes*," I said, poking him in the chest with my finger. "You too, buddy boy."

It was when I reached the truck and turned the key in the ignition that it hit me. The tiny connection that just might or might not prove my feeling that the shooter last night was not aiming at me or Sissy, but at Emma. But I had to go to the museum to make sure.

CHAPTER 18

April 20, 1995
Thursday

*I*T TOOK ME ALMOST FIVE MINUTES OF SEARCHING EMMA'S intricate quilt before I found what I was looking for—on a small dark blue velvet triangle located near the top right of the quilt was an eggshell blue embroidered lute. To look at it closely, I had to fetch a ladder and climb half-way up the rungs. Because of the busyness of the quilt and because this patch was so small and nondescript, it would take a very observant eye to see that within the intricate embroidered depiction of this lute was a date: 12-21-52.

I stood for a moment on the ladder, trying to wrap my mind around this fact. Luke—or rather Lute—was some-how related to Emma? But how? Was she related to his mother? His father? I don't remember Gabe ever men-tioning Luke's father. Who was he? Was he still alive? That explained one thing, the letter with the LAPD return address I'd picked up a few days ago when she dropped her notebook. They'd obviously been in touch. But for how long? And more important, why?

Questions swirled like dust devils in my head. I called

Gabe, but he had already left for Santa Barbara. When I tried his cell phone, I got voice mail. He was obviously in one of the sections along the road to Santa Barbara where service was interrupted, so I left him a message telling him it wasn't important, that I'd see him in a few hours. Actually, I was sort of glad. I wanted to contemplate this new information myself before Gabe knew about it. With Emma's thin, but obvious connection with Luke now, I knew Gabe would pull me back and have his detectives question her.

Had Luke been in touch with Emma when he was here? Did Emma know he'd been killed? Why hadn't she said something to me or Gabe?

She had to know about Luke's murder. It was on the front page of the paper. And how in the world did my stalker fit in? Were there two stalkers? One for Emma, one for me? This was getting way too confusing and way too coincidental.

I hesitated for a moment, and despite the fact I knew Gabe would probably have a conniption fit now that she had a real connection to Luke, I dialed Emma's number. I wanted to talk to her before the police descended upon her. I owed her that much. It was something I knew I'd pay for later with a lecture from Gabe, but sometimes there were things more important than proper procedure. If she hadn't heard about Luke's death from the paper, it had to be better hearing it from me rather than the police.

She picked up on the fifth ring.

"Emma?" I said.

"Yes." Her voice was low and hesitant.

"This is Benni."

"I'm sorry." The tone of her voice lightened. "I didn't immediately recognize your voice."

I filled my lungs and then exhaled slowly before answering. "Emma, I was wondering . . ." I faltered for a moment. Maybe this wasn't such a good idea; maybe I should have just dumped the whole thing in Gabe's lap, let him and his detectives question Emma . . . and tell her about Luke's death.

But I just couldn't. Though maybe it was childish or even reckless on my part, if I went to the police first about the clue I'd found in the quilt, it felt like I was tattling on her. And I owed her, at the very least, time. Time to get ready for all the questions that were coming her way.

"Yes?" she said in an encouraging tone. "You were wondering about what?"

"Your quilt," I finally blurted out. My stomach rumbled with a sour feeling. "I found the lute on it. The lute with the date."

She gave a sharp "oh," then was silent. The silence went on for a minute, then stretched into two minutes.

"Emma?" I finally said. "I have to tell Gabe because . . ." Then I stopped. What if she didn't know Luke was dead? How could I explain to her why or how I found out about Lute/Luke without telling her about his murder? "Emma, have you read the *Tribune* in the last week or so?"

She cleared her throat. "No, I never read the paper. Why?"

I sat back in my chair, utterly dismayed at my lack of good judgment in calling her. Well, I was in it now and it would be cruel not to tell her. And frankly, no matter how hard or awkward it was for me, wasn't it better for her to hear it from me than in Gabe's office?

"Emma, we need to talk," I said. "It's really important." I glanced over at my wall clock. Three o'clock. I was already late to the setup for Farmer's Market. There was no way I could drive over the pass to Paso Robles and make it back in time to help at the booths. Not to mention I'd promised Gabe I wouldn't go traipsing off by myself. A thought hit me. "Are you going to Farmer's Market tonight?"

"Yes, Lou and I were going to leave in about a half hour."

Good, she wouldn't be alone. I wouldn't have let her drive from Paso Robles by herself.

"I'd like to talk with you someplace where we have some privacy."

"I understand." Her voice sounded tired, resigned. "Where shall we meet?"

"How about the folk art museum booth? I'll be working there all night. We can go someplace quiet from there."

"I'll be there at six o'clock."

We hung up without saying good-bye. I felt wrung out, as if I'd ridden twenty miles of bad trail. Was I doing the right thing? Maybe I should have waited for Gabe, let him handle it. But there was no turning back now.

At three-thirty Scout and I drove downtown, where Lopez Street was already being cordoned off for this special Farmer's Market. Normally they didn't start closing off the streets until five o'clock but this Farmer's Market, which they were calling *El Mercado*—The Marketplace— in honor of the festival, was twice as large as the normal Thursday night gathering of artists, farmers, restaurants, and various organizations trying to get the word out about their agendas. I parked in the municipal parking lot next to the courthouse, a block away from the festivities. I headed first for the altar ladies booth where Señora Aragon and her fellow altar ladies were having trouble setting up their striped awning.

"Here, let me help," I said, tying Scout's leash to a wrought iron light pole and rushing over to help them with the sagging blue-and-white awning.

"Good, some young arms," Señora Padilla said, wiping her perspiring brow. "My son Manny was supposed to help us, but there was a three-car accident on Rosita Pass a half hour ago and he said he didn't know when they'd be here." Manny and his son, Junior, owned two tow trucks.

"I think I can figure this out," I said, climbing up on the folding step stool. In about ten minutes, with the help and encouragement of Señoras Aragon, Padilla, Sauceda, and Nuñez, I managed to stretch and secure the canvas awning over the aluminum frame.

"I think that will hold," I said, climbing down off the stool.

"Gracias, Benni," Señora Aragon said, giving me a hug. "We can get the tables set up now. We expect *muy grande* crowds."

"You'll probably be sold out in an hour," I said, looking over at the piles of white bakery boxes. All five women had been baking all day, and since there was only one Mexican bakery in town and it didn't carry every type of Mexican pastry, there were people who waited for *El Mercado* every year specifically to buy the altar ladies' sweet breads.

"Did Gabriel like his lunch?" Señora Aragon asked.

"You bet he did. He ate every bite, but saved his sweets for tonight."

Señora Aragon beamed at my words. "He is a good *niño.*"

"Once in a while," I said, causing the other señoras to laugh.

"Poor little *niña,*" said Señora Padilla, winking at the other ladies. "She didn't know what she was doing when she married a *macho hispano,* did she?"

They all chuckled and shook their heads.

"Ah, he's a man," I said, laughing with them. "Doesn't matter what ethnic background he is, aren't they all the same?"

All the women nodded and murmured in agreement.

"See you all later," I said, untying Scout from the light pole.

The early crowds were already starting to fill the street as I wound my way around half-erected booths toward the folk art museum booth across from Blind Harry's. A couple of the artists, Art and Willie, had volunteered to go early and put the booth together. Three women were al-

·

ready arranging the merchandise while Art and Willie sat on the curb drinking cans of orange soda.

"Hey, boss," Willie said. "Wondered when you'd get here."

"It's only"—I glanced at my watch—"four-thirty. We still have an hour and a half before you can start selling." I tied Scout to another light pole next to Willie's basset hound, Leland.

With another set of hands, within the next hour, the booth was organized. Quilts, carved leather wallets, pillows, wall hangings, folk art paintings, papier-mâché piñatas, pottery, and woodcarvings were priced and displayed in a way that we hoped would tempt hundreds of buyers. The city expected record crowds tonight since they'd gone all out and advertised this event up and down the state from San Francisco to San Diego. They expected it to be as large as our annual Mardi Gras celebration.

By six o'clock, when the official ringing of the Mission bell signaled the start of *El Mercado,* the air downtown was alive with the mingled scents of smoky tri-tip steak barbecued over blazing red oak fires, hot, sweet kettle corn, the meaty smell of frying tacos, and the excited brass-heavy sounds of two separate mariachi bands as well as a polka band featuring a huge accordion.

Though it was called *El Mercado* and there was a larger amount of Latin-influenced craft booths and food stalls, other nationalities were also represented in this celebration of our town.

There were Japanese booths featuring fantastic origami cranes, turtles, and dragonflies. In their food booth they sold sushi to go and tempura shrimp. The Chinese of San Celina, integral to the building of the railroad and to the once bustling Chinese section of town, had a booth that sold replicas of old postcards of San Celina back in the early 1900s as well as incense and perfume oils and those wonderful little pincushions with the Chinese children all holding hands around the padded applelike cushion. Dove had one of those in her sewing basket that had been given to her by Mrs. Chang, whose family had lived in San Celina County for five generations.

The Portuguese sold their hot and peppery linguica sausage while the African-Americans had a booth that sold brilliantly patterned and colored table runners and potholders made by a local quilting guild, who'd patterned their guild mission after the Tutwiler, Mississippi, quilters and used the money from the quilt sales to help with college scholarships. The Irish sold corned beef sandwiches, silver four-leaf-clover bracelets and hair clips, and KISS ME, I'M IRISH buttons, and Italians tempted us with gnocci, spicy, wet Italian beef sandwiches, and anise-flavored homemade biscotti.

A Dutch booth sold wooden shoe pins and chocolate *Hagel,* strong chocolate-flavored sprinkles that the Dutch eat with bread and butter like Americans eat peanut butter and jelly. Scandinavians, many of whom came up from the town of Solvang, a few hours south, peddled the traditional Swedish red-painted Dala horses and the Danes' famous abel skivers, a puffy, lacy pastry made in a special iron pan and sprinkled with powdered sugar.

There were representative booths from Scotland, Norway, Polynesia, the Philippines, Poland, and Germany. The Cajun booth was manned by none other than my much-loved assistant, D-Daddy Boudreaux. Anyone who bought some filé gumbo and a cup of rich, eye-popping, black-as-homemade-sin Community brand coffee was invited to sit on the curb next to their tent and be treated to one of his detailed, slightly unbelievable Cajun folk tales.

As Miguel had told me earlier, law enforcement presence, both city police and county sheriff, was strong tonight. It both soothed and agitated me. The fact that they felt the need to come out in such numbers made me nervous, but as Gabe often said; sometimes just having a large visible amount of officers could quell a possible disturbance. Though I thought I saw young men who looked as if they might belong to some sort of gang, it was hard to tell these days. Good kids who just hung around in groups wearing the typical, sullen expression of adolescence, dressed in identical ways to gang members with shaved heads, multiple piercings, baggy wool shirts, and even baggier cotton duck work pants.

At six-fifteen, Emma had still not arrived. I glanced through the crowd apprehensively, hoping everything was okay. I was distracted for a few moments by two college girls who'd worked as part-time docents at the museum during the previous year to obtain college credit for their fine arts degrees.

"Hi, Benni," Beth said. "We have a question for you." Her friend, Kiki, giggled behind her hand.

"What's that?" I said as I folded quilts that people had pulled out to look at.

Beth gave me a wide, cajoling smile and tugged at her caramel-colored braid. "Can we borrow Scout for a little while? We'll take good care of him. Promise."

Kiki giggled again.

"Why?" I asked.

They pointed at a couple of young men across the street who had a black Labrador puppy on a red leash. Beth and Kiki let out simultaneous sighs.

"Oh, I get it," I said, laughing. "You need a conversation starter. Sure, you can take him. Just be back before we close up at nine." They were good, responsible girls who I enjoyed hearing chatter about their activities at school as well as their different romances. They brought back good memories of when Jack, Elvia, and I were attending Cal Poly.

"Okay," they said and eagerly untied Scout's leash from the light pole.

He picked up on their excitement and started barking.

"You be good now, Scooby-Doo," I said, patting his ribs. "You make sure these girls are safe."

They walked away giggling, darting through the crowd toward the boys.

Emma and Lou showed up at the booth at six-thirty.

Dusk was approaching, hanging heavy and cool on the sparkling sounds of competing mariachi trumpets and guitars.

When I walked over to greet them, I saw that Emma's face was frozen in an expression of sadness, and for the twentieth time in the last few hours, I regretted setting up this meeting. "Emma, are you all right?"

Lou's arm came up and touched the small of her back for a quick moment, then dropped to his side. She turned her head to look at him, her face relaxing for a moment when he nodded his head.

For the first time, it occurred to me that he wasn't just her ranch manager, that there was a personal relationship between them that went beyond employer-employee.

"I'm fine," she said. "I apologize for being late but there was a horrible accident on the grade."

"Yes, I heard," I said, glancing around the crowds. This was not the best place in the world to talk, especially about the sensitive subject of the death of someone who obviously meant something to her. "Look, do you want to go over to Elvia's store? I'm sure she'd let us use her office. It would be much quieter there."

"That sounds good," she said, visibly relieved.

Was she afraid I was going to blurt everything out right here in this noisy crowd? Again, shame washed over me. "Emma, I'm so sorry for bothering you about this. I know it's none of my business and I—"

She held up her hand to stop my words. "No, Benni, I'm glad you did. I need to talk about this. I *want* to talk about it. And I trust you. I have something to tell you that pertains to what happened last night at the museum. I feel terrible that my past has put you in danger and I believe you deserve an explanation."

So my suspicion was correct. Though I was relieved that Gabe's past was not involved, I didn't gain any satisfaction from being right. "Let's get out of this crowd," I said, touching her hand.

She turned to Lou. "Go ahead and get something to

eat. You haven't had your dinner and you know how shaky you become if you don't eat on time." She reached up and tenderly touched his face with her fingertips. "I'll meet you downstairs in the bookstore's coffeehouse in an hour or so."

He nodded, gave us both a worried look, and said in a gruff voice, "Be careful, Emma."

"Hey, Willie," I called over the noisy booth. "I'm taking a break." I clipped my cell phone to my belt and made sure my pepper spray was still in my back pocket.

"No problem," he called back.

We started walking toward the bookstore, pushing our way through the crowd of shoulder-to-shoulder people. It was like fighting a current of molasses; the noise and voices were so strident and confusing we didn't even attempt to talk. When a large group of shaved-headed adolescents with tattoos on their necks and arms surged past us, I grasped her arm and we moved through them. It felt like I was paddling a cardboard canoe through a school of sharks. Their heavy scent, that particular aggressive smell of adolescent male sweat and hormones, caused my back to stiffen and I held Emma's arm a little tighter.

We were in the middle of the young men when there came a shout, a couple of curse words, and out of the corner of my eye, I saw another crowd of young men surge in from the left.

In the flash of a moment, Emma and I were in the center of a kicking and punching group of men. Glass shattered, a shot rang out, more swear words. Emma screamed and I threw my arms around her trying to protect her. Two men, fists swinging and heavy boots kicking, knocked us over. Another terrified scream burst from Emma's throat. Clinging to each other, we teetered, then both hit the ground.

"Emma!" I screamed, throwing myself on top of her. From the corner of my eye I saw only moving legs, a swinging bar, a sharp pain in my thigh as a boot grazed it. Emma lay underneath me, frozen still in terror.

"Oh, God," I prayed, trying to protect both our heads.

Though it felt like an hour, it was only a matter of minutes when the police and sheriff's deputies surged in. By that time, many of the gang members had fled and those who had been caught by the police were laid out facedown on the pavement.

I loosened my hold on Emma. "Are you okay?" I asked, taking deep breaths as if I'd been running for miles.

"I think so," she said, her voice trembling.

I helped her up, brushed off her denim skirt, and helped her move away from the ruckus. "Oh," I said when we had reached the sidewalk. "You're hurt."

Bright red blood trickled from a deep scrape on her cheek. She touched it gingerly, giving a pained grimace. A nearby woman handed her a clean tissue.

"Thank you," she said, holding the tissue up to her cheek.

"We should go to the emergency room," I said.

"Oh, no. Really, I'm fine."

But I didn't like the paleness of her complexion. She looked ready to faint any moment. "Emma, you need to sit down. And I really don't like the look of that cut." The tissue she held to her cheek was already soaked with blood. "I really think you need to go to emergency."

She gave me a desperate look. "No, really, I . . . can't we go somewhere else? Isn't your house nearby?"

I hesitated, then said, "Yes, but . . ."

It was starting to get dark and I didn't have Scout with me. To be honest, the thought of walking into my own house without Scout's ability to smell if anyone was there made me a little nervous. On the other hand, it *wasn't* dark yet, it was only two blocks away, and the streets were full of people. My neighborhood was an active one, being so close to downtown, with people working in their yards or sitting on their front porches even after dark sometimes.

Besides, a stubborn part of me was mad. If I let this person make me afraid to walk to my own house, then he's won. He's won because he succeeded in making me change my life. I checked to make sure my cell phone was clipped to my belt and turned on and that my pepper spray was in my back pocket.

I took Emma's arm. "I do have first aid supplies at home and you can sit down for a moment, maybe have a cup of tea. By that time, everything should be calmed down here and we can find Lou at the bookstore."

"Thank you," she said gratefully.

We walked the short distance without saying a word. I kept glancing around to see if anyone suspicious was following us, but all I saw were people familiar to me. I'd nod at them, feeling a little more at ease as I neared my house. I helped her up our front steps and unlocked the door. The house was quiet and cool. After settling her on the sofa, I started toward the kitchen. The swinging door flew open and a man walked in.

"Oh," I said, freezing in my tracks. My heart started beating at five times its normal rate.

The man, as average-looking as someone advertising tires on television, looked over my shoulder and said to Emma, "Hi, Ma. It's been a long time, hasn't it?"

CHAPTER 19

❖

April 7, 1978
Friday

"DO YOU STILL WANT TO GO RIDING TODAY?" I ASKED Jack the next morning while we were eating breakfast. "This afternoon is the only time I can go. When I was at the Farm Supply yesterday, I picked up Dove's special chicken feed so I thought I'd take it to her. Then I need to drive up to Mrs. Baldwin's house and give her a copy of my term paper. I couldn't sleep last night so I finished it."

He lifted up his cereal bowl and, after drinking the last dregs of milk, said, "Great, now you can finish mine."

"In your dreams. Besides, isn't that journal the only paper you have to write this semester? How hard can that be?"

He grinned and tilted his wooden chair back on two legs. "It's harder than you think. Those are my deep, *personal* feelings I'm laying out for the world to see."

"And I'm sure the world just can't to wait read them," I said, picking up his bowl and taking it over to the sink.

"I'll have the horses tacked up by five. I don't have any classes today so, to keep Big Brother happy, I'll probably be tinkering with the tractor until then."

"Okay, that'll give me plenty of time after my one o'clock class to go by Dove's, then see Mrs. Baldwin. I just want to make sure there's nothing in my paper that's inaccurate before I type the final draft."

When I dropped the chicken feed off at Dove's, she was sitting on the front porch hulling strawberries, preparing them to be packed in plastic bags for the deep freezer out in the barn.

"Pull up a knife and sit down," she said, pointing to the rocking chair next to her.

"I can't stay long, but I can do a couple of baskets." I went into the kitchen, found another chipped ceramic bowl, and joined her.

"How's things at the Harper ranch?" she asked, her reddish-blond hair, half white now, pulled up in a long ponytail. For a moment time seemed to rush at me like a locomotive. I tried to picture Dove completely white-haired, me and Jack middle-aged with a couple of teen-agers nagging at us to borrow the truck, our ranch prosperous and thriving. It was beyond my imagination.

I shook my head and picked up a bright red strawberry the size of a baby's fist. "Jack and Wade are fighting, as usual. The pastures look great. We probably won't have to buy as much feed this year, which is good because our savings are getting real low. I don't know how much longer the tractor will hold out, but you know how good Jack is at patching mechanical things. He says he can probably baby it along for another year or so."

Dove nodded, not breaking one second of rhythm in her hulling. "Your daddy says you have a real nice crop of calves this year."

"Yeah, they're looking good. Some nice-sized heifers and one bull that Jack and Wade are arguing over. Jack thinks he's got potential, but Wade said his bloodline isn't worth perpetuating."

Dove stopped her hulling for a moment. "Wade should

listen. Jack has a good eye. He's a natural rancher, that boy."

"That might be some of the problem between them. I think Wade is jealous."

Dove pursed her lips and threw a finished strawberry in the bowl on the table next to her. "Brothers spit and snort at each other. Watched my husband do it with his brothers, watched my sons do it with each other. It's the way of the world."

I sat back in the rocking chair and stared at my bowl of shiny strawberries. A breeze came through swirling the sweet scent around us. It felt as if I could lick the air and it would taste like a strawberry malt. "I just wish that they could work out some kind of compromise, put this thing between them to rest. I just have a bad feeling that someday one of them will go too far and . . ." I wasn't sure what. Hurt each other? Hurt themselves?

Dove stopped rocking, set her bowl on the porch, and leaned over to pat my knee. "Honeybun, you remember what it says in Proverbs. 'There are many plans in a man's heart, Nevertheless the Lord's counsel—that will stand.' Whatever happens with those boys, whatever happens in our lives, God already knows what it is and how we'll react, and if we surrender ourselves up to His counsel, we'll know the right thing to do."

I leaned my head back and closed my eyes, soothed yet again by my gramma's words. "Sometimes I just wish I could see how it all turns out. Then everything wouldn't be so . . . I don't know, scary, I guess."

She gave my knee a squeeze before picking her bowl back up and continuing with her task. "No, you don't. We think we want to know what will happen in the future, but we really don't. Our future is best left in God's hands. We have enough on our plate just pushing around the peas of the present."

I opened my eyes and giggled. "The peas of the present?"

"Oh, you," she said, waving a hand at me. "You know what I mean."

Lightened by her words and loaded down with a grocery bag of fresh strawberries, onions, tomatoes, green beans, and two loaves of home-baked wheat bread she insisted I take, I drove over Rosita Pass to Mrs. Baldwin's house.

It was a little before three P.M. when I pulled onto her long gravel driveway. There were no cars in front of the farmhouse. Silence was punctuated only by the sound of chattering birds and a slight rustling in the bushes surrounding her wraparound porch. All the window blinds were drawn, giving the house a locked-up deserted look. That was odd. People out here in the country usually never locked their houses unless they were going away on a long trip. Sometimes not even then. But they certainly didn't do it just to go to town.

I knocked on the front door and waited. After a minute or so, I knocked again, harder this time. "Mrs. Baldwin?" No answer. I rang the doorbell and heard it echo through the house.

I glanced at my watch. It was already past three and I really wanted to get her approval before I turned in my paper. Finals were next week so I probably wouldn't have time to drive back up here. After a few more minutes, I scribbled a quick note on the front of the manila envelope that held my term paper.

> Dear Mrs. Baldwin,
> I dropped by to give you this copy of my term paper. I'm turning it in this week. Hope you like it.

I contemplated my words for a moment. They sounded so stupid and bland. Why did I feel so awkward writing her? Because she was a writer, I supposed. I imagined her critiquing my letter, shaking her head in dismay at my boring, unimaginative words.

I added:

*Thank you so much for taking the time to talk to
me. It was truly an honor and a privilege.*

I reread it, wishing I had a dictionary. Was that the
right way to spell "privilege"? It didn't look right. Dang,
I should have only said "honor."

Sincerely, your friend always, Benni Harper.

Again I agonized over the words. Your friend? Would
she think I was trying to make something more of our
relationship than what it was? Annoyed at myself, I pulled
my term paper out of the envelope and stuck the folded
envelope in the back pocket of my Wranglers. Back at
my truck, I found an old hay receipt and wrote a quick
note on the back of it.

Dear Mrs. Baldwin, I started. *Here's my paper.
Please call me if there's anything you find*—I
thought for a moment—*objectionable.* Was that
the word I really wanted?

"What do you want?" barked a gravelly male voice
behind me.

Startled, I jumped and dropped my pen. I swung
around to face the man. It was Cody Baldwin. The red in
his glassy eyes was bright enough for me to notice from
twenty feet away. Though I wasn't all that familiar with
it, he sure looked like he was high on something. I stared
at him a moment, speechless.

"You again," he said, his eyes narrowing. "I just can't
seem to get away from you, can I?"

"I . . . I was leaving a note for your mother," I said,
eyeing the distance to my truck, which was, unfortunately,
behind him. And my keys were in the ignition. I started
inching around him, hoping to distract him with a flood
of inane rambling. "I wrote this term paper about her
books and I was giving her a copy and I . . . well, she

wasn't here and I don't know when she'll be back and I'm so busy next week 'cause of finals and all and then there's the parade which my best friend is the queen of so I'm leaving her a note—"

"Ah, shut up," he said, his eyes darting back and forth as if he were looking for something. "She isn't here, but I'm sure she'll be *so sorry* she missed you. She just loves her little groupies." His eyes stopped moving for a moment and bore directly into mine. "Especially *you*. My mother took quite a shine to *you*."

The ugliness in his voice was so vehement, I stepped back in surprise.

"Well, I . . . I . . ." I stuttered, trying to find a moment to make a run for it. I could jump in the truck, lock the door, and hope like heck that our often temperamental truck started with the first crank of the ignition. "Could you tell her I was here and—"

"I'm not her freaking servant," he snapped. He covered the distance between us in two seconds and grabbed my upper arm.

"Hey!" I cried, trying to pull out of his grasp. "Let me go!"

His face came within inches of mine. His breath was sour, like garbage on a hot day. Up close, his eyes looked like two shiny marbles, hard and glassy and without feeling. "The cops have been asking me questions. Too many questions. Did you go to them? What did you say?"

I jerked my arm trying to free myself. "You were trespassing on our land. What were you doing there?"

He squeezed my arm harder and I swallowed a squeal of pain. "Did you tell the police? Did you?"

I glared up at him, anger overcoming fear for a moment. "So what if I did?"

The moment I said the words, I regretted them. What was I thinking? It wasn't even the truth. It was Jack who'd called the police and reported seeing Cody on our land. And they'd told us they couldn't do a thing unless we had some kind of proof that they were involved in illegal activity on our land.

He kept squeezing my upper arm until the pressure brought tears to my eyes. "If they come to talk to me again . . . if I get arrested because of you . . ."

Before he could finish, I hauled off and kicked his shin as hard as I could.

"Shit!" he yelled, letting loose of my arm. "You little . . ."

I dashed for my truck and had it started and halfway down the driveway by the time he was able to stand up. Thank goodness for my good old Justin boots. My last sight of him was in the rearview mirror of my truck. He stood in the driveway, his hand held up in anger, giving me the finger.

On the drive back home I wondered if I should call Emma and warn her about her son. But what could I say that she didn't already know? It was obvious he was taking drugs, maybe even selling them. I'd ask Jack when I got home what I should do.

When I got home, Jack's Jeep was not parked in front of our house. I carried the groceries Dove had given me inside the house and saw the note on the kitchen counter.

Babe, me and Wade got into a fight. I went for a drive. Don't wait up for me.

DON'T WORRY. I LOVE YOU.
JACK.

"Oh, Jack," I said out loud to the empty kitchen.

I put the away the groceries, then stood outside on the front porch and stared over at the new house. I could see my sister-in-law, Sandra, moving about the big kitchen, probably fixing dinner. Wade's truck, the newest of the three red Harper's Herefords trucks, was parked in their wide circle driveway. Obviously only Jack took off in anger this time. For that, I was relieved. Jack wasn't a drinker like Wade. He probably went driving up the coast, letting the ocean calm his angry feelings. He often did that when he was really upset. At least we wouldn't have to be traipsing around to bars all night, at the request of his mother and Sandra, looking for Wade.

After making myself a peanut butter and jelly sandwich, I took out my American history book with the plans of studying for my final next week. After fifteen minutes of rereading the same paragraph about the Louisiana Purchase without comprehending a word, I gave up and turned on the television. And that's how I spent the rest of the evening, stretched out on the sofa, eating a complete bag of Tootsie Rolls, watching *Little House on the Prairie* and an old Doris Day movie, waiting for my husband to come home.

CHAPTER 20

❖

April 20, 1995
Thursday

"*C*ODY," EMMA SAID CALMLY, STANDING UP. "WHAT do you want?"

I stared at the short-haired, middle-aged man wearing a dark blue T-shirt and faded jeans, my thoughts flashing back seventeen years to the brief encounters I'd had with her son outside our land and her house in Paso Robles. He looked so different, but I could see vestiges of the young brash Cody in his still sullen mouth.

"I thought you were dead," I blurted out.

He narrowed his eyes and laughed. "Yeah, that's what Ma would like people to believe, but here I am, alive and well. Unlike your *other* son, huh, Ma?" He spat her name out as if it were a swear word. "Luke, the *good* son."

I glanced over at Emma. Luke was her son?

"You may as well be dead to me," Emma said, her voice emotionless.

"You may as well be dead," he mimicked. "Give me a break. So you don't like my friends—is that any reason to reject your only *legitimate* son?"

The tone of his voice was growing uglier by the minute. Would he hurt us? By the look on his face, I was afraid that was exactly what he intended.

"What do you want?" I asked. "If you need money, I have some here in the house. You're welcome to it if you'll just go." Stall for time, my mind commanded. Then punch the automatic dial on your cell phone. Could I do that without Cody noticing? It would ring Gabe and he'd be able to hear everything that was going on. Maybe I could somehow tell him where we were.

"Money's not going to do me any good now," he snapped. "No, I just want my dear mother to see what she's done. And I want her to know that I am her only son left, at least until we all join Luke where I sent him, in hell."

Emma gasped. "Luke is dead?"

Cody's face tightened, his lips turning up into a smile. "Yep. Thanks to me, I am again an only child."

Emma's face paled. "You killed Luke? Cody, he's your brother!"

"No," he said, spittle collecting around the edge of his mouth. "He *was* your son. Big difference."

"You have the same blood," she insisted.

"Only yours," he said. "And that's worth nothing to me."

While they talked, I tried to slowly work my hand around to punch the cell phone hooked to my belt. Cody saw the movement, took the distance between us in two strides, and ripped the cell phone from my waist. Then he backhanded me, the hard metal of a ring hitting the bridge of my nose. I screamed and fell to the wood floor.

"Benni . . ." Emma cried.

"Stay where you are!" he yelled to his mother. "Do you think I'm stupid?"

I lifted my head to look at him, touching my throbbing nose. Blood stained my fingers and stars twirled in little cyclones in front of my eyes.

He threw the cell phone against the brick fireplace. Plastic pieces flew all over the floor.

I lay there for a moment, contemplating the distance

to the door. Should I try to make a run for it? What about Emma? Would he kill her in the moments it took me to get help? Should I try or should I stay? My mind buzzed with indecision; my whole face throbbed in pain.

"Get up," he said, grabbing my upper arm and jerking me up. He shoved me over toward Emma. "Stand over there until I decide what to do."

"Look," I said, my voice sounding thick in my ears, as if I were talking with a mouthful of molasses. "If you just leave now, we won't tell anyone about this. You can take all our money—"

"Shut up!" he yelled, pulling a small pistol out of his pocket. "Shut your mouth until I tell you to talk." He started pacing back and forth.

"Cody," Emma said, her voice calm. "You can do whatever you want with me, but Benni has nothing to do with this. You must let her go."

He stopped pacing and sneered at his mother. "Fat chance, Ma. I know you care about her. Why do you think I've been harassing her all this time? For my own fun?" Then he gave a nasty smile. "Though it certainly has been."

"My husband is Gabe Ortiz," I said, not quite certain if what I was hearing was true. "The police chief . . ."

"Yeah, yeah, I know. So what? I admit, that made me think twice, but actually, I found it kind of a challenge." He rubbed the barrel of the gun alongside his jaw.

It was true then. He hadn't stalked me because of anything in Gabe's past. A big part of me was relieved, glad that whatever happened to me, Gabe couldn't feel responsible.

"What do you mean money's not going to do you any good now?" I asked, thinking that the longer I kept him talking, the better chance I'd have to figure out a plan of escape.

"Prison's an ugly place, Ma," he said, not answering me. "They do horrible things to new guys in prison. Want to hear all about your baby boy's adventures?"

Emma closed her eyes, touching her hand to her forehead. "I'm sorry, Cody. You know I didn't want you to go to prison. But you were the one who chose to deal drugs. You chose that life."

"You didn't have to turn me in," he cried. "What kind of mother does that?"

She opened her eyes and looked at him, unblinking. "A responsible one. A mother who cares about other mothers' children who bought your dope. Cody, they were *children*. You sold drugs to junior high children. I'm so sorry for wherever I failed you as a mother, but I couldn't continue letting you hurt other people." She hesitated, then said, "I still love you, Cody. Your father—"

"Shut up!" He pointed the pistol directly at her. "Leave Dad out of this. If he'd been alive, none of this would have happened."

"Your dad would have hated what you do."

His arm trembled slightly. "Do you know what dad would have hated? He would have hated that I've got AIDS now, Ma, and that I'm going to die. You gave it to me by selling me out to the cops seventeen years ago and now I'm going to die. You deserve to die too."

She continued to stare at her son, the expression on her face unchanging, as if she'd expected this confrontation for years. "Why did you come back?" she asked.

"Why did you?" he countered.

"I wanted to live my last days out here," she said simply. "Your father is here. And Lou."

He lowered the gun to his side. I let out a small breath of relief. "Oh, yeah, Lou," he said, his voice thick with sarcasm. "The great cowboy, Lou. Dad's good buddy. The guy who screwed his best friend's wife while he was in Korea."

Emma's face twitched at Cody's graphic words. "What we did was wrong. We've paid for it many times over in guilt and grief. Trust me on that, Cody."

He ignored her words. "I bet you were just tickled pink when Luke showed up at your door, weren't you? He found me first, you know? I was the one who told him where you lived."

Her face blanched. "Luke came by the ranch? We'd spoken on the phone, but we never . . ." Her words choked deep in her throat.

Cody let out a whoop of laughter. "You mean you never met your dream son? That's rich, that's just too funny. I didn't realize when I met him that night that he hadn't seen you yet. I would have certainly said something when I stabbed him."

My heart sank at his words. If he was so bold as to tell us that he'd killed Luke, that meant he had no intention of letting us live. Every nerve in my body felt like it was on alert. I had to find an opening. The weight of the pepper spray in my back pocket gave me a small light of hope. It wasn't much against a pistol, but it was all Emma and I had unless, by some miracle, Gabe walked in.

Cody raised the gun up and walked toward us. "We're going to go for a ride, ladies." He glanced over at me. "You'll drive."

When he got close enough to Emma, she reached out a hand to him. "Cody, please," she said, tears now rolling down her soft, wrinkled cheeks. "I love you . . ." She touched his shoulder.

He jerked back and raised his hand to strike her. In that split second, I pulled the pepper spray out of my pocket and sprayed it in the direction of his face, praying desperately for divine intervention.

He screamed. Emma screamed. The gun dropped to the wood floor with a thump. I sprayed until the pepper spray's fifteen seconds ran out. Cody fell backward against the fireplace, his hands clawing at his face. I scrambled after the gun, grabbed it, and ran for the phone.

Emma crawled toward her screaming son, her voice calling out to him with an agonizing sadness, "Oh, Cody, Cody . . . I'm sorry . . ."

"Nine-one-one," the operator answered.

"Please," I said. "This is Benni Harper. Send the police . . . 1954 Canyon Street. The police chief's house. Hurry!"

CHAPTER 21

❖

April 20, 1995
Thursday

"THERE'S NOT EVEN GOING TO BE A TRIAL," GABE SAID hours later when I was sitting in his office. "Mrs. Baldwin's and your statements will go on file but you won't even have to testify. Cody Baldwin confessed to killing Luke. That with all the other charges, not to mention his parole violations, means he will probably be in jail for a good portion of his life."

I sat back in the visitor's chair holding an ice pack to my still throbbing nose. I pulled it away to speak. "What did Emma have to say? What's the story behind Luke's birth?"

"When her husband was drafted and sent to Korea, Emma and Lou had an affair and Luke was conceived. She named him Lute in memory of her grandfather. Before her pregnancy was apparent, she decided to go to her cousin in Georgia and have the baby. She left Cody with some friends in San Celina. Cody was so young at the time that he didn't even remember spending Christmas without either of his parents. While she was gone, she had to make the decision about whether to tell her husband when he came back, knowing he could bring up the affair in the divorce proceedings, and things being the way they were in the fifties, she'd probably lose custody of Cody. So she had to decide which son she would raise, and because of Cody's age, she decided giving up Luke seemed the right thing to do. Her cousin helped find a home for Luke with a friend not too far away in an Alabama town just over the border from Georgia. Then Emma came back to San Celina. Lou knew about his son, but he said he was pretty messed up back then, drinking a lot, not able to hold down a decent job. He left town shortly afterward, drifting around working at different ranches around the West, but he kept in sporadic contact with Emma's cousin, who would tell him how Luke was doing. After Emma's husband was killed, Lou and Emma started writing each other. When she decided to keep the ranch, he came back to San Celina."

I rearranged the ice in my pack and placed it gently on my nose. "So how did Luke and Cody hook up?"

"Luke was a good detective," Gabe said. "I'm guessing that looking for his parents was one of the reasons he became a private investigator. At some point he must have discovered he was adopted, maybe when his adopted mother died, and he felt compelled to find his birth parents. In the process, he also found Cody." Gabe's mouth turned down underneath his thick mustache. "Luke used to tell me how much he wanted a sibling. He hated being an only child."

"In his case it would have been better if he'd never looked for his birth family. That certainly makes you think, doesn't it?"

Gabe pulled at the end of his mustache and didn't answer.

"How's Emma?" I hadn't seen her since the officers swarmed on our house after hearing from dispatch that a crime had occurred at the chief's house. Miguel was on duty, and after contacting Gabe, he took me down to the emergency room, where Gabe was already waiting. My nose was swollen with a small gash across the bridge, though fortunately, not broken.

"She's fine," he said. "Lou came and picked her up."

"Luke's dad," I said softly.

He nodded. "Luke didn't even know that before he died. You know that night we had dinner with him? He'd already been in contact with Emma a few times, by letter and phone."

I sat up in my chair. "That explains the letter from the LAPD that I saw at her house!"

He looked over his glass at me in accusation. "Which you didn't tell me about. At any rate, he had a date to see her the next morning. She didn't tell him about Lou, but was going to save that for when they met in person. When he didn't show up the next day, she just assumed he'd changed his mind or had some emergency come up. She said she didn't realize he'd been killed because she or Lou don't read the newspaper."

"If Luke had seen Emma before meeting with Cody, everything might have turned out differently."

Gabe sighed and sat forward in his chair, resting his elbows on his desk. "It might have. Then again, it might have all ended up exactly like it did. We'll just never know."

"How long has Cody been back in San Celina?"

"For the last six months or so. Like I told you, Mrs. Baldwin said she didn't know that when she returned to San Celina. She didn't even know he'd gotten out of prison. They haven't been in touch for years. Apparently Cody had been in trouble since high school. She said she tried paying for drug rehabilitation, counseling, tried threats. She almost lost her ranch twice because she took out so many second mortgages. So, when he went to prison the last time, she just found it easier to tell people he was dead. That way no one questioned her about him."

I took the ice pack off my nose again. It was now numb to the point of no feeling. Of course, the pain pills the doctor gave me helped too. "So the child she gave away ended up having a better life, being a better person. That just seems so weird."

His mouth became a straight line. "It's ironic, no doubt. But Luke ended up dead so no one really won in this situation."

"All of this just because two people had an affair," I said, shaking my head. We stared for a moment at each other. This hit closer to home than either of us wanted to acknowledge. Neither of us could throw any stones at Emma and Lou. A few months ago we'd both been tempted by the same passion that had obviously overcome them.

He stood up and came around the desk. I met him halfway and we hugged in silence. When we broke apart, I glanced at myself in the mirror that hung on the back of his office door.

"Oh, no," I moaned, touching the side of my swollen nose. "I look awful. I bet there'll be a scar."

Gabe came up behind me, encircling me with his arms. He rested his chin on the top of my head and smiled at my reflection. "I think you look cute. Like a little prize-fighter."

"Oh, great," I said, making a face at his reflection. "Every girl's dream."

"I'm just glad you're safe."

I smiled. "And see, it wasn't because of your past. You have nothing to feel guilty about."

He didn't smile back. "Just because it wasn't this time, doesn't mean it still can't happen."

I kissed his forearm. "As Dove would say, don't be pickin' tomorrow's tomatoes today. The time to harvest them will come soon enough."

"That's what I'm afraid of."

"And whatever happens, we'll face it together."

He kissed the top of my head. "I'm counting on that, *querida*."

CHAPTER 22

❖

April 22, 1995
Saturday

O N SATURDAY, GABE AND I WATCHED THE LA FIESTA
Parade, ate juicy tri-tip sandwiches, and cheered when the
alumnae queen's float passed us. It was like being in a
time warp seeing Elvia and six other former queens up
on the flower-covered float. I remember helping her pick
out the white, lacy empire-style dress in the spring of
1978. The band behind the queen's float was playing
"Happy Together" by the Turtles. Jack had known every
word to that song. He loved to sing it to me when we had
to get up early to do chores and I was grumpy because I
hadn't had my first cup of coffee. "So happy together . . ."
he would sing, trying to get me to smile.

I took the yellow rose I bought from a street vendor
and ran up to Elvia's float.

"Hey, *amiga!*" I called and held out the rose. "You're
the best queen of them all!" Then I blew her a kiss.

"*Gringa loca,*" she called back and hugged the rose to
her chest.

At the lemonade booth Gabe and I ran into Isaac, who
wore a huge Cheshire cat smile. The last time I'd seen

him this happy was the day he and Dove were married.

"What's going on, Pops?" I asked. "Have you discovered a way to win your fair maiden back?"

"Just don't miss my entrance to the Cattleman's ball tonight," he said.

Later that afternoon when we were dressing for the ball, Gabe said, "I guess this jacket isn't *that* bad." He slipped on the black Western-cut jacket Emory had bought. It fit perfectly.

"Told you so," I said, slipping on my embroidered Manuel dress and closing all but the top two pearl snaps.

"Wow," Gabe said. "That fits you really nice." He came over and ran his hands down my hips.

"Don't even think about *that* until after the ball, cowboy," I said, kissing him quickly on the lips and wiggling out of his grasp. "I'm not missing one minute of the festivities."

We arrived at the grange hall down near the Elks Lodge when the band played the first song. Gabe immediately found our table near the stage and joined Daddy and a few other nondancing ranchers at the punch bowl. I wandered over to the hors d'oeuvres buffet and found Emory and Elvia, also dressed in elegant Western wear. Elvia's dress was a deep burgundy lacy outfit with a sort of Victorian look. She wore trim, lace-up high-heel boots in deep merlot-colored leather. Emory's dark Western-cut suit was similar to Gabe's but he'd added an expensive black 100x felt cowboy hat with a cattleman's crease.

"You looked gorgeous in the parade," I said to Elvia, giving her a big hug.

"Thank you," she said, "but I think I even prefer this Western dress to that seventies horror."

"She was adorable," Emory said, winking at me. "I'm going to make her wear that dress just for me."

"You are as *loco* as your cousin," she said, slapping him lightly on the shoulder. Then she turned a concerned face to me. "How's Emma?"

I told them the latest and we all were quiet for a moment, the sadness of the situation overwhelming the need for words.

"How are *you?*" Emory asked, putting his hand on my shoulder.

I shrugged. "Fine, I guess. It was scary, but . . ." What could I say? What can you say about facing a moment in your life that could possibly be your last? "I'm just glad it wasn't my time to go, you know?"

His arm came around my shoulders. "Me too, sweet-cakes." With his free hand, he gently touched my still slightly swollen nose. "Need any money for a nose job?"

I swiped at his hand. "No, the doctor said I'll look as good as new in a week or so."

In the next half hour almost everyone had arrived, including Dove, who was wearing a beautiful red-and-black Manuel dress with black pearl buttons.

"I'm guessing Emory?" I said, pointing to her outfit.

"I think he bought out Mr. Manuel's Nashville store," she said, laughing.

She sat down next to me at our round, ten-person table next to the stage. The centerpieces were clever arrangements of perfect red roses, local wild flowers, and old rusty horseshoes set in replicas of old packing crates with Western-themed labels. Ours was Wild Mustang Strawberries, San Celina, California.

"That's our Emory. Always concerned with keeping the economy rolling along."

The twins, Beebs and Millee, unpredictable as ever, caused a minor sensation when, for the first time in their lives, they wore different outfits. Beebs was dressed in a black, full-skirted, Western-yoke dress similar to mine with butter-colored horseshoes embroidered on the yokes, and Millee wore a bright red broomstick skirt with a white, turquoise, and red Mexican peasant blouse.

"You two look great!" I said when they came by our table to show off their outfits and say hi. "But you're not dressed alike."

Millee gave our table an amused look. "Sharp as a tack, this girl."

"We just wanted to shake things up a bit," Beebs said, smiling at us.

"You're never too old to try something new," Millee said. Then she gazed around the crowded room. "Let's get popping, Beebs. There's cowboys to dance with here."

After sampling all the different Western-inspired hors d'oeuvres including grilled portabella mushrooms seasoned with Cajun spices, miniature Denver omelette quiches, and tiny slices of Portuguese linguica sausages wrapped in a spicy, garlic-flavored pastry triangle ("Am I crazy," I whispered to Emory, "or is this basically pigs in a blanket?"), I started getting a little nervous. The ball had been going on for an hour and still no Isaac.

I went over to Gabe at the punch bowl, where he and the district attorney, who owned a small ranch that bred Arabian horses, were laughing at a story about a local pervert who'd flashed the wrong lady and got a poke in his privates with the metal tip of her sturdy English umbrella. Apparently she actually broke skin on his testicles and he was trying to get his defense attorney to sue her for pain and suffering.

After they had stopped laughing, I asked Gabe, "Have you seen Isaac anywhere?" I looked back out at the hall. There had to be five hundred people here, but Isaac was not usually a hard person to find in a crowd. "They're going to present Dove with her award soon. I can't believe he'd miss that."

Gabe kissed the top of my head. "Don't worry, *querida*. Dove will be going home with her *esposo* tonight. I promise."

I looked up at him. "You know what he's going to do!" I grabbed the silver tips of his Western tie and gave it a sharp tug. "You dirty dog! What's going on?"

He laughed and said, "I promised not to leak a word. Let's get back to the table; they're announcing the awards."

After speeches by our mayor, the head of the Farm Bureau, and the presidents of the Cattlemen's and Cattlewomen's Associations, they finally started giving out the awards. We hooted and hollered, and I rushed up to the stage to snap a fast half-dozen pictures when Dove's name was announced for the Lifetime Achievement Award.

Embarrassed by the large crowd and attention, Dove was practically speechless, though she did manage a quick thank-you and "Look, they usually give out these things when people have one foot in the hearse and the other on a banana peel. Don't y'all count me out yet." Then, with great dignity, she stepped down from the stage.

And there at the foot of the steps, from out of nowhere it seemed, stood Isaac. Tall, wide as a grizzly, and dressed in a beautiful cream-colored Western suit and navy blue shirt, he held out his hand to help her down the steps. By this time, most of San Celina's agricultural and artistic community had heard about their troubles. The tables closest to the stage went almost silent.

"Miss Dove," Isaac said, in his wonderfully deep baritone voice, "I have something for you. Would you care to accompany me outside?"

Dove gave him a wary look. Another thirty seconds went by. Isaac never changed his smiling, genial expression.

"Oh, for cryin' out loud, Mama," Daddy finally yelled. He only called her Mama when he was at the end of his rope. "The man's closing in on eighty years old. He ain't got all year."

The crowd around us tittered with nervous laughter.

"I'll give you one minute," Dove said, taking his hand with all the haughty grace of the Queen of England.

Most of us couldn't resist and followed them outside, where Isaac walked her up to a brand new, candy apple red, one-ton, Chevy pickup with a matching stock trailer. On the truck's passenger side door painted in black script were their names: *Isaac and Dove.* I went around to the driver side and saw painted on that door: *Dove and Isaac*. This man was sharp as a porcupine quill.

But the ranchers were all gathered around the trailer, where the sounds of snorting and snuffling could be heard.

"Isaac, what in the world did you do?" Dove said.

"You're a special woman, Dove," he said. "I wanted to show you how special. That's Black Bart Tucson in that trailer and he's now got a new home, the Ramsey ranch, on one condition . . ."

Everyone gasped. Black Bart was one of the most prized bulls at the Houston Stock Auction last year and was worth a good quarter of a million dollars.

She looked up at him, shook her head, and laughed. "You old coot. You think you can buy yourself back into my good graces with a mangy bull?"

He bent down and whispered something in her ear.

She thought for a moment and said, "Sold."

Then, right in front of everyone, she took his face in her hands and kissed him straight on the mouth.

"Thank you, Jesus," said my father, looking upward.

"What did he say to her?" I asked.

Daddy grinned at me. "He's putting in another phone line with an answering service, he's rebuilding the bunkhouse so I can live out there in some peace and quiet, he's adding an addition to the ranch house where they'll have separate bedroom suites with a connecting door, and they're going on a month-long vacation while it's all being done."

"Guess any woman would have a hard time saying no to all that," I said. Then I smacked my dad's arm. "You old crabapple. You and Gabe knew what Isaac was going to do all along."

"Not all along," Daddy said smugly. "Just since this morning. And I'm here to tell you, after he told me what he was going to do and I knew your gramma wouldn't dare say no, I almost kissed Isaac on the lips myself."

CHAPTER 23

❖

April 8, 1978
Saturday

"WHERE ARE YOU?" I SCREAMED INTO THE PHONE AT Jack. "It's almost three A.M. I've been worried sick!" Rain pounded against the kitchen windows like tiny hands clamoring to get inside. My heart beat almost as fast as the raindrops hitting the glass.

"I'm in the emergency room at General Hospital," Jack said, his voice calm.

"Are you okay?" I asked, realizing the second I did how illogical the question was. If he was speaking to me on the phone, he must be okay.

"I'm fine. Just helped someone else. I'll be home in a half hour, babe. Just don't lock me out." He gave a hesitant laugh.

"Oh, Jack, be careful driving home."

Forty-five minutes later he stood in the doorway, dripping from the rain, his face tired and drawn, looking much older than his twenty years.

"Are you okay?" I opened the door wider.

He nodded, walked across the kitchen, and sat down at the kitchen table. "I'm sorry, babe. I should have called earlier. I was just so mad at Wade that I started driving and totally lost track of time."

I sat down across from him and took one of his hands. It was damp and cold, rough as a corn cob. I brought it to my cheek, where its icy temperature shocked my warm skin. "I was just afraid you'd been in an accident, that maybe you'd been drinking . . ."

He turned his brown eyes toward me. His damp eyebrows moved together in a hurt expression. "I'd never do that, Bonni. Wade's the stupid drunk in our family."

"He came over here looking for you. When I told him I didn't know where you were, that you were mad, he went looking for you. He just got back about a half hour ago himself." I held his hand in both of mine, caressing its roughness.

He shrugged, feigning indifference.

"He told me he felt bad about the things he said. Said he wanted to apologize to you."

Jack gave a harsh laugh. "That'll be the day."

"In spite of your differences, he loves you, Jack. And he wants this ranch to work as much as you do."

"Maybe, maybe not. I've wondered if he wants it to fail so he can go back to Texas. He never has liked it here in California."

"You two have to work it out somehow."

He shivered inside his frayed Wrangler jacket.

"Your clothes are wet. You need to change." I stood up and pulled his jacket off him. Bloodstains darkened the front of his flannel shirt. "What happened?"

He looked down at his shirt, a surprised look on his face. "Oh, man, I didn't realize he was bleeding that much."

"Who?"

"The guy I picked up."

"You picked up a guy who was bleeding?" My stomach did flip-flops. "Where?"

"Over near Sweetheart Hill. I dropped by to see if anyone was trespassing . . ."

"At night by yourself!" I said, smacking the top of his hand. "Jack, that's crazy. Someone could have shot you."

He grabbed my hand and held it tightly. "No one hurt me, babe. But it was a good thing I did. This guy might not have been found alive if I hadn't gone by. Looked like he'd been beat up bad. That's why I was so late. I took him to the hospital."

I shook my head and helped him take off the shirt. "Probably some dope addict. Hope he appreciates someday what you did for him."

I held the shirt out away from me. "This is going straight in the trash. I'll never get that blood out. I don't even want to try."

After he'd showered and we were in bed, he pulled out his journal notebook.

"What're you doing?" I asked, turning on my side to look at him.

"Recording what happened with that guy tonight. I have to turn this in tomorrow, and if this isn't a good last entry about meeting someone outside your daily life, I don't know what is."

I leaned over and kissed his cheek. "I'm glad you're home safe. I don't know what I'd do if I ever lost you."

He pulled me to him and I rested my head on his smooth, solid chest. "You'd get by just fine, Blondie. But don't worry, you can't get rid of me that easy. I plan on being around to track mud on your clean floors until we're both old and gray."

CHAPTER 24

❖

April 23, 1995
Sunday

*A*FTER OUR STRESSFUL WEEK, GABE AND I SPENT most of Sunday just reading the paper and puttering around the house. That evening, I was downstairs in the study putting away more books in the mission-style bookshelves when I finally decided to go through the box labeled *Jack.* Sitting at the bottom of the box was the blue journal notebook from his long-ago college class. At the top of the first page, in Professor Hill's spidery handwriting, was written: *Intriguing, honest, powerful. Good job, Mr. Harper. A.*

Upstairs, I could hear Gabe talking to Scout, discussing the run they were going to take together. Outside the wind blew hard and cold, another late April storm brewing. I'm glad it waited until the parade and the Cattleman's Ball was over. I'd have to remind Gabe to wear a sweatshirt.

I sat down crosslegged on the floor. I'd read a few of Jack's entries when he first wrote them, but when he asked me not to read them again, I honored his request. When he died, I'd packed all his stuff away without looking at it. Back then, I couldn't endure even seeing his

handwriting. At the time I remember thinking that I'd
never be happy again. How certain I was of that. When
you're in the middle of such deep grief, it's hard to imagine feeling anything except that emptiness, that frozen anger, that dark, bottomless sadness.

But the old cliché that time heals wounds does work,
to some degree. Do the wounds ever heal? Maybe not
completely. Maybe they just soften around the edges, like
a headache right before aspirin starts to work. You know
the pain is still there, hovering around you, light as a
butterfly, but it is almost imperceivable, it is almost gone.
It's bearable. Instead of feeling like a smothering strait-
jacket, it almost feels like a time-softened quilt, a little
too warm sometimes, but comforting somehow. Maybe
that's the way grief is supposed to be, not something to
experience and then get over, like a fever, but something
you take inside you, something that becomes as much a
part of you as blood and bones and muscle. As much a
part of you as love.

Yes, the pain of losing Jack still surrounded me. It
would always be right there framing the picture of my
life. But the deep voice echoing above me, teasing Scout,
whistling a tuneless song, was a bandage over the wound.
Just as I hoped I could be a bandage over his old wounds.

I hoped that's how it would be for Emma and Lou.
They had a whole lifetime of pain to heal from and now
this new pain. For the physical loss of their son, Luke.
For Emma, the emotional loss of her son, Cody. But there
was still hope for him, as long as he still lived.

Yes, Emma and Lou had hope. And they had each
other. And forgiveness, if they chose it. As we all do.

I opened Jack's notebook and read a few of the entries.
Jack's strong, young voice came back to me as clear as a
church bell.

The words written in his heavy scrawl brought back in
a rush all the moments we had together—riding bareback
around the ranch, our hands free, gripping the sides of our
horses, our young thighs strong as steel, daring each other

to perform wild stunts; eating a whole cherry pie straight out of the pan; watching the first heifer we jointly owned give birth the night of our senior prom, after we'd ditched the dance early so we wouldn't miss it. I closed my eyes and remembered the first time we made love, the night we were married, young, inexperienced, but so thrilled by each other's touch. An avalanche of feelings and memories poured over me, so much of my young life, such a huge part of my soul.

I turned to the last entry. I remember him sitting up in bed writing it at four A.M. the night he came in so late. While he wrote, his face screwed up like a little boy's, concentrating on writing neatly. He'd always hated his handwriting, though I'd found it entrancing and unique, so much a part of him. After he finished, we made love. I remember feeling so at peace, so happy he was home and safe. I felt like we'd be safe forever.

> *April 9, 1978—Sweetheart Hill, Ramsey Ranch—1:00 a.m.*
>
> *I was out driving around after having a fight with my older brother, Wade, about our ranch when I decided to go check my father-in-law's land where we'd found evidence of trespassers a week or so ago. When I got to the gate I thought I saw some movement over by a clump of bushes. I took my shotgun and checked it out. It was a guy. He was Mexican and a little older than me, maybe twenty-eight or thirty years old. It was hard to tell because of all the blood on his face and how swollen it was. He had a black goatee and the one time he opened his eyes, they were blue, a weird sort of gray blue. He spoke to me in Spanish and I helped him into my truck, told him I'd take him to the hospital. He was barely conscious the whole time, talking under his breath in Spanish. Once he called for his mother which kinda made me feel sad. At the hospital I helped him in-*

*side and asked him if I could call anyone for him.
It was really weird. In English he mumbled a
phone number to me and said to call it and tell
the machine that Gabe, no, Gilberto is at the
emergency room. I asked him which it was. He
said Gilberto. I did what he said and then went
into the room where he was waiting for a doctor.
His eyes were swollen completely shut now. But
when he heard my voice, he grabbed my hand and
said in a chokey kind of voice, "Gracias, compa.
Maybe someday I'll be able to help you." I said,
yeah, right, buddy and told him to take it easy.*

    April 10, 1978—10:00 a.m.
    *I went back to the hospital today and asked
about the Mexican guy. For some reason I just
couldn't stop thinking about him. I kind of felt like
maybe I saved his life or something. I mean, if I
hadn't have come along when I did the guys who
beat him might've come back or he might have
died out there. Anyway, the lady at the desk said
they didn't have any record of a Mexican man being brought in earlier that morning. I said that
was crazy, that I brought him in myself, but I
never could get her to change her mind. She kept
saying there was no record. Maybe they don't
keep records of people who don't pay, I don't
know. It seemed like he just disappeared. But
there was something about that guy. You know
that deja vu thing people are always talking
about? It kind of felt like that, like he was familiar
or something. I know that's kind of nuts, but he
really got to me. Maybe it was just how late it
was or how messed up he was or how he grabbed
my hand before I left him there. He was barely
conscious but, I don't know, it seems stupid now,
but it sure felt like he was someone important to*

my life . . . that's what it felt like, like he was some-
one real important to my life.

"What're you reading?" Gabe asked from behind me.

I turned to look at him. He was dressed in sweatpants and a T-shirt that showed a picture of a brown trout that a friend bought him on a fishing trip to the Sierra Nevada Mountains. BIG, BAD AND BROWN, the words under the trout said. His familiar blue eyes studied me, intense with concern. His figure grew wavy in my sight.

What was it Einstein once said? "God doesn't play dice."

"Querida," Gabe said. "What's wrong? Why are you crying?"

"Sit down. I want to read you something."